A PUNISHING BREED

a novel

DC Frost

CANIS MAJOR BOOKS

Book design by Mark E. Cull

Library of Congress Cataloging-in-Publication Data

Names: Frost, DC, 1956– author.
Title: A punishing breed: a novel / DC Frost.
Description: First edition. | Pasadena, CA: Canis Major Books, 2024.
Identifiers: LCCN 2023047260 | ISBN 9781939096173 (trade paperback) | ISBN
9781939096180 (ebook)
Subjects: LCGFT: Detective and mystery fiction. | Novels.
Classification: LCC PS3606.R644 P86 2024 | DDC 813/.6—dc23/eng/20231010
LC record available at https://lccn.loc.gov/2023047260

The National Endowment for the Arts, the Los Angeles County Arts Commission, the Ah-
manson Foundation, the Dwight Stuart Youth Fund, the Max Factor Family Foundation, the
Pasadena Tournament of Roses Foundation, the Pasadena Arts & Culture Commission and
the City of Pasadena Cultural Affairs Division, the City of Los Angeles Department of Cultural Affairs, the Audrey & Sydney Irmas Charitable Foundation, the Meta & George Rosen-
berg Foundation, the Albert and Elaine Borchard Foundation, the Adams Family Foundation, the Riordan Foundation, Amazon Literary Partnership, the Sam Francis Foundation,
and the Mara W. Breech Foundation partially support Red Hen Press.

    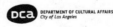

First Edition
Published by Canis Major Books
An imprint of Red Hen Press
Pasadena, CA
www.redhen.org

Printed in Canada

Dedicated to my husband and son.
Great companions in the City of Angels.

And to Marian.

PART ONE

The Watcher

Footsteps. Eyes open. Night.

A girl walked by the house, propelled forward by the Santa Ana wind. Her long hair funneled into the air like black cotton candy.

The Watcher spied her from his second-story window. Suddenly, the girl jackknifed forward as if gut punched and retched on the sidewalk. Wiping her mouth with the back of her hand, she straightened up, looked at his house. Ivy invaded the yard, a riot of scarlet bougainvillea climbed up the wood and brick wall obscuring three black windows.

The wind had calmed. The girl's hair fell around her shoulders as she stared at the spot where he hid in the dark. Her cheekbones, nose, and lips caught light, her eyes still in shadow. Her right hand reached up and clutched at the edge of a gold oval that gleamed at her throat.

The Watcher bent forward, studying the girl.

He leaned right, her head bent left, a mirror image.

She sees me.

The Watcher's hand covered his mouth. His fingers smelled of sour apple candy and musk. He breathed in and closed his eyes. The inside-out world played across his eyelids in random order; night, wind, moon, pale neck. A prick of desire and something deeper, an ancient longing, burrowed into his core.

Eyes open.

The wind gusted, carried the girl forward. No one lingered on his sidewalk. Not elementary school brats, goth teens, or college coeds. They all ran from the haunted hole. That's what they screamed as they hurried past. "The haunted hole." His black hole. His house.

"I. See. You," he said in his high singsong voice.

His reflection stared back from the glass; a white asymmetrical face, eyes askew, a gaping mouth.

He stretched his good arm, pushed himself up, muscles popped, tendons loosened. Goose pimples rose on the flesh down his back. Hard veins surfaced on the side of his body—a thousand pricks, a hull of scars.

As he stood, the pain of bone on sinew grounded him.

His eyes bore past the walls of his room into the night.
The girl was young, frightened, ill.
Her beauty struck deep inside his charred heart.
An ember embedded in his entrails. "I am here, pretty one. I'll protect you."
She was leaving.
He would follow.

CHAPTER 1

The Man Who Wasn't There

Danny Mendoza woke one morning at 3:00 a.m. from horticulture dreams dredging up the names of plants: *Petalonyx thurberi, Wyethia mollis, Erodium texanum,* a list he compiled to say aloud in the dead of night to shut out other noises. He drifted off to sleep and the memory rumbled into his dream like an oilcan bouncing down a rutted road; the screech of brakes, the dull thud of a body hitting the hood of his car. The end of two lives: the beginning of this one.

The radio alarm sputtered on at four. Danny heard its whistling static, followed by a man's voice reading the news at the top of the hour. His wake-up call to a wonderful world; the casualties of war fought on foreign soil, a tornado that tore through a Midwestern town upending mobile homes, splitting the timbers of old farmhouses like a monster on a bender.

Swish, swish, swish. Outside, the sprinklers sprang into action; the rat-tat-tat of water against the bedroom window greeted him as he turned on the lamp. Light spilled onto the scuffed floor and his cot covered by an old army blanket. He shut off the radio on his bedside table, a repository of despised self-help books.

Danny made a mental note to adjust the sprinkler. He kept a tally of projects that needed attention on a to-do list in his head.

Stepping outside onto the porch that ran across the front of his house, Danny lit the first of two daily self-allotted cigarettes. The inhaled heat warded off the chill of morning. He saw a flash of white stripe from a fat skunk waddling down the sidewalk.

"Good morning, *compadre,*" said Danny. "*Buenos días.*"

The skunk disappeared behind a hedge at the end of his property. "That's okay. I'll catch you tomorrow." Cigarette smoke formed an unholy halo above his head.

Back inside the house, Danny wrestled his six-foot body under the showerhead and washed away the nightmares. As he shaved in the mirror, the green eyes of his late mother, Isabella, restless and worried, stared back at him. The imprint of the one person who had loved him. They had planned to leave Eagle Rock and start over; a new life. But six months ago, she gave up her heroic, losing battle to breast cancer. She never lost her faith—not during his trial or prison sentence. For that, he'd never forgive God or himself.

Danny checked out his reflection. He was muscular from the hours spent pumping iron in prison, a practice he continued. Putting on his work uniform of khaki shirt, dark green work pants, boots, and baseball cap, he walked two blocks to Hesperia College.

He didn't begin work until six. But he arrived early Friday morning to pick his assignments for the day. Otherwise, he might get stuck digging holes with chatty Charlie Janes or sharing a tree saw with Benny Martinez, who laughed at his own jokes and farted at each punch line.

Inside the Facilities office, Danny perused the tasks on an old-school bulletin board. He chose a two-day requisition to clean up the walled cactus garden inside the Sliming Administrative Center. Lionel T. Sliming was the ninth president of Hesperia College. Some genius decided to name a building in his honor.

Danny pocketed the requisition card and opened the cabinet with the pegboard of various keys. There were two for Sliming, an exterior door override key and an access key to the interior courtyard. He signed them out, noting the date and time.

Most of the campus was built in the Spanish Revival–style of the early twentieth century, with stately white walls and slanting red tile roofs. The Sliming Administration Center, constructed in the early 1960s, was designed in the International style. The large glass and concrete cube perched on the high point of campus, looming like a metaphoric thumb in the eye to the surrounding architecture. The building had aged badly inside and out. Officially, it was called the SAC, but everyone called it "Sliming."

Danny brewed a strong pot of coffee for the office. He bought fresh coffee beans and prepared them with his own grinder. He worked a lot of overtime and didn't have many ways to spend his paychecks. He poured the dark brew into his travel mug and left the rest for his colleagues. Danny avoided any conversation beyond "Morning" and "See you later." Making gourmet coffee was the smallest balance of his penance to the world.

"Danny," said Rita Clay, the Facilities secretary, on the rare occasion she caught him in the office, "one day you are going to make some girl very happy."

Danny tried to avoid the relentlessly cheerful Rita. She was brunette with bright caramel streaks and double-D breasts displayed in low-cut blouses. He blushed in her company.

"If a girl can ever get your attention," she said.

A small gold crucifix dangled along a trail of red freckles into the deep cleavage that led to Rita Clay's heart. Danny ducked out of the office before she could engage him in conversation. Alone at night he remembered the trail of heartache and imagined double-D delights, as he twisted in his sheets, burning and hollow in equal measure.

He loaded an electric cart with gardening tools, trash bags, and gravel. As Danny left the Facilities yard, he passed the Chiller, a modern concrete and glass structure that cooled campus buildings along an infrastructure of tunnels and pipes.

Jerome Blight, the Facilities director and Danny's boss, passed by in his black Dodge truck.

"Morning," Danny called out. Jerome nodded, eyes hidden behind black wraparound sunglasses. Danny always suspected his boss had an unrequited crush on his mother, Isabella Mendoza. It was probably the reason he had a job in Jerome's department.

A few fingers of light streaked the sky as Danny drove the cart up Tillman Road, past the graceful columns of Robinson Auditorium and through the stand of jacaranda trees that bloomed purple each May before graduation. The old ache formed in the center of Danny's chest.

Ten years ago, Danny had strutted his stuff as an eighteen-year-old freshman; eager, sure of himself. On the first day of college, a new world unfurled at his feet, a seductive red carpet welcoming him aboard. Long-legged girls in tight shorts with thick curtains of hair turned to smile at him. Danny was going to own this place.

He shut down these memories with hard-earned practice. The ache in his belly curdled into something stronger, deeper and harder to contain. At sunrise when the grass and roses glittered with dew, and dark transgressions faded, his old feelings of invincibility surged. Before reality sank back into Danny's bones and frustration bloomed like smoke from a doused, steaming fire. Bitterness eating him alive.

Danny stopped the cart and pulled to the curb to steady his breath. His shoulders slumped into submission as he once again became the faceless man who pruned shrubs, dug holes, and picked up the trash for a new crop of students. He was invisible and faceless as the trees, rocks, and columns of Hesperia College. A fix-it man who could not repair his own mistake.

CHAPTER 2

Age Is Just a Number

Will Bloom's final day on earth, a Thursday, began the same as most. He spiraled down into a black nightmare, first jerked left, then pulled right, now spinning freestyle. He emerged awake.

Will squinted, gingerly opened his eyes. The sandpaper light scraped his eyeballs.

"Goddamn," he said.

The aroma of coffee bloomed from the kitchen. An automatic coffee maker was a marvel of the modern world.

Will tried to stand; instead, he swayed. He was bare-chested and wore his jockeys. His clothes draped the chair beside his bed.

Thank God. He was grateful. *Nothing worse than sleeping in your Jos Bank suit.*

A surge of last night's scotch mixed with a liquefied filet mignon shot up his esophagus. Will held his ground and the dinner retreated.

Slinging on his sunglasses from the bedside table, he lurched toward the kitchen. He opened the cabinet door above the coffee maker and emptied four aspirin into his mouth. The powdery bite of pills stung his tongue. Will liked it.

He poured a half cup of coffee as his hand shook. Unscrewing the Jameson Irish whiskey that stood discreetly behind the aspirin bottle, he filled his cup to the brim. The aspirin and coffee went down like velvet, followed by a tall chaser of tap water. Will stood up straight and held out his hands.

"Steady as a rock," he said.

Today he woke up by himself. His lover, Hoa Phan, was out of town at a conference, and though Will had an impressive list of ladies-in-waiting to take her place, he had gone to bed alone.

"Thirty-nine years," Will said. He wore the boyish smile that only a well-maintained man of sixty-four could muster. It was the number of years between Hoa Phan, age twenty-five, and himself. He savored their age difference at odd moments of the day. It was a lifetime.

He visualized her stretching across his bed; the graceful frame of her shoulder, the flat belly, the firm line of her jaw as she turned to look at him. Her dark eyes always seemed to know a secret. His secret.

"Goddamn," he whispered.

Hoa meant flower in Vietnamese.

Will Bloom screeched into a fire lane and illegally parked his car. He was the vice president of Development at Hesperia College, and he was late for a meeting with the president. No one in Campus Safety would dare issue him a parking ticket. But President Bill Reese was pissed when he was late, which was always for their 9:00 a.m. Thursday morning meeting. It was Reese's own fault. It was an ungodly hour to meet.

Will strolled into his office at 9:05 a.m., pausing at Trish Ballentine's desk.

"Morning, Trish," Will said to his executive assistant. "The big man looking for me?" Trish had peacock-blue eyeshadow. She sported a blonde shag hairdo that was popular in the eighties. Though ten years younger, she was decades past hot to Will.

"Oh, didn't I tell you?" Trish said in a weary Southern drawl. She didn't bother to smile, "The president's office is moving your Thursday standing meeting to nine thirty."

"Now that," said Will, "is a good idea. You should have told me that yesterday!"

"Um-hmm," said Trish. She turned away to tend to a ringing phone and muttered to herself, "But then you would have arrived at nine thirty-five."

"What was that?" Will asked.

"Nothing," Trish grunted.

Will hummed as he walked down the hallway. Now he had time for another coffee. Things were looking up! Hoa Phan would be home tonight. And yesterday he had closed a three-million-dollar gift from a fat cat alum to fund one of President Reese's special initiatives. Will felt invincible! The dirty little secret of a small liberal arts college was its voracious appetite for cash. Tuition didn't begin to cover the day-to-day expenses of Hesperia College, the small class size, ten-to-one ratio of faculty to students, the ivory of the towers, the feeding of students' hearts and minds. And the pet projects of the president. They needed a crackerjack fundraiser like him. Damn, he was good!

Will worked in an office of women; the majority of fundraisers were female. That suited him fine. There wasn't one type of woman Will preferred; all females were catnip to him. He loved the pursuit of women as much as the money. But lately the chase was getting old. Maybe, after all these years, he was finally tiring of it.

He tiptoed past the office of his associate vice president of Fundraising Operations, Serena Rigby, and stopped at another office, the director of the Annual Fund. He touched the nameplate on the door, Hoa Phan. In a few hours she would be flying back from her conference in Arizona. He had big plans for her tonight, beginning with a gift. Will imagined her on his bed, blouse unbuttoned and her short skirt riding above the swell of her thighs. He was getting hard just thinking about her.

Will slipped into Hoa's office and sat down in the chair facing her desk. The sharpened pencils all pointed skyward in a porcelain cup. He came to a decision and made a quick phone call. Lazily pulling at a slip of paper, a receipt, tucked beneath the desk pad, he wrote himself a note on the back. Tonight would mark a new beginning. It was time—after all the other women, all the years, he was finally ready to settle down. He stared at what he had written and smiled. Standing up, he stuffed the paper into his pocket and headed up to the president's office. Damn it, he'd be early for his meeting. He didn't need more coffee!

The receipt, a slip of thermal paper, would lead to Will Bloom's undoing. Will whistled as he strode down the hallway, filled with anticipation.

CHAPTER 3

Ladies of the Canyon

Trish Ballentine performed her late afternoon ritual. She straightened, then cleaned her desk with a tissue dipped in alcohol, collected her belongings into her Vera Bradley tote bag, getting ready to head home. It was Thursday at 5:00 p.m., one more day before she could sleep in for the weekend, dream of an early retirement in Florida if her husband could get their finances together.

Will Bloom's office sat to her left. She looked down the hallway that ran perpendicular to her work area. The worn blue patterned carpet resembled a muddy river. Trish was a Joni Mitchell fan. In her mind she called the corridor *the ladies of the canyon.* She'd read a book about women musicians in the sixties who lived in Laurel Canyon. None of their ilk resided here.

Everyone who wanted to see Will Bloom had to pass by Trish's desk. Dolly Ruiz loitered at the end of the hallway. Trish called her *Little Red.* Her office was directly across the patio courtyard from Will's. Dolly was young, ambitious, and already the associate director of Office Management. Trish snorted at the thought.

Dolly Ruiz was at the beck and call of Will Bloom. He'd flash his lights across the courtyard or he'd shout for her through his open door. He never remembered anyone's name—so Trish became "Tish" or "Tess." Sometimes he called Dolly "Dilly Dally," which Trish thought appropriate. And once "Mads," as in Dolly Madison.

"Dilly," Will Bloom bellowed, "get in here." Dolly came running, Trish rolled her eyes. Dolly pretended not to notice. A Hesperia blanket was draped across her shoulders to ward off the late afternoon chill.

"Oh," Dolly said. "Are you leaving already?"

"Yes, ma'am," Trish answered in her Southern drawl. "I have a husband to get home to."

Dolly forced a smile. "Must be nice."

"It is," Trish said. "You should try one of your own."

Big Red, Serena Rigby, the associate vice president, bustled into the office suite from the lobby like thunder before a storm. Everything about Serena was oversize. A thick spew of ginger hair, a flat voice that penetrated walls, and a zaftig body ensconced in revealing bodices and wide swishing skirts. Will Bloom's door closed with a decisive bang.

"Oh, Trish," said Serena. "Is Will in with somebody?"

Trish closed her tote bag. She looked at the shut door and back at Serena. "Yes, ma'am," she said.

"Oh," said Serena. She stood before Trish's desk, staring at the closed door. "Do you know how long he'll be with . . . ?"

Trish could have told Serena that Will was with Dolly Ruiz, but it was really none of her business. Besides, Trish liked Serena even less than Dolly.

"No idea, dear."

Stymied, Serena didn't bother to say goodnight. She bustled off to her office down the hallway. At the end of the corridor on the opposite side was Hoa Phan's office. For the last few months, Trish had observed it was the one office Will could never pass by without poking in his head. Hoa Phan was Vietnamese, a slim, dark-haired beauty who seemed mature beyond her years. She was one cool customer, and nothing like Little and Big Red.

The other members of the fundraising team, gift officers and back-office worker bees, were shipwrecked on the far side of the building.

Trish stuffed one last item, a blue steno notebook, into an outside pocket of her tote bag. It was her practice to jot down the names of the numerous women who called Will Bloom, crestfallen if he was unavailable. She also taped in copies of incriminating receipts of alcohol-fueled lunches, dinners, and overnight business trips. Trish considered herself the chronicler of a Casanova. It might come in useful one day.

Her paisley tote slung over one shoulder, Trish flicked off her overhead light and headed toward the lobby. Director of Campus Safety Hedy Scacht was roaming the hallways in one of her pastel pantsuits, her ring of keys jingle-jangling.

Trish watched as Hedy tried several office doors to make sure all was secure. Trish thought she could lock all the doors in the building, but that wouldn't contain Will Bloom or his antics.

"Poor thing," she muttered under her breath. "Good ni-ight," Trish called out.

The other woman gave her quick wave.

As Trish sat in her Volkswagen Bug gearing up for the freeway ride home to the Valley, she had a premonition of disaster, the same way she had felt before the death of Princess Diana. Trish shook it off. She'd had little empathy for anyone after Diana died. The late princess was the last of the unicorns and now Trish lived in a world of donkeys.

In her office, Serena Rigby concentrated on a spreadsheet. The department was behind on its fundraising goals, over their budget. That meant trouble for Serena, and worse trouble for her staff. Serena was known for her organization and data skills. The tangibles. For Serena, numbers told a story—the only story she believed in.

Serena was five-foot-eight inches, a generous size sixteen, with red hair and flinty brown eyes that bored through the strongest man's confidence. Serena considered herself womanly, and there were enough men in her life to affirm her belief.

Today, she mused that her allure might be a curse. A recent encounter had rocked her sense of order and decorum. She didn't like surprises. They led to chaos.

But there was that note. Not a love note, more an admiration of her attributes. The writer had described her as a *burnished copper Venus*. She doubted the usual men she dated could muster that phrase. Serena might have written it about herself.

"Hi, Serena." Dolly Ruiz stood at her office door.

Dolly always showed up without forewarning like that pop-goes-the-weasel game. Tonight, she looked pale, a little under the weather.

"You said you wanted to meet with me before I headed home?" Dolly's cloud of strawberry-blonde hair surrounded her artfully construed "how can I be helpful" expression. She resembled Little Red Riding Hood, though Serena knew she was more the wolf in disguise. Serena saw her as a younger version of herself, except for her eyes. Dolly's were ice-blue.

"I'm just finishing up something," Serena said. "Can you give me five minutes?"

"Of course," said Dolly. "I'll go back to my office."

Something was wrong with Dolly, thought Serena. She was giving up without a fight or even a snarky comment.

"No," Serena said. She felt the fine grip of control returning, her world clicking into place, one gear at a time.

"I'll be just a few minutes—if you would wait outside? I'll call you when I'm ready."

"Of course," Dolly said. She stepped backward, closing the door with deference. Dolly would sit in the corridor in a metal chair waiting for her. Serena felt a flush of superiority. Let the younger woman wonder why Serena called the meeting. Though in her experience, Dolly knew exactly what everyone in the office wanted or needed.

Dolly was close to Will Bloom. They had some connection that Serena didn't understand. Was she his confidant?

Serena put down her pen. She hoped not. Serena pressed the fingers of her left hand across her forehead and then down over her face, lingering on her lips. This was what he had done; three days ago. She had been annoyed. What was he doing? His fingers on her face, gently moving from her forehead to her mouth. She had been working on the departmental budget. Trying to make everything balance—which wasn't easy, given Will's penchant for taking out his "women friends" on the college's dime. She felt her full lips, now a bit chapped, and the wet inside of her mouth. His fingers had then moved downward between her ample breasts, her nipples suddenly standing at attention. His fingers had lingered there and he looked her in the eye, not with expectation but pleading and something else. Was it need, hunger, anguish? Sleeping with Will Bloom wasn't anything she had ever considered, but at that moment, he wanted her more than anything or anyone else. Even with his terrible reputation, Will had an animal magnetism that was palpable and a strange vulnerability that caught her off guard.

"Did you get my note?" he said. "I wouldn't blame you for turning me away."

Then he fucked her like his life depended on it.

After the encounter earlier this week, not one word from Will acknowledging what happened between them. Serena almost thought it was all a dream except for the copper Venus note she kept in her wallet.

Serena heard a muffled sound and imagined Dolly Ruiz, ear against the door, reading her thoughts through the wood.

"Dolly," she called out.

Serena knew it wasn't true—but she said it anyway. "I'm ready for you."

CHAPTER 4

Buzzsaw

That Thursday night went sideways for Will Bloom.

A power outage left Will standing in the dark.

"Hoa Phan," Will said. How could she do it?

Saying her name tore a hole in his armor. He loved her and she had betrayed him. Betrayal; an ancient word.

Will had other women to take her place. Plenty. He didn't need her. He was waiting for her replacement right now. A repeat performance; an old flame.

Old flame. Words that made him feel ancient. He didn't like the direction this was heading.

Where the hell was the woman anyway? And how long until the power came back on? The building was old, the wiring shot. He hated waiting. His own power on the wane. She better get the hell in here or he would have an outage. Viagra was all about timing. He didn't have four-hour erections anymore like the commercials promised. The old buzzsaw winding down.

He gulped down a waiting shot and felt the sting in this throat.

Whiskey and memories hit him like a sledgehammer.

He was twenty-one years old, standing before Katy Simpson in his dorm room at Notre Dame. She was wearing white cotton panties and a Playtex bra. No thongs in those days, but it wasn't the underwear he was after. He had played her for months. The perfect gentleman, opening the door, closing the door, asking if he could hold her hand, kiss her cheek, her lips—a soft sweetheart kiss. "Goodnight, Katy. I'll see you in my dreams."

The whole time, he was doing the groupies who hung out at the local football pub after he said his innocent goodnights to Katy. Getting them juiced up on alcohol to lose their reluctance or inhibitions. Some were ready to jump in the back seat of his car with no prelude. The Fighting Irish men were gods, and the town girls were kneeling angels ready to provide succor—or anything else he wanted.

Man, those were the days of kiss and don't tell, good girls and bad girls. Will liked the bad girls, but he yearned for the good ones. He loved the thrill of the chase, the slow tease, the build of desire and expectation. The tuck in your side when the girl smiled at you—innocent of your intentions. The girls he had to coo and coax into submission, the cool and steady chase, the warming up, the brush of skin against skin. "Oh, I'm sorry Katy, I didn't mean to . . ." But after weeks of chaste kisses and accidental brushes against each other—Katy was breathing harder now, pulling at the collar of her sweater. Pulling at the collar of his shirt. *What was up with him? Was he gay? Was it her?* She made the first move. Her mother had warned her about football players—but this one was six feet tall, the best-looking hunk on campus. Rumors swirled around him, but she knew him best, his intentions, his heart. He was shy. *Sorry, Mama, but I'm not passing this experience up so I can end up with a desiccated old man who works all day and then shuts himself up "in the library" with a decanter of scotch when he finally comes home.*

To Will, it was beyond delicious when the good girls finally caved in. His arm over her shoulder, his hand lay awkwardly near the rise of her breast. Like a football he was hankering to grab onto if he could just find his grip. Her thick padded bra could have protected fine china, but he followed the seam to the tip of her nipple. He groaned dramatically, pulled away.

"We should stop," he said. "I'm afraid I can't control myself."

"Who said you should stop?" said Katy. Her voice had dropped an octave and her labored breathing in his ear made him worry he actually wouldn't be able to control himself.

"I don't want the first time to be in a car," he said. "It's not right."

That's how he got her into his dorm room, lying on his bed, moaning in her white cotton panties and begging him to take her. The uptight ones read romance novels. It was always about taking, conquering, sweeping them away. As if this was a legendary romantic climax and not just a good long monumental fuck. But Katy was right, he would enjoy taking her, the end to a long, patient, and skillful hunt.

He always started soft and slow. He wanted them to come first; it was a point of honor that she enjoyed her first time. Katy began to moan, faster and urgent. She climaxed like a wave breaking against a cliff, to use romance novel terms. And that's when he let go, he closed his eyes and started his moan, Mmmmmm, mmmmm, mmmmm. His voice grinding low and rhythmically like a buzzsaw.

He closed his eyes; Katy deserved his best. He kept going, pushing deeper. "Yes," she said. "Oh, yes!" The bed hit the wall, again and again until the buzzsaw broke through, the crash, her high squealed yips of approval, his voice groaning like a madman. She loved it, man. Moaning and yelling, "Yes, yes, yes."

The jealous idiots on the other side of the wall ruined it. "Shut up, man. Not again. Fuck off! Who is she this time? Goddamn it, Will, enough! I'm calling the RA again to complain!"

Katy took the truth like a glass of ice water thrown in her face. It had all been a game. She was just another conquest. Will felt her body tense, then go cold. He stopped—the fun was over. She slithered out from under him and stood up, furious, holding her clothes in front of her tits—now off-limits. Will licked his lips, because he had just had a mouthful of them.

"You lousy son of a whore." The Catholic girls always swore the best. She threw on her clothes and turned for the door.

"Let me walk you home, honey."

"Fuck you. I'll walk to my dorm by myself. And don't ever call me honey again. In fact, never call me again, ever! And not a word to anyone . . . or I'll cut your fucking dick off."

"You tell him, sister!" said the losers on the other side of the wall.

He was a gentleman, at least in that regard. He kept her secret and his from the next unsuspecting good girl.

His dormmates called him *Buzzsaw*. They thought it was a joke, a poke in the ribs.

But Will loved it.

Tonight, sixty-four-year-old Will Bloom stood alone in his dark office holding his flagging erection. Pain radiated from his lower back, and he felt a tickle on his skull, the bald spot he tried to hide with his longer strands of hair.

What the hell was he doing? He had slept with women during his relationship with Hoa Phan and felt no regret. He was just playing the game. A few nights ago he hit a new low. The moment when he really knew. Will had only wanted Hoa the whole time he was screwing Serena Rigby.

Did Hoa know about the others? She must. Is that why she had betrayed him? She was beautiful, young, made him feel hopeful—like he had a chance to start over. Thinking of her made him hard again. He could leave right now, drive to her apartment, beg for a fresh start, for both of them.

Will heard the click. A cold draft grazed his back. Too late, the other woman was here. A flashlight flickered on, then darkness again. Wait, where was she coming from?

"It's about time," he said. "I'd about given up on you." He stopped attending to his born-again erection. He didn't even bother turning around. It wasn't Hoa Phan. He didn't want anyone else. Not even a last hurrah for the old Buzzsaw.

"Listen," he said. "It's not . . . not . . . about you." He didn't know what to say. He'd never turned down sex before.

Will had a bigger problem. Something gleamed in the window; long, sharp, and deadly. He felt a rush of air, something thrown across his back, covering his head. Complete blackness.

"What the hell?" he asked.

Disoriented, Will tried to move, but it was too late. A shock of cold sharp steel penetrated his back with force and intention; an off-center thrust that missed his spine, plunged through cartilage into the soft tissue of chest cavity and pierced what all his life had been his least vulnerable organ: his heart.

CHAPTER 5

Fern

At 8:10 p.m., Ferencia Lake stood outside her professor's house. A twig wreath hung on the scarlet door. One thin branch, an accusing finger, pointed at her.

Earlier that day, she had visited Professor Gabriel Bounty during office hours.

"Hello, Fern Lake," the professor said.

Professor Bounty said her full name as if hundreds of girls named Fern roamed campus. She was named Ferencia after her grandmother, but a cousin had called her Fern and the name stuck.

Most of the female students and a few of the guys had a crush on Professor Gabriel Bounty. With a hipster vibe, he was tall and slim with a full head of black hair and intelligent blue eyes behind black-framed glasses. His wife, Loretta Bounty, monitored many of his classes. She wore skinny jeans, a leather jacket, and a beehive of jet-black hair. Last week, with a pang of envy, Fern saw the professor and his wife walk across campus holding hands.

Sitting in his office, Fern said, "I don't understand why you gave me a C on my abstract."

Most disturbing was the red ink scrawled across the first page. A massacre that bled through to innocent sheets below.

It was important for Fern to get an A on her paper.

"You're not," said Professor Bounty, "moving past your emotional response to the subject."

Her paper focused on the role of war and culture in Etruscan art.

"You need to analyze, assess, and reconstruct."

The starving Etruscans migrated to modern-day Tuscany. They waged war, but for a brief period their art flourished in colorful tomb paintings.

Professor Bounty walked behind her, retrieving something from a bookcase.

"Not simply react," he said.

The Etruscan murals showed their obsession with fighting, death, and funereal scenes, rendered in saturated colors of saffron, blood red, cerulean blue. The palette is what resonated with Fern.

"You need to remove your emotional response to the drawings," he said. "I don't care how you feel. Tell me how the Etruscan's warlike nature informed their art."

Fern pulled at the necklace inherited from her grandmother, a gold oval with an ascending Virgin Mary on an iridescent sky.

Professor Bounty's hand touched her shoulder.

"Why don't you come by my house after dinner," he said. "Bring your paper, and we'll go through it point by point."

"You mean slash by red slash."

Fern sounded petulant even to herself.

"Is that how you prefer," he asked, "to react?"

The professor's posse of favorite students were occasionally invited into the inner sanctum of the Bounty home a few blocks from campus. Fern imaged herself in sweats and a tank top and Mrs. Bounty, a hip Lady Macbeth, flanking the professor as he attacked her prose and stripped each literary outburst from her paper.

"Professor," she said, "I don't want to disturb you and Mrs. Bounty."

"Gabriel," he said. "Call me Gabriel. Listen, Fern Lake, my wife is out of town. We'll focus on your paper—get you moving in the right direction."

Fern turned around to look at him. Her cheek brushed against his hand, still resting on her shoulder. He didn't flinch. A warm flush spread from her cheek down to her neck and chest. Jeez, she was blushing.

Fern needed an A in his class to be in contention for a Fulbright.

"Okay," she said. "That would be helpful. Thank you."

Tonight, standing outside the circle of light from Bounty's front porch, she could smell him on her fingers, patchouli and regret. She wiped her hands on her pants, but the remorse stayed with her.

"I can drive you to your dorm," the professor had said as she buttoned her shirt over her grandmother's necklace.

"I have my roommate's car," Fern lied.

"Okay," he said quickly. His eyes flitted from her face to a spot six feet behind her. "I mean, if you're sure."

Fern realized that purging emotional responses wasn't just about her paper, it was Professor Gabriel Bounty's way of life.

"Yes," she said. "I'm sure."

"Take care, Fern Lake."

He didn't walk her to the door. She left without looking back.

Outside, Fern slung her backpack over her shoulder, turned away from his house, and walked down the street toward campus. She didn't have a car or a roommate.

Leaves and debris tumbled in the Santa Anas. Suddenly an image of Fern's father flickered in her mind. After her mother died, when neither of them could sleep, he would stay up late with her, reading the newspaper while Fern read her mom's collection of Agatha Christie books. When the Santa Anas came, they would sit behind the screen door and watch the dry desert winds whip around the branches of birch trees that lined their street.

"Tipsy ballerinas," her dad called them.

Fern was twelve, and from that point on it was just the two of them.

A gust of wind caught her from behind, blowing her hair above and around her face. Fern doubled over, a sudden pang in her belly, a nauseous sludge rising up her throat. She heaved, throwing up red wine.

Wiping her face on her sleeve, Fern straightened and assessed her surroundings. She was outside the old derelict house a block from campus. Her friends called it the haunted hole. Ivy and black branches of red bougainvillea climbed up brick and rotted shutters to the second floor. No light penetrated its shadows. She felt a quiver run down her back. Was someone watching her from the black windows?

She wiped her mouth again and quickly moved on.

Students were cautioned not to walk in the neighborhood alone late at night. Each year a few student muggings occurred. Fern couldn't call Campus Safety; her cell phone had died along with her decision-making prowess.

Fern walked along the perimeter of Hesperia College, past the football stadium and a squat stucco building tucked between overgrown shrubs; the rat lab, where she had struggled through her psychology class.

She finally reached the west gates of campus and immediately felt safe. Newman Hall was on her left, where she had lived as a first-year student. She had dated a cute guy named Jonah. But he was obsessed with video games and pot. It didn't last.

She met Jim Singer, the center for the basketball team, in her psychology lab her sophomore year. He was from the East Coast, smart and handsome. Their relationship burned hot for two years before cooling over the long summer break. He returned from a semester in South America questioning everything, including the relevance of their relationship. He broke up with her two months ago.

Fern focused on her schoolwork, pretending she wasn't devastated. She had applied for a Fulbright, a year in England where she could figure out the rest of her life. Sleeping with a professor, and a married man to boot, was not in her plans.

Earlier that evening, drinking a third glass of wine Professor Bounty poured for her, he pulled at her grandmother's necklace, his fingers brushed her neck.

He studied the Virgin Mary on her pendant.

"You're a believer?" he asked.

"Yes," she said. "I mean, I want to believe in something."

Gabriel Bounty pulled Fern closer.

"Your eyes," he said, "are an unusual color."

"They're amber." That's what her dad said anyway. The room began to spin. "I mean, thank you. I'm feeling woozy." She was close enough to smell his patchouli oil and see a cut on his chin from shaving.

"Hey, lean back, just relax," he said.

She touched the wound on his chin with her finger.

Right after that, Fern broke a Commandment; the one about adultery.

Fern gazed up at the scaly limbs of tall eucalyptus trees lining the road on Hesperia campus. Across the way, a grove of olive trees populated the hill leading to upper campus, where her dorm, Ramble Hall, and bed waited for her. There was an old asphalt shortcut through the trees, used by students who didn't want to spend an extra ten or fifteen minutes taking the three vertical staircases on the other side of campus near the Sliming Administration Center.

She headed up the hill through the canopy of branches. There was a full moon. Shadows scattered in the wind, making it difficult to see. Fern took out her phone to use the light before remembering it was dead.

"Goddamn it," she muttered. Add swearing to tonight's list of sins.

She heard something rustle behind her.

"Hello," Fern said, turning around.

Nothing. She almost tripped but caught herself, then continued onward.

She heard it again; something moving through the branches.

Fern walked faster up the path and to the edge of a clearing dead center in the grove.

Here the asphalt path ended in a treeless open space dotted with a few large boulders before a short rougher trail continued up the hill through the brush. She'd heard a rumor that a student Wicca group practiced rituals here. The moon and wind cast dancing black shadows across the clearing. Tonight, Fern would have welcomed the Wiccans' presence.

A group of female students to light the way.

"Is anyone there?"

Wind whistled through the branches, whipping her long hair across her face. She thought of her father's wayward ballerinas and laughed uneasily. She sounded like a frightened little girl, even to herself.

A dust devil wound its way across the clearing toward her.

She caught a stink from the breeze; dense, sickly sweet.

A faint drumbeat came from the trees to the east.

She stood, listening, unable to move.

The drumbeat grew louder. And another sound . . . a tearing, a breaking of twigs.

The stink closer . . . dense, dark. Familiar.

Footsteps sluicing branches.

She recognized the smell from that terrible day her childhood ended; her mother's aneurysm. Hot, copper, and cloying like blood.

Fern tried to run, but her legs felt like cement. She stumbled, hit the ground. Pain exploded in her knee.

A high-pitched scream pricked her hearing.

Black filled the sky as a wet heavy shroud covered her face and arms. A weight pressed down on her trunk, pinning her arms, her legs.

"What's happening?" Fear ricocheted through her mind, her body.

Fern struggled to breathe, to free her limbs.

She gulped for air.

Something grabbed her from behind, pulling at her backpack. Blackness turned sideways, the wet thing peeled away, the night sky reappeared, North Star burning bright.

"Run!" screeched a high-pitched voice with a commanding push to her back.

Fern scrambled to her feet, ran for her life up the hill. She didn't know if anyone or anything still followed her. She scurried through brush until she reached the paved road that circled the campus, then sprinted until the lights ringing the perimeter of Ramble Hall came into view.

A boy she knew, not well, was smoking pot on the bench near the front door. He looked up, obviously stoned, and walked away in the opposite direction.

"Thanks for your help, asshole," Fern screamed. Soaked with sweat, she turned back and saw the road behind her was empty. She stepped into the lighted entrance and pulled off her backpack to grab her key card. That's when she saw it. She wasn't soaked in sweat. She was covered in blood.

CHAPTER 6

The Poet's Wife

Ema Treet began her shift at three thirty Friday morning in the Sliming Administration Center. She wore the cleaning crew uniform of scarlet pants and jumper. Unlike her colleagues, Ema wasn't Latina and didn't speak Spanish. Her family had emigrated from the former Czechoslovakia, and she had a year of community college under her belt, which didn't count for much in Hesperia-land. She had met her husband, Marco Treet, in a creative writing class at Highland Community College. Marco was a poet.

Ema was recently promoted to the early morning shift in Sliming. "In early, out early," the Facilities director, Jerome Blight, assured her. Being moved to an early shift isolated her from colleagues who tried to teach Ema Spanish and put some meat on her bones with homemade tamales and refried beans. Her body and language skills remained resolutely thin.

Sliming had three floors. Ema worked from the top down. The third floor housed the president's office—William "Just call me Bill" Reese—twelfth president of Hesperia. President Bill was a minimalist, his office, the largest, was sleek and tidy. The dean of the college and the vice president of Finance's offices were also clear of clutter. Ema zipped through these offices, vacuuming, dusting, and emptying the trash. She carefully maneuvered through the assistants' cubicles, careful not to disturb the overflowing stacks of paperwork crowding their work areas. She also tidied the kitchen, bathrooms, and third-floor conference room.

Ema called the middle floor "The Terrarium." Sliming's main entrance was a three-sided lobby of glass anchored by a gray marble floor. A wooden wall made up the north side. Three steps led up to a conference room used quarterly by trustees, an elevator, and an emergency stairwell. Dead center in the lobby, a wide circular stairway wound down to the bottom floor of Sliming, home to financial aid, the Office of the Registrar, and the Fundraising Department.

Ema spent about twenty minutes on the lobby—running a mop across the marble floor. Though the glass walls were too high for her to clean, she wiped down the fingerprints and smudges at eye level with Windex. As she cleaned the windows, her reflection floated in the glass.

Ema was suddenly seated back in her high school English class. Her teacher was named Mrs. Monserrat. Ema believed her teacher had wandered into her inner-city high school from the moors. Mrs. Monserrat had a meager and head-forward frame as if all extraneous bits of flesh had been scoured away and she had staked her body to the earth in defiance of ferocious headwinds. Her brow was furrowed and marionette lines ran from her nose down to her prominent jawline. She read poetry to the class. No one but Ema paid attention. It was Mrs. Monserrat's eyes that Ema couldn't forget and now saw in her own reflection. They were pale blue, as if life had bleached them of color. Mrs. Monserrat's eyes clenched open and shut as they searched the classroom, astonished that she had somehow ended up at such a god-awful place. "My husband is a poet," the teacher had announced on the first day of class.

Ema sprayed the Windex again and breathed in its scent. She wiped at her reflection in the window and moved on.

She sent the cleaning cart down to the first floor on the elevator as she walked toward the circular stairway in the center of the lobby. It was 5:15 a.m.

At six, fellow cleaning woman Maria Lorena would start working on the far side of Sliming, the portion of the odd-shaped building where the lower floor extended underground on the opposite side of the courtyard. Ema tried to avoid Maria and her constant barrage of chatter she didn't understand or have the energy to return.

Ema doused her dust cloth with lemon oil and wiped down the long curved wooden banister of the circular stairway, descending the marble steps to Sliming's first floor.

Without overhead lights, the basement lobby was pitch-black. Even during the day, the only natural lobby light came from the dribs and drabs of sunlight that slipped down the massive stairway. Ema switched on the auxiliary lights. They cast a sickly yellow glow on the circle of marble floor that mirrored the bottom of the stairs.

She retrieved her cleaning cart from the elevator and wheeled it toward the fundraising suite of offices directly opposite the stairs. She mopped the pockmarked floor around the stairs, which was bordered by a worn blue-and-gray paisley carpet. Something dark like chocolate had dripped on the marble, then disappeared into the old carpet. Ema had to scrub hard to clean up the mess.

The entire first floor had been divided into a maze of ill-conceived offices.

It was almost impossible to clean them all, even with Maria Lorena's efforts, before the staff began to arrive at eight.

Ema began with Will Bloom's office, the largest in the suite. She knocked hard. No answer. During the past six months, Ema had found whiskey bottles under Mr. Bloom's desk, a pair of woman's high heels, a lacy black thong, a red bra, and other unmentionables on the floor. Recently, she discovered a jaggedly opened box of Trojan double-ring condoms. All of these items she had collected wearing rubber gloves, tucking them inside the credenza. She knocked again. No answer. Ema listened as the building creaked and settled itself.

She opened the unlocked door. Inside the dark office, Ema saw a sliver of the inner courtyard through the open exterior door. Cold air ruffled her hair.

From the glare of yellow lobby lights, one side of the room was visible. A riot of papers, books, and a fossilized elk hoof sat on the credenza. The right wall was bare. Yesterday, a long Japanese blade had hung on a dark wood plaque alongside a framed degree from Notre Dame. The breeze from the courtyard door scattered bits of debris across the floor like frightened mice.

Ema turned on the office light.

Will Bloom was sprawled halfway across an oval conference table, arms stretched out in front of him, hands rigid on its rim, pants pooled around his ankles. His head, cocked back like an animal roaring in pain, listed to the left, his dead eyes were open in horror and shock. The missing sword protruded from his back, pinioning him to the table.

Ema quickly switched off the light. Her hands went cold, then her feet, as if she might turn to ice, beginning with her extremities. She tried to scream, but her voice failed her.

She backed out of the room and outer office into the sickly yellow light and heavy scent of Pine-Sol in the lobby.

Bending over, she heaved and threw up, with regret, on her freshly mopped floor.

CHAPTER 7

Cold in California

Danny Mendoza drove the cart to Sliming Administration Center to begin his second day of work in the courtyard. Cold crept inside his jacket and work uniform as he stood outside the lower east entrance. His memory crept back to frigid mornings in Chino's prison yard as he shifted from foot to foot waiting for the head count. It was California cold, a chill born between mountains and sea that seeped into his bones, lingering until the midday sun warmed his scalp, face, and forearms.

Danny unloaded the gravel, shovel, and pickax from the cart. None of the office workers came in this early, before 6:00 a.m. It lessened the chance Danny would run into folks he wanted to avoid. Those who remembered his mother and the younger, more promising version of Danny Mendoza.

Carrying heavy bags of gravel across the hall, through the Finance office, into the courtyard was a pain, but tending the cactus and cleaning up gravel pathways was mindless work. His favorite kind.

Danny unlocked the exterior door of lower Sliming with the override key and a twenty-five-pound bag of gravel on one shoulder and headed inside. The moment he stepped into the corridor, he knew something was wrong. He had developed a visceral ESP for danger at Chino; an electric current originating in his cervical spine that barreled into his sphincter muscle.

Danny set down the gravel, walked slowly down the hallway toward the lobby. The yellow auxiliary lights were on.

"Hello, anybody there?"

Danny heard mewling as if a cat was trapped inside. No, it was whimpering. In the sickly glow of lights, he saw a woman sitting at the base of the circular stairs, one of the cleaning women. Which one? He moved closer. Ema Treet, skinny and pale, was curled into a near-fetal position on the bottom stair. What was she doing? Was she hurt, was she praying? Then he smelled it; vomit and Pine-Sol. *God*, he thought. *Which scent was worse?*

"Hello," Danny said. "Are you all right?"

The crying continued. Of course she wasn't all right. What a stupid prick he was. Danny didn't want anything to do with a crying woman. Maybe she was hurt, or worse, heartbroken. She looked ill. Maybe she was pregnant with morning sickness. His high school girlfriend, Rina, had been pregnant, but no one else knew about that. She had taken care of that lickety-split. She wasn't going to let Danny Mendoza's rambunctious sperm stop her forward trajectory. No way.

"I'll get over it," Rina had said.

Ema Treet finally looked up at him, let out a strangled cry. "There!" She turned and pointed to the darkened office suite and the open door that yawned like a black hole.

He was staying right where he was, thank you very much. Danny wanted to shake Ema Treet's pointy shoulders until she quieted down. Then he would lead her up the stairs where sunlight broke across the campus, promising a calm day after the winds.

All clean and swept away.

But he couldn't bring himself to touch her. For ten years, he hadn't touched a woman other than his mother. Perhaps he never had touched a woman—not even Rina, his high school girlfriend. Not really touched her in the way that counted. Danny had let her walk away without protest or an offer to help. He had his own forward trajectory.

"What is it?" he barked. She cowered away from him, cried louder and pointed again to the dark office. He felt like an asshole, yelling at the terrified woman.

Danny dragged his unwilling feet toward the threshold of the office. The room was black and still as if nothing had ever lived inside and never would again. His eyes adjusted to the dark room, barely touched by the yellow lobby light and now the glint of morning slipping through the courtyard's open door.

There it was again, death. The white bloodless skin, the long curving sword, the body splayed out on its stomach and arms. The neck rigid as if the victim was overdoing his role. "You got me!" The shocked eyes frozen in morbidity that knew what was coming. Murder!

Will Bloom was dead.

Ema Treet whimpered again, louder now, a howl. He wanted to yell at her, "Shut up! Please shut up, I need to think!" I'm the one that should be worried. I'm the convicted felon staring at a dead man. What should he do? Run? Pretend he was never here? But Ema Treet knew he was here.

Finally, he turned back into the outer office. There was something shiny on the old carpet; he reached down, put it in his pocket, and made a phone call. He walked back into the lobby, to the wide marble stairway. His legs buckled beneath him, but he managed to remain standing.

"It's going to be all right," he said to Ema Treet.

It wasn't going to be all right. A man was dead. Danny would be a suspect and Ema Treet would have bad dreams for the rest of her life. He knew that for sure. She looked up at him with fear in her pale blue eyes. It steadied him. She reached for the hand he reluctantly offered. Then she threw herself into him, a small avalanche of awkward arms and elbows, unwashed hair, Pine-Sol, and dried vomit.

It was a connection; flesh to flesh, human being to human being. Danny Mendoza let himself be embraced. The first time a woman other than his mother had touched him in ten years.

"It's okay," he said.

It wasn't okay, and nothing would ever be the same again.

PART TWO

Hurt

The Watcher followed the girl down Campus Road. He moved quickly using his walking stick. Forward, sideways, stabilize, repeat.

Under streetlights, her silhouette bloomed crimson, then darkened to purple, the color of bruised plums, tart on the outside, ripe at the core.

She passed through the gates of campus, then stopped and looked skyward.

The Watcher slipped behind the thick-trunked eucalyptus tree, battened down his wings, stopped all extraneous movement.

Above, branches shivered in the wind.

Leaves fell, camphor arrows from above.

He watched her beneath the full moon; so lovely, so alone.

The girl started again, heading north into the grove of Jesus trees, what his mother called olive trees, from the garden of Gethsemane.

He followed; forward, sideways, stabilize, repeat. Moving from shadow to shadow along the asphalt trail.

The girl stopped again; this time she looked over her shoulder.

"Hello," she said. "Is anyone there?"

He swallowed the long ribbon of her voice. Down it journeyed into his core, threading his entrails, pulsing through him. She sounded delicious.

She resumed walking, faster now.

He followed, again shadow to shadow, keeping her in sight.

Moonlight caught the curve of her shoulder, the luster of her hair.

He breathed heavily through uneven lips, lungs protesting. The girl stopped dead center in a clearing, a dirt circle, the end of the olive grove, before a thin path wound uphill through scrubby oaks.

He went still, hidden among the trees, afraid to venture into the open.

She called out again, "Hello?"

A gust of wind answered, a swish of tree limbs, a warm breath on a cold night.

It stirred the leaves and the soul.

The girl laughed; her voice a wind chime in a tempest.

He saw it first, from where he stood hidden.

Something stirred along the shrub and oaks to the right of the clearing.

The girl straightened, her feet cemented to earth.

A sound like a dull gallop, something pounding dirt.

The girl wasn't laughing now; her head swiveled toward the sound, then away.

It moved in the brush, pulsing leaves, parting branches.

She was frozen, the whites of her eyes bright in the moonlight.

Something burst through the scrub and trees,

A stampede of one.

The Watcher saw it.

Red, wet, dark. Tumbling forward.

She was rooted to the spot.

A sackcloth monster, face hidden beneath the shadow of a shroud.

Scrambling forward and grunting, it fell upon her.

The Watcher didn't hesitate; he threw his crooked body into the fray, holding the walking stick like a saber.

The monster, the girl, and the Watcher were a tangle of kicking legs, punching arms, wriggling bodies beneath the shroud that was warm and wet . . .

The Watcher's claw-shaped hand pushed through the wet thing, found the girl's hair, then her neck, his fingers caught up in a fragile chain. With his good hand, he grabbed the bulk of her backpack, tugged hard, wrested her away from the monster, twisted her sideways, then free.

The Watcher screamed, piercing the night with the whistle-pitch of his voice.

"Run," he screamed, pushing at the girl's back.

The girl stumbled away, ran north and up the hill.

Monster and Watcher twisted together. The Watcher's legs and arms tangled in the wet, clinging shroud that still covered the monster. With his good arm and leg, the Watcher punched and kicked at the grunting creature. He twisted and turned until he was free. The monster reached for the Watcher, for the shroud caught in his crippled hand and arm, but the Watcher tore away, fearing for his life. He threw his crooked arm upward, the shroud disappearing into the trees.

The Watcher fell to ground. He looked up. Everything was quiet. He was alone. His fingers found the walking stick; he pulled himself to his feet.

Like a phantom, the monster had disappeared into the night.

The Watcher, bruised and battered, was sore but whole.

He picked his way up the hill clutching the walking stick. He found pavement, crossed a crescent of road, saw the building he called the fortress on the hill.

Lights burned in the Tower.
The girl must be safe.

At home, the Watcher climbed into the shower, let warm water pour down on his head, his crooked body. The water turned red, then clear. Not his blood.

He reached into the clothes he had discarded, took something from one pocket.

The Watcher fell into bed.

As he closed his eyes, the image of the sackcloth monster waited for him.

"Gooo awaaay," he cried.

There was something hard, oval, and cold pressed inside his clenched fist.

He opened his hand.

A treasure lay in his palm. A pendant, a gold Madonna ascending to heaven in an iridescent sky. More valuable were the fine black hairs caught in its chain. He counted; there were seven of them.

He curled into himself and slept.

CHAPTER 8

Away from Him

Detective DJ Arias was not a morning person. Left to his own devices, he stayed up past midnight, pulling on a six-pack of Bud until the late-night talk shows sputtered out and C-list stars of cable plugged away, selling youth serum and magic kitchen appliances.

Friday morning found DJ sprawled on the living room sofa. In his dream, he was running after a bad guy, three steps behind, just out of reach.

The phone rang at 6:50 a.m.

"What's up," he growled into the receiver. DJ always expected bad news, an occupational hazard.

A homicide at Hesperia College. Not gangbangers shooting each other—the usual cause of death in Eagle Rock—but a bona fide white dude, some vice president, in an office, with a sword in his back. Maybe the butler did it. Or Professor Plum.

There was a secondary incident, a young woman attacked on campus in an olive grove. The woman escaped, emotionally shaken but physically intact.

"Yep. I'm on it—I'll be there in twenty minutes," he said to the watch commander, Sergeant Culley.

"LT SS assigned this specifically to you, Arias," said Culley.

Lieutenant Stella Steele was his officer in charge. Everyone called her LT SS for brevity, and as a sign of respect.

"What is higher education coming to these days?" asked DJ. "Hey, you called Bobtail yet?"

"LT SS said don't fuck with Talbot."

DJ listened to the abrupt dial tone and shrugged. Bobby Talbot was another new partner. DJ thought the nickname Bobtail was appropriate.

Elite private colleges gave DJ the creeps, full of holier-than-thou professors and spoiled rich kids. He had history with Hesperia College. Ten years back he had made his first major arrest there. A drunk frat boy had killed a teenage girl. It had made the *Los Angeles Times*, outraged people across the city, stained the reputation of the college. Gross vehicular manslaughter and DUI murder. The kickoff to DJ's career, the end of his life as he knew it.

The mantel clock struck seven. Five minutes late by his phone, but on time for the clock. DJ took the brass key, wound it tight, but not too tight, and moved the long arm ahead five minutes. He headed to the kitchen, heated the kettle, and found the jar of instant coffee. It was a two tablespoon morning. He didn't go for the fancy stuff at home. The powdered caffeine shot straight into his bloodstream. He saluted his reflection in the window with his cup before heading for a shower.

Two days ago was his birthday. Darius Joaquin Arias was thirty-eight years old, nearing the cusp of forty. No one baked him a cake or tried to guess his wish. No celebration, no candles. His last girlfriend informed him last week she was over him.

"You're a selfish son of a bitch," Zelda had said. Or was it Imelda? He lost count as names and faces blurred into one angry female slamming his front door.

Women couldn't keep their priorities straight. First, Zelda/Imelda had talked DJ into a "relationship" and then she talked herself into bed with her trainer, Ronnie. DJ guessed Ronnie was her new "relationshit." He had more names for it, but it was too early in the morning for that kind of language.

DJ showered and dressed quickly. He walked outside and locked the two dead bolts on his front door. He owned a California bungalow painted chocolate brown with green trim. Today, it looked worn and defeated. He had painted the house with great hope for the future; a new woman, a new chapter, a new life. Since his ex-wife left five years ago, there had been a parade of one-nighters—and a few hangers-on. Women with understanding smiles who sat across his breakfast table as DJ nursed a hangover.

Maybe she didn't look so good that morning, or maybe her voice pierced the last drop of his patience as she said, "It's okay, baby. Maybe you shouldn't drink so much." His least favorite line.

DJ explained what he thought of her chitchat, clichéd dreams, and particularly her "understanding." He watched each woman flinch at the assault to her dignity. Every time he felt equally justified and remorseful. DJ knew the real problem. He was an asshole and none of them were his ex-wife.

Pausing in his driveway, DJ looked up the steep hill standing cheek to jowl with his backyard. The lawn was even and green as a golf course. A third of the way up, separated by a chain-link fence, flat marble stones checkerboarded the sharp rise of grass.

DJ made the sign of the cross.

Buying a home that abutted Forest Lawn cemetery was both genius (no neighbors) and foolish (dead neighbors).

He and his cousin, Frankie, had grown up with their Grandma Amelia's ghost stories. They had chuckled at her tales, but as DJ grew older, he stopped laughing. Whenever he came across a body—a dead gangster, tats crisscrossing his neck; a victim with the void stare of death—DJ said a silent prayer. "Go with God, away from this place, away from me."

Other ghosts could not be banished. As years unfolded, people he loved and lost, like his cousin Frankie, left their mark. Their eyes, their smile, the one crooked tooth among perfection. Their scent. His ex-wife, Lillian, smelled like caramel, her skin, her hair, her favorite T-shirt.

Yesterday, standing in their old bedroom, he caught her scent as if she had just walked by. He reached out his hand and felt her absence like a stab to his solar plexus.

"You broke my heart," she had said. "Worse for you, you broke both our hearts. You just don't know it yet."

She had slammed the door on her way out of his life. Every other slamming door was just her echo. She left him. So had his cousin Frankie. They were gone. Away from him.

DJ got into his Toyota Highlander. It was painted matte black and showed each nick and dent. He studied his bloodshot eyes in the rearview mirror. He was off to find the bad guy. Just like his dream chasing down evil. That made him one of the good guys, right?

DJ pulled on his black Ray-Bans and drove down his driveway to Adams Boulevard, turned right toward the dead man waiting for him at Hesperia College.

CHAPTER 9

Romeo/Juliet

There were three things Hedy Scacht loved: (1) the long arm of justice, (2) a fine-looking man; she had a thing for Latin men but was nondenominational, and (3) smoking an unfiltered cigarette.

Her fingers twitched at the thought of a nicotine jolt; she was trying to quit. Hedy was the Hesperia College director of Campus Safety. Early this morning, she had been briefed on the student attack and then the discovery of Will Bloom's body.

Even with little sleep, she came in blazing in one of her signature pastel pantsuits. Today, she wore powder blue, a full face of makeup, and a smooth helmet of wheat-colored hair. Her long fingernails were painted metallic silver. She chewed Nicorette gum to dull the headache between her eyes as she assessed the scene. Officers of the Los Angeles Police Department were crawling all over the Sliming Academic Center. It felt like a violation.

Hedy spoke into her walkie-talkie:

"ROMEO/JULIET, this is HOTEL/SIERRA, do you copy? Over."

"ROMEO/JULIET, roger. Over."

Hedy communicated with Campus Safety Officer Rodney Johnson. On air, they went by call names, their initials in the phonetic alphabet from Alpha Bravo to Yankee Zulu. Rodney's were tragically romantic.

"ROMEO/JULIET, give me your location. Over."

"Copy. I'm in lower Sliming. Holding at the elevator. LAPD are securing the murder scene. Over."

"How are Ema Treet and Danny Mendoza? Over."

"Standby." Hedy heard garbled static. "Not sure, they're in separate offices. Police are guarding. Over."

"Who is in charge down there? Over."

"Eyes on lead detective. Name is Arial or Ares. Looks like doom walking. Over."

Hedy paused. "Is his name Arias? Detective DJ Arias? Over."

"Affirmative. That's the dude. Over."

"Thanks, Rodney. I mean ROMEO/JULIET. HOTEL/SIERRA, over and out."

Ten years back, eighteen-year-old Danny Mendoza was hauled away in handcuffs. Vehicular manslaughter. Hedy tried to counsel Danny to keep quiet, but he couldn't wait to confess. His mother, the head of campus dining and her best friend, Isabella Mendoza, had collapsed in Hedy's arms. Hedy didn't easily make friends; women friends were rarer.

"I'm not going to be able to survive this," Isabella had said.

"Remember, you need to be strong," said Hedy. "For Danny."

Isabella stood up and whispered in Hedy's ear.

"He's all I've got."

With any other police detective, Danny Mendoza would be just another suspect. But Danny called in the murder, and worse, DJ Arias was assigned to the case. Doom walking was an apt description.

She had made a promise to her best friend and to herself to watch over Danny. Hedy didn't become the head of Campus Safety by being faint of heart. She always did what was necessary. She committed.

Hedy knew the drill in a murder case. No one in, no one out. The police were stationed at the top and bottom of the curving staircase. Her officers were guarding the elevators and entrances on each floor. She looked over the curving wooden rail down to the bottom level. It was strangely tranquil. The murder scene secured. Death now inhabited the space; silent, cold, fixed.

In the lobby, where Hedy stood, a young detective tried to organize the chaos of the living; faculty, staff, students, and campus lookie-loos. The lobby chatter bounced off the glass walls and marble floor. Hedy could feel her headache blossom into migraine territory. Will Bloom's colleagues, all women, were herded to one corner. They wore stunned looks of shock; a few cried.

Hedy caught a few of their eyes. One sent a clear accusation. It said, "You should have prevented this. It was your job." Hedy turned away.

The detective, a man in his late twenties, had a twitch: he cricked his neck and rolled his shoulders when he talked to a civilian. He nodded at each answer like a bobblehead doll.

Hedy straightened her posture, adjusted her pantsuit like armor, and moved in.

"Excuse me," she said. "I need to speak to the detective in charge."

"I'm Detective Bobby Talbot," he said. "You can talk to me."

I could, Hedy thought, but she didn't want to.

"Is the lead detective onsite?"

"He's busy."

"I'm Hedy Scacht, the director of Campus Safety, and I need to talk to Detective Arias."

"It's nice to meet you," Bobby said, "I appreciate that your officers are helping us cordon off the building. But we're extremely busy right now. Someone got murdered last night."

"No kidding," she said.

"Ma'am. I'm sure you know that murder is when the LAPD take over."

"It's Ms. Scacht. Hedy Scacht. That's why I need to talk to DJ," Hedy said in a purr that edged into growl territory. "Now."

"How do you know his name is DJ?"

Now she had Talbot's full attention.

"We're old friends," she said.

"Highly unlikely," he said.

"What do you mean by that?" Hedy's eyes grew cold.

"He doesn't have any friends," Talbot said. All the cops in Robbery-Homicide knew that.

The junior detective had a point.

"I need to see him now."

Bobby studied the middle-aged blonde standing nose to nose with him. She wore an Easter egg of a pantsuit. Her eyes were the color of the Mediterranean Sea. The years and job had sculpted her into one formidable female. The kind that made men, even Talbot, who admired strong women, uneasy.

"Well," Bobby hesitated. "He's going to ask me why you need to speak to him."

Hedy knew DJ was busting Talbot's chops every chance he got.

"Tell him I need to discuss Daniel Mendoza."

"Excuse me?"

"Just give him the message," she said. Hedy held his gaze.

Talbot rolled his shoulder blade, his head leaning left then right, weighing his options. Finally, he came to a decision.

"All right," he said.

Taking a deep breath, Talbot physically braced himself as he headed to the stairs. He would deliver the message to Arias in person, and it would likely be ugly. "I'll be back."

Hedy watched him go with no sense of triumph or pity. For years, she had been at the beck and call of men like Arias who liked to humiliate their subordinates. That part of her life was over. She turned on her walkie-talkie with a scratch of audio.

"ROMEO/JULIET, this is HOTEL/SIERRA. Do you copy?"

"Affirmative, ROMEO/JULIET here. Copy."

"A suit, Detective Talbot, just headed down looking for Arias. Over."

"Eyes on the package. Over."

"Copy, ROMEO/JULIET. I hope to be heading down soon."

"With love's light wings, HOTEL/SIERRA. Over."

"ROMEO/JULIET. You never disappoint. Over and out."

Hedy smiled. One pleasure of working in Los Angeles was that several Campus Safety officers, like Rodney Johnson, had once had ambitions of becoming actors. Rodney knew Shakespeare and was good-looking to boot, not that she was in the market. Still, it was nice to feel that tang in the dang once in a while.

Hedy watched Will Bloom's colleagues standing in line, waiting for Detective Talbot, for their moment to share what they knew, if anything, of what had transpired.

All this effort, all these fools trying to determine which one of them had a motive to kill Will Bloom. Hedy knew the real question.

Who didn't have a reason to murder Will Bloom?

CHAPTER 10

Cash for Gold

DJ Arias studied the victim, Will Bloom, white, around sixty-five years of age. Naked, except for a pair of boxers and dress pants pooled around his feet. His bare torso was pinned to a rectangular table, the pelvis hinged over the edge above collapsed legs. DJ crouched down. Will Bloom wore a condom when he died; a sad sight, a deflated black balloon clinging to a dick that would rise no more.

The victim's splayed arms were well-muscled, the back around the midsection was fleshy. His head was thrown back, eyes bulbous in shock, mouth open, tongue out. His hair was dark brown, a dye job, possibly in a quest to keep himself youthful. Death still caught up with him; a long curved sword rose out of his spine. DJ noted a lack of blood splatter. Most people were killed with guns, knives, a screwdriver, something handy. This murder weapon appeared to be a samurai sword. On the wall kitty-corner to the victim hung a mounted black sword rack with a gold dragon imprint, now empty. DJ loved *Seven Samurai*, a movie about honor and ancient nobility. Maybe the choice of weapon meant something to the killer or the victim?

DJ slipped on rubber gloves as he stood in the dead man's office. Bowing his head, DJ prayed, "Dear God, bless this soul, who has passed into your realm. And away from mine. Help me find justice for this man . . . whether he deserves it or not. Amen."

DJ made the sign of the cross.

"Will Bloom," he said. "I'm DJ Arias." The woman officer guarding the door looked in. DJ waved her away. It was the beginning of an important relationship. The kind DJ was good at.

DJ turned, noted the glass door behind the victim, open to the courtyard. Is this how the murderer entered the room? DJ walked outside into a quadrangle of white walls and the tall windows of other offices. Mature prickly pear, barrel, and cholla cacti dotted the space, divided by concrete paths and mounds of white gravel. Trash bags and garden implements were stashed in the corner. One other entrance, a closed glass door, stood on a perpendicular wall.

Back inside, DJ took a quick mental inventory of Will Bloom's office. A bookcase held leather-bound history books and slim pamphlets of poetry. There were mementos—including an elk hoof paperweight that only an old white guy could love. Dress shirts wrapped in a dry cleaner bag hung from a coat stand. DJ noted the bottles of whiskey under the desk. In a half-opened drawer, he spied a variety pack of condoms.

On top of the desk, stacks of paper and yellow legal pads shared space with an overflowing inbox. One item, a dry cleaner's receipt held scribbled words and a drawn lopsided heart. DJ made out "three o'clock, Gdale SP" and a phone number written over the faintly printed numbers. What caught DJ's interest was the letter opener that impaled the drawn heart, piercing the receipt and plunging into the body of the leather desk blotter. It was an eerie echo of Bloom's death. DJ took a photo of the receipt on his phone.

DJ had noted that Will Bloom wore no wedding ring. There were no pictures of the missus or girlfriend on the desk. A man who died as he probably lived, fucking up his life.

"Takes one to know one."

DJ took out his Swiss army knife and, with the longest blade, carefully flicked through the inbox; expense reports listing several bars DJ knew, a presentation with red and green graphs, opened and unopened mail in no particular order. Next to the inbox, casually discarded, was an advertisement that read, "Cash for Gold."

DJ stood still as a memory from his past unwound in his head like an old family movie—faded and poorly edited.

A voice said, "Be right back, Darius."

Seventeen-year-old DJ was standing on a Las Vegas street corner. Blood stained the sidewalk. Yellow tape cordoned off the busy men and women wearing Las Vegas Police Department uniforms, cleaning up the mess they had made. Lying on the ground was DJ's beloved cousin, Frankie, a now-dead gangbanger who had moved to Vegas to straighten up his life. That's what he told their Grandma Amelia. His cousin looked *fuerte*, strong, even in death, as if he'd decided to take a nap before he hit the clubs. Only he wasn't in the casino district; he had died on the backstreets of Vegas, inhabited by pawnshops and instant check cashing storefronts promising easy money to the suckers who took one last chance to make their fortune.

Was Frankie really trying to rob one of these places like the cops said? Or did he just look like a guy who was? Frankie had told DJ to wait in the car. He had a buddy who owed him some cash. He'd be right back.

DJ was so green that when he heard the pop–pop–pop, he thought it was kids setting off firecrackers. Fireworks in Vegas.

Bobby Talbot's voice brought him back to the present.

"Detective Arias," Talbot said. "I need to speak with you, sir."

"Hey, Bobtail," said DJ. "You spoke to the woman who found the body?"

Talbot took a breath before he continued.

"Yes, the maid. She's in an office down the hall for further questioning."

"You mean the cleaning woman?" DJ didn't like the word maid. White women used to call his grandmother their maid, as if they owned her for the one day a week she cleaned their house.

"Yes, sir, the cleaning woman. Her name is Ema Treet."

"Did she do it, Bobtail?"

Talbot didn't smile. He hated the name Bobtail. Everyone knew DJ was an asshole, but the man felt the need to prove it.

"Good one, sir," Talbot said.

DJ looked up at Talbot. Another new partner. He wore one of those form-fitting suits he'd seen in the windows of H&M, and his leather shoes were polished. Talbot looked so new and shiny, he probably ate peanut butter and jelly sandwiches for lunch. DJ had heard he was a Buddhist.

"She found the body at approximately five thirty this morning."

"She's sure of the time?"

"She's on a tight schedule. The secretaries begin their shift at eight—and once they arrive, forget cleaning the offices. She checked her watch when she headed down here—five fifteen. It took ten or fifteen minutes to clean the staircase and lower lobby."

"Okay, then the cleaning women called in the murder?" asked DJ.

"No."

DJ stared at Bobtail again, hoping to encourage an answer.

"So who called the police?"

"That's why I need to speak with you. The Facilities guy, his name is Daniel Mendoza, he called the police and . . ."

"Daniel Mendoza?" DJ interrupted.

"That's his name. Do you know him, sir? We have him in an office down the hall."

DJ knew Daniel Mendoza, the young man he'd sent to prison ten years ago. He lost track of him after the conviction. What were the chances another Daniel Mendoza was involved with a death on the Hesperia campus? DJ didn't believe in coincidence.

"There's a Hedy Scacht upstairs. She's the head of Campus Safety. She wants to talk to you . . . about this Daniel Mendoza."

Hedy Scacht, another name from the past. DJ didn't believe in coincidence and now there were two.

Cousin Frankie's death tore a hole through DJ's family. Grandma Amelia was never the same. She drifted in and out of an ether visited by ghosts, including Frankie, until she died from a stroke in her home.

DJ graduated from Cal State Los Angeles, a college with no private cactus gardens, just miles of crowded parking lots. With a degree in criminal justice and forensic studies, DJ was planning to attend law school until one of Frankie's old pals attended his graduation.

Manny Saldano was only five years older than DJ but looked closer to forty. A bone-and-gristle gangster who wore a bandanna on his head, black wraparound shades, and a flannel shirt. When he took off his sunglasses, DJ saw the black teardrop tattoo at the outer corner of his right eye.

"Hey, man!" Manny gave DJ a fist bump and then a vicelike hug. DJ felt the tough sinew of the man. "I'm proud of you, *compadre*."

"Thanks, bro."

"Yeah, you're all right, not a gangster like your cousin or me."

DJ stepped back. "Hey, Frankie was the man. He was my hero."

"I ran the streets with him," Manny said. "I know what Frankie was."

DJ's face went slack, his chin bumped up. He gave the other man a cold look. Manny's dead-man eyes stared back, punctuated by the prison tear tattooed with a needle and ink from a Bic pen.

"I just came by to say congratulations," Manny said. "And don't be a fucking gangbanger like your cousin Frankie."

"Asshole," DJ said under his breath as the other man started to walk away.

Manny turned around and smiled. It didn't reach his eyes. He pushed his hand into his pocket. DJ wondered if he was going for a gun. Instead, he pulled out a pack of cigarettes and lit one, blowing a perfect ring of smoke in the air.

"I'd rather die on my feet than live on my knees," DJ said. It was Frankie's favorite quote from Mexican revolutionary Emiliano Zapata, ripped off by a now deceased rap artist.

"Hey, genius, Frankie lived and died on his knees. You're a college graduate and you're still a no-nothing punk like your cousin."

With a last ring of smoke, Manny was gone.

DJ signed up for the Police Academy two weeks after graduation. He was going to infiltrate the bad guys—the men in blue—to prove that Frankie was innocent. He would be the good cop who didn't finger every Latino as the bad guy; he was going to turn it all around.

Day after day, week after week, year after year, as DJ patrolled the streets, rose from police officer to Detective I, Detective II, he stepped across the remains of dead gangbangers, kids, teens, his people, *La Raza*, killed on the streets of Los Angeles, mostly by their own. Every time he saw another life extinguished, he saw his beloved cousin Frankie, lying dead on the warm cement of Las Vegas, lit by the white and yellow neon lights flashing, "Cash for Gold."

CHAPTER 11

Circus of Smoke

DJ left Will Bloom's office followed by Bobby Talbot.

"I'm sending you a photo," said DJ, punching his phone. "It's a receipt, someone stabbed it with a letter opener. There's writing on it. Call the phone number and see who answers."

"Yes, sir," said Talbot as he glanced upward.

Hedy Scacht watched them from the lobby, her face visible above the banister of the spiral staircase. DJ looked up. Talbot thought he caught a flicker of interest in DJ's eyes.

"That's the woman I told you about," said Talbot.

"Yes," said DJ. "I know the woman." He motioned her to come down. Hedy quickly descended, her heels clapping the marble.

To Hedy, DJ Arias looked leaner, meaner than she remembered. Ten years ago, he was almost handsome, with a sculpted face, brown eyes, full lips. When he smiled, which was rare, his mouth stretched into a crooked grin. He was bad news when they first met.

Now he was worse.

"Hedy, how are you?" he asked.

"Not so good," she said. "Now that you've returned to Hesperia."

"You're hurting my feelings."

"I doubt it."

"I was invited here," he said, "by a dead man."

"Will Bloom."

"You knew him?"

"I did," she said. "But . . ."

"But that's not why you asked to see me."

"Can we speak in private?"

"I was hoping you'd ask."

"Still the charmer," she said.

Hedy nodded at Officer Rodney Johnson stationed by the elevator. He pressed the call button.

"ROMEO," said Hedy as she approached with DJ.

"Ms. SIERRA," he replied.

DJ joined Hedy in the elevator. Hedy hit the "close door" button, and the doors closed as Talbot approached.

Talbot looked to Officer Johnson, who shrugged. The younger detective would have to climb the stairs. At the top, he took a few deep breaths to shake off DJ calling him Bobtail and doors closing in his face.

DJ and Hedy emerged from the elevator in the second-floor lobby. DJ almost collided with a woman. She had glossy black hair, caramel skin, large brown eyes reddened from recent tears.

"Oh, Hedy, I heard about Will," said the woman. "I can't believe it!"

"Yes, it's a shock," said Hedy. "Ravi, this is Detective DJ Arias."

"Oh, hello," the woman said in a British accent. "I'm Professor Ravi La-Val, head of faculty council. Sorry for rushing in, I'm heading upstairs for an emergency meeting with the president."

"Hello," said DJ. "No worries."

"Any idea," asked Professor LaVal, "how Will died?"

"Too early to tell," said DJ.

"Well," said Professor LaVal, "let me know if the faculty can be helpful in any way."

"Of course," DJ said.

"Goodbye, then. See you later, Hedy," she said, stepping into the elevator and heading upstairs.

"I bet you'll run into Ravi LaVal again," Hedy said after the elevator door closed. "She makes it her business to know what's going on at Hesperia."

"And what is going on at Hesperia?" said DJ.

They were now thrust into the chaos of the main lobby, where Campus Safety and police officers were stopping people from entering and exiting. Bloom's officemates were being kept in one place for further questioning, while the other Sliming dwellers were relegated to another area against one wall of windows.

A tall Campus Safety officer escorted a petite young woman wearing a sweater and black leggings across the lobby. The girl carried a large plastic trash bag.

"That's Luke Benson," said Hedy. "This must be the girl who was attacked last night."

Hesperia was a small college, and Hedy recognized the student, but she only knew her name from the Campus Safety report regarding the attack. The girl looked pale and tired, as if she hadn't slept. Her long black hair hung like a shroud around her lovely face.

"I'm Hedy Scacht, director of Campus Safety." She reached out to shake the girl's hand—short nails, no fingernail polish. The girl stared at Hedy's well-manicured hand which had one ragged fingernail. DJ noticed the chink in Hedy's armor.

"Yes, of course," the girl said. "I've seen you on campus. I'm Ferencia Lake. I go by Fern."

The women shook hands.

"I'm Detective Arias." He nodded at the girl, then looked around.

"Bobtail," called DJ. "Bobtail! Hey, Talbot!" He gestured to the junior detective now standing among Bloom's officemates. "Show Officer Benson which room Ms. Lake can wait in downstairs. I'll be there shortly."

DJ ignored Talbot's face, reddened with anger.

He turned to Hedy. "There's a lot happening at Hesperia College these days."

"Tell me something I don't know."

Hedy pulled one key from dozens that hung from a retractable key ring clipped to her belt loop. She unlocked the double doors adjacent to the elevator. "I can arrange for you to use this room for your investigation. It's centrally located and private. It's the Wick Conference Room, where our trustees meet."

"Sounds good." Hedy was one of the few women DJ knew who could rock a pastel power suit and a retractable key ring clip. DJ's lopsided grimace quickly appeared and vanished as they entered and she closed the door. "So, what's up?"

Hedy adjusted the front of her jacket, gathering her thoughts.

"I want you to treat him fairly."

"Who?"

"You know who," said Hedy. "Danny Mendoza."

"He called in the murder," DJ said.

"That's not a crime."

"He was at the murder scene."

"That's coincidence and bad timing," Hedy said.

"He's a convicted felon. I couldn't ignore that if I wanted to," DJ said. "And I don't want to."

"He's trying to rebuild what's left of his life."

"He still has his life."

"Don't think," Hedy said, "he doesn't remember that every minute of every day."

"I'm sure the girl's parents remember."

Hedy pressed her lips together. After a beat she said, "I haven't forgotten. The girl's name was Sally Smith. Nothing will ease her family's loss," said Hedy. "But I've promised to be the guardian of my best friend's son. I'm here to protect Danny."

"Okay, Hedy, you had your say," DJ said. "But he's a suspect."

"His mother died six months ago. He's almost a year out of prison, sober, and he's an exemplary worker. No trouble. Danny and Will Bloom had nothing more than a passing acquaintance, if that. A small liberal arts college is like a feudal village. Vice presidents don't hobnob with facility workers."

"That I believe. We'll check out his alibi," said DJ, "if he has one."

"That Danny was even in Sliming this morning is pure chance," said Hedy.

"Isn't it all chance?" asked DJ. "Someone has too many beers, whiskey, or both. He gets behind the wheel of a car. Someone crosses a street and doesn't remember to look both ways. All chance; all tragedy. But I have another dead body—and a man at the scene with a record."

Hedy controlled the anger that flared to hide her fear. It would be so easy to point a finger at Danny.

"Any thoughts," said Hedy, "on how Will died? Could it be an accident?"

"Can't say," said DJ. The chance that Will Bloom accidentally impaled himself in the back with a samurai sword was zero.

"No?" asked Hedy. "And he wasn't the type to take his own life."

"You knew Mr. Bloom?"

"Not well," said Hedy. "When can I see Danny?"

"After I question him. Now, tell me what you know about Mr. Bloom."

Hedy studied DJ and made a decision.

"Will Bloom came to Hesperia about two years ago from Montclair College. He was trouble there and trouble here. I worked with him briefly, a long time ago. He was forced out of Montclair. Some people never change."

"What kind of trouble?"

"He is . . . was a notorious womanizer," said Hedy. "And a mean drunk."

"Well, that's a terrible trait on a college campus. Did he sleep with students?"

"I think he learned, the hard way, to stay away from students. Everyone else was fair game; secretaries, professors, coworkers, he wasn't picky. And it's not just gossip. Several of our cleaning staff have walked in on Mr. Bloom in compromising situations with other employees. I've had to personally calm them down."

"Why wasn't he fired for that?" asked DJ.

"He seemed to be immune," said Hedy. "Maybe someone was protecting him."

"Who?"

"Can't say," said Hedy.

"Look, I'll bend over backward to be fair," said DJ. "To Danny."

"I'll hold your feet to the fire on that," said Hedy.

"Well?" DJ asked again.

"Will Bloom made a lot of money for Hesperia College, for every place he worked. But he was a liability. Let's just say when a powerful man makes a mistake, he'd rather make excuses than admit he was wrong."

"The president?"

Hedy gathered up all five foot ten of herself, adjusted her jacket, headed for the door. "Can't say. But I'll remember your promise."

Hedy circled her chest, then put her fist against her heart. "It's in the vault."

"Hedy," said DJ, "if I ever get into trouble, I'd want you to have my back."

DJ crossed his heart in solidarity. He might very well need her help.

Hedy looked him over from head to toe and back again.

"You are trouble," said Hedy.

She smiled at DJ for the first time. A smile that made him think of pork chops, sex, and twenty-year-old scotch—not in that order. In her day, she was a woman someone might have risked anything for. Maybe still would.

Hedy walked out of Sliming to her illegally parked car. Being head of Campus Safety had its privileges. She knew Hesperia inside and out, the century-old buildings, the academic quad studded with California oaks, the wild scrub of Malo Hill. Uneven sidewalks and sprawling lawns covered an aging infrastructure of pipes and wires buried in old concrete tunnels that ran to all corners of campus.

Hesperia's beauty usually lifted her spirits. Not today. She drove through Eagle Rock's gentrifying neighborhood of old bungalows, many freshly painted.

Turning left, she quickly covered the five blocks up York Boulevard to the tobacco store, Circus of Smoke. She bought unfiltered Camels. Standing outside the small shop, with a shaking hand she lit a cigarette and inhaled. She wished that Isabella Mendoza was standing beside her so she could talk to her old friend, confide her fears, her worry about Danny and her own daughter, Delores. But Isabella was gone and Hedy was alone.

How could Hedy keep her promise to Isabella? What could she do to protect Danny?

Ten years ago, Danny Mendoza was a first year at Hesperia, being initiated into Alpha Tau Omega, the fraternity of football and rugby players. Drunk from a night of pledging and egged on by his would-be frat brothers, Danny drove the four blocks back to campus. He forgot to turn on the headlights. He didn't see seventeen-year-old Sally Smith walk into the street, but he heard the sickening thud as the car plowed into something soft and pliant. He turned on the lights. The older boys got out of the car and ran. Not Danny.

Suddenly sober, he jumped out and saw what he had done. He couldn't find his cell phone, so Danny ran from door to door begging for someone to call an ambulance. But it was too late. Sally Smith was dead.

Hedy inhaled deeply. The hot nicotine reached her lungs but didn't fill the void. A dull throb of pain rooted inside her chest. She chose to ignore it.

Dropping the butt to the sidewalk, she ground it out with the toe of her shoe. Hedy almost threw the rest of the pack into the trash, but instead tucked it into her purse and headed back to Hesperia College.

CHAPTER 12

Witness

DJ and Talbot headed downstairs to conduct the first interviews of the investigation: Ema Treet, the cleaning woman who found the victim; Danny Mendoza, the groundskeeper who called in the murder; and Fern Lake, the student attacked in the olive grove. Talbot had taken down their names and basic information. Now DJ, with the younger man's assistance, would conduct interrogations.

"Hey, Bobtail," said DJ.

Talbot considered not responding until he used his real name.

"Get me the job description for Daniel Mendoza and his work assignment. I want to know what he was doing in this building and if he was authorized to be here."

"Already in progress, and it's Talbot," said the younger detective as he led DJ to the office where Ema Treet waited.

DJ ignored the comment. He knew his colleagues thought he was an asshole. He liked it that way. It nixed the extraneous chitchat and forced camaraderie of the blue brotherhood. DJ didn't need brothers, blue or otherwise. Cousin Frankie had been as close as a brother. That led to loss and two lingering questions; what and why. He knew the when and where. He relived it every night before he fell asleep.

Talbot opened the door to the office where the cleaning woman, Ema Treet, waited. She sat like a small obedient child in a black ergonomic office chair suitable for a starship captain, with movable head and armrests, levers and knobs, chrome legs and wheels. Ema had pale gray eyes surrounded by dark circles. The fingers resting on her lap resembled twigs that might break with a firm handshake.

DJ waved to avoid any fractures.

"Hello," he said. "I'm Detective DJ Arias, in charge of the investigation."

He immediately ruled her out as a suspect based on the lack of any tangible evidence of upper body strength. Her Hesperia uniform ballooned around her slim shoulders. He wondered how she had the muscle to clean offices.

Talbot stood at attention near the closed door with a legal pad ready to take notes.

"I need to go home," she said. "My husband, Marco, will be worried."

"A few questions," said DJ. "Then you can go home."

"Does Marco know what happened?" she asked. "I couldn't reach him."

"We've called your home," Talbot said, "and left a message."

"He must be writing," said Ema Treet. "Marco's a poet."

"Uh-huh," said DJ. He had little interest in poetry, even less in poets. "How well did you know Will Bloom?"

"Not at all," Ema said. "He was a very bad man."

"A bad man? You said you didn't know him."

"I cleaned his office," said Ema. "I knew him."

"How's that?"

"Whiskey bottles, women's undergarments on the floor, and worse in the wastebasket."

DJ nodded. Trash spilled secrets. If you let others dump it, you deserved what you got.

"Not a good man," said Ema. "Not like my Marco."

DJ grunted and thought Marco probably disposed of his own detritus.

"When you cleaned his office, Will Bloom was never present?"

"No," Ema Treet said. "Never. I always clean his office first, early in the morning."

"Did you ever see anyone else, perhaps a woman, in Will Bloom's office?"

"No," she said.

"You said there was a woman's . . . clothes, underwear."

"Women's undergarments. Many shapes, many sizes."

"Many women."

"It would seem so," Ema Treet said.

"Did you hear any gossip about his women friends?"

Ema Treet looked him in the eye. "I don't do gossip."

"Mrs. Treet," said DJ. "You are one in a million."

Ema said nothing, unimpressed by his admiration.

"Okay, let's begin with this morning. What time did you start your shift?"

"Three thirty a.m."

"Tell me what happened before you entered Mr. Bloom's office. Did you hear anyone, see anything unusual?"

"No," she said. "I start on the third floor, then the main lobby. It was an ordinary morning." Ema Treet whimpered, realizing there would be no ordinary anythings in her immediate future.

"I know this is upsetting," DJ said. "But we have to document everything you saw and heard. Tell me what happened next?"

Ema Treet took a moment to calm herself.

"I sent the cart down in the elevator to the bottom floor and I walk down the stairs. It was five fifteen, I check my watch. First, I mop the circle of marble by the stairs, usually it takes a few minutes, but this morning, someone had spilled a few drops of something dark and sticky, like chocolate. I had to scrub it with Pine-Sol."

DJ caught Talbot's eye. The younger man made a note to have the forensics team concentrate on that area.

"Then I go to Mr. Bloom's office. Like I said, I always clean it first."

"Was the door to Will Bloom's office open or shut?"

"His door was shut."

"Okay. And then?"

"I knock on the door. I always knock in case Mr. Bloom is inside. No one answered so I open the door." Ema's hand flew to her face, fingers fluttered around her lips.

"What happened next?" asked DJ. "Describe what you saw."

"I turned on the lights. I saw his face, his eyes were open," she said. "And the sword. It was horrible."

"Yes, sorry. I know it was. Did you notice anything else?"

"No," she said. "I mean, yes."

"Go on."

"The courtyard door was open. To the cactus garden."

"Did you see anyone or anything outside?"

"No," said Ema Treet. "I only saw Mr. Bloom."

"Okay," said DJ. "Tell me exactly what happened next."

"I backed out, I was frightened, and I felt sick to my stomach. I made it to the lobby and I threw up all over the floor I had just mopped." Ema Treet began to cry. "The floor, I was worried about the floor and a man was dead."

DJ didn't like crying women. He had enough of those in his private life.

Suddenly, Talbot produced a bottle of water out of thin air.

"Here, take a drink," Talbot said. "You're doing great."

Bobtail was a real Boy Scout, thought DJ. Always prepared. He stared at the floor until the tear-storm abated, the cleaning woman's breathing returned to normal.

"You okay now, Mrs. Treet?"

After a few sniffles, Ema Treet nodded.

"What happened next?"

"I was at the bottom of the stairs when Daniel found me."

"Daniel Mendoza?" asked DJ.

"Yes, one of the gardeners."

"You know him?"

"Not well," said Ema Treet. "He is a very quiet man. We both work in the Facilities Department."

"Where did he come from?" asked DJ. "Which direction?"

"From the left, the hallway," said Ema. "I was relieved to see him."

"And what was his demeanor? Was he disheveled, dirty, panting, out of breath?"

"No," she said. "Daniel was in his uniform. It was pressed and clean."

"What was he doing there?" asked DJ.

"I don't know."

"Did he say what he was doing there?"

"I didn't ask him."

"And what did he do when he saw you?"

"I want to go home," said Ema.

"We're almost done here," said DJ.

Going home wasn't going to help her forget what she saw, but she'd know that soon enough.

"What did Daniel Mendoza say or do?"

"He asked me what was wrong. I pointed to the office."

"What did he do?"

"He walked over to the office, I didn't want to look, but I couldn't help it. He turned on the light and stood at the doorway. And then he went to the assistant's desk and called someone. I think Campus Safety."

"You're sure he didn't step inside the office?" asked DJ.

"No, he stood in the doorway. I watched him. I didn't want to be alone," she said in a barely audible voice, "I'm afraid of the dead."

"What?" asked DJ.

"I was frightened," said Ema Treet. She gathered her thoughts. "This man, the dead man, part of him is trapped here. Looking for a way out. I saw his eyes."

"Well, I just examined the victim," said DJ. "He is dead—over and out." DJ didn't need any ghost stories either.

"You are one of those men," Ema Treet stared at him with pity, "who think they know everything."

Talbot cleared his throat. DJ threw him a look as he ran a hand through his hair. "So you and Mendoza stayed until the police arrived?"

"Yes," said Ema. "Daniel was very kind. He sat with me until the Campus Safety officer arrived, and then the police."

"Uh-huh," said DJ. "That's nice of him. Did the Campus Safety officer step into Will Bloom's office?"

"Officer Benson? He's very tall. No, he looked into the room from the doorway. Said he needed to secure the area."

"Okay, good," said DJ.

He had heard enough. He didn't want any more "tales from the crypt" from this spooky bird.

"Well, I think that's enough for now. Thank you for your help."

Ema Treet stood up. Talbot gently took her elbow, escorted her to the door with the usual admonishments about not leaving town and being available for further questions. Ema Treet turned and looked at DJ.

"The dead," she said, "speak to the living."

DJ met her eyes, pale and haunted, surrounded by lashes and circles so dark, she might be a fashion model or heroin user.

"But," said Ema, "I think you know that."

"I do my best, Mrs. Treet."

Ema Treet lowered her eyes. "*Bůh ti žehnej*," she whispered.

"What does that mean?" asked DJ.

"Something you need," said Ema Treet.

She left the room accompanied by Detective Talbot, presumably to return to her husband the poet.

DJ shook off an involuntary shudder.

CHAPTER 13

Person of Interest

Danny Mendoza was pacing. Walking back and forth in a small rectangle—the exact size of his cell at Chino Prison. He now occupied a large office with plenty of space, but part of Danny remained in that eight-by-six-foot cell and would for the rest of his life.

Detective DJ Arias and the younger detective, Talbot, entered the office. The younger man looked miserable. This didn't surprise Danny. Detective Arias was an asshole when Danny was eighteen. Now he was a black hole, a man that emitted no light.

Danny, planting both feet on the floor a ruler's-length apart, stood ramrod straight, broad shoulders back. He took up space as he had learned to do in the yard when a predator came sniffing around.

DJ stopped and took note of the man before him.

Talbot wasn't sure what was happening. He had briefly met Daniel Mendoza thirty minutes ago. The man had transformed from a humble gardener into the Hulk. This version of Daniel had presence, a thick muscled boxer's physique, a man to take seriously if challenged.

"This is Daniel Mendoza. Daniel is ground maintenance, fourth level. He reports to Grounds Supervisor level five."

Talbot produced the job description that DJ had requested earlier with a flourish and handed it to the older detective. The paper fell to the ground.

This time DJ didn't mean to humiliate Talbot. He couldn't take his eyes off Danny. The last time he saw Daniel Mendoza, he was an eighteen-year-old with an arrogance that had almost survived the vehicular manslaughter verdict. Daniel had no idea what lay ahead of him in prison. The ten-year sentence had taken its toll. Each day, week, year was stamped on the skin of the man before him. Not tats like most felons, but early crow's-feet riveting down cheeks that owed more to doing time than sun damage.

Danny Mendoza was now the taller man, lean and muscled. Not much else to do in prison but lift weights and run the yard. Danny stood with his chin out, eyes forward, mouth closed. DJ saw veins standing at attention in his neck and temples. This was a man who would not hesitate between fight or flight. Given any provocation, he would hold his ground.

Except for the eyes. DJ recognized those eyes, not just of the boy, but from his late mother. Hedy said she had passed away. A particular shade of green with a nobility that almost coaxed out DJ's sympathy for her son. But not quite.

"That's all right," said Talbot. He bent down to retrieve the job description. "I've got it." He held it out for DJ, but to no avail. Talbot sighed.

"Hello, Daniel," said DJ Arias.

"Sir." Danny stood ramrod straight and otherwise kept silent. Another lesson learned, offer nothing that's not asked.

"So, here we are again," said DJ.

"Oh," said Talbot. "You know each other too?"

"You better catch up, Bobtail," said DJ. "The train has left the station and you're miles behind."

Talbot retreated to the corner. "Of course I am."

The punk of a boy DJ had put away was now a beast of a man. "This is Daniel Mendoza," said DJ, "convicted felon."

"I served my time," said Danny.

"Trouble seems to have a way of following you around, son."

Danny flinched. This asshole would never call him son if they were standing man to man in a dark alley. He kept his mouth shut.

DJ smiled like he knew what Danny was thinking. Danny didn't smile back.

"All right, Daniel, so tell me what happened this morning," said DJ. "In your own words."

For Danny, everything was on the line. He was a convicted felon; by law, he had to declare it on every job application. His mother had begged the president to give Danny a chance with this job. He couldn't lose it, for her memory, or for himself.

"I had a two-day assignment to clean up the inner courtyard of Sliming. Today was the second day. I started early, got here around five forty-five. I unlocked the exterior door and heard something, someone crying. I walked to the lobby and found Ema Treet sitting on the bottom stair. She wouldn't stop crying. She pointed to the vice president's office."

Danny paused.

"Go on," said DJ.

"I went to the door and saw Mr. Bloom was dead. I walked over to the phone on Trish Ballentine's desk. I called Campus Safety, they said sit tight. They would call the police. I walked back to Ema Treet. Officer Benson arrived in a few minutes. Told us to stay put until the police arrived."

DJ was quiet, nodding his head as if he was considering Danny's story, ready to say, "Okay, thank you! You are free to go." That wasn't what DJ was considering and Danny knew it. Talbot scribbled down Danny's statement. "Did you go inside Bloom's office?" asked DJ. "Think before you answer."

"No," said Danny. "I stood at the threshold and turned on the light." He didn't need to think about it.

"Did you ever go into Will Bloom's office?" asked DJ. "Before today."

"No," said Danny.

"Never worked in his office? Fixed something, screwed in a lightbulb?"

"I'm grounds maintenance. That's building maintenance."

Talbot checked the job description. "He's right. He's grounds maintenance. That entails sports fields, landscaping, and general grounds."

"Thank you, Bobtail," growled DJ. "I was asking Daniel."

Talbot straightened up, reddened at this rebuke.

"Detective Talbot is correct," said Danny. "I don't work in the buildings."

"Thank you," said Talbot.

DJ glared at the younger detective, who glared back.

"And yet," said DJ, "here you are. Inside Sliming helping Ema Treet in her time of need."

Danny pulled the requisition for the courtyard maintenance out of his back pocket.

"There's no outside access to the courtyard. Facilities enters through the business office door."

DJ remembered the other door in the perpendicular wall of the courtyard. He barely glanced at the paper. "I'll be keeping this for evidence."

Danny said nothing.

"So two interior doors access the courtyard. You're saying you used the other door?"

"I did yesterday," said Danny. "The business office door is in a corridor. The other is in a private office."

"Will Bloom's office. And the doors are kept locked?" asked DJ.

Danny shrugged. "All doors are supposed to be locked at the end of business day."

"So to enter the building," asked DJ, "you needed a key, right?"

Danny pulled the neatly labeled keys out of the same pocket.

"Two keys. Exterior door, which I used, and the interior door to the court-yard through the business office, which I did not."

"So that door should be locked?" asked DJ.

Danny didn't answer for a moment. "I locked it yesterday at the end of my shift." He felt DJ was leading him into a trap and would love to slam it down on his neck.

"I don't know about this morning," said Danny. "I never got to that door. I heard the crying, I followed the sound to the lobby and found Ema Treet on the stairs."

"You know that we'll check Will Bloom's office and his courtyard door for fingerprints," said DJ.

Danny said nothing, just met DJ's eyes as if to say, "Do what you have to, motherfucker. Doesn't matter to me." Instead Danny said, "Yes, sir."

"And what were you doing last night? Between 5:30 p.m. and midnight. "

"As I told Detective Talbot, I was home. I watched women's basketball, pre-season game, Connecticut won. Lights out at nine thirty."

"Not much of an alibi," said DJ.

"I got pizza delivered around seven thirty."

"What restaurant?"

"Domino's," said Danny. "I have the box and receipt at home."

"We'll need it," said DJ. "And we'll check it out too. Anything else you want to tell me? Anything else you saw out of the ordinary?"

"Just Mr. Bloom, dead, sir. With a sword in his back." Danny didn't say it was a horrible way to die. All dying was horrible: in bed like his mother, pin-ioned to a conference table like Will Bloom, or on the pavement of a street lit by headlights like Sally Smith.

"You're a person of interest in this case. Go home and don't even think of leaving the city."

"Yes, sir."

Part of Danny felt dead and had for the past ten years. But the rest of him remained, having to listen to this asshole, DJ Arias. He shifted his weight and felt something in his pocket press against his thigh.

"Come back tomorrow morning. And bring the receipt for pizza and any-thing else that can prove you were at home last night," said DJ. "We can go through all this again. From the top."

Danny nodded. "Sure."

Why not? He had nowhere else to go but home and no one else to see.

CHAPTER 14

Truth Is Not My Friend

Ferencia Lake waited in an office on the bottom floor of Sliming.

"Someone will come by shortly to interview you," said Campus Safety Officer Luke Benson.

"All right." Her voice sounded young and afraid, even to herself.

"I need to take possession of these clothes. They're evidence now." He took the bag of her bloodstained clothes from last night. "The LAPD will provide you with a receipt."

"My backpack's inside," said Fern. "Forget the receipt. I never want to see those things again."

"It's procedure," said Officer Benson before he closed the door.

Fern thought she heard the lock click.

She curled up her knees, her feet resting on the seat of the office chair. Last night she had slept with her professor, a married man. It was as if her guilt over that fact had manifested into a monster. And that monster had attacked her. What if she hadn't escaped? She hadn't known then that someone on campus had been murdered. What if the attack had something to do with the death of that vice president? The thought terrified her.

Fern heard voices and footsteps heading her way. She made a quick decision. She was not only growing more guilty about sleeping with Professor Bounty, but she also worried there might be a morals clause in her scholarship grant. Fern couldn't lose her scholarship. Her widowed father was a high school teacher and football coach. She had to protect herself and her father too. Right now, truth was not her friend.

The door flew open. *Not locked*, thought Fern. Two men entered. Fern had briefly met them upstairs. One was hard to forget. Dark, lean, even handsome in a Heathcliff kind of way. Like he might enjoy hurting those he loved.

The younger man who had accompanied her and Officer Benson earlier looked awful, stressed out. He followed the other man into the office, shut the door, stood against the wall like a sentry.

"So, again, Ms. Lake, I'm Detective Arias and this is . . ."

"Talbot," the other man yelled out. "I'm Detective Bobby Talbot."

Arias scowled at the younger man. Talbot winced, prepared for a rebuke, then stood tall when nothing came his way. He nodded at her, slid down into a chair, and positioned a yellow pad on his lap.

Police! thought Fern. Was this good cop, bad cop? Who knew what they were up to. It appeared as if they were pitted against each other, but it was probably a trap. It solidified her decision to keep Professor Bounty a secret.

"Now, tell me your full name and your age," DJ said.

"Ferencia Louisa Lake," she said. "People call me Fern. I'm twenty-one, a senior here."

"Fern," he said the name as if he disapproved. "So, you're almost done with Hesperia?"

"I graduate in May." She looked down at her hands. Her fingers involuntarily rubbed against each other like Lady Macbeth washing away imaginary blood. She clamped her left hand over right to still herself. Both men watched closely.

"Are you all right?" asked DJ.

"Yes, of course," she said. "I mean, no. Someone attacked me last night, so no, I'm not all right."

"Okay. Fair enough. In your own words," said Detective Arias, "tell us what happened."

Fern decided to only cover the relevant event. "Last night, I took the shortcut up the hill to my residence hall. I thought I heard someone walking on the path behind me, so I stopped. But I didn't see anyone. I called out—asked if anyone was there. But no one answered. So I walked faster, and when I reached the center of the grove—which is an open area . . . I heard something in the trees to my right."

"Wait, wait," said DJ. "Just a few questions before you continue. Did you have your cell phone with you?"

"It was dead," said Fern.

"And what time was this?" asked DJ.

"I'm not sure. Maybe around eight, eight ten or so?"

"And what were you doing at the west side of campus that late at night with a dead phone?"

"Eight p.m. isn't late, Detective. I had my phone with me all day. It just ran out of power."

DJ stared at her. "Okay, so what were you doing 'not so late' walking through a dark wooded area without a phone or light?"

Fern made a quick calculation. If she had studied in the library and arrived before 5:00 p.m., she didn't have to swipe her card to enter. Fern always studied in a hidden cubby in the old circular core of stacks where no one ventured.

"I was studying. In the library. "

"But isn't it closer from the library to go directly up the stairs just north of Sliming here, to your dorm?"

Damn. This detective had the campus map tattooed on the back of his hand. "I needed some air," Fern said, "after studying for a couple of hours, so I went for a walk. In the neighborhood."

"After eight p.m.?"

"No, I started at seven or so. I just wanted to clear my head."

"Uh-huh," said DJ. "Did you get a cup of coffee or go to the taco truck on York?"

"No," she said. He would check her whereabouts. She hadn't stopped for coffee or a taco.

"No dinner last night?"

"I wasn't hungry." *I was too busy fucking my professor. Just straight up sex, sir, thrilling in the moment, and as soon as it was over, I knew it was the biggest mistake of my life.* Fern wasn't going to tell this cop anything about that. It was done, needed to be erased from her memory bank. Anyway, what the hell? Did she need an alibi for being attacked on her own campus? No, she did not! Cops always blamed the victim. She needed to remember that.

"Okay," DJ said. "You were wandering around the neighborhood for about an hour, walked back to campus, and decided to take a shortcut at night through a grove of trees."

"Is that against the law, Detective?" Fern asked. Two red spots surfaced on her cheeks. "Because the last time I checked, walking up a campus path to my residence hall is not a crime. And I was the one who was attacked!"

"Calm down. Just trying to get the facts." DJ knew the girl was lying. She was frightened, but trying to control the narrative. He didn't know why or what she was lying about.

"So you got to a clearing in the trees?" he said.

"Yes," said Fern. "And I heard something coming toward me, on my right, behind the trees and shrubs."

"Did you see who it was?"

"No, at first it sounded like pounding, maybe someone running hard. I ran to the other side of the clearing. But I tripped, fell on the ground. My knee hurt, there was a gash. And then . . ." Fern stopped. A visible shiver ran through her. DJ glanced at Bobtail to make sure he didn't run to her rescue with another bottle of water. Talbot sat quietly, listening to her story.

"Go on," said DJ.

"Then everything happened at once. Something fell on me; it was wet and gross. It felt like an animal skin or something. And smelled awful. My backpack got tangled up in it. I felt a hand run across my neck and shoulders. Something pulled at me. And then pushed me out from under it. Suddenly I was free, free of the skin and the monster thing. And then a high-pitched voice, really creepy, screamed and told me to run. And I did."

"Wait, who told you to run? The monster?"

"I don't know," said Fern. "It was like there was someone else there. With a high-pitched scary voice. I know this sounds weird, but it sounded like someone speaking with a falsetto voice. At the time, it terrified me, but now I think it was like my guardian angel or something."

"A guardian angel?" asked Talbot before DJ could say anything.

"I think it was protecting me, pushing me away from that terrible thing. It told me to run. So I ran."

"And you didn't turn around to see who attacked you, or this guardian angel?" asked DJ.

"No," said Fern. "I was terrified. I didn't know if that monster was coming after me. I was free and my instincts kicked in. I ran."

"And the blood?" asked DJ. "On your clothes and backpack."

"When I got to my residence hall, I took off my backpack to get my key card. That's when I saw that my backpack and my clothes were covered with blood. It must have been that thing that fell on me. That animal skin."

"Okay. Now, the guardian angel, the person that told you to run with the high voice. Did it sound like a woman?"

Fern stared at the floor. Her face had cooled to pale caramel.

"Officer Benson asked me that too. I called Campus Safety on the emergency phone as soon as I was inside my dorm. When I told him what happened, he asked me if it might be the Wiccans."

"What are Wiccans?" asked DJ.

"They practice pagan witchcraft," said Talbot. "They worship the goddess."

DJ stared daggers at Talbot. Bobtail was a vestibule of useless knowledge. Wiccans, Buddhists, guardian angels; he was surrounded by religious nuts.

"There's a group at Hesperia," said Fern. "Sometimes they meet in the grove. Mostly women."

"Okay. Do you think this was the Wiccan group?" asked DJ. "Maybe you interrupted one of their gatherings?"

"This wasn't women casting spells," said Fern. "This was something else. Something evil. It wanted to hurt me."

"Maybe kidnap you?" asked DJ.

"I don't know, the more I think about it, I wonder if I was just in its way. Like it was trying to get somewhere and it stumbled over me," said Fern. "And there was that smell."

"That what?" Talbot asked.

Fern looked at DJ, then Talbot. "The thing is, I know what the smell was, on the thing it threw over me. It was blood."

"You smelled blood?" asked DJ. "Or you think so now because you were covered in it?"

"My mom died when I was twelve. She had a bleeding disorder. She was pregnant. I found her when I came home from school." Fern Lake was quiet, thoughts inward, reliving something from long ago. "I recognized it, but didn't understand it."

"Understand what?" asked DJ.

"That smell. When I came home that day and found my mother. She'd hemorrhaged. She'd fallen and kept trying to get up. She'd crawled all over the house."

"You don't have to talk about that now," said DJ.

"We think she was trying to find her phone as she bled out. Blood was everywhere."

"I'm sorry this brought that memory back," said Talbot.

"Yeah," said DJ. "You don't have to relive that."

"But it was that smell," said Fern. "Strong and coppery. You know?"

"Yes," said DJ. "I know it."

"It was death," said Fern. "Whoever attacked me last night was covered in it, covered in that smell."

CHAPTER 15

Dollar Socks

DJ stood up. He wanted out of the room. He nodded at Talbot. Let Bobtail walk the young woman out and give her the 411. What kind of name was Fern anyway? What's wrong with the name Ferencia? God, he wanted a cigarette. No, he wanted a beer, preceded by a shot of tequila. Then a cigarette.

There was an exterior door at the end of the office suite. He took it. The story of Fern Lake's mother got under his skin. His Grandma Amelia had died alone. A stroke. Blood everywhere. She was on the back porch, where she did laundry. She fought hard to stay alive.

After her death, his mother, Cari, short for Caridad, Spanish for Charity, went through his beloved grandma's house like a bulldozer. She demanded DJ be present to "help out." Truth was, DJ wanted to be there. He would stand witness to his grandmother's treasures even if she didn't need them anymore. The old timber house felt fragile without her, as if a strong wind would carry it away.

He felt his grandma's presence as if at any moment she might walk in and say, *"Hola, mijo."*

She was everywhere, her baby-powder scent on the sheets, the clear plastic tablecloth protecting the fine hand-embroidered linen on the dining room table, her freshly cooked enchiladas in the fridge. DJ threw them in the trash. You can't eat a person's last intended meal. His mother, Charity, for once kept silent.

He always called his mother Charity.

It didn't suit her.

She was a person who kept busy organizing, putting things in their places, slamming drawers. That's how she dealt with life. She'd punished a rebellious boy by slamming things, a yardstick on his fingers, an open hand across his mouth, a book that hit his head. One day DJ had retreated to Grandma Amelia's house with a bloody nose and stayed there.

"Let's start with the bedroom," Charity said.

DJ watched mutely as she piled his grandmother's white cotton panties into a trash bag. They reminded DJ of innocence, as if his grandmother never grew beyond her twelve-year-old self. Maybe there were years of silk and lace, but he didn't want to believe it.

"You take this drawer."

DJ knew her impatience was due to the fact that his aunts, Hope and Faith, would soon arrive to fight over the linen, old jewelry, and china. Keepsakes of their idealized childhood. DJ didn't have one of those.

He shook open the plastic trash bag and started shoving in the white rolled socks. One pair was a black sock and a white sock. Because he had his own sense of order, he pulled them apart. That's when DJ found four twenty-dollar bills rolled inside. His mother perked up at that. She dumped all the socks on the bed and started unrolling each pair. DJ jumped in. By the time they reached the bottom of the drawer, they had eight hundred and twenty dollars in cash and countless orphan socks. His mother started unfolding the underwear.

When the aunts arrived, the cash disappeared into his mother's oversized purse.

"We'll deal with this later," she whispered. DJ didn't care. As his aunts and mother bickered over the remnants of his grandmother's jewelry, he cleaned up the enclosed back porch off the kitchen.

His grandmother died beneath the yellow laundry sorting table wedged into the corner. She had struggled after the stroke, fell, and hit her head. She must have tried to rise up over and over again. Blood was everywhere, the sick-sweet coppery smell Fern Lake had described. He shut the door to the kitchen and the women's arguments. DJ wept as he scrubbed the floors and adjoining wall.

In the end, for Charity, Hope, and Faith, it was all for nothing. His grandmother had a will and left everything, including her house, to DJ and Faith's son, Frankie. By that point, there was no Frankie, so it all went to DJ. He didn't care about the cash, linens, china, let his mother and her sisters fight over those. He kept the mantel clock that he used to wind for Grandma Amelia each morning when he was a boy. It ran five minutes late.

He sold the house because the person that saved his childhood, who loved him, had died there. He bought a new house for his wife, Lillian, for their life to begin.

Memory made his heart ache. His grandma's house was gone, and his own home felt hollow and fragile, as if a strong wind might carry him away.

CHAPTER 16

Campus Politics

DJ sat in the conference room drinking coffee. It was set up as their temporary headquarters, visible by thermos carafes, Styrofoam cups, a bag of fruit from the Buddhist, and a box of doughnuts scattered across the table. Two patrol officers had left to search the olive grove and found nothing of interest.

DJ read a message on his phone. The forensics team found drops of blood on the carpet around the staircase that Ema Treet had attempted to clean earlier. They matched the rare blood type, O-negative, to Will Bloom. The same blood type on Fern Lake's backpack and clothes. It would take weeks for DNA results, but it was clear Fern Lake had tangled with the murderer.

He considered this as he stared out the window watching students head to class, lunch, or destinations unknown. Girls with giraffe-like legs visible beneath short-shorts and boys with haystack hair peeking out under baseball caps strolled by. Even on a fall day, most students wore flip-flops as if there were a campus-wide ban on wearing shoes.

Hedy Scacht suggested Hesperia's president had protected Will Bloom. DJ wanted to interview the president ASAP, set parameters on the murder investigation. He'd sent Talbot to set up the meeting.

The former Hesperia College president, the one DJ dealt with ten years ago, was an old gray-hair named Jordan White. He was hands-off with the suspect, gave DJ carte blanche.

"Church and state," White had said. "You lead the way, young man, and we'll deal with the consequences."

That was music to DJ's ears. Later, DJ realized that his suspect, Daniel Mendoza, was inconsequential to President White. He was the son of an employee, Isabelle Mendoza, the head chef, not a rich kid with a donor parent who could sue Hesperia College. The frat boys who poured whiskey down Danny's throat came from wealthy families. President White went to bat for them. But Danny could be hung out to dry, to atone for all sins. The case helped DJ's career but soured him on Hesperia College.

A quick knock on the door brought DJ out of his reverie. Talbot escorted a tall, bony woman with a cap of smooth black hair into the conference room.

DJ felt the coffee sour in his belly. The woman wore a Scandinavian sweater over a gray skirt, turquoise tights anchored by red clogs. Not likely one of Will Bloom's conquests unless the dead man had a stronger stomach than DJ did.

"Detective Arias," said Talbot. "This is Larissa Wren. She's the president's secretary."

Larissa's face, bare of makeup, was the human personification of an owl; bushy, close-knit eyebrows, amber irises in round unblinking eyes. Heavy black glasses sat on a sharp beak of a nose. She wore a severe haircut, more monkish than modern.

"Executive assistant," said the woman. "You may address me as Larissa. President Reese will see you now, Detective Arias."

"We're finishing up preliminary interviews," DJ said, glancing at his watch. He didn't like to be ordered around, and he wanted to finish his coffee. "Give me ten minutes."

Her eyelids, naked of embellishment and perhaps lashes, finally blinked. "Now would be best."

DJ was about to protest, but her stare unnerved him. Larissa Wren was a woman who completed her mission with an unwavering belief in the power from above. In this case, the third floor, where president was king.

"I'm sure your staff will understand your absence," said Larissa.

DJ caught a smirk from Talbot that disappeared so quickly he might have imagined it.

"I need the president to answer a few questions right away," said DJ, trying to wrestle back control of the situation. "So by all means, lead the way."

"President Reese was devastated by the passing of Mr. Bloom. He has a full day of meetings, but he had me clear the next thirty minutes to meet with you."

"A whole thirty minutes," said DJ as they left the conference room, "of devastation."

"Thirty minutes for you, Detective," said Larissa. "The devastation is on-going. Please follow me."

She was impervious to sarcasm.

DJ admired that.

The third-floor executive lobby was a rotunda, the decor vintage 1960s. Under the domed ceiling, polished wood counters housed a reception area. Beige Berber carpet covered the floor and bright blue and orange leather cushions graced midcentury chairs that had seen better days.

"Wait here, please," Larissa said in a whisper. She disappeared into a side office. As DJ sat down, he heard a muffled knock and hushed voices.

She reappeared immediately.

"President Reese is ready to see you."

DJ rose and followed the woman through an inner reception area, past another minion's desk, and through a tall oak doorframe. The president's offices took up half the third story. A compact man with an athletic build and a mane of Kennedyesque hair stood before them. He immediately held out his hand.

"William Reese," he said. "Please call me Bill."

He had a firm grip, bright blue eyes, and an open youthful face beneath his chestnut wave of hair. DJ guessed "please call me Bill" was in his midforties. Young for a college president. DJ couldn't detect the thirty minutes of devastation.

"I'm Detective Arias."

"I'll close the door," said Larissa as she disappeared into the outer office.

"Detective Arias, this is a terrible tragedy for the college and for me personally."

"You and Mr. Bloom were good friends?"

"Will was a colleague. He came on board several years ago. This is a terrible shock." "Bill" clenched his jaw and lowered his eyes in a show of the aforementioned devastation.

"So you weren't personal friends. You didn't know his family or women friends?"

"No, no, no," said the president. "Well, I know he had an ex-wife, no children. His ex lives on the East Coast, I believe."

"You can provide us with her information?" asked DJ.

"Yes, Larissa will send it to you," said Reese. "We've been trying to reach her. Please sit down. I want to hear your thoughts on Will's death. Hedy said that you don't believe it was an accident?"

The president led DJ to a circle of leather chairs around a center table. On its surface stood ceramic bowls of blueberries, shelled pistachios, and flower buds. DJ wondered if a Japanese tea service would arrive.

They sat down opposite each other.

"There's no possibility," said DJ, "of accident or suicide."

"No," said Bill Reese. "Will wasn't the type for suicide."

"So perhaps you and Will Bloom were more than colleagues?"

"I just meant that Will was very sure of himself. It made him a damn good fundraiser. One of the best. It's not easy raising money for a small liberal arts college committed to social justice and community."

"From a search of Will Bloom's office and conversations with witnesses, it appears Mr. Bloom's community focus was on the ladies. Did you ever hear rumors of that?"

Bill Reese's set smile tightened until there was a white ring around his lips.

"President Reese?"

"Look, Will Bloom was the best fundraiser in the business. Raising money is a top priority; this college lives on a razor's edge. I needed the best."

"You didn't answer my question."

"This is confidential. It wasn't until about nine months after I hired Will that I realized he had personal issues. They didn't interfere with his job performance."

"What were those personal issues?"

President Reese formed a triangle with his two hands. He stared into his improvised steeple of fingers, searching for an answer. "I don't want to gossip about a dead man."

"A murdered man," said DJ. "It's not gossip. Your information could lead to his killer."

"I doubt that."

"Please," said DJ, "go on."

Bill Reese leaned forward, combed manicured fingernails through his glossy wave of hair, and came to a decision.

"Will drank. A lot. It got out of control and I addressed it. He curbed the drinking, but he didn't entirely stop. An occupational hazard. It comes with the job. I've never seen more consumption of alcohol in my life than in the pursuit of raising money."

"Mr. Bloom has whiskey bottles under his desk," said DJ.

"Not a good idea," said Bill Reese. "But not unheard of. Donors drop by after work."

"He also had an open box of condoms in his bottom desk drawer, along with women's lingerie. More donors dropping by?"

Reese's face went pale. "I would have no way of knowing that."

"He didn't pursue women on campus? Have sex in his office?"

"Not to my knowledge," said Bill Reese. "I can't know what each employee is doing on campus. But we have very strict rules about administrator/student relationships. Anyone abusing that rule would be immediately dismissed."

"But if Mr. Bloom was sleeping with anyone other than a student in his office? No big deal?"

"Of course it would be a big deal," he said. "If I had known. If he was caught. Not just gossip."

"Or maybe he was just too good at raising money?" asked DJ.

"Are you accusing me of something, Detective Arias?" said the president. "Bill's" tight smile turned into a snarl. "Shouldn't you be finding Will Bloom's murderer instead of insinuating something about my character?"

DJ barely suppressed a smile of satisfaction. There can only be one big dog in the yard, and it wasn't going to be "Just call me Bill."

"I'm sorry," said DJ. "Just doing my job. Mr. Bloom was killed before or during sex. And in his office."

"What?" said the president. "I didn't know that."

DJ thought there were a lot of things that "Bill" conveniently did not know. "Can you tell me," asked DJ, "where you were last night from 5:30 p.m. until around 5:30 a.m. today?"

"Why? You can't think I had anything to do with Will Bloom's death."

"Maybe you found out what he was up to and decided to stop him?"

The snarl returned. "I was in a very public meeting at Eagle Rock Library with faculty and community members last night until ten o'clock. And then I went home to my wife and children. Just for the record, Will Bloom was heterosexual, as am I."

"Good to know," said DJ. "We'll check your alibi and . . . I'll take your word, for now, on the other thing."

DJ couldn't keep the sarcastic smile from his face.

A knock at the door. President Reese tried to once again become "Bill," the in control politician. He settled for pale fury.

"Come in."

Larissa Wren stepped in; a heat-seeking owl protecting King Owl. "John Lonica is here. Is everything all right, sir?"

DJ's thirty minutes must be up. He felt the interview went well.

"Everything is fine," President Reese said tersely. "Bring him in. I've asked John to join us for the last ten minutes of our meeting. He's our Head of Communications. I want to make sure we get the right message out to the community about this terrible loss. Detective Arias, meet John Lonica."

Lonica was a tall, thin, no-nonsense man, his smile slight as his silhouette. He shook DJ's hand and folded his long legs to fit into one of the low chairs surrounding the small circular table. He carried a reporter's notebook and a pencil.

"Now, John," Bill Reese said to the communications man, "the important thing we want to convey to our trustees, parents, faculty, and larger community is that our students are in no danger."

"Yes, sir," said John Lonica. "And that is correct, Detective?"

"Can't say," said DJ, "until I know who killed Will Bloom."

"Surely, the person involved with Will Bloom's death," said President Reese, "has nothing to do with our students."

"Surely, the person who killed Will Bloom," said DJ, "was on campus last night."

"Our students aren't in danger from the person who did this!"

"You keep saying 'the person involved,' 'the person who did this.' You're describing the murderer. Someone committed a cold-blooded killing on your campus. I don't know if the students are safe. I don't know if anyone is safe—I don't know if you're safe."

"Please don't concern yourself with my safety, Detective Arias." The snarl on the president's face was becoming a permanent fixture.

John Lonica cleared his throat and pulled out a printed piece of paper.

"Sir, fall break starts on Monday. Why don't I put out an immediate statement via email saying that you and the college were deeply saddened to learn that Will Bloom, vice president of Fundraising, was found dead in his office early Friday morning. The death appears suspicious and police are investigating. This incident occurred in an administration building. No students were present in the immediate area. Hesperia College's week-long fall break begins on Monday, but because of . . . present circumstances, classes are canceled today, Friday, and students are free to leave immediately. We will provide timely updates to the community as the investigation proceeds."

"I can live with that," President Reese said. He stood up, leaning over the still-seated DJ. "It will create an interruption in the faculty's syllabi."

"You heard a student was attacked last night in a separate incident?" asked DJ.

"Hedy said the girl is fine," said President Reese. "She thinks it's unrelated."

"Is that so?" asked DJ. "It's still unclear. My sense is that you better hope it's related or you might have two predators on your campus."

"I don't care what 'your sense' is," said President Reese. "It's time for you to leave, Detective. And you better have this investigation wrapped up before our students return to campus. You have one week."

"My job is to find the murderer," DJ said. "However long it takes."

"This needs to be resolved by next weekend. The earlier, the better," said Bill Reese. He leaned in, his face white as if all blood had pooled into the index finger being waved in front of DJ's face. "I know the police chief. He is a friend, and my next call will be to him. Consider yourself on notice."

Bill Reese stormed out of his office suite, followed by Larissa Wren, who looked coldly at DJ before leaving.

Lonica stood up. Tall, thin, and understated, his clothes and glasses were the same unremarkable brown. He would tell a version of the truth but, like a good flack, would omit the dirty details. A melancholy smile made the man appear wise and tired.

"The president," he said, "is used to people following his orders."

"Did Will Bloom follow his orders?" asked DJ.

"Will didn't think orders or rules applied to him," said John Lonica as he headed to the door. He turned around, the melancholy sinking into his eyes.

"And until last night, they didn't."

CHAPTER 17

Penance

Danny Mendoza sat on his porch, staring at the unopened beer in his hand. Wet with condensation, its label peeled off like a woman seducing her lover. He could hear the metallic click, the dull pop of effervescence escape from the amber bottle. Almost taste the cold hoppy foam push against his soft palate as golden liquid slid down his gullet, hit his belly, exploded into his bloodstream. Feel the brain freeze as he drank the beer down in one long vertical swallow. After three or four more bottles, the true brain freeze followed by the mercy of forgetting. Even for a little while.

Danny had stopped by the liquor store on the way home, wearing a hoodie that covered his uniform, hid his face. He couldn't risk bumping into Hedy Scacht or Jerome Blight. Drinking was on the verboten list of his employee contract with Hesperia College. He made it home undetected.

Then he sat on his front porch because he didn't really give a shit. Jerome Blight never looked him in the eye, and so what if Hedy drove by his house. He was a man. He could handle a six-pack of beer. He wasn't going to drive anywhere. His mother's Ford Aerostar van sat in the garage, untouched. An electric cart on the Hesperia campus was his speed now.

It had been a long day. A long life. How old was he anyway? Twenty-eight? When he was in prison, he had counted the minutes, days, weeks, years. Ten years. Then he was released, and he counted the hours, minutes, seconds his mother was in pain. Until the next morphine drip released. When she wasn't in pain anymore, he prayed to God she would come back—even with the pain, so he could be with her for one more hour. What good did counting do? What good did praying do? What good did God do?

Danny held the unopened beer bottle to his face. It was cold and wet against his skin. A touch of the dead. He threw the bottle against the wall and watched as the amber glass shattered and brown foam spewed across the cement floor. It smelled like vomit. One bottle down, five to go.

Danny covered his face with his hands. He could still see the dead girl, Sally Smith. Not only when he slept, but sometimes her image flashed before his eyes during the brightest part of the day when sunshine lit the sky and warmed the grass beneath his feet. There she lay in the glare of headlights. After his car slammed into her. She had no marks on her legs or arms. She looked as if she was sleeping. Until he saw blood leaking from her lips, nose. Then he knew. He couldn't save her. He couldn't save himself. He couldn't save anyone, not even his mother.

Now another death, a deliberate murder. Danny didn't know Will Bloom, other than stories from his mom. He would see the man on campus, occasionally nod hello, and that was it. Who would the police look to for an easy arrest? Not just the police, but Detective DJ Arias, the son of a bitch who put him away ten years ago. To Arias, he was Daniel Mendoza, the Latino ex-con who killed a teenage girl.

The charge was vehicular manslaughter; eighteen-year-old Danny was bereft, felt terrible at what he'd done. He knew he had caused a terrible accident, that he was responsible for an awful lapse in judgment, but he believed he would avoid the most dire consequences. He always had.

In the courtroom, everything became real. Sally Smith's parents howled in pain as they grieved their only child. The weight of the girl's death and the loss to her parents bore down on Danny. He felt their devastation, their empty future without their daughter. He was sentenced to ten years in jail. Sally Smith was dead and Danny was responsible.

Prison changed him. Danny began to smell his own self-pity. He recognized the stink from his fellow prisoners: it was always someone else's fault, a cheating wife, a lying friend. Danny blamed his dead father for his own anger, an alcoholic Desert Storm vet who wrapped his car around a tree when Danny was five. His mother tried to fill the empty space, make up for what was missing. But it wasn't enough.

As a child, he always felt the tick, tick, tick. An embedded time bomb waiting to implode. Danny was smart; he zipped through homework. In high school, he dulled the anger at his fatherless state, at his mother's tenuous finances with bravado, pot, and beer. He still aced his tests. When girlfriend Rina took care of their "little problem" on her own, Danny felt instant relief; he had dodged a bullet. Still, self-pity and fury inside grew like an embedded fire, grasping, out of control.

He attended class, played football, partied all weekend. Drunk or high day and night, the ticking accelerated. He hid it from his mother with wall-to-wall activities, cocksure teenage bravado, and peppermint mouthwash. She worked hard and was proud of her busy *big-man-on-campus* son.

And then at last, he was a first-year Hesperia college student; a free ride his mom had worked twenty years at the college to guarantee. One night during Greek rush, Danny proved to his would-be fraternity brothers, boys with private school educations driving their parents' secondhand Mercedes, that he was their equal. He could take whatever they dished out. A bottle of Jack Daniels? Sure! He was a man, not a boy desperate to prove he was one of them. "Come on, Danny. Don't be a pussy. Drive us back to campus!" Sally Smith crossed the street, maybe she didn't look right or left. Danny in the secondhand Mercedes was too wasted to see her, to react, to hit the brake.

Tonight, Danny Mendoza popped the cap on each of the five remaining beer bottles, poured the amber brew on his mother's azalea bushes. Azaleas liked acidic soil. Was beer acid?

"It is to me," Danny said.

A holy trinity, shame, misery, and regret; rooted in his mother's chest during Danny's prison sentence. Breast cancer consumed the one person he loved. After he was released, they had four months together.

Isabel Mendoza died as she requested, at home with her son. Body failing, she opened her eyes, seeing Danny, the man he was, not the boy she had struggled to save.

"I love you, Mom."

"Love you," she whispered.

"Don't leave me," Danny said.

"I have faith."

"I'm afraid, Ma." Danny cried like the boy he had never been.

She inhaled, gathering the last of her strength.

"I have faith. In you."

She was gone. The emptiness filled the room.

As a boy he had chased his father's ghost. Now Danny would put one foot in front of the other, walk tall, and try to be his mother's son.

He didn't know if he could do it.

Living with this truth was his penance.

He walked inside, turned off the lights, and lay down on his bed. The dark would come. Danny just had to wait for it.

CHAPTER 18

Ladies-In-Waiting

Trish Ballentine

DJ left the president's office and took the elevator to the lobby. On his way to the conference room, he observed Will Bloom's colleagues, sitting on folding chairs against the lobby's perimeter. Most were quiet, some in shock, except for one thin middle-aged blonde with peacock-blue eyelids. She fidgeted, her foot tapping with agitated excitement as if waiting for a game show to begin.

Bobtail had conducted quick initial interviews, asking for job titles and length of service at the college. Now DJ and Talbot would conduct deeper interrogations. They had decided to keep the murder weapon confidential.

DJ thought about Daniel Mendoza. After ten years in prison, he had grown into a bitter man, perhaps a dangerous one. DJ had played a major part in that transformation. An ex-con at the scene of a crime was a prime suspect. Did a woman connect Daniel and Will Bloom? According to Hedy Scacht, Daniel was a monk. Women had been wrong about men before—they usually were.

Talbot called out a name. "Trish Ballentine, we're ready for you."

Trish was the blonde with the peacock-blue eyelids. She entered the conference room in a cloud of rose perfume and sat down, her foot still tapping.

"Hello again, *Dee-tec-tive*," she said to Talbot. She had a Southern drawl and a flirtatious smile. DJ guessed she was in her fifties. A real Blanche Du-Bois type. She took the proffered chair at the head of the table.

"Hello, Ms. Ballentine," Talbot said. "Now, for the record, Trish Ballentine, you were Mr. Will Bloom's personal assistant, is that right?"

"I was his 'executive' assistant," she said. "I didn't let things get 'personal.' And it's Mrs. Ballentine." She smoothed her hair and lowered her heavily mascaraed eyelashes. "I am a married woman. But you may call me Trish."

"Why, thank you, Trish," said Talbot.

God, thought DJ. Bobtail was blushing.

"When was the last time you saw Will Bloom?"

"Well, yesterday, before five o'clock p.m. He came in from an 'errand.' Went to his office and shut the door." Trish Ballentine had the annoying habit of air quoting certain words with her fingers.

"What was the errand?" asked DJ.

"He didn't say."

"Was that usual?" asked Talbot. "Leaving without letting you know where he was going? Did he seem upset?"

"There was no usual with Will Bloom," said Trish. "He had a mercurial temperament. Yesterday he started the day out 'jaunty.'" Trish made the word sound dirty.

"By the end of the day he was in one of his black Irish moods. Came in without even a how-do-you-do and 'slammed the door.'"

DJ interrupted. "You said shut the door earlier and now you said slammed the door. Which was it?"

Trish screwed her eyes on DJ's face. "And who do I have the pleasure of speaking with?"

"DJ Arias, ma'am. Lead detective."

"Hmph," said Trish. DJ waited for her to answer his question. She was silent.

"Well?" asked DJ.

"He 'slammed' the door. I was clarifying my statement," said Trish. She looked back at Talbot with a conspiratorial smile and eye roll as if they'd already discussed the bothersome DJ Arias.

"Was that the last time you saw Will Bloom?" asked Talbot.

"Yes, but I heard him before I left. As I was getting ready to leave for the day he opened his door and hollered for Dolly Ruiz. And she came running. Went into the office and 'shut' the door."

"What time was that?" asked Talbot.

"Five o'clock on the dot. I gathered my things and left. I never saw him again."

"Dolly Ruiz and Will Bloom—what was their relationship?" asked DJ.

Trish frowned and paused before she answered.

"Sycophantic."

"Can you elaborate?"

"Dolly acted like the sun rose and set on Will Bloom, and he lapped it up."

"Do you think there was more going on there?"

Trish wrinkled her nose. "I don't know," she said irritably. "Dolly loved to spread office gossip, and Will loved to hear it. They were very similar."

"All right," said Talbot. "What did you do last night after you left the office?"

"I went home, took a nap, and then Mr. Ballentine arrived and we had dinner."

"And did you go out again?"

"No, I did not. I watched television, had a glass of 'chardonnay over ice,' as I have done every night for more years than I can count, and fell asleep. You can ask Mr. Ballentine. Just another day in paradise."

She smiled again at Talbot.

DJ interrupted her reverie with Bobtail.

"I have to say, you don't seem terribly upset that your boss was murdered."

Trish's long fingers smoothed a few loose ringlets of hair at the back of her neck. Everything about Trish Ballentine was long; her fingers, legs, vowels.

"Well, Detective Arias," she said. "It was only a matter of time."

"A matter of time until what?"

"With all the comings and goings of female inter . . . action that man conducted, it was only a matter of time until some cosmic collision occurred . . . you get the picture."

"I don't get the picture. What exactly do you mean?" asked DJ.

"Well, maybe one of them just snapped." Trish punctuated her statement with the sharp click of her fingers. "It happens. I watch those shows about women who have had enough with a capital E."

"This isn't cable TV, Mrs. Ballentine," said DJ. "This is real life."

"I know that, Detective," she said pointing her finger at him. "Who do you think you are talking to? I am a grown woman who graduated from college with an English degree. I do not deserve that tone of voice. You asked me a question and I answered. If you do not want my opinion, do not ask."

DJ felt his face redden. Talbot squeezed his lips together, unsuccessfully hiding a smirk.

DJ was silent. He knew when he hit a brick wall. Trish Ballantine was a Southern citadel.

"You were his trusted assistant," Talbot said. "Did you know his women friends?"

Trish composed herself, pulled her glare away from DJ and turned to Talbot.

"There were any number of women calling him," Trish said, "all day. And he was surrounded by females here at Hesperia College. Many succumbed, but I was not taken in by his 'charm.'"

"Any names you can give us?" asked DJ.

She glowered at DJ and appeared to come to a conclusion. "I certainly cannot."

"No?"

"Decidedly not," Trish said. "Women called him all the time. Some for work, others for I-don't-know-what, some for both. It would be supposition on my part."

"What about a call log, or one of those carbon message pads."

"Mr. Bloom demanded I use the pink message pads. No carbons. And he kept his own calendar."

"Why is that?" asked DJ.

"Oh, I don't know, let me think," Trish said. "No record, no evidence?"

"Was it difficult to keep track of everything?" DJ asked.

"It sure was," said Trish. "I tried to make sure he didn't miss meetings. I scheduled important ones in the morning. His sweet spot was eleven a.m."

"Not in the afternoon?" asked DJ.

"Not after lunch," said Trish. "Some days his lunches stretched to three hours and he smelled like a distillery on his return."

Talbot cleared his throat and Trish Ballentine once again turned her attention to him.

"Just a couple of loose ends. You mentioned he had an errand yesterday afternoon," said Talbot. "Do you know what it was?"

Trish smiled at Bobtail, playing her own version of good cop, bad cop. DJ knew who he was.

"He said he had to pick up dry cleaning. He was gone a long time and didn't return with any clothes."

"When he arrived yesterday morning, you described him as jaunty," said Talbot. "What did you mean by that?"

"He was humming," Trish said. "That usually meant a woman. He hummed a lot."

"Any idea who the lucky lady was?" asked Talbot, smiling at her.

"I have an idea," she said, "but I don't want to gossip."

"Would you give it a shot," Talbot asked. "For me?"

DJ sat silently through this verbal intercourse. Trish smiled. She was enjoying it.

"Well, his director of Annual Giving was arriving home from a conference last night. He was in her office yesterday morning. Mooning around like a schoolboy."

"Her name?"

"Hoa Phan," said Trish. "She is. Twenty-five. Years old." She punctuated the sentence for the greatest possible impact.

"You think there was something going on?" Talbot asked.

"She has worked here for eleven months. And been promoted twice," said Trish. "They traveled together. 'A lot.'"

"Maybe he was mentoring her," said DJ.

"Is that what they call it in your office?" Trish asked.

Talbot coughed loudly. *By God*, thought DJ. *He is laughing. At me.*

DJ glared at Talbot. The younger man blanched.

"Where is this Hoa Phan?" asked DJ. "I don't see her on the interview list."

"She called in sick," said Talbot. "We've scheduled her for tomorrow morning."

"Hmph," said Trish with a shake of her head.

"One more question," said DJ. "In complete confidence."

"Well, of course," said Trish, leaning forward.

"Can you tell us the last time you were in Will Bloom's office?" asked DJ. "And was the Japanese sword on the wall?"

Trish narrowed her eyes, deep in thought. "Ye-es, it was around three p.m.," she said. "I left a memo on his desk. The sword was there, same as always. An ugly relic. I think an uncle of his took it off some poor dead soldier. Why do you ask?"

"Verifying details." He was saying move along, nothing to see here.

"Oh, dear Lord," said Trish. "Was Will Bloom killed with that old sword?"

"We can't say," said Talbot. "Everything we have discussed here is confidential."

"Well, isn't that something!" Trish almost smacked her lips.

DJ had enough of Mrs. Ballentine. "Okay, we are all done here."

"Hmph." Trish stood up and smoothed her skirt. "Goodbye, Detective Talbot. I wish you good luck."

To DJ, she nodded curtly. "Excuse me."

Dolly Ruiz

Dolly Ruiz was next. She was young, early twenties, attractive, with strawberry-blonde hair and blue eyes bright with tears. Unlike Trish Ballentine, Dolly Ruiz visibly mourned Will Bloom's demise.

"I can't believe it," she said. "He is . . . was a wonderful boss."

"I know it's a difficult time," said Talbot. "We need to ask a few questions."

Dolly wiped her eyes, blew her nose with a tissue. "Yes, I understand." She sat down.

"You are the associate director of operations? Is that right?"

"Yes," said Dolly. "I worked with Will for almost two years."

"How would you describe your relationship?" asked DJ. If Will was messing around with colleagues, Dolly Ruiz seemed like a prime candidate. Young, adoring, and not a student.

"The best," she said. "I mean, he was the best boss I ever had."

"So you were close to Will Bloom?" asked DJ.

"Close? Yes," Dolly said. "Sometimes others didn't understand him. Will was a complicated man."

"He was a man," said DJ. "That much is clear."

"He appreciated," said Dolly, "my work."

"Were you in love with him?"

"What?" asked Dolly. "In love with him? He was old . . . older. It wasn't like that."

"He was a father figure?" asked DJ.

"I admired him," said Dolly.

"And you and he weren't," DJ paused. "Intimate?"

"No. Never." Dolly blushed. "I don't like what you are insinuating. Our relationship was," she cleared her throat, "strictly professional." Tears moistened her eyes. DJ noted they were a particular shade of blue.

"What about everyone else in the office?" asked Talbot. "Were all of his relationships strictly professional?"

"I . . . I . . . I, I don't . . . I think so," Dolly said. She looked at the floor.

"Who was he close to?" asked DJ.

"He was friendly," said Dolly, "with everyone."

"Someone mentioned that he and Hoa Phan were particularly friendly."

"Trish said that, right? I'm sure she said something about me? She likes to stir the pot."

"What does that mean?" asked DJ.

"Oh, you know the type. Make innuendos, spread rumors. I tried to warn Will, but he didn't seem to care."

"Tell us about Hoa Phan," said Talbot.

"She's smart," said Dolly, "serious, and ambitious. That's not a bad thing."

"They were close," asked DJ. "Outside of work?"

"I can't say."

"Is that because you don't know?" asked Talbot. "Or don't want to tell us?"

Bobcat made a rookie mistake, thought DJ. Giving her an out.

"Oh, because I don't know," said Dolly, shaking her head. Her pink lips curled into a grateful smile.

"And Hoa Phan is not here today," said DJ. "She called in sick."

"Yes," Dolly said. "She called me."

"What's wrong with her?"

"I'm sorry?" asked Dolly.

"Why couldn't she come in?" asked DJ.

"She . . . she . . . she has a . . . cold."

Dolly was a liar. A bad one.

"Yeah," said DJ. "It's going around."

"May I go now?" Dolly asked. "I don't feel well."

"Trish mentioned that Will Bloom ran an errand yesterday. Do you know what that errand was?"

"Oh," said Dolly. "Oh no!"

"What?" asked Talbot.

"His house," said Dolly. "I think it had something to do with his house. Have you checked his house?"

"We will," said DJ.

"Will you check it today?" asked Dolly.

"Yes," said Talbot. "Does this have something to do with his errand?"

"No," she said. "I mean maybe." The tears came again. "I don't know."

"When was the last time you saw Will Bloom?" Talbot asked.

"Yesterday afternoon. He called me into his office around five."

"What did he want?" asked Talbot.

"He seemed upset," said Dolly. "He asked if I wanted a drink."

"What was he upset about?" asked DJ.

"I don't know."

"Wasn't it a bit early for a drink?" DJ asked.

"Will liked to have a drink after work. He didn't like to drink alone. But yesterday, he seemed different."

"In what way? Did he say something?"

Dolly stared at the floor, then shook her head. "I don't know. It was like he was upset about something."

"So you had a drink with him?"

"No, I couldn't stay. I had a meeting with Serena about the budget. Will said, 'better you than me.' That was the last thing he said to me. Ever."

"He didn't like this Serena person?" asked DJ.

"No one likes . . . I mean," said Dolly, "he was joking. Will was very funny."

"What time did you leave the office yesterday?" asked Talbot.

"I finished the meeting with Serena about six and went home."

"And did you talk to anyone or see anyone?"

"Just my ex-boyfriend, Jesse. On the phone. We spoke around seven thirty."

"We'll be checking everyone's alibi."

"Alibi? You don't think I had anything to do with Will's death?"

"We don't know who killed Will Bloom," said DJ. "We're following every clue."

"We're suspects? We all work together. We're like a family."

"Uh-huh." Family members were prime suspects. "When you were in Will's office yesterday at five o'clock, was the Japanese sword on the wall?"

"I guess so," she said. "It's always there. Why?"

"Just checking."

"Oh my God," she said. "That's not how Will died, is it?"

"We can't disclose that," said DJ. "Everything we discuss in this room is confidential."

She stared at DJ as if taking his measure. "I see."

He sensed that behind her baby blues, a cunning mind whirred. "Anything else you want to tell us?"

"No. Well, yes. I'm missing something. I may have left it in Will's office. My Hesperia blanket. I wear it as a shawl when it's cold. I had it with me yesterday."

"Everything in that office will be held as evidence, for now."

"If we find it anywhere else," said Talbot, "we'll let you know."

"All right. It was a gift from Will," Dolly said. "If you find it, I'd like to have it back."

"We'll see what we can do," said Talbot.

"Thank you," Dolly said. "It's very precious to me."

Serena Rigby

Talbot called in the last of Bloom's suitemates present today, Serena Rigby, associate vice president of Fundraising Operations, and second-in-command. As she arrived, they heard a whoosh of skirts and the whistle of nylon-clad thighs rubbing together. DJ didn't think women wore pantyhose anymore.

Rigby was in her late thirties, early forties. She had thick ginger hair, parted and pulled back into a haphazard ponytail. Brick-colored freckles spattered her face, neck, and décolletage like raindrops on a sidewalk. She wore a tight blazer, confining her broad shoulders. Her cleavage was on display in a V-neck blouse. The whole effect was disconcerting, like a busty football half-back.

"This has been a terrible morning," Serena said. She had the flat voice of a former prep school girl. "I think it's best for everyone to get back to normal as soon as possible."

"Except Will Bloom is dead," said DJ. "So that's not going to happen."

The woman's mud-brown eyes focused on DJ; not liking what she saw, they slid back to Talbot.

"I think he would want us to carry on," said Serena.

DJ didn't say that Will Bloom's days of wants and wishes were over.

"When was the last time you saw Will Bloom?" asked Talbot.

"Yesterday." She thought it over. "I saw him walk by my office when he came in around nine forty-five. But I didn't talk with him then. I was in meetings until five and Will was in his office with the door closed."

"How did you know he was in his office?"

"Trish said he was, but she declined to tell me who he was with."

"Why was that?"

"Trish Ballentine isn't a particularly helpful person," said Serena.

"And what was Will's relationship with Dolly Ruiz?" Serena's eyes met DJ's, then fell to the floor.

"Close," she said.

"How close?"

"You'll have to ask her."

"I'm asking you," said DJ.

"I'd say Will loved hearing office gossip and Dolly was happy to provide it. She listens in at open doors. She's not above exaggerating."

"You're saying she lies."

"She tells stories. She may even believe them. You should remember that."

"It sounds like you and Dolly have a difficult relationship."

"I've worked hard and many years to get where I am. Dolly was my assistant for several months. I gave her a break, she only has her high school diploma and a year or so at a junior college. But with a few blinks of her lashes, she's an associate director working with Will."

DJ looked at Talbot to make sure he wrote that down. The younger detective seemed annoyed by Serena Rigby's characterization of Dolly Ruiz.

"And you're intimating that something else was going on?" Talbot asked.

"I don't know, maybe, maybe not. They're so alike. I mean they were."

"What about Hoa Phan?"

A superior smile appeared on Serena Rigby's face. "The princess? Will doted on her. But she was out of the office this week, wasn't she?"

"What do you mean?"

"Nothing. I simply meant it was quiet this week. We got a lot done."

"Because Hoa Phan was out of the office?" DJ asked.

"Will was focused. On what was important. One of the reasons I was hired at Hesperia was to organize this department. I soon learned that meant controlling Will."

"Really? And were you able to do that?" asked DJ.

"Will is . . . was uncontrollable. And don't ask me who he was dating, messing around with, or whatever. Who knows. Most women were fair game to him. Some of us have too much self-respect and focus on the future to indulge in that nonsense."

DJ stared at Serena. He hadn't asked who Will was dating.

"Where were you last night, Ms. Rigby, from five o'clock on?" asked Talbot.

"I met with Dolly Ruiz at around five thirty to six or so and then I finished up my work around seven. Will called me as I was getting ready to leave. About the budget meetings I had with Finance."

"He called you from his office?" asked DJ. "What time?"

"About seven ten or seven fifteen? We weren't scheduled to meet. A few minutes later and I would have been gone."

"So you met with him at seven fifteen in his office?" asked Talbot.

"No. I couldn't, and then the lights went out."

"Wait," said DJ. "The building's lights went out?"

"Yes, I received a call on my cell phone, one of those emergency calls from Campus Safety right after that. They said there was a blackout in Sliming and to leave the building immediately."

"Campus Safety called your cell phone?"

"Yes, they have our cell phone numbers in case of emergency."

"Who called you? Do you remember their name?"

"No," said Serena. "It was one of those scratchy sounding calls from a walkie-talkie. I honestly couldn't say if it was a man or woman." Talbot and DJ exchanged puzzled glances.

"And did you see Will Bloom before you left?"

Serena Rigby stared at her folded hands on the table. She blushed scarlet from her décolletage up to her face, into the pink part that divided her hair like the red sea.

"No."

Bobtail was about to say something, but DJ caught his eye, held up his hand. "You didn't wait for him before you left the building?"

"No," she said. "I didn't want to wait for him. Particularly not in the dark."

"Why is that?" asked DJ.

Serena's color returned to muddy pink. "It's no secret that Will was a womanizer. Our relationship was always professional. But a few days ago . . ."

She kept staring at her hands and the blush caught fire again.

"A few days ago?"

"He made a pass at me. It took me completely by surprise. I said no, of course, but it was awkward after that."

"And what day did this happen?" asked DJ.

"Tuesday. It was Tuesday because I avoided him Wednesday. But last night he called me and said he wanted to meet . . . about the budget."

"And you said?"

"I said no, I had to meet someone. Look, I'm on the VP track. It's tough being a woman with ambition. I wasn't going to let Will Bloom's proclivities get in my way."

"And then the lights went off?"

"Yes, I'd already gathered my things when Campus Safety said I should leave. I used the light on my cell phone. I went out the door near the career center. I thought I was the last one in the office. Except for Will. The building was dark. And then . . . I thought I saw something."

"What?" asked DJ and Talbot in unison.

"The doors are glass. I saw something moving inside along the hallway. I looked in and tried the door, but it wouldn't open. My key card didn't work, I guess because of the outage."

"Did you see a someone inside?" asked DJ.

"I don't know. I thought I saw a flash of light, but when I looked through the door I couldn't see anything."

"There are mechanical locks on the door, right?" asked DJ.

"Yes, there are keys that override the scanners. But only Campus Safety and maybe Facilities have access to those keys."

Talbot wrote that down.

"Did you see anyone on campus," asked DJ, "after you left Sliming?"

"No, when I got to my car in the parking structure, I called the Blue Hen for takeout. It's Vietnamese food. I picked it up just before they closed. I think it was around seven forty-five or so. I'm sure I was their last customer."

"And then where did you go?"

"I went home, Detective. I didn't have an appointment, except for *The Great British Baking Show*. But there was something strange."

"What?" asked DJ.

"When I left to get my car, the rest of campus was lit up like a Christmas tree. Only Sliming had the blackout. I looked back at the building and it was completely dark. It gave me the creeps. Like something bad was going to happen. And then when I heard about Will this morning, I thought my premonition had come true."

CHAPTER 19

Blue Orange

Serena Rigby exited the room in a swish of skirts and hosiery. Detectives Talbot and Arias stared at each other.

"So this blackout?" asked DJ. "Did anyone else mention it?"

"No," said Talbot. "But everyone else we talked to left the building by six except for Serena Rigby and Will Bloom."

"And the murderer," said DJ. "If the murderer isn't Ms. Rigby. My gut says she's lying about something, but Christ, Will Bloom could hear her coming a mile away unless she was in ninja mode."

"I agree," said the younger man. "And I don't think she knows ninja mode."

DJ smiled, a deadhead grimace. "Bobtail . . ."

"That's not my name," said Talbot. "I find it insulting."

"Okay, okay, don't get your boxers in a twist. Aren't you supposed to be calm? Isn't that the Buddhist way?"

"How do you know I'm a Buddhist? That's private."

"Christ," said DJ. "I'm a detective, aren't I?"

Talbot gave DJ a non-Buddhist fuck-you stare.

The conference room table held a chaos of coffee cups, doughnuts, bagels. The bag of apples and oranges sat among the sugar and caffeine. DJ detected a faint aroma of something sickly sweet as Talbot raked through the bag and grabbed two apples. DJ needed the younger man on this case even if he was a fucking Buddhist.

"Well, what do your friends call you?" asked DJ.

"My friends call me Bobby. You can call me Talbot, sir, or Detective."

DJ was bulletproof to insults from inferiors. And he considered everyone inferior.

"All right, Talbot," said DJ. "So what do you think? Any of those three women lying?"

The younger man gathered his thoughts.

"Each one is hiding something," said Talbot.

"Hiding is lying," said DJ. "Omitting things from fear or embarrassment. Maybe they all slept with Will Bloom."

"If Trish Ballentine slept with Bloom," said Talbot, "she should win an Oscar."

The right side of DJ's lip curled, the beginning of one frightening smile.

"Yeah, not Bloom's type. The other two don't like her, well, none of them really like each other. I think Trish knew who her boss was sleeping with. Maybe she took down names and numbers."

"Even when Bloom asked her not to? Why?"

"For power. Secrets are power, Bobttt . . . Talbot," DJ caught himself.

"And Dolly?" asked Talbot. "What about Dolly Ruiz?"

"Why was she so insistent we check out his house? She knows what Bloom did yesterday afternoon. It has her worried."

"So why not tell us?" asked Talbot.

"She was his right hand. She's still keeping Will Bloom's secrets. Even in death."

"She's loyal," said Talbot.

"Trish called her a gossip, Serena called her a gossip and a liar."

Talbot screwed up his face. "I don't think so."

"Listen, Tal-butt." DJ couldn't help himself. "Sometimes the sweet pretty young things are the worst."

Talbot slumped in his chair. He couldn't wait to finish this case and ask for a transfer. He didn't believe Dolly Ruiz had anything to do with Will Bloom's death, nor that she was a liar. Talbot changed the subject.

"And Serena Rigby?"

"You tell me."

Talbot took a moment. "I think she's lying about Will Bloom. Maybe he made a pass, maybe not, but she's lying about something. No one turns that red from telling the truth."

DJ's lip curled again. "Agreed, perhaps it was pass completed."

But did she kill Will Bloom? DJ thought that Serena, of the three women, had the strength and height to lift a sword and bring it down. But did she have the rage? Whoever pinned Will Bloom to his conference table was full of rage.

"I'll have the second unit start checking alibis," said Talbot.

"And the other one," said DJ. "The young woman who made Will Bloom hum?"

"Hoa Phan," said Talbot. "I spoke to her sister today. She said Ms. Phan was too distraught to come to the phone. But she'll be here tomorrow morning for an interview. Nine a.m."

"Good. And I want you personally to check out the photo I sent you. The receipt under the letter opener. I think it's from a dry cleaner. I'm sure your friend Trish can give you the name of Bloom's regular dry cleaner. And check out his car. See if there is anything of interest there."

"Yes, sir," said Talbot. "What about the blackout?"

"Now that is interesting. Serena said she saw something moving inside. And the rest of the campus had lights."

"But how would the murderer know Will Bloom would stay in his office during a blackout?" asked Talbot.

"Maybe he was waiting for someone? A woman? Maybe an angry husband or boyfriend showed up instead."

"We can check with Campus Safety about the blackout and the call."

"I'll ask Hedy Scacht about that." DJ grabbed Will Bloom's key ring from the evidence bag. He took off the house key and gave the car and office key to Talbot. "I'm going to check out Will Bloom's house this afternoon. See what Dolly Ruiz is worried about."

"You want a unit to accompany you?" asked Talbot.

"No," said DJ. "I'll go solo."

No surprise there, thought Talbot as he left.

DJ wanted to be alone, but not for reasons Talbot might think. He liked to take his time, get to know the victim. There was always a small detail, sometimes hidden, that told the crux of their story.

DJ peered into the bag of fruit. There was only an apple and orange left. He decided to take the bag with him.

He stepped outside into the bright sun, checking the time. It was 2:00 p.m. Students were dragging suitcases and catching rideshares to the airport to take advantage of the early holiday. He imagined Will Bloom, the womanizer, alcoholic, and ticking bomb tarnishing this pretty little fiefdom of Hesperia College. What damage did the man inflict on this place and its inhabitants before he was murdered?

According to President Reese, he had seven days to close this case. DJ had scoffed at the president's demand, but he felt the urgency to find the murderer. The killer walked on this campus, among students, staff, and faculty.

DJ pulled out the last orange in the bag. The scent of mold invaded his nostrils as his fingers dug into a mush of spoiled fruit. He threw the orange to the ground. It made a sickening thump sound, something rotten falling to earth.

"Goddamn it."

His fingers dripped with the smell of rot. Metabolic gas feeding on pulp, juice, and skin, invading the sphere, until the fruit was porous, blue, and the center could no longer hold.

DJ picked up the orange remnants from the ground, threw them into the trash.

There was nothing good about a blue orange.

CHAPTER 20

Evidence

(Friday afternoon)

DJ Arias called Hedy Scacht from his car. Her phone went straight to voice-mail. He left a message describing Serena Rigby's story of a blackout in Sliming at seven last night. And that someone identifying themselves as Campus Safety had told her she should leave.

"Hedy, give me or Talbot a call about this as soon as you can."

He hung up, driving east on the Ventura Freeway.

DJ took exit twenty-eight, climbed into the hills of Sierra Madre above the San Gabriel Valley. Sun-drenched houses clung like scraps of brush to parched hillsides.

Will Bloom was murdered in his office. His home would provide clues to his life, if not his death. Maybe DJ would find out why Dolly Ruiz insisted someone check on the dead man's house as soon as possible.

He wound his car around Morning Glory Road to Morning Glory Circle to Happy Valley Circle. Who named these streets? Doris Day? Miss Day had founded an organization to save cats and dogs, another factoid from late-night television. While others slept, DJ, bleary-eyed, gathered little ingots of information.

DJ didn't like pets. His grandmother rescued strays that fought with her tough little cockapoo named Jack. DJ called the dog Jack Ruby, the assassin. Yap, yap, yap.

DJ kicked at the mutt, who was always biting his ankles, when he didn't back off.

Morning Glory Road again.

"Jesus H. Christ," he said. "Where the hell am I?"

One day his grandfather, his mind already beginning to fail, backed over Jack Ruby as the dog attempted to bite the car's tires. That was the end of Jack.

DJ pulled over, thumbed through his Thomas Guide. Most people used their cell phone's GPS, but DJ was old-school. If he stopped reading maps, his brain might atrophy like the other assholes tethered to their phone's navigation system.

The page was a maze of switchback streets and circles—all with similar names. He found the address: 1333 Little Knell Road.

It was up ahead around the next series of curves.

DJ pulled into a long narrow driveway; Will Bloom's house. Isolated by shrubs and steep hillsides, it was unlikely any neighbor knew of Bloom's comings and goings. The exterior of the house was white stucco, dark gray wood. A midcentury modern with clean lines. DJ unlocked the front door painted glossy red. He entered a cream-colored living room furnished in varying shades of beige. There wasn't an alarm system.

Unlike Bloom's office, the house was immaculate, almost sterile. There was a faint chemical scent, perhaps from the carpet and new paint. There was an emptiness to the living room; no photos, the books, mostly nonfiction, were organized by genre, mostly history and a few slim volumes of poetry. Art pieces, modern and muted, were scattered across the walls as if the house had been staged by an indifferent decorator to hide the character of the man who dwelled here. DJ took off his shoes; he didn't want to dirty the dead man's carpet.

Bloom's home was open concept. He knew this from late-night television. Another 2:00 a.m. diversion that featured bickering couples hell-bent on a better life with a bigger house and sight lines running from entrance to backyard. DJ's bungalow had small boxy rooms, each with its own door. He liked it that way.

DJ was interested in four areas; the kitchen, home office, bedroom, and bathroom.

First was the kitchen. The stove and oven were high-end, looked brand new and pristine. He opened the refrigerator; tonic water, wine, beer, olives. Nothing with an expiration date. The freezer held several brands of vodka.

"That's my boy," said DJ.

The coffee maker was a fancy gadget that dominated the center counter. DJ opened the cabinet above it, found coffee beans, a grinder, a giant-sized bottle of extra-strength aspirin, a fifth of Jameson Irish whiskey.

"The Breakfast of Champions."

DJ knew this was a first aid station. He had one in his house.

"I know you, Mr. Bloom," DJ said. "How you felt each morning when you woke up. A hammering headache, but not enough to stop, not yet."

He closed the cupboard doors.

For Will Bloom, "not yet" had never come.

DJ headed to an office area right off the kitchen. Unlike his office at

Hesperia, this desk was orderly, with bills in a hanging file under the heading "To Pay," which was filled with utility, dentist, dry cleaner bills; "Paid," the same bills, only older; and "To File," the same, only much older. He couldn't find any personal correspondence. Part of a dry cleaner bill lay crumpled on the otherwise tidy desk. DJ smoothed it with his gloved hands. It was from The French Laundry.

There was nothing else of interest except a receipt indicating that Will Bloom recently underwent an expensive tooth whitening treatment.

"What a waste," said DJ.

Next, he headed into the bedroom. Here was the same generic color scheme. Light beige, medium beige, dark beige. How much beige could one man stomach?

A king-size bed, a night table, and a chair made up the furnishings, along with a chest of drawers with socks, jockey shorts, T-shirts. Beneath the socks was a stockpile of Viagra.

"I knew you wouldn't keep it in the bathroom medicine cabinet, pal. Where some snooping Nancy might see it."

Other drawers held neatly folded sweat clothes, casual shirts. Nothing feminine was tucked inside, no nightgowns or errant panties or bras.

Once again, DJ thought the house oddly sterile. As if Will Bloom bought it fully furnished and took up residence like a hotel guest.

In the closet hung six expensive suits—the seventh never made it home. One for every day of the work week, two spares. There were labels where each piece of clothing hung indicating color and fabric.

"Organized," DJ said. "Or obsessive compulsive."

One trench and one heavy wool coat rounded out the suits and jackets. Dress shirts, mostly white, wrapped in dry cleaner's plastic hung on the other side. Expensive built-in shelving completed the closet. Everything was coordinated down to the oak wood shelves and matching clothes hangers. Shoes with smooth leather soles stood at attention on individual caddies. DJ glanced down at his socks. His big toe poked through a hole. His worn shoes by the front door had soles pockmarked with dirt and debris. He needed to go shopping when this case was over.

There was one last place he wanted to check out off the bedroom—the en suite. Another phrase from late-night TV that meant a connected bathroom. The door was shut tight. DJ opened it, experienced the scent of something odd in this pristine house: shit.

There in the middle of the floor, next to a puddle of pee and pile of excrement, was the last thing DJ expected to see.

"What the hell?"

A small dog lay on a round shag rug. It was trembling. The dog looked like a golden miniature pinscher. DJ knew his breeds. Grandma Amelia was a dog show devotee. The creature was reddish brown, short-haired, and, like a bathing beauty, lay stomach down with its long spindly legs capped by delicate white paws. Other than lifting its head with a direct gaze at DJ, it stayed put.

The dog's large amber eyes stared at him with gravity and intelligence as if taking stock of its reluctant rescuer. Resting its head back on outstretched legs, the dog awaited its fate. DJ closed the door and took out his phone, ready to call Talbot to send animal services over to pick up the mutt. He expected to hear the dog scratching at the door, the inevitable whimper, whining, yapping of his grandmother's pack of mutts. The house remained silent. There was nothing so quiet as a dead man's house. He put down his cell phone.

DJ opened the bathroom door again. The dog remained as he left it, lying on the rug, staring at him.

It was the dog's eyes that undid him. Its gaze exhibited some kind of wisdom and a soul. DJ couldn't turn away. "Come here."

The dog rose cautiously, tail between its legs. DJ bent into a crouch and the dog perched on DJ's knees, sniffed his face, his nose, finally licked his left eye.

"Okay," DJ said. "I could live the rest of my life without my eyeball being licked again."

The dog immediately jumped into his lap as DJ teetered above the floor. He'd been right, it was a girl.

Despite the mess on the floor, the dog smelled of baby powder.

DJ stood up, cradling her in his arms. They looked at each other eye to eye. He stroked her ears, her head lolled backward, her eyelids at half-mast.

"Fuck it," DJ said.

He headed to the kitchen and found a plastic grocery bag under the sink. He wrapped the bag around the dog's bottom half.

"In case of accidents."

The dog sniffed his face again. This time her tongue barely brushed his lips. DJ was a goner.

"Evidence," DJ said.

"That's what you are, and that's what I'm going to call you."

CHAPTER 21

Mindfulness

Bobby Talbot, wearing latex gloves, sat in the passenger seat of Will Bloom's Buick Regal Sportback. He took a deep breath, held to the count of one, two, three, released slowly, four, five, six. He repeated the breath. Mind and body connected, a sense of calm flowed through his body. He breathed in a third time. "Ahhh." Better, much better. Equilibrium restored until the next time he spoke to DJ Arias.

Bobby suspected LT SS, Lieutenant Stella Steel, teamed him with Arias because he was a Buddhist; she thought there would be less conflict. LT SS was wrong.

Still, Talbot was focused and efficient. He had ordered their second unit, Officers Browning and Butter, to check out witnesses' alibis. It was grunt work, calling up spouses, partners, friends, showing up at stores and restaurants for receipts. Each date and time carefully noted and corroborated. Kathy Browning and Bonnie Butter were good cops. He knew they would be thorough.

Before he left Sliming, Talbot had checked in with Trish Ballentine. She was still in the lobby, chatting with colleagues.

"It has been *quite a day*," she said, cheeks flushed, a twinkle lit in her eyes. Talbot realized Trish would be front and center during the French Revolution, excited for the beheadings to commence.

"Yes, it certainly has," said Talbot. "Hey, do you know off the top of your head the name of Will Bloom's dry cleaner?"

"Will Bloom frequented The French Laundry on Lake Street in Pasadena," said Trish. "Only the best for Mr. Bloom."

"Thank you," said Talbot as he jotted down the name. "I appreciate your help."

"Anytime!" With a girlish smile, she turned on her heel and sashayed away in her personal scent cloud of roses.

Will Bloom's Buick was parked askew in a no parking zone near the Sliming Academic Center, no ticket on the windshield. This was either normal Will Bloom behavior or vice-presidential privilege. He thought the former. Will Bloom appeared to have been a *rules don't apply to me* kind of guy.

Bobby searched through the glove box. The car was registered to Hesperia College, a stack of receipts told the story of full tanks of gas pumped free from the Facilities garage. Bloom had a company car, endless gas in the tank, a college full of intelligent, attractive women. A hunting ground with all the trappings.

Other than a green parking tag hanging off the rearview mirror, the car's interior was clean. Talbot popped the trunk, walked to the back of the car.

The space was tidy, with a gym bag of clean workout clothes and running shoes. A grocery bag of old books sat next to it. A plastic garment bag and hanger was crumpled into a heap toward the back of the cargo space. Talbot pulled out a man's dark blue suit. Bobby checked the label, size 36, slim, Brooks Brothers. Will Bloom was tall, 6'1", with broad shoulders and round muscles; an ex-football player, not slim. At least a 42L.

"You should have hung this in the back seat," said Talbot. The suit was wrinkled, not that Will Bloom had to worry about that anymore. He checked the dry-cleaning bill and receipt stapled to the plastic. Not The French Laundry. Retrieving his phone, he saw it was a duplicate of the receipt in the photo DJ Arias had sent from Will Bloom's office. The larger slip of paper was old-fashioned carbon; the customer filled out their own name. The address and phone number were left empty. The letters were smeared, but the customer wrote in neat cursive, "Hoa Phan." The suit was not from Bloom's regular dry cleaner, The French Laundry in Pasadena. It was from Lau 'N Dry in Eagle Rock.

"Now, how about that," said Talbot.

Bobby Talbot sat in one of the conference room chairs. He studied the written inventory of Will Bloom's office and found what he was looking for. An item listing a garment bag from The French Laundry hanging from a coatrack. Bobby slipped downstairs to Will Bloom's office; still wearing his gloves, he checked out the suit encased in plastic. He was right. "Jos Bank, Custom Tailored, 42L."

Back in the conference room, Talbot made a telephone call to Lau 'N Dry Cleaners. A woman answered the phone.

"My name is Detective Bobby Talbot, from the Los Angeles Police Department," he said.

"Yes."

"Who am I speaking with?"

"My name is Mitzy Schnirring."

"Good afternoon, Ms. Smearing . . ."

"It's Schnirring, Ms. Mitzy Schnirring."

"Sorry, Ms. Schnirring. I need you to ask you for information on an investigation I'm working. A murder investigation. It concerns a customer and something that might have occurred yesterday, Thursday afternoon?"

"I cannot help you," said Mitzy. "You need to speak with the owner, Mr. Lau."

"Cannot or will not?" asked Talbot.

"Cannot," said Mitzy. "I work part-time. I didn't work yesterday. And Mr. Lau locks up paid receipts in the safe."

"Okay, may I have his phone number?" asked Talbot.

"No," said Mitzy. "I am not allowed to give it out. But he'll be in tomorrow at 10:00 a.m."

This was ridiculous. Bobby would look up his phone number through police computers.

"What is Mr. Lau's first name?" asked Bobby.

"It is Bennet," said Mitzy. "There is no phone in his name. He's very private."

Bobby wondered if Mr. Lau was in witness protection.

"Can you call Mr. Lau and have him call me?" asked Bobby.

"No," said Mitzy. "Mr. Lau is not to be disturbed on his day off. Only in case of emergency."

"This is a murder investigation, Mitzy," said Talbot.

Talbot could hear a rustle of paper.

"Is this a fire, robbery, or imminent death?" asked Mitzy.

"No," said Talbot, "a past death."

"Then Mr. Lau's instructions state it's not an emergency."

"I could force you to call Mr. Lau."

"If you try to force me via a court order it will take effort and time. I know, I'm in law school. It might be more convenient to come by and see him tomorrow morning in person," said Mitzy. "At ten a.m."

"Yeah, right," said Talbot. He started the deep breathing to calm his growing frustration.

"What's that sound?" asked Mitzy.

If his breathing made Mitzy uncomfortable, he was okay with that.

"It's the sound of life passing us by," said Talbot.

There was a beat of silence. "Oh," said Mitzy.

"I'll be in to see Mr. Lau first thing tomorrow."

"Good idea," said Mitzy. "We open at ten on Saturday." She hung up.

Talbot was pissed. He started to breathe deeply again, but only counted to two. No mind-body connection now.

Mr. Lau would have to answer his questions tomorrow face to face. He could make it unpleasant for the man. And Mitzy too, if she was present.

To distract himself, Talbot took off his shoes and sat cross-legged on the chair, proud of his hard-earned flexibility. He moved his attention to the coroner's report. The preliminary examination, which charted the victim's temperature, rigor mortis, visible condition of skin and eyes, and blood pooling estimated Bloom was murdered between the hours of 7:00 p.m. and 11:00 p.m. More likely the earlier part of the timeframe.

They would have a closer time of death after the autopsy.

Either someone stayed behind in the building, or the murderer got into the building after-hours. If they got in after the power was out, that meant someone had an override key. The blackout was a surprise? Did the murderer cause it or take advantage of happenstance?

Talbot felt sure Campus Safety could track who went in and out of the building if they used a key card, but if the murderer used a manual override key, there would be no trace.

It was almost 5:00 p.m. DJ Arias would be back soon.

The week before Arias and Talbot caught this murder case was spent catching up on old paperwork. DJ Arias never smiled and barely talked to Bobby Talbot. The joke at Homicide Division was that DJ Arias only came alive when someone died.

Talbot's gut exuded a low and melancholy growl that echoed his mood. The heavy wood door of the conference room opened. DJ Arias walked in, cradling something in a Target plastic bag. The older detective stared at Bobby with his legs folded in the chair.

"You meditating, Tal-butt?" DJ asked.

Bobby's chair wobbled as he untangled his legs and feet. His carefully compiled notes fell to the floor.

"Oh, shit."

"Now," DJ said, "you're going to make me blush with that kind of language."

"Sorry," said Bobby, diving under the table.

DJ walked to the head of the long U-shaped conference table and sat down. The dog settled into his arms, with ears cocked and eyes watching the seat that Bobby Talbot had just vacated.

When Bobby popped up from under the table, the dog growled in a perfect echo of his nervous stomach.

"What the hell is that, Detective Arias?" Bobby asked.

"You swear a lot for a Buddhist."

"You're not an expert on Buddhism."

Bobby Talbot wanted to punch DJ Arias in the face, but instead closed his eyes and concentrated on his breathing.

"What are you doing?" asked DJ.

"Breathing," said Talbot. "Mindfully. You should try it." He threw the stack of papers on the table with a thud.

The dog barked.

"Hey, Tal-butt," said DJ. "First you made her growl, and now you've made her bark."

"I didn't know you had a dog," said Bobby. He was trying to reorder his interview notes.

"This is Will Bloom's dog."

"He didn't own a dog."

"Well, the dog was in his bathroom."

"Trish Ballentine, in our initial interviews, said he lived alone."

"Well, maybe she was only counting humans."

"No," Bobby said. "I asked about pets."

"You asked about pets?"

"I try to be thorough, sir." Bobby considered it one of his best traits.

"Well, who the hell does this dog belong to? This must be what Dolly Ruiz was worried about."

"I don't know, sir. Is it wearing a tag? Shall we bring in Dolly Ruiz again?"

"No. Call her and tell her we found a dog in Will Bloom's house. See what she says. I want to investigate on our own first before we talk to her again."

"Perhaps the dog has a chip. We can take it to a veterinarian or the pound and have it scanned."

"What are you talking about?" asked DJ.

"Some owners inject information chips between their pet's shoulders in case the pet is lost."

DJ felt faint. It was like 1984. His grandma had never done such a barbarous thing.

"I can take it to the pound tonight," said Bobby.

"Forget it," DJ said. He couldn't fathom Evidence locked up in a cage with strays. "I know a vet. I'll take the dog by later. It's a girl, by the way."

"She's probably dehydrated," said Bobby. "If she was locked up all day. Did you give her water?"

"What? Water?" DJ asked. "Of course I did."

It was obvious DJ had not.

"Yes, sir," Bobby said.

"Are you smirking, Tal-butt?"

"No, sir. Buddhists don't smirk."

DJ looked at the junior detective. There was evidence of a spine buried in that tight shiny suit.

"Anything with the car, Talbot?"

"Yes, sir," said Bobby. "The car was clean, but the trunk held a wrinkled men's suit from a dry cleaner."

"Unfortunate," said DJ. "But I think Mr. Bloom is past caring."

"Except it wasn't from Will Bloom's dry cleaner. Trish Ballentine told me that Will Bloom only used a Pasadena dry cleaner called The French Laundry. This bag was from Eagle Rock, Lau 'N Dry."

"I saw something in Bloom's house for French Laundry," said DJ.

"And the cash register receipt matches the photo you sent me. From Bloom's office, the receipt pierced by the letter opener."

"Well now," said DJ, "that is interesting."

"More interesting is that Hoa Phan's name was listed on the dry cleaner's receipt."

"Hoa Phan, and a man's suit," said DJ.

"The owner, Mr. Lau, will be in tomorrow at ten. His clerk didn't have access to any records."

"Good work," said DJ. He meant it. "You can head over there tomorrow after the Hoa Phan interview. We can ask Ms. Phan about the suit then."

Talbot reflexively smiled. Words of encouragement from Detective DJ Arias. The grin curdled as he pressed his lips together. It might be a trick.

"Tomorrow, after the Phan interview let's focus on Will Bloom's movements during the middle of the day. His errand. Where did he go, who did he see."

An actual assignment. Better to leave on a high note.

"Yes, sir. If that's all, I'll say goodnight, Detective Arias."

"Sure," said DJ. "Call Daniel Mendoza on your way out. Tell him to come in tomorrow morning. Have him bring the physical receipt from the pizza place. Did you hear from Hedy Scacht about the blackout? I left her a message to call you or me."

"No," said Talbot. "I can call her before I leave."

"I'll try her again tonight," said DJ.

Talbot made his exit before the dark shadow of DJ's personality reappeared. He didn't know what to make of the dog.

DJ grabbed the notes, rolled them into a makeshift tube, and stuffed them into his jacket.

"Come on, Evidence. You need a walk, food and water too."

DJ turned out the conference room lights, thought about the owner's name he might find inscribed on a chip between the dog's shoulders. He was more excited about visiting the veterinarian. It had been too long since he had seen her.

And Evidence provided the perfect excuse.

CHAPTER 22

God Bless the Child

(Friday, late afternoon/evening)
Hedy listened to DJ Arias's message several times before she lowered the phone to her desk.

A blackout. In Sliming.

The last of afternoon sunlight slipped between venetian blinds, leaving her office in shadow and light. Hedy had been thinking of Danny Mendoza, one of many children who grew up without a father.

Hedy pulled up the Campus Safety logs on her computer and switched to last night, Thursday night. She searched her officers' written and audio reports to determine if there was any mention of a blackout. Offices officially closed at 5:00 p.m., sunset was at 6:28 p.m. Procedure dictated that Campus Safety secured department and exterior doors and checked the perimeter of each building at the end of day. Hedy herself had been on the Sliming perimeter check last night. She went through each logged call. Standard and routine. No mention of a blackout. She double-checked the time of the call from Ferencia Lake to Campus Safety. That call was logged in at 8:20 p.m. by Officer Luke Benson.

"Student named Fern Lake called in, distraught. Claimed she was attacked in the olive grove by unknown assailant. Driving up now to check it out at Ramble Hall."

Nothing noted about a blackout in Sliming Academic Center. Of course, nothing was noted about the murder of Will Bloom until the next morning. Some things weren't discovered for hours, days, years.

Everyone knew Sliming had electrical problems. Each winter, employees cranked up personal heaters and blew the circuit. It was a 1960s electrical grid trying to accommodate twenty-first-century needs. The college had myriad demands for its meager budget. Even with its hefty tuition, there was never enough money to fix the basics. Everything was papered over and tied up with string. A dab of glitter to divert the eye.

Hedy marveled at how small private colleges were rife with petty grievances and old rivalries, all stirred together in a stew of genteel poverty. Faculty and students distrusted Campus Safety, called them the Hes-police though her officers carried no weapons. Student transgressions were dealt with fairly, and Hedy usually allowed one warning for small offenses before taking punitive action. But during student protests, some students called her officers *pigs*. That went too far.

Hedy admired her boss, President Reese, but lately found him more politician than wise leader. The college desperately needed money, and Reese wanted a rainmaker. He had hired Will Bloom, a man with a terrible reputation as a drinker and womanizer. Hedy herself had warned the president about the man. But soon large gifts started rolling in and their annual fund increased by leaps and bounds. Hedy had received a cool *thank you* and colder *mind your own business* when she reported the cleaning staff's unexpected discovery of Will Bloom's after-hours activities with numerous women.

"Tell them to knock harder next time." An exhausted Jerome Blight, director of Facilities, tried to wave her out of his office. She started to protest, but stopped when Jerome pointed his index finger up the hill in the direction of Sliming and the president's office. "What can I tell you? This comes from the top."

Hedy's eyes focused again on the campus safety logs for Thursday night. For a thorough accounting to the LAPD, Hedy would follow up with each one of her officers on duty last night. She knew if they had seen something, they would have reported it. Her officers were well-trained and disciplined.

Hedy decided to check in on Danny Mendoza. She owed it to Isabella. She could stop by, but maybe a phone call would be better. Give him his space.

Danny had always been Isabella's vulnerable spot. Danny's father, an Iraq War veteran, died when Danny was a boy, wrapped his car around a tree. Isabella did her best to provide for her son, fill in the holes, love him enough for both parents. But it was never enough.

Hedy made the call; the phone rang twice.

"Hello, Hedy," Danny said. "Is this my two-minute warning? Is the dark lord coming over to cart me away?" He sounded tired. But most important, he answered and sounded sober. It was day by day for an ex-convict, each challenge one knot in a tangled rope. Staying sober was a fucking big knot, particularly after today.

"Just checking in on you," Hedy said. "How did it go with Arias?"

"Not great," said Danny. "I told the truth. I didn't know Will Bloom, except to say hello. But Hedy?"

"What?" she asked.

"It was a terrible way to die. I'll never forget his eyes. It was like he knew what was coming. I hope I can forget that someday."

Hedy stared out the window, darkness now between the slats of her blinds.

"I hope so too," she said and meant it. "You need anything? Food, Cokes, company?"

Danny thought of the six broken beer bottles residing in his trash and the stink of beer on his porch despite his hosing down the cement. "No, I'm good," he said. "I'm going to turn in early. I found the receipt for the pizza that was delivered last night. I'm bringing it to the detectives tomorrow morning."

"Good," said Hedy. "Do you want me to pick you up? Go with you? Double-team them?"

"No, I'll go on my own," said Danny. "It's better that way."

Hedy was relieved Danny was strong enough to stand up for himself. More relieved he had a receipt proving he was home last night. Danny had a target on his back because he was an ex-con, because Arias busted him ten years ago. That damn work-order for the Sliming Courtyard was bad timing. He was a gardener—he should never have been inside that building. Life was full of serendipitous shit.

"Sleep well, Danny," Hedy said.

"I will," he said. "How's our girl?"

Hedy wondered the same thing.

"Not sure," said Hedy. "We haven't spoken in a while. Let me know if you need anything."

Hedy hung up. She had been calling her daughter all day. Straight to voicemail. The silence felt like a stab to her heart.

Hedy wanted to head home, have a stiff drink, a bath, fall into bed. But she always had one more task, one more burden, one more mile to go before she could rest.

CHAPTER 23

Roller Bag

It was dusk, Friday night, the end of day one of the investigation. DJ stood with the dog, Evidence, at the entrance to Hesperia College. Before they left the conference room, DJ had filled an empty coffee cup three times with water. Evidence drank each one dry. She ate a bagel and stray bit of lox.

As Evidence finished doing her business, her paws scratched at the ground. Chunks of earth and feces flew.

"Hey, knock it off," DJ said. The dog cringed, waiting to be struck, ears flat against her head. Remembering she was a stray, DJ crouched down and rubbed behind her ears. "Hey, it's all right, girl. It's all right."

DJ looked back toward the campus. Lights illuminated a steel fountain that shot an asymmetrical spray of water into the air. Past a set of jacaranda trees, a wide concrete stairway led to the quad, now empty of students. Wooden benches nestled under mature oaks, limbs pulled earthward by age and gravity. The Sliming Administration Center rested at the top of another set of steep stairs flanked by twin academic halls. Behind Sliming, various buildings and dorms dotted the hillside. White walls topped with red-tiled roofs zigzagged against the darkening sky like towers of a medieval castle. Some might find Hesperia College welcoming. But not DJ. He thought it cold and forbidding, as if he didn't belong.

DJ turned toward the neighborhood surrounding the campus. He needed to think through the interviews they conducted today.

"Let's go for a walk, girl."

He had grabbed an extension cord from the conference room and tied it around the dog's neck, the double plug anchoring the knot. It was a trick he learned from Grandma Amelia and her strays.

Amber streetlights filtered through the canopy of trees along the sidewalk. Homes in this neighborhood were a mishmash of small bungalows and a few Spanish Revivals. DJ remembered that many of these homes were occupied by college faculty and staff; others belonged to regular folks tied by proximity to the life of the college.

They turned south into the neighborhood. Until the murder was solved,

DJ would feel connected to Will Bloom. His colleagues had work, partners, kids. DJ had his victims, each with a story, a beginning, and an end. Not one of them ever articulated his personal shortcomings.

Evidence sniffed at each tuft of grass and stain on the sidewalk, tail wagging.

"Let's head this way, girl," said DJ as they skirted Eagle Rock Boulevard, a main commercial street that bordered the neighborhood.

Through experience, DJ had learned that most crimes were committed by the obvious suspect; the adulterous spouse, spurned lover, devious business partner—the cheated and the cheating, the losers and the lost. It wasn't the strong who killed; it was the weak.

Approaching the busy boulevard, houses and auto body shops lived side by side. A pit bull snarled, then charged against a chain-link fence. Evidence lunged forward, growling then barking, her legs stiff, tail straight up to the sky.

"*Pendeja,*" DJ said as he scooped her up in his arms. "That brute would tear you limb from limb."

But DJ felt a stab of pride at her fierce behavior. He carried her across the street to a quieter place, then lowered her down to the sidewalk.

He breathed in the cool evening air; the blooming jasmine signaled the coming winter. He loved Southern California and its weather. Transplants from the East Coast scoffed at the lack of clear seasons. But DJ, a third-generation Californian, felt his blood quicken at cold fall mornings, fog draping nearby hillsides, hot Santa Anas, and blustery cold winds circling between sea and mountains. In Los Angeles, nature flourished along graffitied walls and within the cracks of a sidewalk like the blood-orange wildflowers that grew at his feet.

As they turned east, DJ conjured up the list of suspects in his head, too early to know if it was complete. He trusted his instincts, but corroborated them with clues and interviews.

The cleaning woman, Ema Treet, was the least likely suspect. No personal connection to Bloom, no upper-body strength. Trish Ballentine couldn't stand her boss, but relished the attendant intrigue and drama. Dolly Ruiz hero-worshipped Will Bloom. There was a bond between them, but he didn't know if it was sexual. Serena Rigby was a plus-size swish of skirts, ginger hair, and freckles. Something happened between her and Bloom. No innocent person blushed like her. Serena had the physical strength to wield a sword, and the opportunity. If her alibi proved true, picking up dinner at the Blue Hen, would that have given her enough time to murder Will Bloom?

Then there was the student, Fern Lake. The attack on her must be connected to Will Bloom's death. His blood type matched her bloody clothes and backpack. Her attacker might have been the murderer—but if she encountered two people in that olive grove, who was the second person?

And there was Daniel Mendoza.

DJ and Evidence turned north where several large run-down houses stood, relics of a once thriving fraternity row. Ten years changed a man; particularly one who did prison time. DJ would not have recognized the boy, Daniel, in the man who stood before him today. Ten years ago, a drunk Daniel Mendoza had killed a teenage girl with a friend's car. The boy's shaking hands, tears, and litany of *I'm sorry*s didn't penetrate DJ's armor. The spoiled college kid had it all, was going to lose it all.

Daniel was so drunk that night he could barely stand. The Alpha Tau Omega (ATO) fraternity house four blocks from campus was now derelict. DJ could almost hear the ghosts of frat boys, egging on their pledge, Daniel. "Are you a pussy? You can't handle your liquor to drive four blocks back to campus?"

The victim, Sally Smith, was a painfully shy seventeen-year-old. Coming home late from the library, she had darted across the street. Daniel didn't see her or wasn't in control enough to stop from hitting her with the car. His headlights were off. The ATO fraternity brothers ran, left the scene of the crime. Daniel had immediately confessed. It was all his fault. He couldn't stop talking or crying. It made the *Los Angeles Times*. The press had used DJ's full name, Darius Joaquin Arias.

He soon learned Daniel Mendoza was the son of the campus cook. He wasn't wealthy or privileged, just a stupid kid bullied by rich frat boys. No one, except his mother and Hedy Scacht, stepped up to defend Daniel. The president and board of trustees circled wagons around the frat brothers. The unfairness of the situation bothered DJ, but he had hardened his armor; the law was the law, and DJ got promoted.

DJ and Evidence stopped at the intersection where the accident occurred ten years ago. He stared at the street where a young girl's life and her parent's world ended.

What motive would Daniel have to kill Will Bloom? A woman in common? A theft discovered? DJ sat down on the curb, holding Evidence in his lap. A teasing clue flickered through his brain, a connection he couldn't quite see. They watched the procession of neighborhood life pass by. A young woman wearing sweats sprinted toward campus. A black Honda propelled by screeching tires turned a corner, sped away toward York.

DJ popped a stick of gum in his mouth. Peppermint rose in his nostrils like a jolt of hope and made him think of his ex-wife, Lillian. He held Evidence even closer, a real reason and excuse to visit his favorite veterinarian.

He heard hard plastic wheels bump and grind against the rough pavement. Expecting a skateboarder, some punk acting like he owned the road, DJ looked up, and saw no one.

The whirring sound came closer. Out of the shadows, in the middle of the street, appeared a skeletal figure leaning sideways, wearing a dark trench coat and black boots. The gait was uneven, one foot forward, a sidestep, the back leg dragging before meeting the first, then stabilizing and moving forward. A long scarf wrapped around the man's head, face, and neck like an old *Invisible Man* movie.

The creature passed in front of them, not checking for oncoming traffic. The dog didn't bark, but rose to attention, ears cocked. By height and figure, DJ guessed it was a man. He walked through the intersection, pulling a suitcase, the top torn off and open; a roller bag.

There were no airports or bus stations nearby. DJ stood, ready to follow, more curious than anything. His makeshift leash, the extension cord, had wrapped around his legs. After a few seconds, he untangled himself from Evidence. When he looked up, the phantom had disappeared into the night.

PART THREE

PART THREE

Cape

Wings collapsed beneath a long winter coat, face hidden under twists of a scarf, eyes focused forward. The Watcher inhaled the night-blooming jasmine, the scent of pine, and car exhaust. He had never felt so alive.

He wore the girl's gold chain and pendant. Was she safe? Was she frightened? He would find her, return the necklace. She would be thankful.

Seven strands of hair, a scent of peony, and a girl tucked deep within his pocket. He kneaded the treasure against his fingertips. Held the fingers to his nostrils. He breathed in like a bloodhound. He would find her.

There were others out in the neighborhood tonight.

A man with a dog as small as a cat. They stood on a street corner. The Watcher halted. The man and dog turned left. He chose right.

Pulling his rolling bag, he stepped forward, sideways, stabilize, repeat. He stayed on the smooth surface of the street.

More people ahead. Riding skateboards, jumping on and off, skidding, falling. Hoots. Cackles. Whistles.

The neighborhood brats. A pit opened. He tumbled inside. They were laughing. At him? His skin burned, face on fire beneath the cloth.

The reason they laughed? His crime?

His scarred jack-o'-lantern face. Twisted spine, dragging leg, torn arm.

Humans were a punishing breed.

"I am nothing," he said.

He shrank inside his coat and scarf. He grew smaller, thin, a shadow. He faded into darkness.

A slam of wheels, they raced past him down the street. They didn't see him. Their voices faded, fainter, then far away.

His blood quickened, the wings bristled. His shoulders expanded. He could barely contain himself.

He was invisible, he was invincible.

"I am everything."

Onward he strode with his uneven gait, along neighborhood streets, pulling his chariot of jewels for the girl. Forward, sideways, stabilize, repeat. On a mission; not looking right, not looking left.

The man with the dog now sat at an intersection. The Watcher did not hesitate. Invisible; invincible; he crossed in front of him and down the street. The man and dog could not see him.

He entered campus through white pillars.

Down the road lined with giant eucalyptus. Darkness swallowed the treetops. Stars stung his eyes. The girl's heavy chain coiled around his neck, bumped along his collarbone. The gold pendant bounced against his heart.

"Tap, tap, tap," it queried.

Come in. Please come in.

Headlights slid across the road.

He shrunk again, inside his scarf and coat. A shadow among shadows.

Music drifted from a car's open window. Voices permeated the air like smoke from a wildfire. A woman, a man. Sparks of laughter, choked words, muffled passion. A blues riff crackled in the night. The wheels caught asphalt, peeled past, the siren call of life expanding, then receding into silence.

They passed him by. No one saw the Watcher. He was invisible as the treetops, invincible as stone. But now being invisible felt cold and alone. As if he wasn't really there, as if he wasn't really a human being among other human beings.

The Watcher entered the grove of trees. The asphalt slippery with fallen leaves. He moved quick in his forward sideways gait. The roller bag bumped and shuddered against the rutted path, threatened to topple. Tonight, everything looked different.

He pushed onward to the opening in the trees, wrestling with the suitcase, through the open space and to the other side. His wings hung heavy down his back.

This was where it happened. Where the monster attacked, the girl tumbled, where he pulled her back, then pushed her away, to freedom.

Muscles in his good leg and arm trembled and ached. His weak side felt numb. Painful breaths squeezed his lungs. He tried to gasp for more air. A long string of saliva hung from lips thick with scar tissue, his mouth opening and closing like a fish.

Suddenly he remembered the neighborhood brats; their laughter, their trudge of names, "fish mouth, skull face, monster man." Hahahahahahaha-hahahaha.

Their eyes. He remembered each and every one. They followed him wherever he went. Rotating in the dark, aglow with hate. Peeking behind tree trunks, peering through branches. He called out, his voice hollow and high as a child's whisper, "I am not what you see. I am not what you call me."

No one answered.

No one heard.

No one was here.

Night jasmine; the scent pricked his memory. He closed his eyes.

Images from the night his world ended unwound in his mind.

The speed, the crash, the echo of a hubcap.

The Watcher pitched forward, reached out to grab a branch, to keep upright. The roller bag tipped over in slow motion. He twisted backward to save it from falling. His legs gave way. His arms scissored for balance.

Thud.

A heavy branch smacked his forehead. Stunned, the Watcher fell to ground.

He opened his eyes.

Stars had scattered, the moon had spun. His beloved's gifts lay splintered among dirt and dead leaves. Broken shards of glass and glitter.

Tears stung his eyes. He looked up to the indifferent sky.

And there he saw it.

High in the tree. A rectangle of something twisted in the branches.

He struggled to stand. His good arm, muscles cracking, climbed up the trunk.

His fingers stretched higher, reaching for it.

What was it? Could it be? Yes!

He touched it, pulled at its edge until it floated down to him.

A cape. Red, the color of life!

He was Warren Worthington III. The Avenging Angel of God.

Invincible, invisible.

He had read it somewhere.

It must be true.

Draped across his shoulders.

The cape finds the man.

CHAPTER 24

Beast

(Friday night)

"Where is it?" Dolly Ruiz asked herself. She stood at the window directly across the courtyard from Will Bloom's office. Earlier, the police had set up bright lights as they conducted their investigation. They had illuminated the cactus garden like klieg lights on a movie set. Now everything was dark.

How many times had Dolly watched this window, waiting for Will's signal. Curtains closed—stay away. Curtains open and a quick phone call, "Desdemona, you're needed."

Will could never remember anyone's name. He called her Dilly, Dally, Desdemona. Will had counted on her. Unlike her first boss, Serena Rigby, who was perpetually annoyed at Dolly and made sure she knew it.

"I was forced to hire Eleanor Rigby, the big guy's idea," Will stated with an air of defeat. "Organizing the books or some such silliness. I need you to work for me on the down-low, keep an eye on the gal, see wherein she is poking her proverbial nose. Would you do that for me? I'd be ever so grateful." Dolly had responded to Will Bloom with an enthusiastic yes.

Dolly made it her business to know what went on at Hesperia. She was young and friendly. People confided in her, she listened. They underestimated her, believed her lack of a college degree made her naive. It didn't.

After a few months, Dolly officially worked for Will. He welcomed her insight on his staff's foibles. Who worked late, which one boasted, who coasted. She was careful not to expose anything that could be directly traced back to her. She kept her boss organized, was good with numbers, and hiding his empty bottles and other indiscretions. Will trusted her. Hadn't she made arrangements for the dog? And then yesterday afternoon, everything went sideways. No, she didn't want to think about that. At least Detective Talbot had let her know they had found the dog.

Will Bloom was a good man, wasn't he? A good boss? He had promoted her twice. It made her ex-boyfriend, Jesse, jealous and her mother suspicious of Will's motives. As if she wasn't smart enough to be successful on her own merits. Today, Will had promised to take her to lunch to celebrate her big promotion. All that was over now.

"Where could it be? Did I leave it in Will's office?"

Her Hesperia blanket was missing. It was made of red and black plush, and the college mascot, a winking panther, was sewn into its center. Will bought it for her months ago. "Here, Delilah, because you're always freezing." It was five feet long, made of 100 percent polyester. After weekly washings it was less plush, more mange.

Will bestowed it a nickname, the beast, in a department meeting as she draped it across her shoulders to ward off the cold in Sliming.

"Dilly, throw that beast out. It's disgusting, and its time has come."

"I wash it every week. It keeps me warm."

"'Twas Beauty who killed the Beast," Will said. "Do what's right and merciful, execute that thing."

Dolly had blushed. Will always said something that made her feel special. "'Twas beauty . . . ," he said it in front of everyone. She had blushed. Now he was gone. No more nicknames, no more secrets, no more Will.

Now the blanket he had given her, "the beast," was missing.

Thien Phan was doing a favor for her little sister, Hoa. She made it to the dry cleaner Friday night, just before closing. Luckily, both Thien and Hoa Phan used the same place, Lau 'N Dry. Mr. Bennet Lau was old-school, formal, ex-military, and benignly flirtatious with the Phan girls.

The sisters still laughed over Mr. Lau's apology when Thien's underwear went missing in the fluff 'n' fold service.

"I regret to inform you, Miss Thien Phan, that we have temporarily misplaced your . . . your . . . delicates." He coughed.

Mr. Lau's glasses were at half-mast.

"My what, Mr. Lau?" asked Thien.

Mr. Lau pushed back his thick black glasses to the bridge of his nose.

"Your deli-cates," he said. "We cannot locate them."

"My deli cuts?" she asked. Thien didn't understand. She tried to imagine what Mr. Lau was trying to tell her as she fingered through her stack of lavender-scented laundry tied with a pale pink ribbon.

"Not deli cuts, Miss Thein Phan" he said. "Delicates!" Mr. Lau made two quick chopping gestures; a V from his crotch along the leg joints and then a horizontal chop across the waist.

"Do you mean my underpants?" Thein asked. A sudden vision of Mr. Lau parading around his bedroom wearing her La Perla panties on his head danced into her consciousness. She had giggled uncontrollably, hiding her face in her hands so Mr. Lau wouldn't see her laughing.

Tonight, Thien Phan was on a serious mission. One she did not fully understand. Even though Mitzy with a z hadn't mentioned it to Detective Talbot, Mr. Lau resided near Lau 'N Dry and closed it every night. He didn't trust staff to deposit his cash and handle credit card receipts. Thien slipped in minutes before closing.

"Good evening, Mr. Lau." She smiled in what she hoped was her most trustworthy manner.

"Hello, Miss Thien Phan." He always called the sisters by their formal names.

"Mr. Lau," she said, "I need a favor for my sister. I'm here to pick up something she dropped off before she left town. It was ready yesterday."

"What?" he asked. Mr. Lau looked upset.

"She lost the ticket. And she's ill and can't come in. But she needs the clothes right away."

Mr. Lau looked at her suspiciously. "I don't understand."

Thien thought Mr. Lau's answer odd since the sisters often picked up each other's clothes, albeit with a ticket.

"Someone already picked up that item," he said.

"They did?" she asked. "When?"

"Yesterday," said Mr. Lau. "A big man. An angry man."

"And you gave him my sister's clothes, Mr. Lau?"

"He had the ticket," Mr. Lau said. "And they were not women's clothes, Miss Thien Phan. It was a man's suit."

"A man's suit?" repeated Thien.

"Yes," he said. "I thought it was perhaps Ms. Hoa Phan's . . . man friend or family member? And he had the ticket."

"You said he was angry?" Thien asked. "What do you mean?"

"He tore through the plastic wrap and stared at the label," Mr. Lau said. "His face turned red. He stood in the middle of my shop and ruined my work. He hunched over. Like a brute."

"Like a brute," said Thien.

"Yes," said Mr. Lau. "Quite disquieting."

"Quite," said Thien. She wondered what her sister had gotten herself into. Whose suit had her sister dropped off? As for the man who picked it up—the brute—she was certain that was Will Bloom.

Danny Mendoza didn't sleep well.

He had the nightmare. Every night. The car rolled down a black highway. A younger Danny listened behind the wheel to the motor's monotone hum. He struggled to keep on the right side of the center line as the car accelerated. A hollow-eyed man in the rearview mirror stared back at him. He knew what was coming.

Danny tried to hit the brake. His leg couldn't reach the pedal. His foot pumped air. He lurched back into the seat as the car accelerated, faster, out of control. The headlights swung erratically, left to right, illuminating stop signs, bare branches, ghosts, an X-ray world; every skeleton bright and sassy.

Danny tried to stretch his arms to the steering wheel, his foot to the brake. Nothing could stop this car. The man in the rearview mirror, mouth open, a silent scream, knew what was coming.

Danny heard it, the pounding thud. The body flew up, onto the hood, against the windshield. He shut his eyes. The car rolled to a stop. He heard the body's slow, dull descent like a bag of wet sand hitting the pavement.

Danny knew what was coming.

Headlights illuminated the girl. Blood pooled in her eyes, nose, and mouth. The dream always had the same ending. He stood in the glare of lights; a guilty man, a sinner, a murderer.

Twelve chimes: midnight. The campus was silent, forsaken. A murder will do that—set people's nerves on edge, scatter them to kingdom come. Tonight, everyone who could find a place to go was gone.

The shadows of buildings, trees, scrub melted together. Under a full moon, the grove glowed, a pattern of silvered darkness. Limbs hung heavy in a toothless wind; a lone whistle of breeze sounded, like a master calling its hound back home. Among dead leaves, fallen branches, and stones, someone walked, crunching debris beneath their feet like bones of the dead.

Searching for one thing.

A blanket.
Steeped in blood.
A clue embedded in thread.
Damned, damning.
An amalgam of despair.
The beast was missing.
And must be found.

CHAPTER 25

Ghost Dog

"Why am I here?" DJ asked. It was five minutes past midnight. The start of Saturday morning.

Evidence licked his hand.

"Yes, girl, you are why I'm here."

Lying to himself made DJ feel better.

He stood a few yards from the entrance of the Emergency Pet Clinic. The building was shipwrecked on lower Eagle Rock Boulevard, close to Hesperia; a double-wide street of auto body shops, run-down mom and pop eateries, massage parlors.

Tonight, Lillian Sing, doctor of veterinary medicine, was in residence. DJ's ex-wife, Lillian, ran the Emergency Pet Clinic every Friday night through Saturday morning. Lillian didn't keep his last name; in fact, she never bothered to take it in the first place.

DJ kept tabs on her; some people might call it spying. After she left him five years ago, Lillian received her degree in veterinary medicine. Crushing his dreams allowed Lillian to pursue hers. DJ couldn't help feeling sorry for himself. It had become a habit.

For the first time that day, Evidence began to whimper. DJ hated whining, but tonight he sympathized.

"I'm afraid to go inside too. But I need to find out who you belong to."

What if Evidence did belong to someone? Better to know now. Before he grew attached. DJ had a way of ignoring attachments until part of him went missing.

The door to the pet clinic opened and a couple came out clutching a cat that resembled a gray feather duster. They looked at him suspiciously until they saw Evidence in his arms. The couple smiled sheepishly and waved.

DJ looked behind himself. Were they waving at him? Maybe holding Evidence made him appear to be a regular Joe, a nice guy with his dog.

He waved back.

The clinic's front door was heavy plastic, fake tree rings etched into its surface. DJ stepped through the entrance into an antiseptic linoleum-tiled lobby.

The walls and fluorescents were so white it hurt his eyes. A sign instructed, "Ring the bell."

He rang and waited.

A young man wearing doctor scrubs greeted him from behind a door. His badge indicated his name was Rolf. DJ disliked him immediately.

"I need to see Dr. Sing," said DJ.

"And how about your friend?" Rolf said.

DJ looked down at the dog. Rolf was making a joke. Dislike confirmed. Rolf wore his hair short on the sides, longer on top. He had smooth caramel skin. DJ thought women probably found him handsome.

DJ pulled out his badge with his left hand and showed it to Rolf.

"Listen, funny boy, I need to see Dr. Sing on police business. I'll explain the dog to her."

DJ hoped his woman didn't find Rolf handsome, even if she wasn't his woman anymore.

"Are you the ex-husband?" asked Rolf.

Young Rolf didn't intimidate easily.

"It's police business. I don't answer questions. You do."

"I guess that would be a yes."

"Shall I take your smart ass down to headquarters?"

Rolf sighed deeply and rolled his eyes. "Follow me."

The younger man turned around and walked down the hallway. Rolf had broad shoulders and muscular arms beneath a short-sleeved smock. He opened a door into an even brighter examination room.

"Wait here," Rolf said. "I'll tell Dr. Sing that you and your friend are here. What's the dog's name?"

"Evidence."

"Of course it is," said Rolf. He shut the door before DJ could reply.

As DJ waited, he held the dog on his lap. Evidence looked up at him. Her eyes resembled golden raisins; her cockeyed ears framed a wizened face. The dog reminded DJ of something. The answer blazed into his mind. Yoda. Her face looked like Yoda! No wonder he had fallen for her. The original *Star Wars* was his favorite movie. He'd watched it at least twenty times when he was a kid. It was his cousin Frankie's favorite. He felt a pang of loss for his cousin, for his ex-wife, for the life he had meant to live.

DJ looked down at Evidence.

"Yes, it's true. Love her, I still do."

The door opened, Lillian walked in. His ex-wife wore mint-green scrubs under a white doctor's coat. Her long black hair was pulled back into a messy ponytail. She had dark circles under her large almond-shaped eyes; her pink lips were chapped. She was beautiful.

"Hi, DJ," Lillian said. She crossed her arms and leaned back against a counter that held swabs, stethoscopes, and other medical equipment. She wasn't surprised to see him, as if she knew that after all these years he'd show up tonight with a dog. At least the dog should have surprised her.

"I'm on a case," he said.

"No doubt," said Lillian.

"You look good," DJ said. He couldn't help it.

"Why are you here?"

"It was my birthday a couple of days ago."

"I know. I remember. Everything," said Lillian.

"I need a veterinarian," said DJ. Perhaps it was better to switch the subject.

"Of all the gin joints," Lillian said, "in all the world."

They had watched *Casablanca* before the first time they had made love. He had lived in a tiny one-room apartment so small he slept on a futon that doubled as his couch. The movie was in black-and-white. They held hands as they watched it. DJ cried. Lillian's left hand shook. When the movie ended, she lay back on his pillow and he kissed her. It wasn't his first kiss, but it was the best kiss of his life.

"I found this dog in a dead man's home," he said. "I named her Evidence."

"Clever."

"My partner said that some dogs have a chip that contains the owner's name and address. Is that true?"

"Yep, that's right," Lillian said. "It's common practice."

"Is it?" DJ asked. "My grandma never did that with her strays."

"So do you want me to scan her?"

"You can do that here?"

"I can. Bring her up on the table."

DJ carried the small dog and put her on the stainless-steel platform. Her long legs splayed as if trying to find her footing on ice. Evidence stared accusingly at DJ.

"Will it hurt?" he asked.

"No," said Lilian. "If she has a chip, I'll recover a number. I'll have to contact the national database to determine who's the registered owner."

"Will I need to return her?" DJ asked.

"Ethically, I'm obligated to contact the owner."

"You always follow the rules," said DJ.

"Yes," Lilian said. "I do." What she left unsaid spoke multitudes.

"So, are we ready?"

She held a scanner that was bright green with a big red button. It read iDentifier. It looked like a Christmas toy that might be mistaken for a spaceman's gun.

"How big is the chip?" asked DJ

"About the size of a grain of rice," she said. She moved the scanner over the back of the dog between her shoulder joints. "Okay, she's chipped. Here's the number."

She showed DJ a line of numbers that she recorded on a notepad.

"Our Wi-Fi's down, old technology here. I should have the information tomorrow. Hopefully it's current."

"Thank you," he said. DJ took her hand. He wanted to hold it forever. He noticed the tremor in her other hand. It had begun in earnest after they were married. She called it a BET, a Benign Essential Tremor. He had read up on it; it was exacerbated by stress. DJ wondered if without him her hands were steadier.

"No problem," she said. She extricated her hand and started examining Evidence. She squeezed the flesh beneath the dog's front legs, examined her neck and paws.

"She's a miniature pinscher, right?" asked DJ.

"I don't think so," said Lilian. "I think she might be a mix. Like me. Maybe Chihuahua and miniature greyhound."

Lillian was an aristocratic Cuban-Chinese princess. Born to be extraordinary, she was whippet-thin, with high cheekbones, eyes almost too large for her delicate face, and a voracious intellect. DJ had a slim chance in hell of attracting her in the first place.

"I'll stop by to get the owner's information," said DJ.

"I'll text or call you," Lilian said. "No need to waste your time."

"It's never a waste of time to see you," said DJ.

"Don't," she said.

"Don't what?" asked DJ.

"Don't put me through this again."

DJ looked down at Evidence, who was gazing at the doctor. Lillian was running her hand across the dog's back.

"I miss seeing you," said DJ. "Can't we be friends?"

"I wouldn't survive it," said Lilian.

"I might not survive without you," he said.

"You chose," said Lillian. "A long time ago. And you're still standing."

There it was.

The truth. He had chosen. He didn't know it at the time. He thought love was elastic, that it could stretch to accommodate his moods, his actions. But it snapped, with a sting that penetrated deeper into his core with each year that went by.

"I'll text you," she said.

"Or maybe Rolf will text me." He couldn't keep the nastiness out of his voice.

"Perhaps," she said. "You should apologize to him. He's a good guy." Her lips formed a sad smile that caused the familiar blow to his solar plexus.

"Oh," she said, "happy birthday."

DJ watched Lillian turn and walk out of the room. Head held high, back straight, her shoulders squared beneath her starched white coat. He saw the tremor in her left hand. It always betrayed her. Just as DJ had done.

He had burned through his marriage as his fortunes waxed and waned. Booze, gambling, women. He did it all. One day he woke up and realized he had lost the only person that mattered to him.

He picked up Evidence and held her in his arms. With a dry tongue, the dog licked his cheek. A kiss from a ghost.

DJ had a slim chance of attracting his wife in the first place and zero chance of winning her back.

CHAPTER 26

Flower

When you lived alone, no one cared where you fell asleep. DJ lay tucked into his couch in the living room, Evidence pressed against his back. He turned over and the dog crawled onto his chest, stared, then nudged at him with her nose. It was time to get up.

He fed Evidence from the bag of dog food he'd received the night before. Rolf presented it to him—at no charge, along with a collar and leash.

"A birthday present from the doc," Rolf said. "Remember, a dog is the only creature on earth that loves you more than you love yourself."

DJ wanted to push Rolf's face in, but he needed the kibble.

As DJ drove to campus Saturday morning, the instant coffee he pounded down took effect. He ran over his mental notes on Hoa Phan. Early Friday morning, she called in sick, spoke to Dolly Ruiz. And now a new question, whose suit did Ms. Phan leave at the dry cleaners, and how did it get into Will Bloom's car trunk?

Talbot was already inside the lobby, pretending to scroll through his phone but surreptitiously studying the twenty-five-year-old woman sitting a few feet away. DJ expected a grieving young girl. Someone pretty and flashy who had caught Will Bloom's eye.

Hoa Phan was slim, somber, entirely in possession of her emotions. She wore a short-sleeved navy pin-striped jacket and matching skirt. Her hair was straight, black, shoulder-length. An array of features, brown eyes, full lips, high cheekbones, that separately might have been attractive and unremark-able were arranged with mathematical precision from God or Darwin. Hoa Phan wasn't pretty, she was beautiful.

"Miss Phan?" DJ shook her hand as Talbot unlocked the conference room door. "Detective DJ Arias. I'm leading the investigation into Will Bloom's murder."

Hoa Phan reached out her hand. Her nails were short, neat. No nail polish. She had a direct gaze and melancholy smile. She wore very high black heels.

She knelt down, balancing perfectly on those heels to pet Evidence. The dog lay on its back and Hoa ran her fingernails across Evidence's belly. A radiant smile broke across the woman's face.

"Oh, what a darling," Hoa said.

They stepped inside the conference room. DJ and Talbot exchanged looks. What Will Bloom saw in Hoa Phan was obvious. But what had this woman seen in Will Bloom? Bloom was old enough to be her father; hell, he might have been her grandfather.

"I'm sorry for your loss," DJ said.

"Will was beloved by many."

"I think," said DJ, "we can dispense with pretense. We know about you and Bloom."

"All right, no pretense. Will and I had a personal relationship."

DJ was pleased, hunch and idle gossip confirmed.

Then Hoa Phan studied him. "Is this your dog?"

"I found her at Will Bloom's house," he said.

"Did you?" Hoa looked perplexed. "Will didn't own a dog."

"Well, he did yesterday," said DJ.

"That's impossible," she said. "But today, everything is impossible."

She sat down in one of the chairs and crossed her legs. Talbot grabbed his yellow pad and sat across the table. DJ remained standing, pretending not to notice Ms. Phan's legs.

"In your opinion," asked DJ, "did Mr. Bloom have any enemies?"

"Yes," she said. "I would think so."

DJ's eyes slid up to Ms. Phan's face. She had his full attention. "I'm sure Trish filled you in on all the details," said Hoa. "Her little blue notebook?"

"No," said Talbot. "She didn't mention a notebook."

DJ shot a look at his partner. Few witnesses tell the whole truth, Talbot hadn't learned that yet, particularly when they batted their eyelashes.

"She listed the names of women who called Will," said Hoa. "She boasted about it. And incriminating receipts. She made sure I overheard her."

"Why would she do that?" asked DJ.

Hoa shrugged.

"To hurt me? To put me in my place." The smile reappeared. A break-your-heart smile like Lillian's.

"And did it?" asked DJ. He sat down and moved his chair closer.

"I'm made of sterner stuff."

From this distance, DJ saw her eyes were swollen from crying. Her skin beneath the makeup was pale. Hoa Phan may have been one of the youngest people working in Bloom's office, but she was the most contained.

"But yes," she said. "It hurt."

"And these women? On the list," said DJ. "Who were they? Perhaps women he . . . he . . ."

"Slept with," said Hoa Phan. "I think that's the term you're searching for."

"Yes. Do you think one of these women might have a reason to hurt Will Bloom?"

"I don't know," said Hoa. "Will was brilliant, witty, charming. But he had a hunger, or a failing, depending on your point of view. He was a little boy in a candy store. Women were candy."

"And once consumed?" asked DJ.

Hoa shrugged her shoulders again. "Old candy."

"And what would you call it?" asked DJ. "Hunger or failing?"

Hoa Phan thought it over. "An addiction," she said. "Like an alcoholic or drug addict."

"He was a woman addict," said Talbot, writing everything down like a good little detective.

"I would characterize it," said Hoa, "as compulsive sexual behavior."

"Do you know the names on Trish's list?" asked Talbot.

"Will interacted with woman all over campus," said Hoa Phan.

"Anyone outside of Hesperia?" asked DJ.

"Probably," said Hoa.

"That's a lot of people," said DJ.

"And their boyfriends and husbands presumably weren't happy, if they found out."

"When was the last time that you saw him?" asked DJ

"Six days ago. On Sunday afternoon, before I left for a conference in Phoenix."

"Trish Ballentine said that he was in your office Thursday morning. Mooning about is how she put it."

"Did she?" asked Hoa Phan. "Oh . . . that is interesting."

"You didn't see him Thursday evening when you returned from your trip?" DJ asked.

"No. We had talked on Wednesday, he said he wanted to pick me up at the airport."

"Okay? So you did see him."

"No, he called me when I landed and said he wasn't coming."

"Why was that?"

"He was angry. Furious, actually. He accused me of cheating on him."

"Were you?"

Hoa appeared to be considering the question. "No."

"Were you seeing someone else?" DJ asked.

Hoa pressed her lips together.

"Will and I weren't going steady," she said. "He hadn't given me his class ring."

"Or any ring?"

"That's right, Detective," she said. "No ring. No commitment."

DJ thought Will Bloom had been a fool.

"But he was angry, you said furious? Why?"

She stared down at her hands, fingers folded tightly together.

"No idea," DJ prodded, "why Will Bloom would suddenly be furious and accuse you of infidelity?"

Hoa Phan was quiet, as if she was calculating a math problem. "I don't know."

DJ thought she had come up with the wrong answer.

"So he was wrong? About you seeing someone else?" Hoa breathed out and DJ realized she had been holding her breath.

"I'm twenty-five years old. I've dated other men," said Hoa. "Not seriously. My personal relationship with Will was new."

"Can I ask you why?" DJ couldn't help himself. "Why, why . . . were you . . . ?"

"Why was I with him?" she asked.

"He was almost forty years your senior, he drank too much and he, he, he . . ."

"He slept around," said Hoa.

"Uh, yeah."

There was moment of silence.

"I thought I was different," she said. "I thought we were different."

"Really?" asked DJ.

"He gave me tremendous opportunities for my age, trusted me to do a good job. He promoted me when I did."

"You were grateful?" asked DJ.

"It wasn't that. I knew what Will was because he told me. He had an abusive, alcoholic father, a mother who abandoned him. But he was also different than anyone I knew. You wouldn't understand."

"Try me."

"Will had survived his past; imperfectly, but he survived. We had that in common. My family immigrated from Viet Nam when I was three. We landed in Garden Grove. My father was a university-educated lawyer. But here, in the United States, he managed a convenience store. Back home, he saved people's lives. Here, he sold Slurpees to spoiled white kids. My sister and I cleaned and stocked the store after school while those brats called us 'gooks' and other terrible names. We scraped by, we survived."

"That must have been a comedown for your father," said DJ. "For your family."

She looked out the windows at campus. "All of this . . ." Her hand swept the air.

"Hesperia?"

"This school, this country, this culture. People here take everything for granted."

"And Will Bloom didn't?"

"No," said Hoa. "He did not. Will was voracious, intellectual, curious. The first day I met him, he took my hand and said, 'Hoa, a beautiful name. I believe it means flower, and rightly so.' Most Americans can't pronounce my name, and this man pronounced it perfectly, knew it's meaning, and . . ." Hoa Phan blushed. "Managed a courtly compliment."

DJ thought Will Bloom had decided to make a move on Hoa Phan the moment he saw her.

"Will made me feel that I was special," said Hoa, "capable, and successful."

DJ stared at Hoa. Did she really need Will Bloom to tell her that?

"What brought you to Hesperia College?"

"Students like me, who come from families like mine? They need opportunity, they need access to institutions like Hesperia."

DJ didn't think there were many like Hoa Phan.

"So when did your relationship become personal?"

"Three months ago," said Hoa. "A business trip."

"Dinner and too many drinks?"

"It wasn't like that. We had a meeting with a wealthy donor. Will asked for a very large gift. The gentleman declined, became angry, then nasty. He humiliated Will. Seemed to enjoy it. Particularly in front of me. Afterward, Will was devastated, he was vulnerable. We talked about what had just happened. We were real with each other. That's rare in my experience."

"That's when it began?"

"Yes," she said.

"And after that?"

"We saw each other almost every night. Will told me—actually, he warned me—that he had inherited three things from his father: alcoholism, womanizing, and that damn Japanese sword that killed him. His great-uncle fought in World War II."

"The police haven't disclosed to the public how Mr. Bloom died," said DJ.

"Oh," said Hoa. "A good guess, then?"

"You're being sarcastic. But no one knows how Will Bloom died except the murderer."

"Detective, you've entered the cloistered world of academia," she said. "A feudal village."

"We've kept the cause of death confidential."

Hoa Phan shook her head. "The cleaning women know, Facilities know, the president's office and Will's officemates know how he died. At this point, the dishwasher in the cafeteria knows. There's no power greater at Hesperia than knowledge, and nothing more porous."

DJ leaned forward across the conference table.

"I find that hard to believe."

Hoa shrugged her shoulders. It didn't matter to her what DJ believed.

"Well, I certainly didn't do it," Hoa said. "I could never hurt Will."

DJ disagreed. Hoa Phan might be the only person who could have hurt Will Bloom.

"And what about the suit?"

"Excuse me?" Hoa's face grew pale beneath the makeup.

"Talbot here found a man's suit in Will's car with your name on the receipt."

Talbot looked up and said, "From Lau 'N Dry."

Again, Hoa stared at her hands. DJ could see her calculating an answer.

"I had no idea Will picked up that suit." She wasn't a bad liar.

"Whose suit is it?"

"It's . . . mine."

"Yours?"

"An old friend of mine's. No one special. I wanted it out of my apartment."

"Will Bloom was angry, accused you of cheating on him, because of 'no one special's' suit?"

"He doesn't live in Los Angeles anymore. I was going to give it away. And . . . and he's married."

"Did Will know that?"

"I don't know. When he telephoned, he was completely irrational. He accused me of cheating and said we were through."

"What did you say?"

"Nothing. I hung up. I don't play those games. I thought we could discuss it the next day. When he was sober."

"And that was your last conversation?"

"Yes," she said.

"Can you verify where you were Thursday night? An alibi? Did you see anyone else?"

"I called my sister," she said. "I told her that Will and I had a fight on the phone. She came over, picked me up, and I stayed at her place."

DJ studied Hoa. Her eyes were downcast, her lips pursed with the memory. DJ thought of Lillian. Her image kept popping up like a ghost he couldn't banish.

"Will had his demons to bear," Hoa Phan said. "I thought when he was sober, he'd realize he was being unreasonable and call to apologize. The next morning, I found out that Will was dead."

"How did you discover that?" asked DJ.

"From Dolly Ruiz," said Hoa. "She knew we were close."

"So you didn't call in sick?"

"I called her back after she told me," said Hoa. "I left a message that I felt ill. When she first telephoned, I couldn't say anything. I couldn't breathe."

DJ saw grief suffuse Hoa Phan's face. Her eyes teared for an instant before her composure returned. He felt his phone vibrate and saw Lilian's number. "Excuse me, I have to take this call."

He turned away as he listened to his ex-wife speak to him in her brisk professional "don't-fuck-with-me"voice, as if he was nothing more than a client.

"Thank you," he said. "Hey . . ." She hung up the phone.

". . . yeah, let's grab a coffee," DJ said to the dial tone.

When he had composed himself, he turned back to Hoa Phan.

"Are you sure Will Bloom didn't talk to you about getting a dog?"

"Will said a dog wouldn't survive one day in his care," she said. "I'm the one who wanted a dog. But I couldn't have one in my apartment complex."

Another mystery.

"Am I free to go?"

"Yes, for now. Don't leave town. We may need to follow up."

As Hoa Phan walked out of the conference room, DJ couldn't help but notice her long legs, her slim figure, her regal bearing. She turned around, gave him an enigmatic smile that could haunt a man for the rest of the day or rest of his life.

"I thought Will and I were special," she said. "That was just ego and folly."

"Don't be so hard on yourself," said DJ. "Ego is the only thing that saves us from folly."

"You know, you remind me of him."

"Who?"

"Will. You remind me of Will."

DJ opened his mouth but had nothing to say.

"Goodbye, Detective."

DJ watched her leave. Across the lobby, out the door into the bright blue Saturday.

Talbot rustled his papers to grab DJ's attention. "The suit. It's important."

"I think so too."

DJ thought over the brief phone call from his ex-wife. The dog found in Will Bloom's bathroom had been chipped at the Glendale Animal Shelter. "G-dale," was scribbled on the receipt. That's where Will Bloom adopted her.

"One more question, sir."

"Yes?"

"Do you think Trish Ballentine is in any danger—with that list of women who slept with Will Bloom? It sounds like she talked about it openly in the office."

DJ considered Trish Ballentine, her balled fist, her angry pinched face.

"We'll interview her again on Monday." Trish Ballentine was a monumental pain in the ass. Hardly dangerous. "And ask about her blue notebook."

DJ looked down into Evidence's face. She belonged to a dead man.

CHAPTER 27

Chance Encounter

Danny Mendoza was ready.

It was Saturday morning. The receipt for the Domino's pizza he ordered Thursday night sat in his pocket, a permission slip. "I am excused from prison this week, thank you very much." He wore a blue broadcloth shirt and dark-wash jeans. Instead of his usual work boots, he dug out suede loafers from the back of his closet, shoes from another life.

Hedy Scacht had offered to drive him to campus. But he preferred to walk, deal with Detective Arias on his own. Hedy tried to protect Danny, but he chafed under her well-meaning interference. *Maybe she should tend to her own child*, he thought, not something he would say out loud.

Danny walked the two blocks to campus. He had nothing to do with Will Bloom's murder. But after prison, he knew bad men did terrible things and sometimes good men paid for their deeds.

Walking through Hesperia's main entrance gates, past the steel fountain, through the oak-studded quad, Danny started up the steep stairs to Sliming Administration Center. He could have taken a more gradual route, but Danny appreciated the climb.

He quickly ascended the wide vertical steps. Halfway up he felt the twinge in his thighs and calves, his heart quickened, sinews tightened. He had learned to push his body hard at Chino. Any kind of muscle ache was better than thinking about where you were, what you were missing.

Danny had almost reached the top when he saw the girl, her head bent down, hidden in her arms. She sat where the steps to Sliming collided with older stairs to Collins Hall. During the workweek and wearing his uniform, Danny would have turned the other way, pretended she didn't exist. A groundskeeper didn't fraternize with students. The girl looked up, wiping her eyes. Just his luck: twice in two days, he had walked into a weeping woman.

The girl watched him with a curiosity Danny forgot he could elicit.

"Hey," Danny said reluctantly. "You all right?"

The girl stared at him. She was beautiful, with long chestnut hair, eyes flecked with gold.

"Not so good," she said. "How about you?"

Surprise, he thought, *a truthful answer.* And she asked a question. He could answer that he walked a tightrope between life on parole and a menial job. Or that last night he almost drank a six-pack of beer, aching to swallow the bitterness he tasted every minute of every day.

"I'm okay," said Danny. He wasn't going to burden this lovely creature with the weight of his existence. "Are you hurt?" Danny asked. Her lovely eyes were glassy with impending tears.

"Hurt? No, I mean . . ." the girl said, "just my knee. But not bad."

Hurt, God! What a stupid question. He hadn't been alone with a young woman in years. And she was a beautiful young woman.

"I'm just under the weather," she said. "My name is Ferencia Lake. Everyone calls me Fern." The girl stood up unsteadily, offering Danny her hand like an earnest applicant interviewing for a job. "I'm a senior here. You look familiar. Are you a student?"

Danny took her hand. It was a miracle of a firm grip and soft skin.

"I was once," he said. That much was true. "I'm Danny Mendoza. Nice to meet you."

"Oh, you're an alum," said Fern. "So you know what it's like. To be a senior, about to be cast out into the world. All this pressure to be someone."

Danny didn't know what to say.

"And what if I mess up?" She looked at him with genuine angst. "I'm sorry. I'm usually more in control. It's been a tough couple of days."

She was right about the pressure to be someone and fucking it up. He could teach a course on it. Now was the moment to tell her who he was, what he did every day. Weeding gardens, planting trees, picking up litter. End any misunderstanding.

But Ferencia Lake was the loveliest woman Danny had ever seen. "You already are someone," he said. "You don't have to worry about that."

Fern blushed, then wobbled, losing her balance on the steep stairs.

"Whoa," she said.

Without thinking, Danny reached out, caught her before she stumbled. "Hey!"

She fell against him, into his arms. Danny breathed in the scent of her hair, honeysuckle. He forgot how good a woman could smell up close.

"Are you really okay?" Danny stepped back to look into her face.

That's when it all poured out.

"I'm sorry. I wrecked my knee the other night. Something awful happened and I haven't been able to sleep or eat since. I came here to speak to the police," Fern said. "It was Thursday night, and I . . . I don't know . . ."

Emotions ping-ponged within Fern; guilt-ridden over Professor Bounty and traumatized from the attack. The aftereffects of fear wrapped in shame permeated her body and mind, made her dizzy with regret. Now the police had summoned her to return for further questioning. It was too much.

"Is this about the murder?" Danny asked.

"I'm not sure," said Fern. "I was attacked Thursday night. On campus. I was walking through the olive grove."

"Who attacked you?" asked Danny.

"I don't know," she said. "I didn't see his face."

"Oh my God. How terrible."

"Someone was following me. They threw something over me, I couldn't see anything or move my arms. I was pushed to the ground. I didn't know what they were going to do to me."

Without thinking, he reached out again, a firm hand on her shoulder. "Only a coward would hurt someone like you, or any woman."

Fern looked up at Danny. He was handsome, muscular, strong. She thought he was the kind of man like her father, who would put himself in danger to protect someone.

"I finally managed to get away. But it was terrifying."

"It makes me furious someone would try to hurt you." He looked into her eyes. "This attack, it will live with you for a while, but after a time, it will fade. You were really brave to escape."

"Was I?" No one said she had been brave, that the attack would stay with her, haunt her. Not the Campus Safety Officer, not the police. She didn't even get a chance to tell her friends. Her fellow students and ex-boyfriend had already left Hesperia for early fall break.

Danny reached out to wipe away an errant tear. Her skin was velvet, the tear wet.

He couldn't stop looking at her.

"Hey, you're safe now, you're here with me."

Fern felt tears flood her eyes. Without thinking, Danny pulled her close again. Miraculously, she melted into him, her cheek again his chest. That scent again of honeysuckle. It felt good to hold someone, it felt amazing to hold Ferencia Lake.

She could feel his strong, steady heartbeat. Danny wasn't a boy; he was a man. She breathed in his scent, clean like soap; her skin grew hot where he held her. A thick, slow bead of desire slipped down into her belly, a warmth grew up her back, her neck, reached her face. Leaning into him made her feel everything would be all right.

"When was the last time you ate something?" He reluctantly pulled back and looked at her with concern.

Fern took a deep breath.

"I don't remember."

Danny knew she was in need of a good meal, a place to sit down and gather her thoughts. He wanted nothing more than to spend a few hours with her in a parallel world where he was a regular guy who could walk on campus and meet a girl. But the longer he delayed revealing the truth of who he was, where he spent the last ten years, the harder he'd fall from grace. He pulled back, keeping his hands on her arms to make sure she was steady.

"Let's get you some food and coffee," he said. "Maybe the cafeteria is open. The police will still be here when we get back."

The young woman needed to eat. And the cafeteria where his mother had worked for years would be the cold splash of reality he needed. A server would recognize him. Ask what he was doing in civilian clothes. He would be forced to tell her then and there. And that would be that.

"Okay," she said quickly. Fern smiled up at him; Danny could feel the pull of her beauty, the long hair that brushed his arm, her scent that drew him in. She had a gravity that anchored him to a different world.

"Wait," said Fern. "Are you here to see the police about the murder?"

"Yeah," said Danny. "I knew the victim, Will Bloom. Not well."

"Wow, they are bringing everyone in, aren't they?"

"This detective is thorough," said Danny. "No loose thread, no stone unturned."

"Oh," said Fern. The shadow of Thursday night darkened her face.

Did the police already know about Professor Bounty? She didn't think Bounty would say anything. It would ruin his career, her senior year, and worse, her father's trust and belief in her. But maybe someone had seen her leaving his house. That night she had the feeling of being watched.

Looking up at the man standing before her, she felt that meeting Danny Mendoza was going to change her luck, maybe her life. He didn't have to know that she'd slept with a married professor, did he?

"Hey, are you okay?"

"I am really hungry," Fern said. "Ravenous."

"All right, Ferencia Lake," Danny said. "Let's find you something to eat."

He held out his elbow, she slipped her hand through his arm.

Danny knew this would end badly. Women expected a better life, a better man. A college graduate might tolerate a starving artist, but not a man who pulled weeds, picked up garbage for a living. Definitely not a convict.

They walked together down the steps to the Hesperia cafeteria arm in arm. Danny savored every second. For the moment, he wasn't an ex-con, a maintenance man, or the callous, grasping college student he once was, but the man he could have been, might have been if life had a different fate in mind for him.

CHAPTER 28

Thorn

DJ Arias walked out of Sliming with Evidence in tow. Several industrial-size cement planters containing Palo Verde trees were housed on the patio surrounding the building. He lifted Evidence inside one to do her business.

While the dog was otherwise engaged, DJ googled *Japanese swords* on his phone, compared them to the photo he'd snapped yesterday. He knew from the conversation with Hoa Phan it was from World War II. That narrowed its provenance. As DJ swiped through screen pages of samurai swords, he came upon a *shin guntō* sword, produced just before World War II by master craftsmen. They were the highest quality weaponry Japanese soldiers carried. Their contemporary guns and other equipment proved inferior in combat with their Western adversaries. According to several websites, the swords sold for anywhere between $1,500 and $3,000.

"Pardon me, aren't you the police detective?"

DJ looked up and saw the silhouette of a woman against the sun. His immediate impression was caramel skin wrapped in a tight black T-shirt and white jeans.

"Yes. I'm Detective DJ Arias. And you are?" DJ moved counterclockwise around the planter for a better look. He recognized the woman.

"We met briefly yesterday. I'm Ravi LaVal," she said, smiling. "Professor of history and chair of the faculty council." She was medium height, with dark sparkling eyes and full coral lips that revealed perfect teeth. She held a white rose in one hand.

"Is this your dog in the planter?"

"This is Evidence," said DJ.

"Really," said Ravi LaVal. "Now that is interesting. Does the dog play good cop? Disarm your suspects?" She had a British accent and a mocking smile.

"It's a good idea," DJ said. "Where are you headed this Saturday morning, Professor LaVal?"

"Call me Ravi. Third floor. I have another emergency meeting with the president. They're becoming a regular occurrence. But do let me know if I or any faculty can be of help or answer any questions."

"Thanks, I'll keep that in mind."

To be surrounded by so many beautiful, intelligent women was disconcerting to DJ. How did Will Bloom, with his proclivities, manage his impulses? DJ reminded himself that Bloom was dead.

"The faculty appreciates your efforts," said Ravi, taking his hand, "to keep this horrible incident away, as much as possible, from the students." She held his fingers a beat too long; her version of a handshake.

DJ had done nothing to keep students out of the murder investigation. So far, the one cohort Will Bloom was not diddling were coeds. Supposedly, he had learned that lesson from a former job. But who knew, the investigation was still young.

"You're welcome," said DJ, taking back his hand. He noticed a wedding band on her ring finger. "How well did you know Will Bloom?"

"He was a charming scoundrel. But harmless." She flashed her brilliant smile of even white teeth.

DJ was distracted for a beat by the radiance of that smile.

"Poor Will," she said, the smile fading. "It's such a tragedy."

"Most murders are," said DJ. "I do have a question for you. I met with Hoa Phan this morning."

"Well, that must have been a treat."

"She knew confidential details of the murder scene. When I asked her how she knew the particulars, she said Hesperia is a feudal village, a cloistered world, and there are no secrets. Do you agree with that?"

The smile disappeared. "So, you met with Hoa Phan," she said. "How lucky for you, and so early in the day."

"What about her metaphor?" asked DJ.

"Is it metaphor or analogy? I wonder. How did she describe herself? Princess or courtesan?"

"I take it you don't like Ms. Phan?" asked DJ.

"Oh dear." Ravi twirled the rose in her hand. "I hardly know her. I'm sure she is a fine person, if a bit young."

"For Will?" asked DJ.

"For her job, Detective," said Ravi LaVal.

"She seemed capable. So is Hesperia a feudal village?" asked DJ. "Where everyone knows each other's secrets?"

"Well," Ravi said, "a Japanese sword through the back is quite shocking. That news is not easily contained."

"So you know too," said DJ.

"Hesperia is full of secrets, connections, skeletons in the cupboard," said Ravi. "I'm sure there are a few staring you right in the face."

"You mean people having affairs?" asked DJ.

"Detective, you might be more imaginative," Ravi LaVal sighed. "Not what I meant. Besides, the word *affair* is so bourgeois."

"I'm just a cop, toiling outside the walls and social mores of Hesperia," said DJ. "Help me out?"

"Is this college a feudal village? I'd say, more like an inbred, airless cloister. Faculty, the intellectuals, are practically indentured servants. The administrators are vassals who scrape and bow to the entitled aristocracy; that would be the president and senior management team. And finally, there are the trustees, like gods of old, trying to solve the problem of our existence in the modern world."

"And have they?" asked DJ. "Solved the problem?"

"Detective," said Ravi, "we don't want to be solved. We're a private liberal arts college, not an engineering school. We don't 'solve' a problem. We focus on the question, each one spurring myriad deeper inquiries."

"Sounds like a cult," said DJ.

"Unlike the military or the police?" The mocking smile reappeared. "At Hesperia, we provide an intellectual grounding for essential truths, not the solution of the day. We explore ideas, issues, facts. I tell my students every day to think critically on the nature of things."

"I missed that in college," said DJ. "I went to Cal State LA."

"Nonsense," said Professor Ravi LaVal. "Critical thinking is central to all college educations."

"Most of the students I attended college with just needed a job," he said.

DJ stared at the scarlet flowers of a bougainvillea spilling over a retaining wall.

"Education is not only about vocation, Detective, it's purpose, passion. That spark that makes you want to jump out of bed in the morning, that makes life feel heightened."

"Is that how you feel?" DJ asked. "Working at Hesperia, teaching your students."

Her face darkened. "Not on days like this."

Ravi brought the rose to her face, inhaling its scent.

"Days like this will break your heart."

DJ thought he knew who Ravi LaVal was thinking about.

"So how well did you know Will Bloom?"

"Oh, everyone knew Will," said Ravi. "He was quite the presence on campus."

"Did you spend time with him?" asked DJ. "One-on-one. Have meetings or other types of contact?"

"What a funny question." Ravi didn't smile.

"I've heard he liked beautiful women," said DJ. "I have to believe he must have liked you?"

"Are you paying me a compliment?"

"Was your relationship with Will Bloom strictly professional?" asked DJ.

"I liked Will and he liked me," said Ravi. "But for the last two or three months, I barely saw him. Besides, I don't kiss and tell."

"I'll take that as a yes?" asked DJ. "So, Mr. Bloom became otherwise engaged and left you hanging?"

Ravi stood up straight, the playful manner evaporated.

"I'm devastated Will is dead. It's awful. But I haven't done anything illegal, and I don't believe in immoral." She was now the professor and head of faculty council, smarter than DJ and dismissive. "You will have to leave it at that."

"And you have an alibi for Thursday night?" asked DJ.

"Yes," she said. "I was in a spin class on Colorado with my husband and then we ate Mexican food at Cacao Mexicatessan for dinner. We sat on the patio. It was quite a windy evening."

"We will check your alibi," said DJ.

"I expect nothing less," she said, holding up the flower. "This is a cutting from my garden."

"Nice."

"I brought it for Will."

"For Will Bloom? White for friendship? Surrender?"

"White is sympathy, Detective. I thought I might leave it at his office door. In memoriam."

"Like a shrine?" DJ had an image of flowers and teddy bears, demarcations of a traffic fatality on a lonely road.

"A remembrance of days past."

The stem was wrapped in a paper towel.

"Sorry," said DJ. "The bottom floor of Sliming is a crime scene. No one in or out."

"Well, I'll leave it with you then," she said. "Perhaps you can put it in an appropriate place."

She thrust the flower in his hand. A thorn poked through the paper towel, pricked his finger. A drop of blood bloomed against the white.

"Here's my card if you need to reach me. About feudal villages."

"Thanks," DJ said, taking the offered card, smudging it with red.

Ravi LaVal walked into Sliming. He wondered about Professor LaVal, her husband and their supposed mutual alibi. Was the husband brightened or burned by his wife's fire? And how did Ravi LaVal really feel about being dumped by Will Bloom for a younger woman? DJ stood there for several minutes before lifting Evidence out of the wide planter, setting her back on the ground.

He brought the injured finger to his mouth, tasting the salty blood on his lips. His grandma had taught him thorns grow downward to stop predators from reaching the flower.

He studied his finger.

It was a puncture wound.

CHAPTER 29

Lau 'N Dry

"You're bleeding, sir."

DJ looked up. Talbot had his car keys in hand.

"Where are you going? Isn't that student, Fern Lake, coming in?"

"She texted me," Talbot said. "She changed her appointment to this afternoon. I'm heading to the dry cleaner, Lau 'N Dry. Browning and Butter are manning the command post."

DJ suspected Fern Lake was lying about something. Now she was avoiding them. He looked down at his hand; the paper towel had stanched the bleeding.

"Lau 'N Dry?"

"Yes. Mr. Bennet Lau is the owner."

"Is he expecting us?"

"Us? I just spoke to Mr. Lau. He's expecting me in . . ." Talbot checked his watch. "Twenty minutes."

"All right, Talbot, let's go." DJ, tired of interviews, wanted to take action.

"You mean me *and* you?"

"Why not," said DJ. Evidence barked.

"You heard from the vet?" asked Talbot. "About the dog . . ."

"We can check out that lead after Mr. Lau."

"Nice rose," said Talbot.

"Yeah," said DJ, "but it bites." He threw the flower in a trash container.

Talbot drove. DJ rode shotgun with Evidence on his lap in the younger detective's Dodge Charger. DJ reported his conversation with Professor LaVal.

"Do you think she's a suspect?" asked Talbot.

"We'll have to check her alibi. Said she was with her husband at an exercise class, then went to a restaurant. I'd say she was involved with Will Bloom before Miss Hoa Phan came into the picture. I think the professor was dumped. Add her to the list, and maybe the husband."

"I'll have B&B check their alibi."

The two officers, Browning and Butter, were good cops, ambitious and methodical. Their names reminded DJ of Thanksgiving dinner. Talbot and DJ drove in silence for a few minutes. Evidence hung her face out the window, communing with the wind.

"So how did you get the nickname Bobby?"

"It's not a nickname," said Talbot. "My official name is Bobby. It's on the birth certificate."

"No shit," said DJ.

"Yes, sir."

"After Bobby Kennedy? Bobby McFerrin? I think they were Roberts."

"I was raised by a single mom. She named me after that song. 'Me and Bobby McGee.' It was her favorite. She was a backup singer in her forties when she had me. Mom has the vinyl record by Janis Joplin."

"Great song," said DJ. "Written by Kristofferson."

"Yeah, she knew Kris Kristofferson back in the day."

"And that's why she named you Bobby?"

"She said listening to Janis Joplin on vinyl was like hearing God sing."

"So that's what God sounds like," said DJ.

"According to Mom."

"Well, she sounds way cooler than Charity," said DJ.

"Who, sir?"

"No one." DJ stared out the window.

Bobby slowed down and pulled into a large parking lot of a Smart & Final. At the northwest corner, adjacent to an intersection, was a small white building. Painted on one side were the words Lau 'N Dry Cleaners.

"Smart & Final and Lau 'N Dry," said DJ. "I guess that's a kind of symmetry."

Bobby parked the car in front of the dry cleaner. He wondered if this interview would be an embarrassment. Mr. Lau had sounded uncooperative on the phone. DJ opened his window, left Evidence in the passenger seat where he could see her.

The establishment had two open doors, one as they entered on the south side of the building, the second on the west, facing the street. The two entrances formed a wind tunnel, one's hair and any errant papers were at the mercy of the breeze. There was a bell, DJ rang it without hesitation. Talbot thought, *Okay, here we go.*

A thin middle-aged man wearing a short-sleeved guayabera shirt appeared from behind the automated racks of clothing. He had very straight posture, his hair and mustache were jet-black.

"Mr. Bennet Lau?" asked Bobby Talbot.

"Yes," said Mr. Lau. "You are the policeman I spoke to?"

Bobby hesitated but DJ was quiet. He was letting Bobby take the lead.

"Yes, we spoke on the phone," said Talbot. "I'm Detective Bobby Talbot and this is Detective DJ Arias."

"I wish I could say it was nice to meet you," said Mr. Lau.

"We're here to ask you about a customer pickup that was made Thursday afternoon by a Mr. Will Bloom."

"I don't have a customer by that name," said Mr. Lau.

"Well, here's the ticket number," said Talbot. Bobby showed him a photo of the dry cleaner receipt found in Will Bloom's trunk, which matched the copy found pinned to Bloom's desk.

Mr. Lau didn't look at the photo. He already knew who Bobby referred to.

"Yes, yes," said Mr. Lau, pulling a carbon of the receipt out of a drawer. "The whole incident was most unpleasant. You see, the big man had the ticket and I pulled out the suit and hung it up before I realized that it was Ms. Hoa Phan's dry cleaning."

"I see," said Bobby, jotting down a note. "What time was that, Mr. Lau? And what was the article of clothing?"

"Around 4:00 p.m.," said Mr. Lau. "It was a man's suit."

"You're sure of the time?" asked Bobby Talbot.

"Yes," said Mr. Lau. "See, it's time-stamped on the receipt."

4:03 p.m. was printed on the paper.

"And what did this man look like?"

"Like I said, he was a big man. Older, with a severe haircut like a German. Sunglasses. And he wore a good suit, well-made," said Mr. Lau. "I matched the numbers and hung up the item on this rack. The man grabbed it and stared at the suit before I realized whose ticket it was. You see, at first, I thought he was a new customer. But when I read the name on the ticket, I realized it was Miss Phan's dry cleaning. And then I thought maybe he was a family friend."

"Could it have been his suit?" asked Bobby. "Maybe he picked it up so he could pay for it."

"No," said Mr. Lau. "Not his suit, not his size. And Ms. Hoa Phan always pays in advance. I have her credit card on file. Anyway, he grabbed the suit by the middle and twisted it in his hands. He destroyed my work. Most disturbing."

"And then what?" asked Talbot. "He left?"

"He started yelling."

"What did he say?"

"How could she? How could she?" said Mr. Lau in a monotone voice.

"Did you ask his name?" asked Talbot. "Ask how he got the ticket?"

"No," said Mr. Lau. "At that point, I went into my office and locked the door. The man was very angry. He pounded the counter and then the wall. I left him to it."

"And when you came out again, he was gone?" asked Talbot.

"Yes. I waited until it was quiet. I slipped out into the parking lot from my back door to make sure he was gone. And then I locked up for an hour in case he decided to return."

"Did you contact Ms. Hoa Phan after that?" asked DJ

"No," said Mr. Lau. "I didn't contact Hoa Phan. I wanted to see her in person. To explain."

"Why is that?" asked DJ. "A good customer has her clothes picked up by a stranger. Why wouldn't you call her immediately?"

Mr. Lau looked from Bobby Talbot to DJ Arias.

"First, the man had the ticket," said Mr. Lau. "So I matched the number and pulled the clothes, which was a man's suit."

"Yes, that right. A man's suit." said Talbot. "Wasn't that unusual, for Hoa Phan to clean a man's suit?"

"Not really," said Mr. Lau. "People bring in all sorts of clothes. I don't question. And the big man had the ticket. Some people have 'friends' pick up their clothes, or servants."

"And this man?" asked Talbot.

"Not a servant," said Mr. Lau. "Maybe not a friend either."

"Did any other men ever pick up Hoa Phan's clothes?" asked Bobby.

"No," said Mr. Lau. "No men."

"Anything else you want to tell us, Mr. Lau?" asked DJ. "This is a murder investigation."

"No," said Mr. Lau. "The sisters are very good customers."

"The sisters?" asked DJ.

"Yes," said Mr. Lau. "Both Hoa Phan and her sister, Thien Phan, are very good customers."

"Did Thien Phan ever pick up her sister's clothes?"

Mr. Lau's face was pale and his eyes were glued to the counter. He had promised to keep Thien Phan's Friday night visit confidential. "Occasionally."

"Anything else you can remember?"

"No," said Mr. Lau. "And this man, the big angry man, he won't come back?"

"No chance of that," said DJ.

"Here's my card," Bobby said, "in case you remember anything else about the incident."

Mr. Lau barely glanced at the card as he tossed it on the counter.

Bobby and DJ left Lau 'N Dry, stood for a moment next to the Dodge Charger.

"The suit Hoa Phan dropped off at the dry cleaner belonged to another man."

"No shit," said DJ.

"So was this dry cleaner the errand Bloom went on with Dolly Ruiz?"

"No. I think the dry cleaner was the second errand." DJ looked at Evidence sitting in the car. "I think this was his first errand."

"The dog?" asked Bobby.

"Hoa Phan said she wanted a dog."

"That's right," Bobby said. "But she couldn't have one where she lived."

"Well, absence makes the heart grow foolish. Hoa Phan was out of town. Will Bloom was missing his girl in an awful way. So he makes a decision that will change his life."

"What's that?" asked Talbot.

DJ raised his hand to wait.

"That's our next stop. I'll drive."

"Yes, sir," said Bobby. DJ put Evidence in the back seat and circled the car to trade places with Talbot.

Bobby heard Detective Arias humming off-key: "Me and Bobby McGee."

It was not the voice of any god Talbot believed in.

CHAPTER 30

To Take A Life

Danny and Fern arrived at the campus cafeteria. It was deserted, the doors locked. A handwritten sign said, "Closed until 4:00 p.m." Will Bloom's murder and fall break had shut everything down.

Despite himself, Danny was relieved. This fantasy with Ferencia Lake could continue for a few more minutes, a few more hours. Then he would disappear into his real life, hidden by goggles and a flap cap. One future day he would watch the young woman head to class as he dug a ditch, burying his hope and, let's face it, his lust among seedlings that would bloom in spring.

"Oh no," said Fern. "I think I really need to eat something."

"We could walk to the Char," said Danny. She needed to eat, right? The hamburger place was a few blocks away.

"I've never been to the Char," said Fern. She didn't tell him that she'd been a vegetarian for the last two years. That practice disappeared with her ex-boyfriend.

"Never been to the Char?" asked Danny. "It's a neighborhood institution. We have to fix that."

"I think we should." Fern smiled.

He felt himself smile back.

"Are you okay to walk that far?"

"I think so," she said. "If I need to, I'll lean on you." She took his arm.

"Anytime." Danny felt his muscle flex beneath her hand. If she asked, he would happily carry her in his arms.

The day had turned chilly, thunderheads gathered above the San Gabriel Mountains. It was two long neighborhood blocks to the fast-food restaurant Char #8, home of the charbroiled burger. Fern and Danny talked about music and books. They both liked old seventies rock and hip-hop. Fern was a fan of David Bowie; Danny preferred the Rolling Stones. Both loved Kendrick Lamar. Fern read Jane Austen and Toni Morrison, Danny liked nonfiction; *Dispatches* about Viet Nam was a favorite, as well as Pat Welsh's gardening books. He pointed out varieties of trees, flowers, and shrubs as they walked. They passed by Danny's house; he didn't mention it.

They stood in line at the Char as the scent of charbroiled burgers made Fern's stomach rumble.

"Are you okay with this menu?" Danny asked. "It's not fancy."

"It's great. I'm starving." She ordered a double charburger and fries. Danny insisted on paying for both their meals. Another difference from college boys who meticulously counted out her share and sent her a Venmo request. "Grab a table. I'll bring it over." Fern grabbed Danny's phone.

"I'll pay you back," she said.

"Forget it." He smiled as she pressed his finger on the screen to open his phone.

Fern sat down at a booth, sent her number to his phone, added his to hers.

Danny brought over their order on a red tray.

"I sent you my number," Fern said as Danny watched her slide his phone back to him. He couldn't keep the smile from his face, the worry from his heart.

"Great." He tried to remember back to when he had been like Ferencia Lake. So sure everything was easy, at his fingertips.

They demolished the burgers and fries. He enjoyed watching her. She ate with undisguised pleasure, savoring each bite. The color had returned to her face.

"That was an awesome burger," she said. "I can't believe I never ate here before." There was a smudge of ketchup above her lip.

"It's a neighborhood favorite," he said. He reached across, handed her his napkin. "You have something right here."

"Go ahead," she said. "Make me presentable."

He swallowed hard. "Okay." Danny followed the contour of her upper lip with the napkin. He stared at her, then down at the table.

"Do you live nearby?" she asked.

"Yes," Danny said. "I inherited my mother's house. It's down the street. We walked by it. She died about six months ago." His voice caught in his throat. "From breast cancer."

"I'm sorry," Fern said. She placed her hand on top of his. "I know how hard that is. I lost my mom when I was twelve."

She moved her index finger in a slow circle across the back of his hand. "And your father?" she asked.

"He passed away when I was a kid. He was a vet, had addiction problems." Danny stared at his hand as if it belonged to someone else. She couldn't know that no woman had touched him like this in ten long years. He put his hand over hers to stop her finger. He was about to have an erection right here in Char #8.

"I need to get you back to Hesperia," Danny said. "Before . . ."

"Before what?" she asked. She was looking at him with a mixture of shyness, genuine interest, and something else . . . could it be desire? No, he was dreaming, projecting his own feelings onto her.

"Before things get out of hand," he said.

"What does that mean?" asked Fern. She knew she should back off. Take time to reflect on everything that had occurred over the past two days, the attack on campus, her indiscretion with Professor Bounty. But she felt herself drawn to this man from the very beginning. Danny Mendoza was different. Mature and sure of himself. That old-fashioned phrase came to her mind, "a gentleman."

"Would you regret spending some more time with me?"

"No," he said. "Of course not. But you don't know me. You don't know who I am or what I've done."

"Well," said Fern. "Who are you, Danny Mendoza, and what have you done?"

"Let's head back." Danny abruptly stood up. He was angry with himself. He should never have taken this girl to lunch.

When they were outside, Danny silently walked across York, his hands shoved in his pockets. Fern struggled to keep up with him as they reached the curb, walked into the neighborhood.

"Hey," she said, "slow down. You're leaving me behind."

Danny stopped.

"I'm sorry," Fern said, "I've upset you."

"No, I'm fine. I need to be somewhere, that's all."

Fern suddenly stopped. "Wait!" she cried.

Danny turned around and looked at her.

"Wait a minute." She stared at his face, watching his eyes.

Danny stood paralyzed. Did she know who he was? How could that be?

"You aren't married, are you?" Fern said it with such disgust that it almost made Danny laugh, then cry.

"No," he said. "I'm not married. I don't have a girlfriend. I haven't been with anyone in a very long time."

"Oh," she said, confused. "Okay."

"There are worse things," said Danny, "than being a married man."

"Hmmm," said Fern. "I don't know about that."

Danny stayed quiet as they continued to walk toward campus. "Which house is yours?" she asked.

They were standing in front of it.

"Here." Danny sounded angry. Desire pounded his core, thickening his already hard cock. He could invite her inside. He thought she might say yes. But no, he wouldn't do that.

Fern looked concerned. She was even lovelier when she didn't smile.

He had to break this spell. He wasn't going to lie to this girl. He promised himself. Not now. Not ever.

She moved directly in front of him and looked up into his face.

"Something is wrong," she said as she reached for his arm. "You can tell me; it can't be that bad."

He wanted his mouth on her lips. He wanted to carry her inside his house. Danny heard himself moan as he pulled away from her hand. "Don't," he said. "I need you to listen to what I have to say."

"All right." She stepped back, her face reddening.

He stood silent, gathering his thoughts.

"I'm sorry," she said. "I'm not good at this. I felt something when we met. I thought you did too."

"I did," he said. "I do. But you don't know who I am."

"I know you're Danny Mendoza. You've recently lost your mother. You seem like a really nice guy."

"What I've done and where I've been."

"What is it?" Fern asked. "What's wrong?"

Danny said, almost to himself, "Now I'm just a gardener, a groundskeeper at Hesperia."

Fern let that sink in for a moment. Is that why he seemed familiar?

"All right," she said. "That doesn't seem so terrible."

"What I've done and where I've been," Danny repeated, a whisper now.

"Where have you been? What did you do? You're acting like you murdered someone."

Danny froze, looked into her eyes. He heard her sharp intake of breath.

The passion that burned through his body had turned cold. Ice ran through him like a knife.

"Yes," he said. "Yes, I did. I took a life. And I went to prison for it."

CHAPTER 31

Chiclet

(Saturday afternoon)

DJ drove Talbot's car from Eagle Rock to Glendale, past tall office buildings and squat shopping malls toward San Fernando Boulevard. According to his ex-wife, Glendale Humane Society was where Lady Dog, her previous name, was chipped.

"Lady Dog," DJ said. "We know where you came from."

Evidence, now in the back seat, stared down at the floor.

"No worries, girl. I won't leave you there."

They stopped at a traffic light on the western edge of Glendale. Across San Fernando Road, a littered field bisected by railroad tracks housed a strip joint named The Gentlemen's Club. Farther down bloomed the giant vats of a brewery and its adjoining airplane-hangar restaurant, The Amber Path. The name reminded DJ of pissing in the forest. Microbreweries were for hipsters like Rolf, the veterinarian's assistant. His veterinarian. His Lillian.

DJ pulled the Dodge Charger into a side street, parked across from a cinder-block building. Functional metal letters identified The Glendale Humane Society.

DJ cradled Evidence and walked with Bobby Talbot through the double glass doors into the building. Straight ahead, steel gates barricaded a bedlam of barks and howls. In the office hung a bulletin board named "The Wall of Contentment." Scattered across it were photographs of happy humans with canine companions, dreams fulfilled; a doggy version of match.com.

"Chiclet!"

DJ pulled Evidence closer to his chest.

A straw-haired woman stood behind the counter. She was pale, with round black eyes, a smile punctuated by small uneven teeth.

"I beg your pardon?"

"You're holding Chiclet, aren't you?" The woman's loud voice rang out, perhaps to overcome the cacophony of the residents. "I'd know her anywhere. I have the knack, you know."

Evidence, unmoved by this recognition, snuggled deeper into DJ's embrace.

"I'm Detective DJ Arias, LAPD, and this is Detective Bobby Talbot. I thought she was named Lady Dog."

"That was her kennel name 'cause she's a female and whatnot—but I named her Chiclet. They're my favorite gum. You know, hard candy shell, chewy inside."

DJ stared at the woman's teeth, imagining each one a sharp peppermint wonder.

"Listen, Miss . . . ?"

"Yes, Lieutenant Arias?" The woman stared with black unblinking eyes; straw hair splayed from her scalp as if an electric current shot through her body.

"Detective Arias," DJ said. "I'm a detective."

"Oh." She looked at him blankly.

"You said lieutenant. But I'm a detective."

Bobby coughed.

"I love dogs," she said. "I'm not good with people, you know. No, I'm not. So, what are you doing here with our little Chiclet? She's not in trouble, is she? She wouldn't hurt no one, Mr. Arias."

"No, but . . ." said DJ.

"She's a good girl, aren't you, Chiclet? A rescue dog, poor thing. Found under an apartment stairwell. Survived by her wits and whatnot."

He felt the weight of Evidence in his arms, heard the beginning of a growl emanate from her throat.

"Please," said DJ, losing patience. The woman was hard to interrupt. She took no breath between sentences.

"What's your name?" asked DJ. "Your full name."

"Oh, my name is Cyndy with a y, Louella with two l's, Barnes with an e-s at the end. Yes, sir, I work the front desk Tuesday through Saturday afternoons. Sunday is my day off and Monday we are closed to the public."

"Thursday," said DJ. "This past Thursday, did a man named Will Bloom come in and adopt Evidence—I mean, this dog?"

"Chiclet? Yes, sir. He sure did."

"So what time was Mr. Bloom here? Did he mention why he was getting the dog?"

"Well, I think he was here around three or three fifteen," said Cyndy. "He signed the papers and whatnot. But the girl, she did all the advance paper-work before he arrived."

"The girl? What girl?"

"I thought she was his daughter. He didn't like that. She didn't either, really. But like I said, I know dogs. I'm not so good with people."

"Yeah," said DJ. "I got that. What was the girl's name?"

Cyndy stopped. Her black-eyed stare bored through DJ's forehead. She was offended. Damn it, he knew better than to antagonize a witness, especially one like Cyndy with a y.

And in front of his rookie partner.

"Look." DJ started to mumble his apologies. But Cyndy held up a pale thin index finger, holding her breath.

"Delilah?" Like an oracle, she proclaimed the name.

"Who?" asked DJ.

"No, not Delilah. Not a song. A country music star."

"What? A singer?"

"'Nine to Five' . . . but he did call her other names."

"Oh, for God's sake," DJ muttered.

"Dolly?" asked Talbot. "Was her name Dolly?"

"Yep, Dolly Parton. I try mnemonics with humans."

"Dolly? Dolly Ruiz? Red hair and freckles?"

"Yes, red hair, freckles. She said her name was Dolly, but the man called her Dilly, Dally, or some such, I don't know why."

"So this young woman, Dolly, came in before Thursday?" asked DJ. "She completed the paperwork. Did she pick out the dog?"

"Yes, Mr. Arias. Even got Chiclet checked out by the doctor for Mr. Bloom."

"Did she say anything? About Mr. Bloom, why he wanted the dog."

"She kept saying Chiclet was going to be a wonderful surprise. The man who was adopting her was a great man and whatnot. That's why when Mr. Bloom walked in, I said, 'Hello Dad!'"

"But he didn't like that?"

"No, sir," said Cyndy. "He turned red and said something . . ." Cyndy went into her black-eyed-stare, index finger raised, conjuring up the memory. "He said something like 'keep the lid on the trash, hold in the flies.' I'm not sure what he meant."

"I imagine not," sighed DJ.

"Dolly introduced Mr. Bloom as the best boss in the world," said Cyndy. "He gave her a big smile."

"Did they say anything else?" asked DJ.

"No, just chitchat. Neither of 'em knew a thing about dogs. They were so wrapped up in the big surprise."

"Did they say who the surprise was for?"

"No, but it was a 'she' as in 'she' will be so surprised. Mr. Bloom was real happy. I'm not so sure about the girl. She began to look less happy."

"And they left?"

"Yep, he signed the papers. They took little Chiclet and headed out the door. I yelled after them, saying 'don't forget the dog food and dish,' but they didn't hear me. Off he went with Chiclet in his car. Dilly Dally stood watching after them. I guess she drove away eventually."

DJ thought Cyndy Louella Barnes made a reliable witness.

"Thank you, Miss Barnes. If we need more information, we'll call you."

"I'm off Sunday and we're closed on Mondays."

"Got it," said DJ.

Cyndy pulled a brightly colored package from her pocket, popped five pieces of gum into her mouth. She offered the box to DJ. He declined. She tried Bobby. He took several pieces.

"Reminds me of my childhood," said Talbot.

"Hey," said Cyndy. "So why do you have Chiclet? Where's Mr. Bloom?"

"I'm sorry to tell you," said DJ, "that Mr. Bloom is dead."

"Heart?"

"Murdered."

"Oh. My. That girl is going to be real sad . . . So what's going to happen to Chiclet? Is she in custody or something?"

"Something like that."

"But who is going to take care of her after you find the murderer, Mr. Oreos?"

"It's Arias. Detective Arias."

"Who is going to take care of Chiclet, Detective Arias?"

"I am," said DJ.

"Forever?"

"Yes," DJ said. As he said it, he knew it was true.

Cyndy watched Evidence sleeping now in DJ's arms.

"Well, I guess everything turned out for the best," Cyndy said, chomping away. "For Chiclet anyway. We run a no-kill shelter here—still, every dog needs a home."

She busied herself putting kibble and a dog dish in a paper bag. She handed it to DJ.

"The other people didn't take it. It's yours now."

DJ took the bag in one hand, held onto Evidence with the other arm. At this rate, he wouldn't need to buy dog food for weeks.

"Thanks," he said.

They walked out to the car. The weather had turned cold, clouds crowded the nearby mountains. Talbot got behind the wheel, DJ held Evidence on his lap.

Talbot's phone rang. He put the call on speaker. It was their police technician with results from the lab. No fingerprints or smudges on the sword handle; it was wiped clean. There were microscopic fibers on the edge of the exposed blade closest to the hilt, the part that protruded from the body. The fibers were black, possibly fleece.

The sword entered just left of Will Bloom's spine, cut through the lungs, sliced the pulmonary artery, and ended its journey in the right atrium. There should have been more blood splatter. The coroner surmised there was some type of covering on the victim's back—a sheet, a tarp, or blanket—that had been removed, perhaps cut through with the protruding blade. which might explain the fibers on its base. If there was such a covering, it wasn't found at the crime scene.

DNA results were at least a week or two away. Talbot ended the call.

"I wonder," said Talbot, "if Dolly's missing blanket is significant?"

"Sounds like it might be important," said DJ. "Fern Lake said something wet and heavy was thrown over her. When we get back, take Butter and Browning and search the entire olive grove again."

"Yes, sir." Talbot started the car and headed toward Hesperia College.

"Expand the search to the edge of campus. Maybe we'll get lucky and find that blanket."

CHAPTER 32

Wake Up!

"I took a life. I was drunk and I hit a young girl. And I went to prison for it."

Fern stared at Danny, not wanting to believe him, still waiting for his denial.

Instead, she saw pain, the edge of a deep and yawning chasm that lived inside the man that stood before her.

Fern turned, walked away, sure he would call after her, explain that none of this was real. But he didn't stop her. And if he didn't call after her, she couldn't turn back. Each step carried her away from him, from what she felt, the jolt of recognition that this man would mean something, be someone to her.

Thunder rumbled across the sky as she reached campus. She headed toward her residence hall and saw police cars surrounding Sliming; one car pulled away. Fern had texted the younger detective she would come by for an interview this afternoon. Instead, she made a quick detour up a path behind the McKeon Medical Center and caught the first stairway up the hill.

Why had she thrown herself at a stranger after the disastrous evening with Professor Bounty and then the attack in the olive grove? What was wrong with her?

The sky opened, rain drenching her hair and clothes.

The breakup with her ex-boyfriend, Jim, had unmoored her, wrecked her self-confidence. Fern didn't know where she fit, who she was anymore.

Jim never had that problem.

"Things have changed." His words still stung. "My feelings have changed."

Over their summer apart, he had studied in Brazil, working in the slums of Rio De Janeiro. His texts and Skype calls slowed, then stopped.

Fern had spent the summer in Upland with her dad, working at a local restaurant. Upland was forty miles away but might have been a thousand. She picked up extra shifts, saved every dollar for senior year. Her father, grateful his daughter was home, bent his now graying head over the *Los Angeles Times* each morning, reading aloud anything that might peak Fern's interest. "Listen to this . . ." An ache flickered in her chest, wanting everything in her life to change, yet remain exactly the same.

Her boyfriend *had* changed. When they saw each other again, he had already recast his future; Fern wasn't in it.

"This summer," he said, "I felt alive. I'd forgotten what that was like. This place, Hesperia, and us, I've outgrown it. It's just not enough for me."

Fern's face must have shown her devastation.

"Oh, sweetie," Jim said, "don't feel bad. We are who we are, where we come from. It's not your fault. What you want, what you need . . . we're just so different."

His words stung. Even now. *Her wants and needs? Were so very different from his?*

Fern reached the top of the stairs soaked from the rain. She had gone through several stages of grief over being dumped. Shock, depression. Now anger took root. Her ex-boyfriend didn't need to work all summer at a mind-numbing job so he could buy schoolbooks. His parents were wealthy New Yorkers, his father a Wall Street investment banker. Jim could fly first class to South America, ponder the misery of mankind in a secure apartment carefully sourced by his parents and paid for by their money.

He had made one visit to Upland to meet her dad last year.

"Wow!" They had stopped for coffee on the way. "This is the land of mini-malls and big box stores."

Her dad wore a tight smile throughout their visit. When they were alone together in the kitchen, Fern asked her father what he thought. "He's from privilege and private schools. It's a different world."

"He means a lot to me, Dad."

"Yeah, he's okay. But you are better."

"Jeez, Dad, you always say that."

"Fern, you have to be better. He doesn't."

Fern hugged her old man, annoyed he didn't see the person that she knew lived inside Jim Singer.

Now within the warmth of her dorm room, Fern changed into dry clothes. But her dad had seen the real man and she hadn't. And Fern wasn't the better person, was she? No, she had acted out by sleeping with her professor. And glomming onto the first guy she ran into.

Outside, the rain had stopped. She opened the window and looked out. Directly below, a narrow trail wound around the building, through scrub, and down across the road that led to the olive grove.

Fern reached for her grandmother's necklace as she had countless times since Thursday night, shocked again at its absence. *Al vivo todo le falta, y al muerto todo le sobra.* She remembered her grandmother's voice, cigarette smoke curling above her head, as she gave Fern the necklace after her mother's funeral: *To the living, nothing is enough. To the dead, everything's too much.* Now her grandmother was gone too.

Fern opened her laptop, she skimmed the email from her father; he was old-school and didn't text much. Coach Lake's subject line declared, "We won."

Thank God it was football season and little news of Will Bloom's death had leaked to the press. On Friday, Fern had sent an email saying she was spending the beginning of fall break with girlfriends in Palm Springs. She'd be home by Tuesday. She couldn't see or talk to her dad right now. He'd know something was wrong and the whole sordid story with Professor Bounty might spill out. She had never been able to hide the truth from her father, and she had to keep what she did to herself.

Instead, Fern googled "Daniel Mendoza." Nothing came up at first. She tried different searches and included Hesperia College. Finally, an item from ten years ago appeared from the *Los Angeles Times.* Eighteen-year-old Daniel Mendoza, driving from a fraternity party off campus to Hesperia College, hit and killed a young girl with his car. He was driving under the influence of alcohol during a fraternity hazing. The young woman was Sally Smith, who was seventeen years old.

Late afternoon sunlight seeped into the room. Fern laid down on her bed. watching the shadow of windowpanes ladder up the wall. Danny had told her the truth. God, how many times had she driven home drunk or high from a party? Squirting peppermint mouth spray to "fool" her dad.

Her eyelids grew heavy, sleep, then dreams came quickly. A figure stood shrouded against a massive night sky. Stars collapsed into quicksilver, then black brightness.

"*Levantate!*" a voice said. "*Levantate!*"

Her grandmother's voice. Old and graveled from too many cigarettes, but strong enough to break through dreams and the grave.

"Wake up! *Levantate!*" Fern searched for her grandmother's face in the collapsing sky. "Wake up. Go to the window."

Fern sat up, then stood, a puppet pulled by invisible strings. Shadows had lengthened into the corners of her room. She walked to the open window. It was almost dusk. One last gasp of light broke across the glass.

She looked outside, down to the trail below. Something moved among the dense shrubs, their branches bending from an invisible force. Fern strained her eyes to see what it was. An animal? A person? There was a waving arm. Someone barely visible in the fading light.

Suddenly, she saw it. An upturned jack-o'-lantern face with jagged yellow teeth, crooked jaw, and uneven eyes was watching her. First, she heard a low grunting or gurgling sound. Its misaligned lips were moving. Then the high-pitched screech from Thursday night rang out. "Nooooo, nooooo! Es meeeee!"

Fern screamed.

The creature's hideous face fell away. Turning, it tumbled off-balance into the bushes. She drew back, then peeked outside as it crawled away, sideways, crablike, disappearing into the thick wet underbrush.

From the window, Fern could see that the creature wore something red. No, darker, deeper, it was crimson. He wore it like a cape.

CHAPTER 33

Hedda

Hedy watched Detectives DJ Arias and Bobby Talbot enter Sliming's lobby. She was finishing up a late Saturday afternoon security check on Sliming before heading home. DJ carried a small red dog in his arms.

"What is that?" she asked.

"I found her in Will Bloom's bathroom," said DJ. "I named her Evidence."

"How nice for you." Hedy didn't care for dogs. She had more important things to take care of.

"You got my message?" asked DJ. "About the blackout in Sliming?"

What could she say?

"I've asked all of my officers on duty that night, checked all the logs," she said. "No one reported a blackout."

"Serena Rigby said the lights went out around 7:05 p.m.," said Talbot. "And she received a call from Campus Safety."

"None of my officers called her," said Hedy. "And none reported an outage."

"You don't think anyone called her?" DJ asked. "So what? You think she's lying?"

Hedy felt DJ's stare.

"I think if someone called her, it wasn't Campus Safety."

"And the blackout?" asked DJ.

"If it happened," said Hedy, "maybe it was local. The wiring is old in this building. One circuit does the job of three. Perhaps it overloaded."

"But if almost everyone had headed home," said Talbot, "that doesn't seem likely, does it?"

DJ Arias said nothing, just continued to watch her, holding that ridiculous dog.

"I'm guessing," said Hedy. "I don't know."

She stared back at Arias, straight into his eyes. Who would blink first? Not Hedy.

"Will Bloom was alone, on the prowl that night," said DJ, "waiting for someone. Doesn't seem likely that he tripped the electrical circuit by himself. And wouldn't someone have to switch the circuit breaker on again? The electricity must have been working when Ema Treet started her shift the next morning. She didn't mention a problem."

Hedy shrugged her shoulders as if it wasn't her concern. "Presumably."

A man on the prowl, thought Hedy, *Will Bloom's resting state.* "I'll have an electrician check out the panel," she said.

"Good," said DJ. "Let us know when they do. We want to be there." Hedy headed for the door but was stopped by Detective Arias's final question.

"How well do you know Trish Ballentine?" asked DJ.

Hedy turned around. "I've known Trish for years. We came to Hesperia around the same time."

"Has she ever talked to you about Will Bloom?" asked DJ. "Discuss the women he was with? We heard she keeps a record of his indiscretions in a blue notebook."

"She didn't care for Will Bloom," said Hedy. "That was no secret. We haven't really talked that much lately. I don't know anything about a notebook."

"Hmmm. Maybe not something she'd mention to someone in your position," said DJ. "Someone in authority?"

Hedy thought it over. "I don't know, maybe. But I'll let you know about the electrician."

"Please do," said DJ. "It's important."

Hedy gave a retreating wave as she headed out. *A man on the prowl.* She knew all about men on the prowl.

Hedda Scacht was raised in Fullerton, California. Orange County was home to Disneyland and heart of the conservative party in the Golden State.

In high school, five-foot-ten Hedda towered above her classmates. She was a powerful swimmer with round muscles and a layer of baby fat. Kids called her Hedda Gobbler. Ibsen was required reading in Honors English.

High school had been the apex of her mother Delores's life. It's where she had snagged Hedy's father, the star of the baseball team. Mother lamented that her unpopular daughter was missing out on all the fun.

Hedda attended grad night, at Disneyland, alone, surrounded by high school couples from all over Southern California. As she went on rides, surrounded by boys and girls necking in the dark, Hedda stared straight ahead, locked away her shame at being alone, circled the imaginary vault in her chest with her fingers, fist to her heart.

The summer after graduation, Hedda worked as a counselor at a summer camp. Her father, a reformed alcoholic, owned the local hardware store and was active in AA and the YMCA. He had secured her the job.

"It will be good for you," he said. "Lots of activity. No time to dawdle. Toughen you up."

Hedda said nothing. *Why not?* she thought. It would get her out of her house, away from her parents, who worried over her lack of any social life.

Her brother sniggered, "Fat camp."

In June, eighteen-year-old Hedda shipped out to Bluff Lake in the San Bernardino Mountains. Each week she oversaw a new group of prepubescent girls. They traveled in packs; a constant cycle of fighting, giggling, or crying. Her campers needed a firm hand to propel them through homesickness, dining hall food, and endless physical activity. By the end of the first month, Hedy knew she excelled at her job. Plus, she had lost ten pounds and most of her baby fat.

Several of the older counselors were ex-military. They wrangled the rowdy teenage boys. One was a retired marine, Garth Stull, six foot four of muscle and grit, with a smile that could make a girl feel dizzy. The first time he touched her, they were sitting alone in one of the camp's pickup trucks. He ran one finger down a rivulet of sweat that made its way from behind her knee and down her calf. She turned to look him in the eye.

"Wait," Garth said. "How old are you?"

"Eighteen," said Hedda, now a self-declared Hedy. Hedda had gone along with the baby fat.

"You sure?" he asked.

"I turned eighteen in May."

"All right then." He smiled. "Let the games commence."

Garth had green eyes hooded by blond eyelashes, white even teeth, broad shoulders, and he smelled like the meadow. "Is this okay?" He asked every time his hand moved into new territory.

Oh yes, Hedy thought, *Was it ever!*

He was a break of sun in a cloudy life.

That summer was a revelation. Hedy had power, it emanated from the same body that had caused her so much humiliation in high school. By the end of August, Hedy had lost twenty pounds. She was lean, strong, unstoppable.

Garth was preparing a speech the night before the camp closed for the season. They had arranged to meet in the meadow where the whole thing started.

"You know how special you are to me . . . but . . ." Garth said.

Hedy smiled and shook her head. "No explanations, no regrets."

Garth looked crestfallen. He wasn't ready for a relationship, but was upset that Hedy, who had blossomed into a very hot babe, wasn't interested in one either. "That's it?" he asked.

"The games commenced and now they're done," Hedy said. She was losing her summer buzz. "I mean, right? We don't live near each other. I'm eighteen. I need go to college. You're twenty-seven and you need to . . ."

"To what?" he asked. "And I'm twenty-six." He sounded upset.

"To travel, have adventures. I mean, I'm eight years behind you."

"You think I'm too old for you. And what, not smart enough?"

A thought flickered through Hedy's mind. She might be lacking some essential female component. During the summer, she realized all her lady parts were fully functioning, but she lacked any desire to be tied to a man.

"Is that what you're saying?" Garth asked.

Hedy could see more hurt than anger in his face. She didn't understand the intricacies of her female campers' emotions, but men were easy. They liked to feel in control of the situation, whether it was true or not.

"Hey, baby," Hedy said. She pushed her forehead to his. "If I thought I could hold on to you, I'd follow you anywhere. But I'm green. I still have too much to learn. But I can do this." Her hand was unzipping his jeans. He was hard. She pushed her breasts into his chest. They had remained large and perky despite her weight loss. He unbuttoned her blouse, cupped each breast tenderly.

"I'm going to miss these," he said. She went down on her knees. Started nice and slow like he'd taught her while her hand played with his balls and her finger went into his ass. "Is this okay?" Hedy asked.

"Uh, yeah," Garth moaned.

Garth had not taught her this move into new territory, but he liked it just the same. Hedy had a whole big world to explore, and though Garth was sexy and sweet, she wanted more.

The next two years, Hedy blazed through junior college. It was easy for her; she was disciplined, focused. One day, bored by her surroundings, she found her way to a recruiting office. Missing the order of the prescribed life of camp, Hedy signed up for the army.

Eventually, she landed in the Military Police and found her calling. She worked crowd control, tracked AWOL soldiers, a few crime scenes. Hedy worked out as if training for the Olympics; she lifted weights, building muscle, and ran every day, practicing endurance.

"Who is that?" Hedy heard a young recruit say.

"Son, that's DFW Scacht."

"Who?"

"That's Ms. Don't Fuck With Scacht," said a fellow soldier.

Hedy enjoyed the moniker. She casually dated, preferring Latino men who were respectful to their *guera*, their *white girl*, and talked fondly of their mothers. She kept her wits about her, left every party early and in control. For each new deployment, she packed up, took off for greener pastures. If she left a trail of broken hearts, they would heal. Her own was encased in elegant armor.

At age thirty, she left the military to test herself out in the world. Hedy tried private security—too political—and applied to the LAPD—way too political, and dominated by men who saw their control slipping away as women invaded their ranks.

One day, like a flash of lightning from a long-ago summer, she received a call.

"Hey, Hedy, Garth Stull here. You remember me?"

Of course she did. Garth was now the director of Campus Security at Chapman College.

"I need a second-in-command. I heard you recently retired from the military. You'd be perfect for the job."

Hedy didn't think twice on her way to the city of Orange and its pretty Mayberry circle at the center of town. She was home.

Garth was happily married with two little boys. He now carried an extra thirty pounds on his frame, his green eyes had deep wrinkles that bespoke humor and kindness. He loved his family, his job, and treated Hedy with an affectionate offhand friendliness.

The only thing he said that hearkened back to their past was this: "Don't take this the wrong way, but I have to say it because you're a single woman, and easy on the eyes. Don't mess with anyone on campus. It would be an actionable offense."

Hedy knew he was serious. She was both flattered and annoyed. "Yes, sir. Ten-four." Message received.

Chapman College was like summer camp on steroids; young men and women free for the first time from parental oversight. Sex, drugs, alcohol; the unbridled hormones and hubris of youth coalesced in a murky stew of education and bad behavior. Hedy tried to decipher the ultra-liberal stance of tenured faculty against the conservative policies of the administration. It was exhilarating, stressful, exhausting. After a few years, Hedy began to drop her guard, she drank with colleagues, sometimes too much, dated a few men from her gym.

After all the personal diligence of her military days, her training, her tightly wound sense of order, she made one mistake, the one thing her boss had warned her about. She lowered her guard with a college employee who worked in another department.

. She had been drinking with a group of colleagues at a bar and ran into the man. He was tall, muscular, and good-looking. But he looked as if this had been the worst day of his life.

"They are going to sack me," he claimed. "Unfairly, I might add."

He joined their table. She felt sorry for him; everyone knew Chapman's administration sucked. She invited him to her apartment for a nightcap. She should have noticed how drunk he was, how much liquor he had put away. But she had also drank too much.

Hedy stood in her brightly lit living room, about to hand him a drink. She looked up and realized something was wrong. His face was red, he was sweating, his breaths short and hard as if he'd been running.

"This can't happen to me," he said. "Being fired. It's fucking unfair."

The man's eyes were roaming around her apartment. *What was he looking for?* No, he wasn't looking outward, but inward; he was staring into an abyss. His irises rolled around in their sockets, right then left, right then up, then down, unmoored from the reality of his surroundings.

"That bitch targeted me," he said.

Hedy realized too late that the alcohol and his self-pity had fused into rage.

"I think you should go," she said.

"Come over here!"

Her first thought was that this guy had lost it.

He grabbed her arm.

"Stop it," she said. "What the hell are you doing?"

He twisted one arm behind her back, pushed her off-balance, then down to her knees. Pulling her hair so hard her scalp burned, his face was inches above hers. "I'm in control," he said. "I decide what happens in my life."

"No!" she said. "Stop it!"

He had turned into someone, something else.

"Wait, you need to stop. I said no."

It was no use. He was taller, heavier, stronger. He easily pinned her body on the floor.

"You don't tell me no." His knees straddled her; his eyes roiled in their sockets. "No piece of ass tells me no."

Hedy thought if she yelled, pounded on the floor, someone, a neighbor, might hear and call the police. Her fists and feet struck the carpeted floor. She screamed, "Get off of me!"

His forearm crushed down on her windpipe. She struggled, using all her power to break free. He was cutting off her breath. She slapped at his face, fear replaced by dread. The more she fought, the harder his elbow pushed down on her throat. He pinned her arms above her head with his free hand. Hedy tasted his sweat dripping on her lips, felt the swell of his penis as he lowered himself on top of her. Trapped under his weight, she squirmed frantically, fighting for her life now. He let go of one of her hands as he unzipped his pants. Her arm scissored up and down as if she was drowning in the carpet. She remembered that long ago summer, that understanding of what men want, to feel in control, whether they are or not. This man had complete power over her. She stopped fighting, went still, then numb. The pressure on her windpipe let up.

He penetrated her.

Hedy stared at the ceiling. The building was old, cracks ran under the paint, a spiderweb of fault lines. He rutted like an animal, grunting like a pig. Maybe the roof would come down and bury them both. Pushing harder and deeper, he came inside of her.

He yelled out as if in pain, then fell, a dead weight on her body. She felt him shrivel inside of her, a spent carcass of rage.

Hedy didn't cry out or move. Her body had betrayed her. All the years of strength training, lifting weights. As strong as she was, he had easily overpowered her. He rolled off, staggered up and away. Silently zipped his pants.

During all of it, the lamps still blazed. His hand flew to his face, his eyes hollow, as if he was lost in a brightly lit forest.

"I don't know what happened," he said. He began to cry. Not for Hedy, for himself. He paced back and forth beside her prone body, headed to the front door, then came back.

He stood over her.

"This didn't happen," he said. "You hear me? It didn't happen."

He fingered his car keys and left.

They called it date rape then, some people still did.

She shed no tears, circled her chest with her fingers, fist to heart.

Hedy had her daughter at age thirty-five. She named the baby after her mother.

CHAPTER 34

Other People's Happiness

DJ sat in the conference room facing a wall of windows that stretched from floor to ceiling as the afternoon rain drizzled then stopped. Evidence snored in the corner.

Daniel Mendoza was expected in a few minutes, along with the pizza receipt he was supposed to have turned in that morning. Browning and Butter had reported he was a no-show. DJ had a tense phone conversation with Daniel.

"Sorry, Detective. Something came up, man. I can bring it over now." Something always came up with ex-cons, or maybe there wasn't a pizza receipt.

He thought back to what Hedy said about Serena Rigby. Maybe she never received a call from Campus Safety, maybe there wasn't a blackout. The only other occupant of Sliming at that time, Will Bloom, could neither confirm nor deny her claim. Serena had the strength and heft to wield that sword. It could be the oldest story in the book: love unrequited, a woman scorned? But she had picked up her dinner at that Vietnamese restaurant, in business dress, at seven forty-five. That didn't seem like enough time to kill Will Bloom and not break a sweat unless she was a cold-blooded killer. And had carefully planned out the whole thing.

Detective Talbot, along with four of LAPD's finest, was now scouring the olive grove, broadening the search area. Officers had checked the grove on Friday, but now they were looking for something specific, Dolly Ruiz's missing blanket.

Outside the conference room window, bougainvillea bushes with magenta and ocher blooms receded into shadow, thick leafy shrubs glimmered in the dusk. The campus had an abandoned quality like a story-book kingdom whose residents had fled.

DJ contrasted Hesperia with his alma mater, Cal State LA, where serviceable brick and concrete buildings towered above a maze of sidewalks and asphalt. Scattered patches of grass fought for survival beneath the blazing California sun. As a student, DJ had circled numerous parking lots, praying for a space, while downtown Los Angeles glittered in brown haze like the Emerald City from Oz.

He saw movement at the corner of his eye. Fern Lake appeared out of nowhere. She ran down the stairs from Ramble Hall as if a devil chased her. What was she doing? Finally making their appointment? She stumbled down the last step of the stairway, falling to her knees.

What the hell, thought DJ. The girl was running as if someone was after her.

"Fuck," said DJ. Was someone chasing her?

He pounded the windows with his fists and yelled.

"Fern! Fern Lake!"

The girl looked up with no sign of recognition.

"Wait there!" he yelled. "Don't move!" Her body curled into a defensive crouch, frozen in place. DJ held up his index finger, a signal to hold on, he was coming. He raced out of the conference room, through the lobby, out the glass doors. Afraid that whoever was after her might get there first.

A gust of breeze hit DJ's face, adrenaline, his heart. Turning the corner, he saw Fern fixed to the same spot, cowering close to the ground.

"What happened?" DJ reached for her. She flinched.

"He's following me," she whispered.

"Who?" DJ asked.

"He found me. He was outside my dorm. Watching me."

DJ tried to help her up. Fern pulled away as he took her arm. The left knee of her sweatpants was torn. She walked on her own into Sliming's lobby as he held the door.

Once inside the conference room, Fern sunk into DJ's chair, a broken doll, arms limp, legs askew. One single light from above caught glimmers of gold in her long dark hair and in her eyes, now searching the corners of the room as if looking for monsters.

Wearing a peasant blouse and sweatpants, she appeared impossibly young and fragile. Evidence approached her, sniffed at her tennis shoes.

"Who followed you?" DJ asked.

She looked up as if she didn't remember who he was.

"Was it the man from the other night? The one who attacked you?"

She shook her head. "Maybe not a man."

"Not a man?"

She cocked her head as if listening for something.

"He doesn't look human," she whispered.

What kind of thing was that to say? The girl sat up, alert to a sound.

DJ turned. He heard the slow squeak of the lobby door open and close. Thump, thump, thump. Soles on marble. Up three stairs to the conference room. Despite himself, DJ was spooked. Who had entered the building? The thing that followed the girl? His hand went to his holstered gun. The dog growled.

The room was dark except for the one overhead light that now encompassed Fern Lake.

Someone knocked at the conference room door.

"Who is it?" DJ barked.

"It's Danny. Daniel Mendoza. Detective Arias told me to come."

"Goddamn it," said DJ. "Bad timing." He opened the door.

Daniel Mendoza stood framed against the doorway, backlit by the lobby lights. DJ felt the other man's height and heft against his own slim five-foot-ten frame. Danny was over six feet tall, wore a T-shirt and jeans that defined his muscles. Danny didn't pay DJ any mind. He stared past DJ's shoulder, at the girl.

A bittersweet smile bloomed across Fern Lake's face. DJ looked from Danny to the girl. He felt crosscurrents of strong emotion; recognition, desire, regret?

"Wait, do you two know each other?"

"Danny Mendoza," Fern said. DJ heard her whisper, "I know you."

"What did you say?" DJ asked.

Danny teetered in the doorway, deciding whether to enter or run.

As DJ was about to tell him, "Go home, come back later," Danny entered, pacing to one corner of the room then the other like a panther sizing up its cage. Fern watched him.

"Hello again," Fern said.

"Hey," said Danny, treading back and forth. "What are you doing here?"

DJ had lost control of the situation. The girl seemed to have forgotten him.

"That man that followed me the other night, he showed up again. At my dorm. Below my window."

Danny stopped pacing. "Oh, no," he said. "I'm so sorry."

His face looked pained, his eyes fell to the floor, then slowly took her in, from her feet, up her legs, wincing at her torn knee, and finally met her eyes. She leaned forward, a magnetic reaction.

"I should have walked you home. Protected you."

"No, no, no," said DJ. "The police will protect her."

"Well, you're doing a lousy job," Danny said.

"What did you say?" asked DJ.

A drama was unfolding before DJ's eyes. He was only a bit player. Danny and Fern only saw each other. *Christ,* thought DJ, *how do these two know each other? Do students date gardeners now?*

The conference room door opened again, Talbot returning from his search of the grove. He carried an evidence bag of colored glass shards, bits of tinsel. Talbot looked at DJ, then Danny and Fern.

"What's up?" he asked.

DJ said, "Our murder seems to have inspired romance."

Evidence began to bark at Talbot and Fern broke away from Danny's stare to look at the dog. Danny continued pacing, his eyes focused on Fern.

DJ gave Evidence a reassuring pat for getting the girl's attention.

"Miss Fern Lake's stalker seems to have found her again."

"Where was this?" asked Talbot.

"Outside my dorm room," said Fern. "West Tower of Ramble Hall."

"Do you think he's still there?" asked Talbot.

"No. I don't know. I screamed and he ran into the bushes."

"Can you describe him?" asked Talbot.

"He looked like a monster, bulging eyes, big yellow teeth. Oh, I don't know. I was four floors up."

DJ should have asked the questions, but he was confused by the dynamic of his two witnesses.

"How do you two know each other?" asked DJ.

Neither responded.

"Do you know each other from campus?" Talbot asked.

Fern looked up. "Yes."

Another softball question from Tal-butt, thought DJ.

"We met today," said Fern. "On our way here, to Sliming."

"Ahh," said DJ, staring at Danny. "Something came up, right, Daniel? Stop pacing, for God's sake! Sit down!"

Danny said nothing. He stopped, never taking his eyes off the girl. He sat in a chair opposite Fern.

Jesus Christ, thought DJ. Now they were running a dating service. Meet your mate over death and mayhem.

DJ called Talbot over, they spoke quietly, then broke apart. "Both of you, stay put," ordered DJ. "We'll check out the perimeter of your residence hall and be right back. Don't move. We have a police car outside. I have questions for both of you."

Talbot and DJ left with Evidence in tow. Talbot told the black-and-white car parked outside to guard the front lobby doors. "No one in or out!"

They walked up the set of steep stairs, across the access road, quickly reached Ramble Hall. Talbot still had the flashlight from his search of the olive grove. They turned left to circle the footprint of the four-story behemoth of a building. A muddy path hugged the perimeter, branches wet from rain slapped their faces and torsos as they progressed. Beneath the west tower, they stopped. Here, the mud hardened, and two stiff ruts plowed the path. Shards of sapphire and plum-colored glass embedded the mud.

"What do you think?" asked Talbot. "This is the same kind of debris from the olive grove."

Something played at the edge of DJ's memory. A vision walking through the neighborhood that appeared like a ghost, with a covered face like the Invisible Man, pulling a roller bag. "I think I may have seen this guy."

"Where?" asked Talbot.

"In the neighborhood, last night."

"Did you get a good look at him?"

"He was physically impaired," said DJ. "His face covered by a scarf or something. Someone must know him, a neighbor who knows all the Boo Radleys."

"Boo . . . who?"

"Never mind," said DJ. "Hedy Scacht might know. I think she lives around here, in one of the college-owned houses."

They emerged from the bushes, damp and disheveled, walked down the steep three stairways to Sliming. Evidence wagged her tail, enjoying the whole adventure. On their way back, DJ noticed, not for the first time, that Sliming was built into the hillside. The third-floor entrance, where the cleaning woman, Ema Treet, started work each morning was accessed by a road that wound past Sliming and around the McKeon Medical Center before heading down the hill. DJ thought about all the doors in and out of Sliming and all the things in front of him he didn't see. He began to have a bad feeling, a premonition.

Talbot checked in with the police car guarding the exterior as DJ and Evidence entered Sliming's lobby, up the three steps to the door of the conference room. DJ saw the elevator to his left, and across the wide landing to his right, a second unobtrusive doorway the same color as the wall. DJ opened it. A cramped narrow stairway zigzagged up to the third floor.

DJ checked out the conference room, still lit by the single light. It was empty. He flipped the main switch, the room exploded with light.

Fern and Danny were gone. On the chair where Fern Lake had sat was the Domino's Pizza receipt, Danny's alibi, with Danny's name, signed and dated.

He would task Talbot with tracking them down. If DJ arrested people for being stupid, he'd be busy for the rest of his life. He couldn't hold either of them yet. But he believed someone was stalking Fern Lake. Was it the mysterious roller-bag guy? Was he the murderer? He remembered the halting way the man walked. It would be near impossible to wield a Japanese sword and stab someone if you couldn't even stand up on your own.

DJ shook off the premonition he'd felt a few minutes ago. The lovebirds would be back for questioning tomorrow, here in this room of their own accord or in handcuffs at the station. Maybe that would dampen their ardor, curdle their little romantic dream. DJ's fist tightened around Evidence's leash.

If there was one thing DJ hated more than arrogant faculty, know-it-all presidents, and veterinary assistants, it was other people's happiness.

CHAPTER 35

A Little Adventure

The phone call came at nine fifteen on Saturday night. Trish was on her second glass of Chardonnay over ice. Okay, maybe her third, but it was Saturday night, wasn't it? And it had been an extraordinary week. In the old days, in her youth, she would have been out dancing to a live band, drinking shots of tequila. That was before she met her husband, Billy Ballentine.

Oh, he had been a handsome devil. A roadie for the Allman Brothers. He had barreled through her little Florida town of Geneva like a rock 'n' roll god. Trish wasn't a groupie; she didn't go in for that kind of behavior. But Billy Ballentine, with long black hair and a muscular build, caught her eye, and she had caught him. Easily. Well, why not. She was a Southern beauty with a hippie vibe. Long blonde hair and cornflower blue eyes. Her figure in those days was lean, with shapely legs for miles. He came into the roadhouse where she was hanging out with her gal-friends, and after he tried three times to talk to her, she finally allowed him to buy her a Tequila Sunrise and that was that.

Tonight, sixty-four-year-old Billy Ballentine was snoring next to her in bed and didn't stir when her cell phone buzzed. He worked long hours during the week managing bookings at a concert venue. He still moved the occasional amp and risers in a pinch. It was hard work. Billy was out for the duration.

"Hello," Trish said. "Hold on, Billy's asleep. Let me move to the other room."

She turned down the television and went into the condo's living room. She picked up her watering can while she listened to the caller and tended to her orchids on the balcony. Trish had a green thumb.

"Yes, yes, yes . . . yesterday was chaos. But. What?"

The caller made a plea that Trish was not pleased about.

"Well, I'm not going to drive all that way on a Sunday morning because someone lost a key."

"Tonight? Are you out of your mind? . . . Oh, you're in the neighborhood. Well, maybe that's okay."

She spritzed the air plants, scientific name *Tillandsia ionantha*.

"A drink? That's down Ventura a ways . . . Are you sure? It's a bit pricey."

Trish prided herself on an extensive knowledge of flora.

"Your treat? Well, I guess I could . . . Don't be silly. Those days are in the past. But it's nice of you to say."

Ionanthas were her sentimental favorite. They grew in Florida and reminded her of home.

"Okay, give me twenty minutes. I'll meet you downstairs . . . Yes, I'll bring that too, I guess. But only for that younger cute one. Not for that nasty other one."

Trish put down her phone and slipped back into the bedroom and a pair of jeans. She touched up her makeup in the bathroom mirror and slipped on her leather jacket over the teal-blue T-shirt she wore.

For a moment, she thought of Will Bloom and how he had died. It was the sword of justice as far as Trish was concerned. Will Bloom had chased after almost every woman he encountered. And he had treated Trish like a clerk, some old thing to take down his messages and type his memos. Nothing more. Well, she was much more than that. For one thing, she was a biographer of a Don Juan, and maybe one of his conquests had done him in. It would serve him right. She slipped the blue notebook into her leather purse.

The bar she was headed to was new, she had read it was *boho chic*. She squinted into the mirror and still saw the young Southern hippie girl that made a man forsake a life on the road and one of the most famous bands in rock and roll history. She had been *boho chic* before any of them.

"Billy," she whispered, leaning over her husband. "I'm headin' out for . . ." Billy inhaled a series of staggered snorts followed by a long wheezing exhale. Trish thought, not for the first time, that Billy now more resembled "Yosemite Sam" than the strapping rock and roll roadie he'd once been.

Trish caught herself in the full-length mirror. She looked good; she did try to take care of herself. Her husband worked hard, lived hard, slept hard. Billy wouldn't stir until dawn. She would have left a note, but why bother. She'd be back in an hour. He wouldn't even know she had gone out. And wouldn't that be easier? Didn't an old girl deserve a little adventure?

CHAPTER 36

Mulholland

DJ stood on the pavement of Mulholland Highway. It was Sunday morning, just past seven. If his grandmother was alive, she would be at church, early mass, on her knees confessing nonexistent sins.

The San Fernando Valley, obscured by fog, stretched below him, the main arteries of Ventura Boulevard and the 101 Freeway barely visible. DJ's eyes and nose watered, as if burned by incense smoke from his altar boy days.

Behind him, the blinking red and blue lights of police cars, the field investigation unit, and the medical examiner surrounded the crime scene. Evidence stayed in the car with the window open. No reason to expose his dog to the black heart of murder.

"Sir, would you step this way?" asked Patrol Officer Ben Smith. Smith's partner, Irma Gonzalez, conferred with the medical examiner, a young woman he had seen before, but not met.

DJ followed Smith down an old cement path, the way carefully delineated with police markers. He had visited so many crime scenes over the years he'd lost count. But this morning, foreboding pooled in his feet like blood. Officer Smith stopped. DJ looked down at the body.

"We found her this morning, sir. Five twenty-two a.m. Can you ID her?"

"Yes," said DJ.

Dread rose to his heart, thudding with due regularity inside his chest.

"Her name is Trish, Mrs. Trish Ballentine."

Now the two of them were on a first-name basis. He heard the scratch of radio from Officer Smith verifying the victim's identity. "We got the ID. It is Patricia Ballentine."

Patricia. Suddenly DJ had a vision of a little girl with flaxen hair, then Patty, the teenager, then the adult, Trish Ballentine. He had dismissed her because she was annoying and he disliked her. He thought Trish and her little blue notebook were inconsequential. Patricia "Trish" Ballentine was dead, murdered by an unknown suspect. Her body lay thirty yards off the highway among tall needle grass. Her blue eyes faced the sky, long arms folded over her chest, bruises visible on her neck. She was fully clothed in jeans, blue shirt, leather jacket. The murderer had placed wildflowers under her hands. In death, without her natural agitation, Trish Ballentine looked beautiful.

According to Hoa Phan, Trish chronicled the women who slept with Will Bloom. Bobby Talbot had recognized Trish might be in danger. DJ had ignored him. Tears clouded his vision, not from fog or the memory of incense. It was his personal failing, and worse, a professional one. When DJ made mistakes, people died.

He wiped his eyes on the sleeve of his coat. Officer Smith pretended not to notice. DJ heard the roar of a motor and screech of car brakes on the highway. The police had also notified Bobby Talbot and he had just arrived in his Dodge Charger. From DJ's peripheral vision, he saw Bobby Talbot pause at the top of the hill. The younger man jogged down the cement path to the shallow gully where DJ stood over the body of Trish Ballentine.

Talbot looked down at the victim, then closed his eyes. DJ thought he might be saying a prayer.

He waited for the younger man's crush of anger and righteousness. The accusation that DJ was culpable in Trish Ballentine's death. He couldn't conjure up a defense at this late date.

"Oh. My. God," Bobby whispered. "It's Mrs. Ballentine."

DJ winced at the respectful formality.

"This is my fault," said Bobby.

DJ couldn't speak.

"I should have insisted," Bobby said, "that we put her under surveillance."

DJ started to say something, stopped, and finally reached out to put his hand on the younger man's shoulder.

"This is on me," he said. "Entirely on me."

DJ left Talbot and climbed back up the cement path to the other uniformed officer.

"Did you find a purse? Her ID?" asked DJ. "Any belongings? A blue notebook?"

"No, sir," said Officer Gonzalez. "No ID, no purse, no wallet. No blue notebook. So far, nothing."

"How did you track down her identity so quickly?"

"There was an anonymous phone call that came into Van Nuys station about five a.m., sir," said Gonzalez. "The caller said they saw a body off Mulholland Drive, gave the mileage point and culvert marker. Otherwise, it might have been a long time until someone found her. You can't see the body from the road, and this isn't a trailhead. The cement path leads to an old culvert."

"Did they track the call?" asked DJ. "Was it a man or woman?"

"No identifying number—probably a burner phone. The voice was distorted."

"But how did you get her ID?"

"Well, sir, another call came in forty-five minutes later from a Mr. Bill Ballentine. Early Sunday morning, Van Nuys was relatively quiet. Mr. Ballentine said his wife was missing and he described her, said she had on a blue shirt and sweats last time he saw her. And her leather jacket and purse were missing. He said she worked at Hesperia College, and there was some murder investigation. She talked about it all day like she might know something. He worried his wife was in danger."

"And you'd already found the body?"

"Yes, sir, the description fit our victim. Headquarters found the open Hesperia murder investigation. They called you and Detective Talbot ASAP."

"Where is Mr. Ballentine now?" DJ asked.

"The husband is at the station."

"When was the last time he saw her?"

"Last night in their bedroom. He fell asleep before nine p.m. Mr. Ballentine woke up this morning around 5:30 a.m. and his wife was gone. Her purse and leather jacket were missing. We detained him at the station after you verified the identification."

"All right," said DJ. "Talbot and I will need to interview him."

This was one interview he did not want to do. But it was necessary. Perhaps Bill Ballentine or someone else murdered his wife and it had nothing to do with the notebook. But DJ's gut told him no.

"Any indication how she died?" asked DJ.

"The medical examiner took a first look. You saw the bruising on the neck? Right now, it looks like strangulation. Maybe she was drugged beforehand. They'll do a toxicology screening. She didn't struggle much, no obvious scratches or broken fingernails. She was fully clothed, no sign of sexual assault. She almost looks peaceful, like she was sleeping."

DJ let out a long regretful breath. He looked out over San Fernando Valley. The sun was finally burning through the fog. From where he stood, he could watch the coroner's black SUV slowly wind up the hill from the valley. A Sunday morning drive to meet the dead.

CHAPTER 37

Van Nuys Station

DJ drove to the Van Nuys police station that served several neighborhoods of the San Fernando Valley. Talbot followed behind in his Dodge Charger. The building was a four-story concrete edifice built in the 1960s, when architecture curdled into brutalism.

They were expected. The Van Nuys detectives had been busy; they had pulled footage from the security cameras in Trish's lobby. She left alone, seemingly of her own free will. Dressed in jeans and a jacket, she looked ready to hit the town. The next set of security cameras were on both corners of the street the condominium occupied. Neither one picked her up. Their best guess was that she entered a car parked out of camera range and that car turned into an alley to escape being detected.

DJ and Talbot were escorted to the door of an interrogation room where Bill Ballentine waited for the worst news of his life. He would have to provide a positive ID as next of kin and be interrogated. The most likely suspect was always the spouse.

A few detectives coming off the long Saturday night shift exchanged puzzled glances at the sight of DJ holding his small red dog. One detective came up to him.

"What you got there? Are you like that TV detective with the basset hound?"

DJ stared the man down. He was in no mood for stupid questions or sarcasm.

"I am LAPD, not a TV detective," said DJ. "And this is Evidence, you got it?"

The man stepped back and away. "Sure, okay, I got it."

DJ settled his dog into a nearby chair and peered through a small window in the door. A man with a beard and disheveled hair sat alert at the empty table. He wore a sleeveless black T-shirt and sweatpants. The man was average height and muscular, though time and gravity had done their work. Crepey skin clung to muscles on his arms, a beer belly strained against his shirt. Bill Ballentine appeared dazed. He should be in his kitchen drinking coffee with his wife, not sitting in a police station poised to hear about the end of his world.

They went into the room accompanied by the night watch supervisor, who was relieved to hand over Bill Ballentine to DJ and Talbot so he could go home to his own Sunday morning of pancakes and bacon.

The dread that had pooled into DJ's feet at the murder scene now spiked into his entrails, up his lungs, and pounded his heart. He pulled one palm across his face, donning the mask of executioner to Bill Ballentine's future.

"Mr. Ballentine," said the sergeant before leaving the room. "I want to introduce you to Detective Arias and Detective Talbot. They're going to take over, ask you a few questions."

Ballentine lifted an expectant face to DJ and Talbot. "My wife, Trish, is missing. Have you found her? Have you found Trish?"

They sat down opposite Bill Ballentine. Their chairs scraped the floor, a scream of old wood on worn linoleum.

"Well?" Ballentine asked. "That police sergeant said there was a development."

DJ paused for a beat, looked at Mr. Ballentine. Anxiety and hope flickered in the man's eyes. DJ clasped his hands together under the table as if praying.

"Mr. Ballentine, I'm very sorry. I regret to inform you that your wife, Trish Ballentine, was found dead this morning. It appears to be a homicide."

Bill Ballentine's mouth fell open. He stared at DJ as if he spoke in a foreign language. He shook his head, slowly at first, then more violently.

"No, no, no. I don't believe it!"

"Detective Talbot and I identified her. But we will need a next-of-kin ID."

Ballentine's hand slapped the table.

DJ flinched.

"No! It can't be my Trish. Where did you find this . . . woman?"

"Sir, she was found off Mulholland Highway a few hours ago," said Talbot.

"No, it isn't Trish," argued Ballentine. "You see, Trish was sitting next to me in bed last night. Her car is still in her parking space. How could she possibly get up to Mulholland?"

"I don't know, Mr. Ballentine," DJ said.

"Now, who the hell are you again?" asked Bill Ballentine.

"Detective Arias," said DJ. "My partner, Detective Talbot, and I are investigating the murder of Will Bloom at Hesperia College."

"Oh! Oh, I know who you are now. Trish told me about you. She said you were a nasty piece of work."

DJ looked down at the table stained with old coffee rings and dents from a hundred fists pounded in despair. It was an accurate description.

Bill Ballentine continued his monologue. Talking more to himself than DJ or Talbot. "It's not Trish, I know it's not her. She wouldn't be out there alone on Mulholland in the middle of the night."

"Mr. Ballentine, when was the last time you saw your wife?" asked DJ.

"I already told the other officer. Last night around nine. We were in bed. Trish was watching one of her shows. *Real Housewives*. She likes to watch her shows at night in bed with a glass of wine."

"And then what happened?"

"I had a couple of beers; I was out like a light. But she was right there next to me."

"And you didn't hear her leave your condo?"

"No," he said. "I woke up at five thirty. Trish wasn't in bed. I figured she was in the bathroom, or on the balcony. But the condo was empty. It was too early for the newspaper—but I went down to the lobby anyway, and then I went to the garage and her car was still there. I went back upstairs." Mr. Ballentine gulped down a qualm of disbelief. "It was like she disappeared into thin air."

DJ cleared his throat.

"How was your relationship with your wife?" asked DJ.

"What? What did you say?" asked Ballentine.

"How were you getting along?"

"My Trish and I get along just fine," said Ballentine, bristling. "She is the love of my life."

"No arguments over money or other entanglements?"

"What?" he asked. "No! What are you talking about?"

"Nothing else?" DJ sighed. "I have to ask, did you or your wife have other involvements? Was there anybody else?"

Bill Ballentine stood up, hands curled in fists and ready to fight.

"How dare you!"

"We have to ask, Mr. Ballentine," said Talbot rising. "Just routine questions." His voice was calm, steady. "Please sit down." Ballentine fell back into his chair.

"Did Trish have any trouble with friends, or people at work?" Talbot asked.

"No, of course not. Everyone loves Trish. She's worked at Hesperia for almost fifteen years."

"Did she feel threatened by anyone? Had her behavior or routine changed recently?"

"No!" said Bill Ballentine. He frowned, then continued, "Well, the last few days she was upset, kind of excitable. She told me about Will Bloom's murder, and everyone being questioned. She didn't much like her boss. She said whoever killed Bloom probably had their reasons. And then she said . . . oh my God!"

"What, what did she say?" asked Talbot.

"She said, 'What if I wrote down the name of the murderer in my notebook.' Trish has this blue spiral thing, a secret diary. She says she's chronicling the sins of a Casanova. I don't think it's a good idea, but you can't tell Trish. I mean, what is she going to do with some silly notebook, anyway?"

The notebook wasn't a secret, thought DJ, and it wasn't silly. It was dangerous to someone, to the murderer.

"Did she have the notebook with her this weekend?" asked Talbot.

"Yes. Yesterday afternoon, she was on the balcony while I watched football. She was looking through it."

"Did she indicate who she thought killed Will Bloom?" Talbot asked.

"No," said Mr. Ballentine. "She said there were plenty of angry women and their boyfriends and husbands."

"We'll need to see it," said DJ. "Is the notebook at your home?"

Bill Ballentine looked up at him, his animosity lessened by a tinge of alarm. "I don't know where it is," he said. "When I was searching for Trish this morning, I looked to see if her purse was missing. She has a large work bag, it's quilted with some paisley design, and then she has a smaller leather purse. The work bag, where she keeps the notebook, was empty. Her leather purse and wallet were gone."

"We'll need to search your condominium," said Talbot. "Make sure she didn't put it somewhere else."

"Yeah, fine. Who cares about the notebook," said Ballentine. "Where is Trish?" he pleaded. "Where did she get to?"

There was a quick knock at the door. Ballentine looked up expectantly.

Talbot rose, opened the door, and whispered to a waiting officer.

"We're ready, Mr. Ballentine," he said. "For the identification."

Hope was fading in Bill Ballentine, the fear edging in, and the comprehension that he would have to view a human body. A woman these fools believed was his wife. The dead woman who could not be his Trish.

"Are you okay to do this now or would you like to take a few minutes?" Talbot asked.

"No," said Bill Ballentine, shaking off these men's belief that his dead wife was waiting for him in a dark corner of this building. "I'll do it now. It can't be her." He took a breath, stood up, and with restrained dignity straightened his T-shirt, adjusted his sweatpants, smoothed down his hair.

Mr. Ballentine followed the uniformed officer down a long corridor, the detectives bringing up the rear.

The officer stopped before a double door, turned, and nodded. They entered a waiting room with a torn leather couch and three mismatched chairs. None of them sat down. The light fixture on the ceiling buzzed as if electricity was a fly caught in the harsh fluorescent light. No one spoke.

Bill Ballentine's face was a map of singular tremors; lips, nose, eyes twitching and clenching, trying to comprehend why he waited in this godforsaken room of scuffed walls and scarred furniture, standing with men he didn't know and wouldn't like if he did.

Finally, he reached out his right arm as if expecting his wife, Trish, to take his hand, assure him she was all right. His fingers flailed in the air, curled into an empty fist, then fell to his side.

A woman emerged from the interior set of doors. She introduced herself.

"I'm Gail Torrez, sir. You are Mr. William Ballentine?"

"Yes, ma'am." His posture straightened as if reporting for duty.

"Come in, Mr. Ballentine. I know this is extremely difficult."

This room was bright white, acrid with the stink of disinfectant, the floor tacky with years of old wax. A gurney sat near one wall that held an immaculate steel counter and sink. The industrial faucet had a swan neck. They heard the drip, drip, drip of water hit the metal sink, circle the drain, slip into the black bloody plumbing of what this place really was: a charnel house.

A white sheet covered the body.

The assistant coroner positioned Bill Ballentine a few feet from the gurney. "Are you ready, sir?"

Bill Ballentine would never be ready. A sudden vision of Trish, his lovely wife, standing on their balcony, spritzing her orchids came to him. He took a deep breath. "Yes."

The woman pulled down the sheet to expose Trish Ballentine's face. Her eyes were open, her mouth ajar, the skin a chalk-like pallor. Purple bruises bloomed on her neck at the edge of the crisp white sheet.

Bill Ballentine began to shake, an inner earthquake threatening to disassemble the man, his bones, his life. A harsh bark of pain tore out of Mr. Ballentine's throat as he plunged forward. DJ and Talbot, positioned on each side of the man, tried to catch Bill Ballentine by the elbows and shoulders.

Ballentine screamed, a high-pitched feral sound. "No!"

His legs gave out; a dead weight, he fell to his knees on the floor. The old wax thirsty for another rain of tears, another layer of sorrow to add to its luster.

DJ stood, ineffectually cupping the man's elbow. Talbot held Mr. Ballentine's other arm, waiting quietly until the shaking lessened, then stopped.

Talbot helped Mr. Ballentine stand up.

"I'm so sorry, sir. I have to ask if you can make a positive verbal identification," said Gail Torrez. "I know it's hard, but is this your wife, Patricia Ballentine? Just a simple yes or no."

"Yes." Bill Ballentine's voice was a whisper.

The woman covered the body's face with the sheet.

Patricia "Trish" Ballentine was officially deceased.

Bill Ballentine, Talbot, and DJ exited, walked down the long endless corridor. At the end was the interrogation room, a black hole where no answers waited.

Trish Ballentine was killed because she wrote down the murderer's name in her notebook. DJ knew it. The notebook was gone, and the woman's death lay at his feet.

Talbot and DJ would continue the interrogation, the Van Nuys detectives would search the Ballentine's condo. It was their jurisdiction. Suspicion, as usual, would center on the husband. Like a vulture circling carrion, the police would probe and render the facts of Bill Ballentine's life, then move on when the bones were picked bare.

It was procedure, it was brutal, and it stunk.

CHAPTER 38

Up All Night

Someone had been up all night.

A screech reverberating in the dark.

Tidying loose ends. Righting the ship. Doing what must be done.

For Will Bloom, one downward thrust. Necessary and righteous. Ridding the world of gluttony and lust.

A coup de grâce.

But murder's tentacles grew like cancer.

As birth begets another birth. Murder spawned another death.

Trish.

"Give me the notebook."

"No," she said, "it's mine."

The drug administered by tequila in a silver flask.

Trish laughed,

"I know all the secrets."

She snorted.

"Don't be pathetic, dear. I won't tell yours."

There was a meanness in this world.

"History repeating itself."

The woman devolved into giggles, then snorted again.

"I'm sorry. It's just so ironic."

Nastiness wiggled in Trish's heart like a worm in compost.

The words, the giggling, the snorts.

At the devastation of a soul.

Two hands went around Trish's throat and squeezed.

"Shut. Your. Piehole."

Her neck was birdlike, fragile as a bundle of twigs. So easy to crush.

One last pitiful screech. No more snorts. No more laughter.

Just blessed silence.

Up all night.

A flashlight in the dark grove of trees. A glancing beam flitting and swerving.

The blanket.

Ripped free from the sword standing sentry in the body.

Where was the blanket?

Running, lungs bursting, adrenaline spiking. Almost there, almost home.

Then collision! The stupid girl. The pathetic cripple!

Tangled in a tumble of humans.

"Run!" the cripple screamed.

The blanket torn away, thrown up into the trees, the darkness.

The blanket was missing.

And fear was a metronome.

It beat in the heart, pulsed through veins, pooled in the brain like sepsis.

Blood and DNA.

On the fibers of the blanket."

"Clean up loose ends!" Who had it? The girl? The cripple?

What was one more death?

To an accountant with a bloody balance sheet.

Up. All. Night.

Sunlight broke to the east.

A screech reverberated across the olive grove. Like a gathering of spirits, wild parrots settled on swaying branches.

Feeding on buds, leaves, insects. Necks nodding right, then left, blunt eyes flush on feathered heads.

Following the human's footsteps.

Watching it turn in desultory circles, stagger, shake its fist at the sky, crying to a god that didn't answer.

PART FOUR

PART FOUR

Filament

The Watcher ached from old wounds. His skeleton pieced together with rods and bolts. Metal staples embedded bone, muscle.

Back home, he touched the tender places where skin grew thick over bits of steel.

He couldn't reach the deeper wounds.

The ones inside.

Today, he discovered the truth.

The one that glittered in the deepest night.

He was just a monster to the girl.

What he was, who he would always be.

Something broke inside of him.

Perhaps his heart.

Shards of pain, embedded in his soul.

Cape sodden, necklace leaden on his chest. He fell into exhausted sleep.

Always the same dream.

Warren Worthington alive in the hum of speed.

His body, his bicycle; a bullet on the highway. Face forward. His smile stretched across a bridge of teeth. The shush of wind in his ears. The night bloom of jasmine.

An intersection. The signal clicked from red to green. No slowing down, he stretched both arms, balance perfect. His head rolled back to drink in the stars.

He heard it first. The rumble at his left. Then he saw it, a dark blur at the edge of his vision, a UPS truck.

Time slowed; seconds elongated. Warren turned his head, the headlights flashed on, he saw the driver's face, a grimace of exhaustion, then terrified eyes opened wide.

Cacophony.

The squeal of brakes, metal crumpling, glass shattering.

Bones splintering, muscles ripping, asphalt sluicing skin.

Three percussive pops.

Boom, boom, boom.

*A metal hubcap loosed on the road, a circled ring, velocity dying.
Silence.*

He was once again awake in this world.
   The Watcher sat up in his perch by the window.
   Eyes adjusting to the night. Streetlights dusted the sidewalk.
   Two shadows, doppelgängers, billowed, became whole, then human.
   *He recognized the man. He had named him the hollow man. Blank eyes,
blank face. Home to work, work to home. Always alone. He and the man were
the same. The Watcher's afflictions outside, the hollow man's inside. Like broth-
ers.*
   *Now a girl was with him. The Watcher's girl, the one he'd saved. She walked
beside the hollow man. Her arm touching his. They stopped. The girl looked
at the man, hollow no more. They walked on. Side by side. Shoulders, arms
touching.*
   Passing him by.
   *The Watcher felt a stab to his heart, a keening filled his chest. The necklace
dragged him to ground. He rocked back and forth. Then he was still.*
   The Watcher knew what he must do.
   *The girl was never his. He pulled the necklace out from his collar. Gold
glimmered in dim light.*
   "You thought she would thank you."
   *He heard the ever-present voice of his dead father, the neighborhood brats,
the mocking teens.*
   "You thought you were worthy?"
   Hahahahahaha!
   "Of love?"
   They all laughed.
   He was a fool, a broken-down freak.
   Now he saw.
   They were right.
   *He rubbed the treasure between his fingers, her strands of hair, the scent of
girl, but not for him.*
   *The Watcher straightened the cape around his shoulders, unfolded his body,
stretched out arms and legs. His wings retracted deeper into skin, folding in-
ward like gills on a fish.*
   *Stepping outside, his good hand on the walking stick, he was ready. One step
forward, one step sideways, balance, adjust. Gathering strength. Step by step.*

The hollow man's house was down the block, across the street. He walked up the wet grassy lawn, through azalea bushes, up three steps to the porch, to the door with old glass panes.

A bare light bulb illuminated the entrance.

He spied the woman and man. Standing inside, bodies entwined, lips on lips. Skin on skin. Touching. Moving away into another room.

The Watcher felt their heat from where he stood.

He was invisible. Insignificant.

Cold.

He fell back against the porch wall.

A flame licked the flesh between his thighs, hardened and climbed up his ruined body, desire burned in his belly, acid in his throat.

Fury skittered and blazed, moths combusting in flame.

His right fist clenched.

He could break this glass, shatter the wood.

Humans are a punishing breed.

Claim what was meant to be his.

His hunger, his need.

Shatter it to pieces, to rust, to blood.

Frighten the girl.

Become the monster she thought he was.

His breath sputtered in and out, the old ache squeezed his lungs.

Fire seared along two ridges of his back.

The cuts deep, the wound that never healed.

But his tired heart kept beating, beating.

His thoughts calmed to a whisper.

I am an angel.

An avenging angel.

He closed his eyes, felt the unfurling, heard their rustle, the release of cramped feathers bursting to their destiny. The wings fluttered and preened, then retracted.

An angel first, last, always.

Warren Worthington chased away the monster and saved the girl.

He looked up. Above him, a filament in the bulb, a conductor of electricity, burned nearly to combustion, was suffused in light.

The Watcher opened his hand.

The necklace slithered to the porch.

He turned and walked away.

One step forward, one step sideways, balance, adjust. The real prize curled around his fingers.

Seven strands of hair.

Fragile and dear, a conductor of his heart.

CHAPTER 39

A Better Man

On Sunday morning, Danny watched Ferencia Lake sleep. Everything about her was extraordinary; the dark fringe of eyelashes brushing her cheek, her skin that felt like velvet, her hair across his pillow. He buried his face in the sable silk strands. They smelled of honeysuckle and their commingled sweat.

He was lost in the wonder of this woman; her legs, toes, arms, fingers, like limbs to a tree where he found refuge and release.

Watching her sleep in his bed, Danny felt something else; a pressure expanding in his chest, a lead balloon that might crush his lungs, his heart, his life.

For ten years he had been alone, solitary, and furious at the detective who put him away, at the students who poured alcohol down his throat, at prisonmates whose fear and desperation matched his own. Most of all, Danny was angry at himself.

Fury kept him moving from morning to evening, sober and raging; with each new sunrise, he breathed in another day of slow-burning rage.

If his anger burnt away, what was left?

How would he move through the day without rage pushing him forward?

How would he measure seconds, minutes, hours? In prison, fury pushed him through boredom and despair. He filled each increment of time with loud music, pumping iron, running the yard, reading each night while pacing his cell, blotting out the smell and desperation of trapped men. He transformed himself into a muscular motherfucker no one dared to come near. Each twenty-four-hour period, he marked off the calendar with a red slash.

On parole, living with his dying mother, Danny embraced silence. Anger sunk into his skin, seeped into his soul. No radio, no television, no distractions. The quiet slowed down time. Stretching minutes into hours, hours into days. He embraced those borrowed hours to speak with his mother, listen to her stories, her secrets, her fears. He fed her, doused her with medicine, then morphine.

He ran his fingers across her soft hairless scalp.

"I adore you, Ma."

In the end, nothing slowed her inevitable crawl to death.

Who was Danny without the one person who loved him?

After his mother died, the fury reemerged tenfold, coursed through his blood. Every day he focused on silent rage to propel him forward. It consumed him, numbed him, focused him.

This morning, watching Ferencia Lake, Danny felt the arc of time turn again. Being with her shifted something inside of him. Like a clockwork that stuttered and restarted. This wheel had a different circumference, the sprocket turned at a different angle. Days, hours, and minutes would commence on their own, he could no longer control them. He never had.

Letting go of the fury inside of him would crush Danny's heart. Or save him.

Watching the girl sleep, Danny promised himself to be a better man, to tell her the truth, even if it meant he would lose her. Most likely, he would lose her.

But if he didn't tell the truth, he would lose himself.

CHAPTER 40

Coyote

DJ Arias spent the dregs of Sunday morning with his lieutenant. He dropped Evidence at home with kibble and a bowl of water. The dog watched him leave.

"I fucked up," DJ said. "Now the shit hits the fan and there's nowhere to hide."

Lieutenant Stella Steele had risen through the ranks, climbed up the blue ladder step by step. When most of her contemporaries timed out, went crazy, or retired, LT SS had thrived.

"You are going to wrap up this case ASAP," said LT SS. "And no more murder! Not witnesses, students, or faculty! You hearing me?"

DJ was underwater, drowning in guilt and self-pity. His lieutenant's blue eyes barely blinked, giving her the fanatical gleam of a Scottish preacher. Her hair was white, whether from bleach, the years, or the job, DJ was in no position to ask.

"Do you fucking have anything to say?" asked his lieutenant. She had tanned skin like a sailor, and she swore like one too.

DJ kept his mouth shut.

LT SS didn't like him. She would be happy to push him out of her division, except DJ had the highest murder-solve rate. He boosted the department's numbers, so she tolerated him.

During better days, LT SS had told him, "You have some fucking ability to sniff out murderers. It's like the bastards fart and only you can smell it."

Now the good times were over. No more sweet nothings fell from the lips of his lieutenant.

"Keep the witnesses safe, find the murderer, and return the campus to the students and faculty. Or you are going to be sitting behind a desk chasing paperwork in Pacoima until you go blind. You hearing me?"

DJ nodded his head in the affirmative.

"Are you hearing me?"

"Yes, ma'am." This was the third day of the murder investigation, but already a witness was dead, a key piece of evidence gone, and DJ's expiration date was accelerating. He refocused his attention on his lieutenant's face.

LT SS's makeup was melting from the fluorescents and frustration; black smudges around her icy blue eyes and two hot spots of cherry red burned on each cheek.

"That President . . . Reese? From Hesperia?"

"Yes, ma'am."

"He wants you on campus tomorrow morning, in some conference room, 0900 hours for a meeting with the colleagues of the two decedents. He wants to rally the troops. Reese wants you to give an update. Orders from the chief of police are to assure the gathered that everything will be all right, that they're all safe."

A protest almost escaped DJ's lips. Safe was a lie. No one was safe. Ever. Walking across campus, crossing the street, driving a car; everyone was a target in a giant cosmic pinball game. At Hesperia, an unknown murderer roamed the campus.

"Do you have something to say to me?" asked LT SS.

The last time DJ felt safe was in Lillian's arms. And he'd fucked that up.

"No, ma'am," said DJ. He stared at his hands to avoid her gaze. "I tell everyone they're safe."

"That's right," she said.

DJ was still missing something. The murderer had surveilled the street where Trish Ballentine lived. Avoiding the security cameras was cunning, it took planning. DJ had overlooked the significance of Trish's blue notebook, but there was more; the blackout, Fern Lake, the olive grove, her stalker, the "monster." They were connected, a sequence of events he hadn't quite pieced together until now, staring into the face of his furious lieutenant. If there was a second person, the stalker, present when Fern Lake was attacked, then that person would have seen the murderer. And if the "monster" was the murderer; they had a witness.

"A student was attacked in the olive grove the night of the murder," said DJ. "A man was following her. We don't think he's our suspect. He's physically handicapped."

"We call it differently-abled now, don't we?" asked LT SS.

"I need to find the roller-bag guy."

"Who did you say?" she asked.

"I've seen this guy in the neighborhood. A real Boo Radley character. Walking in the middle of the street pulling a roller bag."

"A roller bag? In the middle of the street?"

"Yes, ma'am."

"I'm listening," said Steele.

"He may be a witness."

"Why hasn't he come forward?"

"He doesn't know he's a witness. I don't know if he's mentally all there."

"Sounds like a fucking terrible witness."

"He might be all we have."

LT SS fixed him with her icy blues, rolled her tongue inside one cheek, across her front teeth to the other side. Watching her accomplish this feat made DJ queasy.

"Damn it," she said. "Find Boo Radley and question him. Maybe he can identify the murderer. God knows we need a break. And for God's sake, keep Mr. Radley safe. And the student too."

"Yes," said DJ.

"Just remember Boo Radley lives in a book with 'To Kill' in the title. And we can't have another body. You copy? Now go."

"Copy that," said DJ. Her comment about 'To Kill' as in *To Kill a Mockingbird* brought him up short. He stood up, thankful to be dismissed.

"And don't torture Detective Talbot," she said. "There's no other prospects to be your partner."

"He's okay," said DJ.

LT SS squinted at him. Her mouth opened, then shut at either a miracle or a convenient fib.

"Scram," she said.

"Yes, ma'am."

"And don't fuck up."

DJ walked out of police headquarters and headed to his car. He pulled out his phone and called Bobby Talbot. He related the relevant points about keeping Fern Lake safe and finding the roller-bag guy.

"We'll need a black-and-white for surveillance. I have to run a quick errand," said DJ. "See you on campus in thirty."

DJ found himself driving up Duane, one of the steepest streets in Silver Lake. He made a left turn and parked his Highlander on Apex. He needed to shake off Trish Ballentine's death, his guilt, the meeting with his lieutenant.

Walking to the crest of the hill, he stared down at the water. It's what passed for a lake in Los Angeles; two reservoirs, one large, one small, surrounded by a fence. On the south end was a dog park, along the northeast side, a newly unfenced meadow area now crowded with hipsters, families, and joggers. Humans had displaced the coyotes who once inhabited the tall grasses between pine and eucalyptus trees.

Standing at the intersection, looking down the steep hill gave DJ vertigo. He returned to his car. Lillian's house was a block away. He always found his way back. His ex-wife flashed into his mind, a bright afterimage of their life together.

It was Sunday. Lillian loved brunch. DJ never understood the meal. During their marriage, he followed her into countless restaurants, pounding down champagne while Lillian happily tucked into a savory omelet, a delicate pastry. Toward the end of their marriage, DJ was too hungover to get up and accompany her. One weekend he forgot to come home. When he finally returned, half of his house was cleared out; she was leaving him for good.

Lillian only took one picture, four frames from a photo booth they visited on their first date. DJ already knew he loved her as they walked across Balboa Island. Although he hadn't had a drink in weeks, he felt high, as if a magic drug bubbled in his veins, lifted a weight off his shoulder. In the sequence of photos DJ knew by heart, Lillian made funny faces at the camera. In each one, DJ couldn't take his eyes off of her.

After the divorce, Lillian, with the help of her parents, bought the small house in Silver Lake. He knew her address because he had to forward her mail and he was a cop, he knew how to run people down. All of Lillian's dreams were accomplished; the nice tidy house with a view of a fake lake, her veterinary medicine degree and her vocation of helping a better breed than humans. Dogs and cats might bite, but they didn't lie or cheat.

One dream she hadn't accomplished was the perfect husband and baby. DJ figured that would happen soon.

He turned left on Fargo, a funky dead-end street divided by a median of wild bushes and scraggly trees with an old traffic sign that directed drivers to "Keep Right." There it sat, across the street, a wood clapboard house with a fresh coat of paint, a yard with white rose bushes. Lillian's car was in the driveway. Back from brunch.

As DJ stared, the front door opened. He hit the gas and sped down to the end of the street. Another sign, "No Outlet," stood at a forty-five-degree angle in the turnaround. He braked the car and gunned the motor. What would he say to her?

DJ felt eyes on him and looked up. A lone coyote stood in front of the car; malnourished, desperate, lost. The animal's amber eyes met his.

Its old habitat gone, the coyote stalked new territory, hungry, hunting for sustenance. DJ rubbed his eyes. Another woman's image burned his corneas, Trish Ballentine, lying on that cold metal gurney.

"God, Lillian, I fucked up. Everything."

The tears, hot and salty, came suddenly.

"What the hell is wrong with me."

He looked up. The coyote was gone. The "No Outlet" sign stood at half-mast.

DJ made the U-turn and headed back up the street. And there she stood. Lillian. Not his sweet girlfriend from the photos, this new Lillian stood stone-faced, arms crossed. Pissed off, she stepped into the street. DJ stopped the car and stared at the steering wheel.

"What's up," he said.

"What are you doing here?" she asked. "First my work, and now my house."

"I need your . . . advice."

"I have moved on, DJ," she said. "When I need advice, I go to a friend or a third-party professional. I am neither of those for you. Not anymore."

"I know," said DJ. He bit his lip to keep it from trembling. "A woman died on my watch. A witness." He looked into her face. He knew he loved her on their first date. That hadn't changed.

Lillian didn't soften. "In your business, people die every day," she said. "That's your world. You told me that."

DJ said nothing. Lillian had changed. He had changed her.

"And the way you fix it is to find the murderer and make them pay. No matter what it takes. You told me that too."

She headed back to her yard, then did a quick turnaround and walked back toward him. "Where is your dog?"

DJ looked at the passenger seat as if Evidence might magically appear. "She's at my house."

"Take care of her," said Lillian. "Don't fuck that up."

This time she walked straight to her front door, which opened as if someone was watching and waiting.

Feeling humiliated, DJ didn't stick around to see who. He turned left on Apex, tires screeching, peeled off to his house to pick up Evidence, then headed to Hesperia College.

Lillian was right, he would find the murderer and make them pay. The other part, about moving on, was harder.

CHAPTER 41

Dead Campus

(Sunday afternoon)

DJ parked his Highlander on the road outside Sliming. The day was long with no end in sight.

Evidence jumped out of the car to do her business. DJ felt the word "loser" etched on his soul. Today, two women in his life told him they agreed with the verdict.

The only creature that cared if DJ lived or died was his dog.

He shook off the self-pity party as Evidence finished up her business. She looked up at DJ, ready to move on.

"Yep," he said. "It's time to clean up the mess."

As they walked toward Sliming, Professor Ravi LaVal climbed up the steps from lower campus.

"And so, we meet again," she said with a smile.

Officers Butter and Browning had checked out Ravi LaVal's alibi. On Thursday night, Professor LaVal and her husband attended a spin class, then ate Mexican food and drank beer across the street at Cacao until nine thirty. Exercise followed by beer DJ could embrace. Both of them were out as suspects.

"Morning," said DJ. He couldn't bring himself to say "good." "I need to follow up on something you said the last time we talked."

"Yes," she said. "What is it?"

"What did you mean when you talked about Hesperia's secrets, skeletons in the closet?"

"Detective, you're going to have to be much more specific, otherwise we could be here all day."

"Look, there's been another murder. So I would appreciate any insight you can provide."

"Another murder?" asked Ravi. The smile disappeared.

"So you haven't heard?" asked DJ.

"I was out of town. The president's office summoned me back for an emergency meeting. They wouldn't say why. Who was murdered?"

"Trish Ballentine," said DJ. "Last night."

"*Très diabolique*," Professor LaVal said.

DJ inwardly groaned but the woman looked shocked.

"But it kind of makes sense."

"What makes sense?" asked DJ.

"Trish couldn't stand Will. She thought tattling on his antics was getting back at him, like poking a bear with a stick. Will didn't seem to care or notice. But anyone involved with Will was fair game to Trish."

"You mean she outed the women Will slept with?"

"Not outed exactly," said Ravi. "Provoked is the better word. Made them aware that she knew they had been with Will. I think it gave Trish a feeling of power."

"That must have made them angry."

Ravi considered this.

"Yes, I suppose it might have. Trish played a dangerous game," said Ravi. "She wanted to take Will down. Everyone else was collateral damage."

"And Bloom didn't care about that?"

"Trish was inconsequential to Will. And he didn't care about anyone's reputation, including his own. He thought no one cared, that it was all a game."

"Well, one person cared," said DJ. "Something Trish knew may have provoked the murderer."

"Oh!" said Ravi. "That is interesting."

"What?"

"Just a thought. Maybe her gossip was like a bullet through someone's heart. Someone with a secret. The irony is Trish wasn't aiming, was she? Just poking the bear, shooting at anything that moved."

DJ nodded at Ravi's logic. "Who are you thinking of? Daniel Mendoza could be . . ."

"Oh, not Danny. Everyone knows about him." She paused, frowning in concentration. "Wait, maybe, no, it can't be . . ."

Ravi's phone pinged. "Oh dear, I've got to go, I have five minutes and need to prep for this meeting." She turned to head into Sliming but looked back. "I might talk to . . . the girl."

"Hoa Phan?" asked DJ.

Ravi opened her mouth to answer, her eyes darting to the left as if distracted by someone or something. She paused and appeared to change her mind. "I have to go! Take care, Detective."

DJ stared after Ravi LaVal. She knew something but had chosen not to tell him. Was she implicating Hoa Phan? Did she have a secret so terrible it was worth murdering Trish?

The seductive waft from a cigarette reached his nose. DJ didn't smoke anymore but yearned for something to burn his lungs, clear his head. As he walked toward Sliming, he saw a figure outside the glass walls of the lobby. Pulling Evidence with him, he took the path through the shrubbery around Sliming.

Answering his dark prayers, Hedy Scacht leaned against the glass, smoking a Camel cigarette. Unfiltered, his favorite kind. If you're going to kill yourself, do it right. Don't be a pussy.

Hedy looked up as if she heard his thoughts. DJ registered her appearance. The woman usually resembled a professional newscaster; blonde helmet of hair, tailored suit, full face of makeup. Today, she wore an ill-fitting denim jacket, T-shirt, and khakis. Several cowlicks stood out on her unbrushed hair. Barefaced, dark circles ringed her eyes.

"Can I have one of those?" asked DJ.

"Sure." Hedy handed him the pack; one cigarette bumped out. She lit it with a heavy silver lighter. DJ noticed her ten ragged fingernails.

"I heard the news. I can't believe Trish is dead," said Hedy.

"You two were close?"

"Like I said, I've known Trish for years," said Hedy. "We went to lunch occasionally. Why would anyone want to hurt Trish?"

"You tell me." DJ kept quiet on the blue notebook. It was a key piece of evidence, no need to advertise his lack of oversight.

"Any suspects?" asked Hedy.

DJ opened his arms, indicated the campus. "You're looking at it."

"Maybe it was random, not connected."

"No chance of that." DJ thought again of the murderer's cunning and planning to make sure their car wasn't seen on security footage. "Had to be on purpose. Not random."

"I guess the husband is torn up," said Hedy. "Does he know anything?"

DJ looked at her. She wasn't a cop or even a colleague. In the end, she played for the other team, and their coach was President "Bill" Reese.

"What are you doing here today?" DJ asked.

"The president called an emergency meeting to prep for tomorrow. The students are off, but staff and administration work through the break. We're having a meeting tomorrow morning with part of the Fundraising Department and several other employees involved in this mess. I hear you're invited." She glanced at her wristwatch. "I better head upstairs."

"When can Talbot and I see the electrician? About the power in Sliming."

"I contacted him. It will have to be tomorrow. He's not local. I've arranged to have Lars, that's the electrician, here after the meeting. Ten o'clock? The electrical closet is on the bottom floor, near the southeast entrance."

"Good. One other thing. You patrol the neighborhood all the time. Do you know a guy, he might be handicapped, he walks with a limp. He's all wrapped up in scarves and pulls a roller bag behind him."

"Are you seeing ghosts now?" Hedy asked.

"No, not a ghost, just a damaged man."

"Hmmm, aren't they all?" Hedy stared out over the campus.

DJ was growing impatient. "I guess that's a no?"

"Doesn't ring a bell."

"I'll see you tomorrow," said DJ, "at the meeting."

"Ten-four," said Hedy. "People are going to be devastated by Trish's death."

"Yeah," said DJ. "All but one."

Hedy looked at him quizzically.

"The murderer," he said. "They're probably feeling lucky right now."

"Oh. I didn't think about that."

DJ watched Hedy take one last inhale of her cigarette.

"Those will kill you." DJ said.

She blew out a plume of smoke in DJ's face. "Back at you."

Hedy ground out the cigarette butt on the ragged pathway beneath the toe of her tennis shoe, headed toward Sliming's glass doors. DJ did the same and, holding Evidence's leash, followed her into the lobby. Hedy took the elevator up to the third floor, to the president's office. DJ headed into the conference room to find Talbot.

CHAPTER 42

Star Crossed

As DJ entered the conference room, he saw Talbot at the table finishing up a phone call with Browning and Butter, beginning the process of confirming Saturday night/early Sunday morning alibis of their main suspects. The toll of Trish's death was apparent on the younger man as he slumped in his chair after the call, propping up his head with both hands.

Losing a witness was the worst rite of passage on a murder case. It had only happened to DJ once before, a gang killing of a witness that had seared him to the bone. He never thought it would happen among the privileged denizens of Hesperia College.

DJ didn't know what to say, not only about Trish Balentine's death, but also about how Talbot had his back this morning. It could have been so much worse. The younger man looked up.

"Talbot," DJ began.

"How was LT SS?"

DJ grunted. "Not happy. With me. She seems to like you, though."

"Really?" Talbot didn't believe it. "Oh, you're trying to shield me from the shitstorm." He shrugged. "Thanks."

DJ looked at the younger man. How did he do it? Say thank you like a Buddhist Boy Scout. And mean it.

Talbot returned to his notes. DJ swayed, indecisive about what to do next. He put Evidence down on the ground. He should say something. "I . . ."

Talbot's cell phone rang, he put it to his ear. "Talbot here. Yep, that's a confirmation. All right. Thanks."

DJ let the moment pass. After all, he was in the middle of a murder case, this was not a time to go soft.

Walking to a chair on the other side of the table, DJ felt a passing sting of regret at not saying something to Talbot. It felt like a pebble in his shoe.

"That was our black-and-white," Talbot said. "Fern Lake was with Daniel Mendoza last night. I had a car patrol his street. They confirmed. She's still there."

"Surprise, surprise." DJ was impressed Talbot had thought to keep an eye on Fern Lake before he had asked him.

"I have Mendoza's address," said Talbot. "He's five minutes away."

"Let's go," said DJ. "Have the black-and-white meet us there. After what happened to Trish Ballentine, Fern Lake needs to have twenty-four-hour protection until we find the murderer."

"Yes, sir."

Talbot drove the Dodge Charger with DJ and Evidence riding shotgun.

"There's a big meeting tomorrow," said DJ. "In the president's conference room, 0900 hours. President Reese will rally the troops. You and I will assure Bloom's staff that everyone is safe, and the case is about to be solved."

"That's not true, is it?"

"Headquarters has a different definition of truth. They call it public relations. LAPD pretends to have everything under control. The citizens pretend to believe us."

"Oh," said Talbot.

"Don't worry, leave the PR to me. I'm a veteran."

At least DJ could do that for Talbot. If it went south, it was his career. Not the younger man's reputation.

"I ran into Professor LaVal again," said DJ. "She said we should talk to the girl."

"Which one?" Talbot asked.

"How many girls are there?"

"Well, there's Hoa Phan, Dolly Ruiz, and Fern Lake? I'd categorize Ms. Serena Rigby as a woman."

"Yeah." DJ hadn't considered the others. His mind had gone directly to Will Bloom's girl, Hoa Phan. "Well, I guess Fern Lake is up first," said DJ.

They were in the car less than five minutes. Daniel Mendoza's house was two blocks away. An old craftsman, it was well-tended, wood shingles with red trim. There were flowers bordering a large front porch and tall bushes on each side of a grassy front yard. DJ knew that Daniel's mother had lived here before her death. The black-and-white arrived right after them. Talbot went over, told them to hold tight, then he and DJ, followed by Evidence, walked up to the house.

The wood door held panes of old glass. Talbot rang the bell and knocked hard while DJ peered inside. Evidence sniffed at the welcome mat. She whined and scratched at something metallic between the mat and threshold.

Danny Mendoza opened the door. Beside him was Fern Lake. They stood close together, bodies touching, hip to hip, shoulder to shoulder. DJ couldn't help but note the post-coital glow.

"What's up?" Danny asked. He stood his full six-foot-one height, shoulders out. The tough guy defending his property. DJ wondered if that now included the girl.

"We are here to talk to Miss Lake."

Despite DJ's disgust that the student was apparently sleeping with an ex-con, he was relieved to see Fern Lake healthy and alive. He knelt down to pick up the metallic chain Evidence scratched at.

"Wait," said Fern. "That's my necklace! It's been missing since Thursday night. Where did you find it?"

DJ looked up at the young woman.

"Hold on," he said as she reached for it. He pulled a pair of rubber gloves and an evidence bag from his pocket. He carefully placed the necklace into the bag with gloved hands.

"What are you doing?" she asked. "My grandmother gave me that necklace."

"I didn't find it. It looks like it was left here. You didn't drop it here by mistake?"

"No," Fern said. "I told you. It's been missing since the night of the attack. It was my grandmother's. How did it end up here?"

"Wait, you didn't mention the missing necklace in our interview, did you?" He looked at Talbot. Talbot shook his head.

Fern looked at the two men, felt her face redden. The last time she remembered seeing the necklace was in Professor Bounty's hand, asking if she was a believer. She wasn't sure where she had lost it. At the professor's house, in the neighborhood, or in the olive grove. But how did it get here?

"I wasn't sure," Fern said, "exactly where I lost it. When will I get it back?"

"When we wrap up the case," said DJ. "We'll test it for fingerprints. You're sure you lost the necklace last Thursday?"

"Yes," said Fern.

Did someone follow the two lovebirds last night? Mr. Roller-Bag? Leave the necklace on Daniel's doorstep? Was it an offering? A warning?

"Wait," said Fern. "You don't think that stalker-guy left it here?"

"Unknown," said DJ.

"Are you saying that guy might have been here at my house?" Danny asked.

"Her stalker," said DJ. "Or guardian angel, depending on your point of view."

"Wait," said Fern. "What are you saying? Was that creature at my dorm a stalker or the murderer?"

"We don't know," said Talbot. "Detective Arias calls your stalker Boo."

"No," said DJ. "I said he's a Boo Radley character. I've seen him on the street. He pulls a roller bag, wears a scarf hiding his face, and has a terrible limp."

"Wait a minute, are you talking about Warren?" asked Danny. "I mean, Mr. Worthington?"

"Who's that?" asked DJ.

"Do you know him?" asked Fern. "The guy who was following me?"

"That doesn't make sense," said Danny. "The guy beneath your window yesterday was Warren Worthington? The poor guy's handicapped, injured from a terrible bike accident years ago. He's like a hermit. Almost never leaves his house."

"But he does leave his house sometimes?" asked DJ.

"I guess so. I've seen him in the neighborhood, usually after dark. My mother used to take over food and other stuff for him. Old costume jewelry and junk. She said he likes things that sparkle. He has a terrible limp, a mangled arm. Half his face is disfigured from the accident. I don't know if he's all there. In the head, I mean. The accident happened when I was in high school. Before prison."

DJ noticed that Fern Lake didn't show any surprise at Danny's reference to prison.

"So you've told Ms. Lake about your prison sentence," said DJ.

Fern turned and looked DJ in the eye.

"Yes. Danny told me all about it. And that you were the detective that put him there."

She leaned into Danny who placed his arm around her shoulder. *Young love,* thought DJ. *Let's see how long it lasts.*

"Where does Mr. Worthington live?" asked Talbot.

"On the next block over," said Danny. "Across the street. It's the run-down two-story house. Neighborhood kids call it the haunted hole. I've chased them off, they can be cruel. Mom said he got a big settlement from the accident for doctors and meds. Since his parents died, no one keeps up the house or yard."

"Why would he have followed me that night?" asked Fern.

DJ thought for a moment and asked Talbot to read his notes. The younger detective flipped open his notebook.

"You said were walking through the neighborhood to clear your head," read Talbot. "Then on campus you decided to take the shortcut through the trees . . . and you heard something behind you."

"Yes," said Fern. She did not want to go through the details of that night and where she had been before she was attacked. She had not confided that to Danny.

"When you were attacked, you said you heard something from your right, behind a stand of trees."

"Yes," she said. "I think so."

"And the attacker threw something over you. And someone behind you, your guardian angel, you said, pulled off whatever it was and told you to run in a high-pitched voice?"

"Yes," said Fern. "That's right."

"Do you think," said DJ, "that perhaps this Mr. Worthington was following behind you? And someone attacked you from another direction, on your right, which would have been from the east, from the direction of Sliming? Maybe Mr. Worthington was the one who pulled you free, told you to run?"

"I don't know," said Fern. "It all happened so fast."

"And you didn't see either person, no one you can identify?"

"No," said Fern. "It was dark, and then something covered my head. And last night when I looked out my window, I saw that terrible face. I heard that high-pitched voice and it brought everything back." Fern turned her head into Danny's shoulder. "Maybe he was my guardian angel. But who was he saving me from?"

"We think it might have been Will Bloom's murderer," said DJ. "And the wet heavy thing might have been a missing blanket from the victim's office."

Fern's face paled. No more rosy post-coital glow.

"The murderer." Fern knew something evil had touched her in the olive grove. "But I still don't understand why Mr. Worthington followed me."

DJ looked at the young woman. He could see now she was beautiful. There was something in her face and slim figure that reminded DJ of a fawn, a creature that needed protecting. As if on cue, Danny pulled her even closer.

"He might have seen you in the neighborhood that night," said Talbot. "Maybe you walked by his house, he saw you and decided to follow you?"

Fern remembered her walk of shame from Professor Bounty's house to campus. Bounty's house was a few blocks south. She had turned toward campus, walked along this street. At some point, she had stopped, sick from the wine, sick at the thought of what had just happened. Fern had felt that someone was watching her. She wasn't going to tell that story to these two cops.

DJ Arias would want to know where she had been, why she was sick. "I don't know," she said. "It's possible. But then . . ."

"Yes?" asked DJ.

"Maybe Mr. Worthington wasn't trying to hurt me that night. But why was he under my dorm window yesterday?"

Any way you look at it, thought DJ, Worthington was stalking her. He needed to find the man, figure out what he was up to, and determine if this Mr. Worthington was a witness.

"We're going to have this patrol car parked outside your residence hall . . . or here . . . you need to stay under police protection until we catch the murderer. For the record, where were both of you from 8:00 p.m. last night until 10:00 a.m. this morning?"

Fern blushed, Danny was stone-faced.

"We've been here, together," said Fern, looking up at Danny.

"That's right," said Danny.

"Playing card games, no doubt," said DJ.

Danny stared hard at the older detective.

"Why do I need police protection?" Fern asked. "Is that really necessary?"

"Yes, it is," said Talbot. "Someone murdered Trish Ballentine last night."

"What?" asked Danny.

"Who?" Fern asked.

"She was Will Bloom's assistant," said Talbot.

"Oh my God," said Danny. "Trish is dead? Does Hedy know?"

"Murdered," said DJ. "Yes, she does."

"Who would hurt Trish Ballentine?" Danny asked. "She was a sweetheart. She worked at Hesperia for years."

"We are working under the assumption that whoever killed Will Bloom also killed Trish Ballentine. We are dealing with a dangerous murderer here."

"Oh my God," said Fern. "You think I'm in danger."

"Yes, we do. Don't ditch the patrol car. No leaving the immediate area or campus."

"She can stay here," said Danny, "with me."

DJ didn't approve of the star-crossed lovers, but thought Daniel's house was easier to manage than an empty residence hall with multiple entrances and endless hallways. That scenario resembled a slasher movie.

"Do you really think someone might try to hurt me?" asked Fern.

"This murderer is calculating and cunning," said DJ. "Don't underestimate who we are dealing with here."

"We'll have the patrol car watching your residence," said Talbot. "Until this is over."

A shiver ran through Fern. "All right."

As the Detective took down Worthington's address from Danny, Fern argued with herself. Did they need to know about Professor Bounty? That she made the worst mistake of her life before everything that happened in the olive grove? Should she keep that information to herself, from these detectives, but most importantly, from Danny?

CHAPTER 43

Boo

Warren Worthington looked out his window as dusk settled on the neighborhood. His companion, pain, throbbed along damaged sinew and muscle. Parallel scars running down both sides of his spine were sore and angry. Warren wanted to sleep, let fatigue and anguish do their work. But tonight, each nerve was alive, bright and winking, fighting for attention.

He needed his pain meds and an orange soda pop to wash it down. *"Don't take those pills, or you'll get addicted."* His dead father's voice ricocheted in his head. *"Not listening, Pa."* Maybe addicted was better. He rode the creaking chairlift down to the living room. Sometimes he managed to get downstairs on his own, but not tonight. The house was dark except for nightlights illuminating the old wood floor. Heavy curtains hung on the windows. The front door had three dead bolts. Almost no one knocked, but if they did, they weren't coming in.

Warren lost track of days, weeks, months. He knew by the carved pumpkins and plastic witches in neighborhood yards that it was October. Halloween was coming. The night when neighborhood brats pounded on his door.

"Hey, Bogeyman! Trick or treat! Hey, Monster-man, how's the haunted hole?"

Their high-pitched laughter and excited hoots pricked at Warren's patience. Last year, he opened the door and in his clear falsetto voice yelled, "Boo!" The dime-store goblins, ghosts, and pirates screamed in terror, then scrammed. His porch stank of bubblegum and farts.

The season of lonely holidays would follow; Thanksgiving, then Christmas with its strings of bright lights, decorated trees, inflatable snowmen rocking on lawns at night, collapsed and forlorn by morning.

But not at his house. Ma and Pa were old when Warren was born; Pa was fifty-one, Ma forty-eight. He was their miracle child. Proof that God worked in mysterious ways. Strict Evangelicals, they brought their shy, stuttering boy to church each Sunday. Their God didn't believe in frivolity. They lived without music, laughter, or holiday decorations.

One Christmas, Warren received a pair of blue striped socks from his mother. Blue stripes, not white! He wore them every day until a hole opened at his heel, then he wore them anyway until his heel grew raw. He wore the ragged socks until the accident, when they disappeared along with the rest of his life.

After the accident, Warren had physical therapy. He was disabled, but learned to walk with a cane; forward, sideways, reorient, repeat. Pa called it the spider crawl.

Tonight, Warren used his cane to retrieve an Orange Crush from the fridge. He balanced against the counter to pop the tab with his good hand. He loved to hear the pop, then fizz. "Umm, good." He drank it all down, his mouth and throat were parched. He grabbed another can.

A speech therapist had helped him work around his crushed larynx. The stutter was gone. Now he had two ways to communicate, one guttural from his chest, indecipherable to almost anyone but his parents, and the other a falsetto voice.

"It's like a ventriloquist," said the therapist. "You're using the tongue against your soft palate to form words."

Breathing into his nasal passages, sinuses vibrating, he found another way to be understood. After six months, Pa had put a stop to physical and speech therapy, as years before he had nixed Warren's dream of attending a four-year university.

"A waste of resources," Pa had said.

"Now, Henry," Ma had said. "Are you sure? There's so much money in Warren's settlement."

"Quiet, woman. God gave us this burden. And we will bear it. And Warren, don't talk like a girl. It's the devil's voice."

Ma, always obedient, nodded. Warren said nothing.

After the accident and its attendant therapy, Warren Worthington disappeared from the world, and no one seemed to notice.

Three years ago, Pa died; Ma, dutiful as ever, followed close behind.

Warren's settlement from UPS was in a secure account. His trustee, Mr. Lester, a church elder, had been appointed by his father. He checked in every other month to make sure Warren was still breathing.

"You are God's miracle, Warren," Mr. Lester said on these visits. "God's miracle."

Warren knew about the real miracle. When he died, the remainder of his settlement money would pass to Saints of the Messiah Church. At first, Mr. Lester attempted to make Warren attend Sunday services with him. Warren, using his guttural voice, moaned throughout the service, louder when the sermon turned to God's grace. He let his mouth gape open and encouraged long ropey strings of saliva to fall on the floor. His fellow churchgoers were horrified by their future benefactor. After three weeks, Mr. Lester relented and gave up on Sunday worship.

Warren despised Mr. Lester, but they had a common goal: to keep Warren out of an expensive facility that would eat up his money, hinder his remaining bit of freedom, and rob the church of its inheritance. The Messiah's saints would eventually have Warren's accident settlement if Mr. Lester would just leave him alone.

Anyway, Warren's basic needs were met. Before her death, his mother set up a standing order of delivered groceries, frozen meals, hot dogs, candy, and orange sodas. His pain meds came like clockwork through the slot in his front door. Her one concession to her son, in defiance of her husband, was the snail mail delivery of Marvel and DC comic books from a Pasadena bookstore. His favorite, *The Avenging Angel*, arrived once in a blue moon.

After his parents died, the neighborhood lady, Mrs. Mendoza, came by several times a week to check on him. She made Warren meatloaf, casserole, pie, and cookies. She cleaned up the kitchen and fussed over him. Mrs. Mendoza always hid something special in the basket of goodies, a glittery angel, a shiny globe, a string of baubles.

"Here you go, Warren," said Mrs. Mendoza. "A good hearty meatloaf. You need to put on a few pounds!"

Sometimes Warren pretended she was his real mother. And, like the *Avenging Angel*'s mom, she loved her son despite his strange appearance and hidden wings. Every six weeks, a van picked up Warren for visits with the morbidly overweight Dr. Taylor. The doc examined his broken body, treated the keloid scars on Warrens back, tender ridges of flesh caused by the truck's axles as his body bounced beneath its undercarriage. "Remarkable, remarkable," Dr. Taylor muttered. "You're a survivor, Mr. Worthington. Remember, you need to keep moving or your body will contract like a doodlebug. Then you'll be stuck in your bed. And that will be the day we move you into a SNF, a skilled nursing facility."

Doc Taylor pronounced it *sniff*, to Warren it was snuff, the end. During these visits, Warren kept his wings hidden; not a feather or spine escaped the encased flesh ridges. Dr. Taylor's bulging belly and the stink of cigarette smoke on his jacket made Warren wonder if Dr. Taylor would soon join Ma and Pa in the great hereafter.

But it was Mrs. Mendoza who left him. Last year, during the rains, her body grew fragile. She covered her thinning hair with a scarf. On her last visit, she touched Warren's face.

"Take care of yourself, Warren. I'm sick and I'm not getting better." Warren held his angel mother's hand.

He opened and closed his mouth, pushing air through his damaged voice box. "*Hhhhaaaannnkk Shhhhhooouuu.*"

"You don't need to thank me," said Mrs. Mendoza. "I've arranged for Meals on Wheels to come by two times a week." She taped a piece of paper to his refrigerator. "If you need anything, call my son, Danny. He's back home. He'll help you."

Warren knew the Dannys of the world didn't have time for him.

After Mrs. Mendoza died, Warren grew thinner. He refused the Meals on Wheels delivery. He didn't want do-gooders with their pitying eyes in his house. But fearful of the SNUFF, he began to walk, venturing out in the neighborhood when it was dark.

He wore Pa's old raincoat, wrapped Ma's scarf around his head like Mrs. Mendoza. Warren hid the left side of his mangled face, the disjointed jaw. He took his Ma's old VersaCart, a black canvas shopping container that he could lean on when he tired, where he could collect treasures.

He rummaged through recycling bins for anything that sparkled. People abandoned beautiful things, glitter and glass, old brass keys, barely used toys, treasures of a life Warren never had.

Tonight, Warren stared at Danny's phone number taped on his fridge. He had spied Mrs. Mendoza's boy from his window, walking to and from Hesperia College every day. A hollow man, no expression on his face, his arms weighted down by his own invisible wounds. Now, Danny was hollow no more. With his second can of orange soda, Warren made his way toward the living room couch and the coffee table where bottles of pills, some still in mailing envelopes, waited. When Dr. Taylor asked if the pills managed his pain, he always nodded yes. But Warren knew the pain managed him.

His left arm and leg stung. The old breaks imperfectly mended, the metal screws protested each movement.

"Stop," they screamed. "Why can't we finally rest? Go to sleep? Why must we keep on?"

As he fell onto the couch, Warren considered this question.

"What if you took the whole bottle, Warren, then we could all rest," his tired old bones whispered seductively. "Just go to sleep."

Tonight, the idea wasn't shut down by Pa's voice in his head warning of addiction or by Warren's own determination to outlive his trustee, Mr. Lester.

Warren imagined the pills, one after the other, sliding down his gullet, burrowing into his belly, the pain fading away. After half a bottle accompanied by gulps of the fizzy orange soda, the rest of the pills would be easy. With a whole bottle at once, he wouldn't get addicted. He'd be past addiction.

Loneliness had a corpulence, dimension, and weight like a tumor in his chest. He sank deeper into the couch. The other night, hope had walked across his sidewalk—a beautiful girl. She stood outside his house, overcome by tears. He felt her pain, recognized it, knew they were bound by the same sorrowful thread. If he pulled that string just a little, he might draw her closer, help her, take care of her. Wouldn't such a sad beautiful creature see through the frog to the prince within?

He had to meet her, follow her. And then, without warning, he saw a monster in the grove. And Warren had saved the girl from the beast.

"Run!" he had screamed.

He became the Avenging Angel. Her avenging angel.

She didn't laugh at him. Worse, she was disgusted by him, screamed at his crooked broken face.

Fearing him, she had found someone else, Danny, his neighbor, the hollow man. Hollow no more.

The bottles on the table gleamed in the low light.

His pain and loneliness had returned. And there was no one to save Warren.

"We will help you sleep; it will be easy. Like a warm embrace, the pain will disappear."

Warren reached for a full bottle of pills. He had to press and turn. Pushing down the bottle with his good hand, he tried to twist the lid. It didn't move. It wasn't easy. They never made it easy.

Knock, knock, knock.

Warren sat up, his muscles tweaking. It was his mind playing a trick on him. He reanchored the bottle on the table, pressed down, tried to turn the lid again. The bottle shot out of his grasp, fell to the floor, rolled beneath the couch, out of reach. No matter, there were plenty more bottles.

Knock, knock, knock.

Was it Halloween already? Had it come so quickly? Maybe he had slept for days or weeks, the world grinding on, time through a blender, all jangled, upside down.

Knock, knock, knock.

The neighborhood kids wouldn't leave him alone. He pulled himself up, muscles straining with effort, grabbed his walking stick. He would get rid of the brats, get back to the pills.

Warren put one foot forward, dragged the other foot sideways. He took a deep breath. He would use his high voice; he was almost at the door.

Knock, knock, knock.

The air filled his belly. He undid dead bolt number one, dead bolt number two, dead bolt number three. "Bbbbb . . . bbbbb . . ." His lips buzzed like a bee.

His hand was on the doorknob. Turning, turning. He took in another breath. The air pushed up from his belly, through his damaged esophagus, his sinuses tickled, into his falsetto, readying the Mickey Mouse voice.

He flung the door open.

Two men stood on his porch, not pirates, ghosts, or cowboys. These men wore rumpled jackets and exhausted faces.

The word launched from Warren's mouth, voice high-pitched and clear. "Boo!"

CHAPTER 44

Doppler Effect

Dolly Ruiz made a phone call. The ringing continued until the message clicked on, a disembodied voice declaring this message box was full. She knew after the first ring no one would answer. Her mother always picked up on the first ring. At least for her daughter. Dolly threw the phone to the floor.

Where was Mother? The last time Dolly had seen her was on Friday. She was tired of her mother's overwhelming presence in her life, her criticism. But when she needed her, her mother was unavailable. And now the news from Danny Mendoza, informing her of another murder: Trish Ballentine.

Dolly couldn't believe it. Still in shock over Will Bloom's death, she couldn't fathom that someone had murdered Trish Ballentine. She had never liked Trish. But why would anyone kill her? The woman was trivial, annoying, just a gossip. Dolly was more irritated by the woman's death than anything else. Now Trish would steal away attention and sorrow that rightly belonged to Will.

She tried her cell phone again. Where was Mother? They had a terrible fight a week ago. That wasn't unusual. What had they fought about this time? Was it that Dolly had broken up with her boyfriend Jesse? Mother never liked any of her boyfriends. But something had really set her off. What was it? Dolly said something about her job. Yes, that was it. That was always it. Will planned to promote her from associate director to director of operations. He was going to take her to lunch on Friday to celebrate. Her mother kept asking why he was promoting her.

She couldn't believe that Will had trusted her, counted on her. Mother didn't understand their special relationship. She had called Will a womanizer; worse, a sexual predator.

Will had never been that way with her. Well, not until Thursday. But Dolly didn't want to think about that. Will was a man's man, a bit of a rogue. Women pursued him, flirted with him, but none of them understood him. Not like Dolly. Until Hoa Phan.

Hoa and Will's relationship was a shock at first. Dolly and Hoa were friendly, close in age, younger than the other staff. Hoa had taken Dolly out for drinks one night, confided in her, told her that she admired and loved Will, wanted to take care of him. Hoa hoped that Dolly would be her ally because Will valued her opinion. Dolly could see that Hoa Phan wasn't like the other women. Not someone easily dismissed.

Dolly had been happy for them, hadn't she? Hadn't she helped Will get that dog? She'd filled out the paperwork, chose the dog. All Will had to do was go to the Glendale Humane Society, sign the final papers, and take it home.

But something bad happened to Will Thursday afternoon.

He had returned to Hesperia in a black rage. She'd never seen him like that. He had called her into his office, same as always. Trish, preparing to go home, snickered, same as always.

Will offered her a drink, not unusual, if a little early. But she could tell right away, something wasn't right.

"I better not," Dolly said. "I have a meeting in a few minutes with Serena. To go over the budget." Will was sweating, his face flushed. He'd already had a few drinks, must have pounded them down. Will could hold his liquor, but not that day. His stare was vacant, as if the man she knew had left the room.

Dolly was concerned.

"Will?"

"Have a drink, Dilly Dally, one little drinkery will help you get through your meeting with the red battle-axe, the voluptuous accountant, the freckled fleshpot."

"What's going on?" Dolly asked. She didn't like Serena, but his comments made her uncomfortable.

"Oh, I see." Will smiled, his lips red, teeth white. "You want me to spell it out? Tell you what's the matter with this guy? What do you think it is, sunshine?" He spit out the last word.

"I don't know."

"It's the fairer sex. Fair; what a word, what a joke. I will tell you all about it. 'Tis pity she's a whore. Does that make it clear?"

Dolly shook her head.

"No? Little Dilly, let me tell you about women. They only have a few years before they run to fat, their bodies sag and dry up. So while they are nimble, they flirt, enchant, douse themselves in sweet perfume to hide the stench. Lower their necklines and raise their hems. All for me. And like the fool I swore I'd never be, I dove right in." He was drinking from the shot glass now.

"Hey, maybe you should slow down." Dolly knew he wasn't talking about Serena anymore.

Will spoke over her. "And then they say no more for you . . . no, not until you are mine."

"What happened?"

"All mine." Will laughed, not a nice laugh.

"And then I find out. She's. Just. A. Whore." The last word roared up from his gut. "Just bedding men from the top down. And I was just the next step on the cracked and filthy stairway."

Dolly reached out to stop him from drinking another shot. That's when he grabbed her arm and pulled her in. His breath was foul with Jameson and old transgressions. "Now I'll tell you about girls. Sweet, slim little girls, rose petals."

"Will! You're hurting me."

"Just like you, Dolly Wolly—just like you." He pulled her closer. "Soft and flesh."

Dolly tried to push away. Flesh. The wrong word, but it rang true.

"No, Will, not like this!"

He held her arm in a vicelike grip. "Like what? You want flowers, candy, courting. You want a fucking dog? Is that what you want, Dolly?" He pulled her closer. Close enough to kiss her. They stared at each other. Dolly saw his eyes, blue irises darting back and forth, up and down. Drowning sailors in a bloodshot sea of veins.

She twisted her arm out of his grip, backed away. There had always been something between them, she felt it from the beginning. But this was wrong.

Will was suddenly present, his eyes focused. He looked down into the shot glass, surprised it was empty. One long lick of hair, artfully placed to hide his bald spot, fell forward, stuck to his sweating forehead. He looked his age, a tired sixty-four-year-old man.

Dolly got herself together, straightened her blouse, wiped away her unease. This was not the Will she knew.

Dolly had to save the situation. Whatever had just happened between them, Will Bloom was her boss. Her future was his future. Tomorrow was the Friday her promotion would be announced. She would be the youngest director at Hesperia College. That would show everyone how smart and capable Dolly Ruiz was, that would show her mother.

This afternoon, something terrible had hurt Will. But he would go home, sober up, come to his senses. She knew he would. And Dolly always did what she needed to do.

"I'll see you tomorrow, Will."

At the moment, her job was to pretend everything was normal.

"It's time for me to meet with Serena. The Red Terror." She pretended to smile. "Wish me luck!"

Will roused himself.

"Better you than me. Luck to you, Delores."

Dolly stood for a moment with her hand on the door. He had never called her by that name.

Anyway, Will would get a good night's sleep and be himself in the morning, once again be the man she knew and admired.

Dolly left Will and headed down the hallway to Serena's office. Unease crawled up her spine, her mother's words reverberated in her head, but she had quickly shut them down.

Dolly didn't see Will the next morning or ever again.

"I have to tell you something."

Danny looked at Fern. They lay entwined on the couch listening to music by Flying Lotus. Danny was still shocked at Trish Ballentine's death. The news brought back the discovery of Will Bloom's murder, his body lying across the table, the sword in his back, the open eyes. He shook it off, looked at Fern sitting next to him.

"I'm sorry. What did you say?"

"I need to tell you something else."

Danny smiled. "Of course, I want to know everything."

The soulful jazzy music had been background noise to their long conversation that evening. They felt comfortable in each other's arms. Danny had talked about his mother and her death from breast cancer. Fern told him about her father, who had married her Mexican American mother against his parents' wishes. How her mom had died when she was twelve. After the funeral, her grandmother, her mother's mom, Ferencia—her namesake—gave her the gold necklace.

"It's just been my dad and me since I was twelve."

"Your father wouldn't like me," Danny said. "I mean, if I ever met him."

"I hope you'll meet him," Fern said. "I want you to."

She told Danny about her ex-boyfriend; his comments on her parochial upbringing and worldview.

"His words wounded me, maybe more than the breakup."

Danny looked at her, lifted her chin. "There's nothing small about you, where you come from, or your love for your father."

She tried to smile. "I know, but it hurt. I really started to doubt myself."

"He sounds like an entitled asshole." Danny pulled her closer. "Believe me, I know the type." He kissed her forehead.

"I threw myself into classwork, applied for a Fulbright. I need an A in my art history class. So I visited my professor during office hours because he trashed the abstract for my final paper."

"Uh-huh."

"He told me that I could come to his house to discuss it."

Danny felt himself stiffen.

"Go on," he said.

His arm around Fern's shoulder felt suddenly heavy, a log caught in a river eddy.

"So I did. I visited him at his house. Thursday, the night of the attack, I wasn't in the library like I told the police. The reason I was walking back to campus was . . . Oh, Danny, I made a really bad mistake."

Danny untangled himself from Fern; he didn't look at her.

"So what happened? He made a move on you?"

"Yes," she said.

Danny stood up and began to pace.

Fern didn't want to continue, but she couldn't stop now. "The professor opened a bottle of red wine and kept refilling my glass. And then . . ."

"You made the mistake." Danny's voice was quiet.

"Yes, it happened so fast. And the second it was over, I knew it was wrong. And I hated myself for it."

Danny studied Fern; she was on the brink of tears, she bit at her bottom lip. He had a silent battle with the old Danny, the one who didn't give a shit about his pregnant high school girlfriend, who chugged down a bottle of Jack Daniels to impress his new college buddies, who, drunk off his ass, killed a girl crossing the street with his car. The Danny present in this room lived every day with the weight of his mistakes. Now Fern told him her secret and asked him to forgive her. And damn it, he was struggling with himself to do it. He knelt down in front of her and took a deep steadying breath.

"Hey," he said, "you made a mistake, right?"

"You think I'm terrible now, don't you?" Fern asked.

"No," Danny said. "Just human." But Danny didn't have a high opinion of humans, did he?

"But you're angry?" Fern said.

She was right. He felt the old familiar ember of fury burning in his chest.

"You bet I'm angry," said Danny.

"At me?" Fern asked quietly.

"At you?" Danny was acting the enraged protective boyfriend now. "No, I'm pissed off that asshole professor took advantage of you. You need to report that *pendejo* motherfucker."

"I can't, Danny, I don't want to ruin his life, and honestly, I don't want to mess up mine. I just want to forget it, get through my senior year and graduate."

"Can you do that?" Danny asked. "Forgive and forget?"

They looked at each other and Danny realized the question was a river with a multitude of undercurrents. Could he let go of what she just revealed, sleeping with her professor? Not visualize it in his mind? Could Fern really forgive him for drunkenly killing another human being in the bright unflattering sunlight of their future lives?

"I can try," Fern said.

Danny sat down again beside her. "Okay, but you're going to have to see this professor in class."

"Yeah, but after fall break we have reading days and then finals. I can pretty much avoid him. But I lied to the police, Danny." She lowered her head. "How do I fix that?"

"Oh, fuck the police," Danny said. "Unless that asshole professor murdered Will Bloom or attacked you in the olive grove, Detective Arias doesn't need to know your personal business, in my opinion."

Fern looked at Danny with a sad, slow smile that made her look older, a woman, not a girl.

God, thought Danny; he wanted her again. She was beautiful and sexy, more real than she had been a few hours before.

"I'll take that under advisement." Fern grabbed his hand and brought it up to her face, her lips.

"You should," he said. "Let me know how I can help."

She was a flesh-and-blood woman who carried her own dark secrets, a weight that brought her down to earth, where he dwelled.

"I will," she said. "I can think of a few things."

Danny felt her tongue flick between his fingers. It made him hard.

He wanted her, to make her his, and only his. Obliterate the existence of that asshole professor, the entitled boyfriend. Everything and everyone.

Danny picked Fern up, her arms encircled his neck. He carried her into the bedroom.

Later, as Fern slept, Danny walked outside, sat on his front porch. It was past midnight. He smoked one of his two daily self-allotted cigarettes. The cops sitting in their patrol car blinked the lights. One cop lowered the window. "Everything all right?"

"Fine," Danny said. "Grabbing a smoke."

The cop waved, then closed the car window.

Danny listened to the night sounds; crickets, a mockingbird calling its mate. Off in the distance he heard the whistle of a train pulling into Glendale Station, two miles away as the crow flies. Earlier, he had received an email, a mandatory meeting tomorrow morning with President Reese.

Danny was once again back in that office, seeing the dead man, Will Bloom. He had crossed to the telephone on Trish's desk to call Campus Safety, saw something on the floor. Something glittery and incongruous that he should have left alone or thrown away. He had done neither; he picked it up and put it in his pocket. He thought again about Fern, about secrets.

The train's whistle slid through the night, three honks signaling its departure. He remembered a quote by that writer he'd read in prison, Bernard Malamud. *We live two lives, the one we learn with, the one we live after that.*

The train was leaving the station and part of Danny yearned to be on it. The old Danny who kept score, thought sex was a game, and winning was everything. That ghost haunted him. Whispered to him in moments like this to think only of himself and fuck everyone else. He imagined that younger Danny hopping into an open rail car and disappearing into the night.

He got up.

"Good riddance," Danny said to the dark and went inside.

CHAPTER 45

The Haunted Hole

"Boo!"

DJ and Talbot jumped back as the door to Warren Worthington's house swung open. It was a child's voice, high and unnerving.

The roller-bag man, framed in the doorway, leaning on a cane, stood before them.

Behind him, the house was dark except for nightlights flickering from the floor. The man was skeletal, with a decided list to the left. A swift breeze might sweep him away.

"Hello, sir," said DJ. "We're LAPD. Could we have a few minutes of your time?"

The man flipped a switch that bathed the porch in ocher light.

The neighborhood kids were right, the house and its inhabitant were haunted. The aftereffects of a calamity lingered here, in the wooden planks of this home, in this damaged man. DJ studied his face. One eye hung lower than the other, that side of his face scarred as if gravel had grated and punctured his skin. The left side of the jaw pushed inward; the other jawbone jutted out. His mouth couldn't close, his lips didn't meet.

"Is this Boo Radley?" whispered Talbot.

DJ said nothing.

The man in the doorway shifted so that his best side faced them. He had a high forehead with wisps of sparse white-blonde hair, a long aquiline nose. It was hard to gauge his age, but DJ guessed late thirties. His asymmetrical eyes were blue, fringed with blonde eyelashes.

The man was broken but standing.

DJ displayed his police badge. "Are you Mr. Warren Worthington, sir?"

The man nodded. Using his lower register, the utterance was made with effort. "Yeeeth."

"I'm Detective Arias and this is Detective Talbot. Do you mind if we come in and ask you a few questions?"

"Commmin?" Mr. Worthington asked. His head leaned left, and his eyes rolled upward as he pondered the question. They waited. His body and the cane threatened to follow the tilt of his head. DJ worried the man might tip sideways without ballast.

"Yes," said DJ. "Is that all right?"

Warren shrugged one shoulder. The other hung limp. He studied the two policemen. Pa had said to obey the police.

"Ohhhkaaay." He turned in a deliberate circle, one leg dragging behind.

DJ looked at Talbot and nodded. The younger man hesitated before entering.

The inside of the house mirrored the tumbledown exterior. Clustered cobwebs clung like stalactites to the ceiling. On the dusty floor sat a threadbare couch, an old chair that, like its owner, listed to one side. Standing in the corner was the torn roller bag DJ had spotted Friday night. Broken Christmas ornaments and bits of old tinsel sat within.

Floor-level nightlights flickered on and off as the detectives walked past, deciding where to sit. No lamps were lit. Half-empty soda cans and plastic pill containers littered a coffee table. A sweetly sick smell from old sugar curdling inside half-consumed pop bottles and cans permeated the stale air of the room. Talbot coughed and held a handkerchief to his nose. DJ silently waved his finger at the younger man, shook his head no.

"What?" Talbot asked. "I have a cold." He put the handkerchief back in his pocket. The detectives took the couch while Warren sank into the chair, put away the cane. Somehow the seat fit his body, leveled him out. If DJ suspected Warren Worthington of any involvement in the murder of Will Bloom or Trish Ballentine, meeting him in person, evaluating his physical condition, alleviated those concerns. Mr. Worthington could never lift a sword over his head, nor drive a car. His body was fragile, his skin draped loose from his bones. Warren Worthington's world was confined to this house, and circumventing the surrounding neighborhood would entail a cane, a walker, or the roller bag for assistance.

DJ nodded at Talbot to begin.

"Do you know why we're here, Mr. Worthington?" asked Talbot.

Warren Worthington stared at the two policemen with unblinking blue eyes. DJ saw intelligence and wariness. The man said nothing.

"Mr. Worthington," said DJ, not unkindly, "we're investigating a murder at Hesperia College."

Again, the blank stare.

"Were you on the Hesperia campus last Thursday night?" Talbot asked.

Warren Worthington lowered his head until his chin almost hit his chest. "Nah suure," he said.

"Maybe you were on campus," said DJ, "but not sure what night it was?"

Worthington nodded his head.

"What were you doing on campus?" Talbot asked.

DJ considered the younger man and made a decision. He knew it was procedure to ask open-ended questions—but they weren't going to get anywhere doing that.

"Mr. Worthington, we believe you might have seen a young woman," said DJ, "perhaps followed her . . ."

Worthington shook his head violently. "Nooooonooonooo."

"We are not here because you did anything wrong," said DJ.

"Garll thad. Garll thad."

DJ didn't know what Mr. Worthington was saying.

"We think you may have been following behind a young woman," said DJ, "who walked onto the Hesperia campus."

"Garll, Garll thad," he repeated.

"That you may have seen someone. Another person who ran into her, wanted to hurt her?"

Worthington was now still. The blue eyes at attention, blinking furiously.

"We think that other person may have been a bad person."

Worthington was twitching in agitation.

"Possibly even a murderer."

Warren nodded his head up and down. "Garll. Thstop." The man was struggling to speak.

"Did you see someone? Did you see the person that attacked the young woman?"

"Garll. Thafe. Garll thafe."

"What happened?" asked DJ. "I'm not understanding you. Can you tell us?"

Warren Worthington shot up from the chair. His face clenched in concentration as he struggled to make his jaw and mouth work in concert.

"Maaaa. Maaaaa. Maaaan. Sthhhe."

Talbot squirmed in his seat. "What's he trying to say?" he asked.

Worthington took in a mighty breath, pushed the air into his sinuses; his voice jumped an octave, high-pitched and clear. "MONSTER! RUN GIRL RUN! MONSTER!"

Talbot sank back, covered his ears.

DJ stood up, moved forward quickly, caught Warren Worthington, afraid he would fall forward with the effort of speaking. He steadied the man.

"Monster, monster, monster . . ." He repeated the word in his high-pitched voice. As if he were a ventriloquist, his lips barely moved. DJ realized Worthington had switched to a falsetto voice. DJ's grandpa, at the end, his brain racked with dementia, had reverted to a baby-like voice.

"Did you save her, Mr. Worthington? Did you warn the girl?"

This quieted the man. He nodded.

"You saw the monster?" DJ asked. "Did you see who it was?"

Warren Worthington pulled back from DJ, looked into his eyes. Warren turned and moved more quickly than DJ could imagine, grabbing onto the back of a chair, the edge of a table to push himself forward. He climbed up a short narrow staircase at the rear of the room like a crab, eschewing the chairlift, using a handrail with his uninjured side to pull himself along, his bad hand landing on each stair for balance.

"Sir? What is he doing?" Talbot stared at DJ.

Before DJ could answer, Worthington was coming back down, descending slowly, his rear end on the banister, his good foot braking his momentum on each step. He had two magazines wedged under the bad arm, and he was wearing something over his shoulders and down his back.

Worthington came forward with his spider-like walk, handed DJ a comic book. The living room was dim, but DJ was afraid to break the spell by turning on a lamp. He dropped to his knees near the nearest nightlight, found the cover, and read it aloud. "*The Avenging Angel.*"

Worthington nodded and pointed one long finger at his chest. "Mmmmeeeee."

And then he handed DJ the second comic book, pulled his good hand across the pages until he found what he wanted. It was a drawing of a villain in a black hood.

DJ read the caption. "Azrael."

That's when DJ noticed what Warren Worthington was wearing on his shoulders and down his back. A rectangle of material with a slit that allowed Warren to drape it over his shoulders. It looked like a poncho, smelled like a dead animal.

"May I?" DJ asked as he touched the fetid material.

Warren Worthington held up his hand to stop him. He pointed again to Azrael, the dark villain on the page of the comic book, and then back at the thing he was wearing. Warren lifted the poncho-like material to encircle his head with one hand, his face now in shadow. He circled the couch with a stumbling gait and came toward them. "What's happening," said Talbot.

"I think," said DJ, "he's showing us what happened that night in the olive grove. Aren't you, Mr. Worthington?"

Warren Worthington pointed to himself and then the page. His voice rising into soprano, he rang out, "MONSTER. MONSTER. MONSTER."

"The monster was wearing this," said DJ. "Over his head?"

"Yeth," said Worthington in his lower register. His voice raw, his whole body fading as if he might collapse into himself. DJ helped him back into the chair.

"May I see this?" DJ asked.

Warren tugged at the stinking poncho as DJ Arias delicately lifted it over Mr. Worthington's head.

"Monstheh," he said one final time.

DJ held the fetid rectangle of material. It was about five feet long, two and a half feet across. He lowered it toward the floor, and in the gleam of nightlights saw the plush fibers of dark scarlet, stiffened and stained with dried blood. At the center, the sewn-in face of a snarling winking panther was underlined with the embroidered words "Hesperia College."

It was the missing blanket.

"Mr. Worthington, this is what we've been looking for!" said DJ. "Where did you find it?"

Warren breathed in and with his high, childlike voice said, "It. Find. Me." Warren pointed upward. "Trees."

"That night?" DJ asked.

"Lat-her," said Warren, switching into his deeper register. The efforts of the evening were catching up with the man.

It made sense to DJ.

In the comic books he had read as a kid, the cape was part of the hero's destiny. Last Thursday night, Mr. Worthington saw Fern Lake in front of his house, decided to follow her onto campus and into the olive grove. He had frightened the girl who heard someone behind her, then probably saved her life when the murderer, running from the direction of Sliming, attacked them both.

Sometime later, Warren Worthington had returned to the olive grove and found the blanket that had eluded the police.

Or, as Warren Worthington believed, he found a cape.

DJ's inner twelve-year-old, and maybe the man he was today, believed the cape had found Mr. Worthington.

Because Warren Worthington was a hero, maybe not a superhero. Bent and broken but not defeated, the man before them had saved the girl.

CHAPTER 46

Azrael

After further questioning, it was clear Warren Worthington had not seen the face of Fern Lake's attacker. He had seen a tall and muscular figure wearing the blanket to hide their identity.

"Monstheh," he repeated.

It must have been a terrifying few minutes for the girl and this man, fighting for their lives in the dark against Mr. Worthington's monster.

"It was a person," Talbot kept repeating.

But DJ believed in monsters; he had arrested a few, some he still chased.

"Mr. Worthington," DJ said. "We're going to have to take the cape; it's evidence. It will help us catch the murderer."

Warren nodded his head. "O*hhk*ay," he said as he watched Talbot carefully fold the cape into an evidence bag with gloved hands.

The two detectives walked outside to wait for a second black-and-white police car to provide surveillance at the Worthington house.

"That place is something," said DJ. "If there was a spark anywhere it would go up in flames."

Talbot was quiet.

"What do you think?" DJ asked. He meant about the case.

"I think we need to call social services. That house is uninhabitable."

"It's not clean and tidy," said DJ, "but I've seen worse."

"Sure, I've seen crack houses that are worse. But Mr. Worthington needs therapy, social interaction . . ."

"A bright new future?" DJ asked.

"That's not funny." Talbot was shaken. Warren Worthington and his monster had gotten under his skin.

DJ held the sheaf of paperwork that was stuck to Warren's refrigerator. On top was a neatly typed list, now yellowed, of the small band of professionals and their contact information that pieced together Mr. Worthington's life. "Mr. Marvin Lester, Elder, Saints of the Messiah Church, Trustee, Estate of Warren Worthington; Dr. Lynwood Taylor, General Practitioner; Mrs. Isabella Mendoza, neighbor, alternate emergency contact." That name was outlined and a carefully printed Post-it note with Danny Mendoza's name and number was placed beside it. Meals on Wheels for shut-ins was written in and messily x-ed out. The rest of the list included pharmacies, handicap van services, neighborhood grocery stores, and a Pasadena comic bookstore. The glue and ceiling wax to patch together a broken life.

How different was this man's house from Will Bloom's home? Despite the dust, clutter, and smell, each home was more notable for its absence. No family photos, love notes on a counter, indentations on a pillow. No breadcrumbs leading to friends and lovers. How different were these homes from DJ's own?

"I know a cleaning service," said DJ, thinking of his cousin, Sylvia, who now ran her own empire, Felicidad Maid Service. "Maybe we can get an agreement from this list of caretakers and Mr. Worthington to have his house cleaned once a month or so."

Talbot was still frowning. "But what about the socialization?"

"Talbot, I think society left Mr. Worthington behind years ago. Maybe even before the accident. He may not be eager to re-up."

"Well, it's not too late to try," said Talbot, snatching the Worthington contact list from DJ's hands.

Their conversation was curtailed by the arrival of the police car. Talbot greeted the two officers who conferred with him on the sidewalk. The male officer, Ricardo Hermosillo, gave a short nod to DJ and returned to the car. The female officer, Maria Lopez, the list now in hand, joined Talbot and DJ as they reentered the house. Officer Lopez looked around the dark interior and at Warren Worthington without a side-eye glance or sniffle at the sickly sweet smell of sugar mold.

"Mr. Worthington, we have a police car outside to watch over you," DJ said.

"Nnnoooo," Warren moaned.

"Just for a day or two." DJ knelt down beside the man. "Mr. Worthington, I don't want to frighten you. But this . . . monster is still out there. He's hurt two people. We don't want him to hurt you."

Warren shook his head and again quietly moaned. "Nooo."

"This is Officer Lopez. We're going to check all the doors and windows, make sure everything is secure. We'd like Officer Lopez to stay here in the living room, by the front door." Lopez was in her late twenties, with long black hair pulled back into a ponytail, warm brown eyes, and a no-nonsense attitude. She shook Warren Worthington's good hand. "It's a pleasure to meet you, Mr. Worthington."

He looked at the woman and, after a moment, gave her a sweet crooked smile.

"Waaarrrn, Ohm Waaaarren."

To Worthington, she looked like a younger version of Mrs. Mendoza. His angel mother.

Officer Lopez smiled back. "Hi, Warren, you can call me Maria." She turned to DJ. "I think we'll be fine here, sir."

DJ and Talbot checked out the rest of the first floor. The cluttered kitchen had a door that exited on an overgrown backyard. It also had three dead bolts. Most of the windows were rusted shut. As DJ and Talbot readied to leave Worthington's house, Officer Lopez turned on lamps, gathered soda bottles, half-empty glasses, and headed to the kitchen. This wasn't expected of her, but she wasn't the type to sit around. Warren watched her, at first warily, then relaxed. This was just what Mrs. Mendoza did, chiding Warren for not putting things away, but always with kindness and a ready smile. He barely acknowledged DJ and Talbot's departure.

Talbot gave a quick wave to Officer Hermosillo in the black-and-white police cruiser. He would be there through the night, watching over the tumbledown Worthington house.

A block away, another cruiser watched over Danny's house and Fern Lake.

The detectives returned to the car, where Evidence waited patiently. DJ felt an electric current run up his spine. The comic books were tucked into his coat pocket and the evidence bag containing the bloodstained blanket was in the back seat. Talbot would send it to the lab for DNA testing.

The results would take weeks, but DJ was certain it contained the blood of Will Bloom and maybe DNA evidence of the murderer.

As Talbot drove back to Hesperia, DJ was quiet. All along, this had been a premeditated, cold-blooded murder. At first, DJ surmised the murderer had made a panicked escape away from the scene of the crime, ending up in the olive grove by accident. But what if the path was carefully planned by someone who knew the campus intimately, the regular comings and goings of students on a school night? It was highly unlikely anyone would be walking through the dark olive grove at night. Why Fern Lake was on that side of campus and took the unlit shortcut to her residence hall was still unclear. But if Fern Lake hadn't taken that path, if Worthington hadn't followed her, the murderer may have escaped with no witnesses or evidence.

But where was the murderer headed? If they were running across campus, through the olive grove, what was on the other side? The street that bordered Hesperia?

"Talbot, where does Campus Road on the west side of Hesperia terminate?" DJ asked.

Talbot had spent hours searching the grove and beyond looking for the blanket. "It dead-ends into a trail that leads up to Malo Hill, then down the other side into a park, a recreation center, and the local high school."

"Could someone make it down that path in the dark?"

Talbot thought it over. "It would be tough at night, but if you had a flashlight and knew your way, you could do it."

Along the street that bordered the Hesperia campus was an affluent neighborhood perched on a hillside.

"All right," said DJ, "and Precipice Drive veers off Campus Road and circles the hill. The college owns several of those houses, and they're occupied by neighbors, faculty, and staff."

Both men were quiet. The murderer could have been a campus employee heading for the safety of home or someone escaping into another neighborhood.

Something, if not someone, was starting to form in DJ's mind. A murderer was right under their noses. Someone not only dangerous, but daring. They wouldn't hesitate to kill again. Talbot pulled into campus and parked outside Sliming.

"Talbot," DJ said. "Make sure that each of the patrols stay in place until the new shift is briefed and takes over."

"Yes, sir."

"And have each of them personally check on the safety of Warren Worthington and Fern Lake before they head out. I want verbal and visual identification on each witness at shift change. Text me when each rotation takes place."

"Of course, sir," Talbot said. "They're good cops on both teams."

"They better be," DJ said. "This murderer has killed twice. I don't think he or she will hesitate to do it again."

DJ grabbed Evidence and headed for his truck. "Get a good night's sleep, Talbot. We have the president's meeting to attend bright and early."

"Yes, sir," said Talbot. "All the usual suspects in one room."

DJ thought it over. "You're right," he said. "Let's get there early to prep. See you at seven thirty."

"Yes, sir," said Talbot.

DJ was glad Talbot's focus was back on the case and away from Warren Worthington's house. Away from the question of what kind of life is worth living.

That night DJ drank no beer, watched no television. He read through the witness reports and the very good and methodical police work of Detective Talbot. Nestled beside him, Evidence slept, tucked into the cushions of the sofa. Before DJ fell asleep, he paged through the comic books that Worthington had given him. One was titled *The Avenging Angel*, a lantern-jawed superhero with wings. The comic book hero's real name was actually Warren Worthington III.

DJ wondered if Warren's parents knew they named their son after a Marvel character. DJ thought not. There wasn't one iota of whimsy in that threadbare, broken-down house.

The other comic book Worthington gave him was a DC *Batman* comic. The hooded figure, Warren's monster, was named Azrael. DJ knew his comic book universe as much as any red-blooded American male. He had collected *Batman* comics as a boy and had liked the DC moniker, Detective Comics.

He vaguely remembered Azrael, a dark hooded figure, his face obscured by the shadow of a hood. DJ looked up the name and comic on the internet. Azrael was a member of a group of assassins in the DC universe and became a minor character in the *Batman* series.

He looked up the name by itself, Azrael, on the Internet. Azrael: the angel of death in Islam and in some Jewish texts. A gruesome and menacing figure in both contexts. A harbinger of the end.

The monster, according to Warren Worthington. The murderer to DJ. He looked at the comic book again; a dark hooded figure, face obscured by shadow and a hood.

It was the last image in his mind as DJ, Evidence at his side, fell into a deep, dreamless sleep.

CHAPTER 47

Meeting with the President

I.

DJ and Evidence arrived on campus at 7:30 a.m. An early morning text confirmed both witnesses, Fern Lake and Warren Worthington, were secure.

Talbot was already at Sliming with Officers Browning and Butter, straightening up the conference room, clearing the table. The president's meeting would now take place in the Wick Conference Room, their temporary headquarters, the largest space on campus to accommodate all the guests. Talbot had okayed the move.

"Some employees need to bring family members or friends for support," said Talbot. "The president's office wants us to know this has been tough on everyone."

"No shit," said DJ.

Cafeteria staff arrived with carafes of fresh coffee, breakfast pastries, fruit. Normally, caffeine and sugar would have delighted DJ, but today, delight was in short supply.

This was President Reese's party with DJ as guest mouthpiece.

Evidence retreated to a quiet corner of the room, laid down, kept a watchful eye on the goings-on.

The two detectives stepped outside to discuss their strategy. DJ's role was to reassure the Hesperia community that all was safe, but he had his own plans for the meeting.

"All right, Talbot, when it's our turn, I'll take the lead. Your role is to observe. If I throw a question to you, only respond in the affirmative or negative, stay out of any political fray."

"I thought LT SS wanted everyone reassured," said Talbot.

"We're here to catch a killer. One of the attendees has to be the murderer. Reassurance won't get us anywhere."

Talbot grimaced.

At eight forty-five, the first to arrive were Danny Mendoza, in street clothes, and Fern Lake, in an oversized button-down shirt and jeans. They were accompanied by sleep-deprived police escorts. Talbot talked to the officers, then whispered to DJ, "Daniel Mendoza was asked to attend. Fern Lake insisted on coming with him."

The officers grabbed a cup of coffee and returned to their car.

The couple, in silent agreement, broke apart, moved to opposite ends of the lengthy conference room table, Danny at the head, Fern at the foot. DJ shrugged. He was relieved to have eyes on his witness. Perhaps Miss Lake would see something among the attendees that would trigger a remembrance of Thursday evening. He made a mental note that a convict-gardener and a college coed had zero chance at a long-term relationship. That made him feel better.

Next came Ema Treet, accompanied by a short muscular man in a tight T-shirt. He assumed this was Marco, the poet-husband. Mr. Treet held Ema's arm, her tiny body lost in an oversize sweater, as if leading a shy child into a raucous birthday party. Ema nodded at Danny Mendoza. Marco positioned his wife and himself at the center of the long table.

He put a protective arm around his little sparrow.

A swish of skirts followed by a loud flat voice announced Serena Rigby. "Come along, the president will be here shortly. Such a smart thing to do, gather us all together!" She was followed by Dolly Ruiz, who looked more distraught than ever in a simple blue dress that matched the color of her eyes. Her misery was compounded by proximity to her new boss. Dolly tried to ditch Serena by making a beeline for a chair to the left of Danny. She saw Evidence sleeping in the corner and did a double take before slipping into her seat.

Serena grabbed coffee and a pastry, then circled the table and sat down on the other side of Dolly, scooting in her chair, spreading out her coffee, tasty treat, and notebook, invading the younger woman's space. Serena looked over at Danny Mendoza, unrecognizable in street clothes, with admiration, trying to place him. Danny didn't acknowledge her.

Ravi LaVal, head of faculty council, sauntered in alone, looking rested, wearing a bright yellow cardigan, apparently without the need of emotional support. "Hallo, everyone!" she said in her crisp British accent as she took a seat near the foot of the table next to Fern Lake.

"Are you all right?" Professor LaVal whispered to Fern. The girl nodded and whispered something back. Professor LaVal gave a sympathetic pat on the girl's shoulder. DJ remembered the small population of the college, not more than 1,800 students. People were acquainted, even if they didn't really know one another.

Hoa Phan arrived with her sister, Thien. They were dressed in shades of gray. Thien was taller and thinner than Hoa; a willow-like woman with slightly stooped shoulders and longer facial features than her sister. The family resemblance was obvious. Hoa held her sister's arm for moral support as they walked around the table to sit opposite Ema Treet and her husband.

Hedy Scacht was almost the last to arrive, accompanied by Officer Rodney Johnson and the very tall Officer Luke Benson. Hedy, making an effort to restore her professional demeanor, wore a pistachio-colored suit, a full face of makeup, and her fingernails, now short, were painted fire-engine red. She led her small delegation, after the requisite coffee and pastries, to the far side of the table, between the Phan sisters and Fern Lake.

They sat down, Hedy flanked by Officers Johnson and Benson.

The room was quiet; the chime of coffee cups on plates, a few creaking chairs, the clearing of throats took the place of small talk. People checked their cell phones and surreptitiously studied their colleagues without meeting each other's eyes.

Talbot, positioned behind the head of the table near Danny Mendoza, studied his notes. He leaned against a wall that held a rogue's gallery of past college presidents, all male, all white, except for one middle-aged black man with a touch of gray at the temples.

DJ, standing kitty-corner near the refreshments, watched the group of suspects. He stood opposite Hedy Scacht near the foot of the table but couldn't catch her eye.

The most illustrious guest by his own estimation, President "just call me Bill" Reese arrived accompanied by his assistant, Ms. Larissa Wren, who wore a purple sweater and yellow tights, as well as the tall, lanky communications director John Lonica, who wore a tie, brown flannel jacket, and slacks, just as the campus bell tower struck nine Westminster chimes.

Larissa Wren strode straight to the refreshment table to pour her boss a black coffee. Noting the head of the table was already occupied by Danny Mendoza, the president lingered momentarily behind him before moving to the other unoccupied space next to him. Danny, realizing his mistake, quickly stood up and offered his chair. Reese demurred.

"No, please sit down. This will be a short meeting." He acknowledged DJ Arias with a nod.

President Reese straightened his shoulders, adjusted his tie, assured that wherever he sat became the head of the table. He unbuttoned the jacket of his navy Brooks Brothers suit as he sat down. Reese's full head of Kennedyesque auburn hair gleamed beneath the room's halogen lights. Glancing around the table, he paused at Hoa Phan, who did not return his gaze. Her sister, Thien, stared daggers at him.

After delivering the coffee, Larissa Wren and John Lonica took open seats to the president's right, pulling back their chairs a bit, as if they weren't allowed to sit at the adult's table.

"Shall we begin?" said President Reese. He commanded the room; the attendees gave him their full attention.

"Good morning, everyone. Thank you for coming today. And thank you to our guests who are supporting their friends and family."

There was a mumble of *mornings* from the assembled group.

"I want to first acknowledge that this has been a very difficult four days. We have lost two beloved members of our community."

DJ reflexively cleared his throat. The sentence stuck in his craw; first, that Will Bloom was beloved, and second, that Will and Trish were lost, as if at sea instead of brutally murdered.

President Reese stood up and ceremoniously removed his suit jacket, carefully draping it on the back of his chair. Reese was five foot nine, trim with an athletic build.

He slowly unbuttoned and rolled up his shirtsleeves, loosened his tie before returning to his seat, leaning forward, elbows on the table. His voice had lowered as if sharing a confidence.

"Now, I gathered you together today for an update. But more than that, I want to check in; listen to you, your concerns, fears, thoughts. Anything you want to share with this group, with me. About those we've lost, memories, anything. I want you to know, I'm here for you."

During the president's ceremonious removal of his jacket, proclaiming himself the common man, one piece of the puzzle had clicked into place for DJ. He looked over at Talbot and the younger detective nodded. They both saw it. The enraged Will Bloom at the dry cleaners, the slim-cut tailored Brooks Brothers suit crumpled in the car trunk, the slamming of the office door, the sudden explosion of anger at Hoa Phan.

An uncomfortable silence had fallen on the assembled group.

Ema Treet sniffled and blew her nose into a tissue. Husband Marco pulled her closer, whispered a Czech endearment to his wife. "*Ticho, lásko, jsi se mnou v bezpečí.*"

Most of the assembled stared at the surface of the conference table. Hoa and her sister, Thien, shared a look. Hoa's eyes were on the brink of tears, but

Thien shook her head. Hoa controlled herself, then looked down. Dolly openly wept, the intake of sobs like a child catching her breath, then shuddering out. It was a long thirty seconds.

DJ looked again at Hedy Scacht, pinioned between her two Campus Safety officers. The men looked solemn, staring down at the floor. Hedy stared straight ahead, her sea-blue eyes expressionless and silver, as if leached of color. For a moment, she caught DJ's stare and flinched before returning to her private reverie.

Serena Rigby twitched in her chair, impatient at the sniffling response of the gathered.

"I'm sure we all are overwhelmed at the death of our colleagues." Her booming voice sliced through the somnolence like a buzzer ending a basketball game. "President Reese, we are all so thankful for your leadership at this time."

Attendees shuddered at her voice. Reese had the good sense to blush. With a strained smile, he bowed his head and the silence commenced anew.

Danny straightened his shoulders and raised his hand.

President Reese turned and said, "Daniel? Please, would you like to say something?"

"Yes, sir," said Danny. "I wanted to say that Trish was a good person."

"Yes, she was," said Reese. "Go on."

Danny hesitated before resuming.

"She was kind to my mom and me. She loved bright-colored clothes, particularly yellow . . . bad jokes . . . and of course, good gossip."

A chorus of subtle laughter lightened the tension of the room.

"She had an incredible knowledge of plants and trees," Danny continued. "If I needed advice on a flower or shrub, she always had a helpful suggestion."

The room seemed to exhale a communal breath.

"Yes," said Professor LaVal. "Trish was a dear. And Will cut quite a figure across campus. Both will be sorely missed."

A murmur of assent issued from the group before silence once again descended. The dead remembered kindly, if not well. Not even Serena Rigby had the temerity to speak again.

"Well, we don't have to say anything more right now," said President Reese. "Just know that my door is always open."

"Thank you so much, President Reese. How grateful we are for this opportunity to share these remembrances with you." Ravi LaVal smiled. "And to know we can drop into your office any time to visit. Such a precedent!" Her voice was tinged with sarcasm, or was it irony?

President Reese's tight-lipped smile reemerged. DJ noted that Professor LaVal's subtle defiance was directed at all representatives of authority, not just him.

"Now, I want to pivot to the Los Angeles Police Department," said the president. "I have known the chief of police, Daniel Charles, for many years. As of this morning, he has assured me that his department is doing everything to bring this situation at Hesperia under control. More importantly, we discussed tactics to keep our community safe. This week, I'm instituting early dismissal at 3:00 p.m. The campus will be closed from 4:00 p.m. to 8:00 a.m. to everyone but essential staff during the rest of fall break. Those that work in lower Sliming, which is still secured, may work in the library or in offices in the Student Center. The chief has assured me that by next week it will be safe to bring our students back to campus." President Reese paused, took a breath, and plunged ahead. "He is confident that whoever did this is likely an outsider." Here the president paused again before continuing, speaking rapidly. "And that the detective in charge is one of their best and the case is close to completion."

DJ wondered how hard it was for President Reese to get out that last sentence.

"Isn't that right, Detective Arias?"

DJ was being reduced to a message boy for the chief of police, a man he had met briefly on two occasions and knew better by his voice floating across a sea of blue cadets.

Standing now behind Ema and Marco Treet, DJ looked at the gathered, some teary-eyed, a few hopeful, several faces cast down to the floor. Talbot tried to catch DJ's attention, shook his head as if warning him, but to no avail.

"Well," said DJ. "That's a nice story, but not accurate. The truth is there is a dangerous predator among you, not an outsider. We have suspects, but we have not identified the murderer."

There was an intake of breath from the gathered. President Reese's face reddened. He was about to interrupt when DJ said, "Yet. But we will. Very soon. And it will most likely be someone in this room."

He looked around the table at each individual face and set of eyes.

"You see, as Detective Talbot and I have been investigating this case, there have been a number of impediments, secrets, half-truths, and a complete lack of confidentiality. I've been told that Hesperia is its own insular world, a place that creates superior beings engaged in the pursuit of critical thinking."

Now DJ had their full attention.

"Me? I went to Cal State Los Angeles, down the freeway in East LA. It's a big rambling campus, open to any student trying to better themselves. But here at Hesperia College, tucked into this quiet neighborhood, I've learned you all engage in the pursuit of essential truth. And that sounds noble. But in the midst of this high-minded educational experience, there's been the bland acceptance of a sexual predator, and that consent bred evil and murder within this little Camelot."

A fist pounded the table, and everyone jumped. "Enough," said President Reese. "I did not call this meeting to hear a hackneyed cop with a state college education tell me what is wrong with my institution."

DJ smiled. "No, you came for a fairy tale. Tell the people what they want to hear so you can resume the daily schedule; prepare for your students' return to campus, keep your revenue streams flowing."

"How dare you!"

John Lonica stood up and addressed DJ in his calm, patient voice.

"Detective, I think we might continue without the drama. We get it. What we must look like from the outside. I assure you, everyone here admires the state college system and your education, and even more your profession. But can we just address where we are in this investigation?" His left hand went up and slowly down, a quiet plea to President Reese to be seated.

DJ gathered himself together. He felt a smug satisfaction that President "just call me Bill" Reese had proven himself to be the snob DJ had recognized hidden inside the common man act. "Fair enough," said DJ. "While we're all gathered here together, let's sort through a few key facts. Right, Talbot?"

"Ummm. Yes, sir." Talbot mumbled, looking miserable.

"This is ridiculous," said President Reese. "Are you going to ask us to sit here while you insult this college and hem and haw over details of this case like a bad detective in a cheap mystery novel? Why should I waste one more minute of my time listening to this?"

"You're free to leave," said DJ. "But before you go, I'm wondering if you could tell me the size of your suit?"

"What?" demanded Reese. "What did you say?"

"Your suit size," said DJ. "It's Brooks Brothers, tailored. Am I right?"

"I don't see how that is any of your business or relevant to this situation."

"Oh," said DJ, "it is relevant. In fact, your suit, in a way, sparked this whole chain of events. The death of Will Bloom, a murder that became inevitable, and Trish Ballentine, collateral damage."

"I don't know what you're talking about," said President Reese, beginning to rise again.

"Sit down, sir," said DJ with an authority that caused Reese to immediately take his chair.

"Unless you'd like me to discuss a key piece of evidence without your presence, a crumpled suit from a dry cleaner." Reese started to object, then closed his mouth. "You see, on the morning of his death, Will Bloom walked through his office suite and popped into Ms. Hoa Phan's empty office."

Reese looked confused.

"We believe Mr. Bloom sat down at Ms. Phan's desk. Maybe he missed her, wanted to feel her presence. Mr. Bloom had come to a big decision. He made a phone call and wanted to write something important down. Unfortunately, he wrote on the back of a receipt from a dry cleaner. Lau 'N Dry—isn't that where you take your clothes, Ms. Phan?" asked DJ.

Hoa looked at her sister, Thien, and then at DJ. "Yes," she whispered.

"Yes. The Phan sisters took their clothes to Lau 'N Dry. They often picked up each other's things. Sometimes they took items that weren't their own, something left behind at their apartments. A friend's scarf, a boyfriend's shirt, a man's Brooks Brothers suit, size 36 slim?"

President Bill Reese said in a controlled voice, "Are you accusing me of something, of murder?"

"Not murder," said DJ. "No, but you left your suit at Ms. Hoa Phan's home at some point in the past eleven months of her employment. So, either you are in the habit of leaving your clothes at random apartments or . . . ?"

"Oh, my," Larissa Wren spoke aloud without realizing it. Her hand flew to her mouth and covered her lips. President Reese shot up, his chair flying back and over. "Enough," said Reese. "I will not sit here and be slandered. One thing is clear. I did not murder Will Bloom or Trish Ballentine. I have alibis for the time of both murders. And whatever else you are insinuating is none of your damn business. We are done here."

John Lonica stood up. He wore his familiar exhausted expression, as if he had witnessed too many human failings to get a good night's sleep. He righted the president's chair and turned to DJ.

"I think we need to head out to the president's next meeting. I believe you've said enough for now."

DJ felt triumphant. "No. President Reese, leaving behind a suit isn't a crime, maybe just an indiscretion, but a dreadful revelation to Will Bloom. It sent him spiraling out of control. And that, I believe, triggered a sequence of events that led to his murder."

DJ saw it all now. The pieces fit. Will Bloom was busy planning his future with Hoa Phan. Arranging a meaningful gift that would cement their relationship, being the good boyfriend by running an errand, picking up her dry cleaning because he had written all over the receipt he'd found in her office.

President Reese donned his tailored jacket over his rolled shirtsleeves. "I will never forget or forgive what you said here today."

"Ah, yes, I'm sure of that." DJ was focused on the crime. "Somehow not forgiving or forgetting is at the crux of these murders."

"Thank you for the mumbo-jumbo psychology, Detective," said Reese, walking over to DJ. "Whatever you presume, I assure you, you are mistaken. There is a perfectly innocent reason for what transpired with my suit and I'm not going to dignify your comments with an answer."

Reese stood so close that DJ could smell the coffee and acid on the other man's breath. "And if I were you, I would start thinking about another line of work."

President Reese squared his shoulders, ran a hand through his auburn hair. With a show of dignity, he turned and nodded his head to his gathered colleagues, avoiding Hoa Phan. "Hedy, come with me, please."

Reese left the conference room, followed by Larissa Wren. John Lonica politely held the door. Hedy quickly made for the exit. She paused for a moment, surveying the room, her face unreadable, then followed the president out of the conference room.

With a weary half-smile, Lonica said, "Let me know when you make an arrest, Detectives."

II.

Everyone that remained glanced at Hoa Phan, then away. Pale-faced, she stared a hole into the table and then looked up and met DJ's eyes. "I hate you" smoldered within them. She and her sister sat glued to their seats.

Attendees began to file out quietly as if leaving church. Talbot followed Danny Mendoza and Fern Lake outside to make sure they took the police car home. DJ watched everyone except the Phan sisters leave.

Professor Ravi LaVal walked up to DJ. "I think, Detective, that you've shattered all rules of decorum. You made your point, but you're a reckless man. President Reese won't forgive you for what you've done."

"I can live with that," said DJ.

"As for me," said Professor LaVal, "I'm disappointed that you really don't understand Hesperia College. Perhaps we overlooked bad behavior, or didn't realize the consequences. But I'm sure even the homely and open-armed Cal State LA has its predators. Colleges are just a microcosm of society. Hesperia isn't so different than your alma mater." She looked out the windows. "It's just scale and architecture."

"It's more than that," said DJ. "Hesperia believes it's creating superior human beings."

"We believe in bettering ourselves. What's the alternative, Detective? Stay in your station with no hope to change your circumstances, your worldview, your life? In England, where I'm from, you're born into your class, and you stay there. I fought my way out, studied hard, went to university. I left behind my country to be here, at Hesperia. I chose to transcend my circumstances. I wonder what you chose?"

"The truth," DJ said.

"Well, the truth can change over time and with perspective," said Professor LaVal, "it's not fixed."

"Two people are dead," said DJ. "Time or perspective won't change that."

"Well, Detective Arias, for our sake and yours, I hope you find the truth about the murderer. I believe your time is running out."

"Tell me something," DJ said. He looked over at Hoa Phan and her sister, who sat at the table whispering to each other. "Yesterday, when we were discussing Hesperia's secrets, you suggested I talk to Hoa Phan."

Ravi LaVal looked at him blankly.

"You told me to talk to the girl," said DJ.

Ravi sighed. "You really have to learn to think with your head rather than other parts of your anatomy."

"What?"

"I meant Will's girl. Girl Friday. Dolly Ruiz. Talk to her."

"Oh," said DJ, taken aback. "Dolly? Why didn't you just say her name?"

"Something distracted me. A person I didn't want to upset, whose wrath I didn't want to incur. Didn't you see her standing there?"

Now it was DJ's turn to look confused.

"You know, Detective," said Professor LaVal, "you really aren't that bright."

She started to leave, but turned back, spoke quietly. "I'll admit I never liked Hoa Phan, but what you did today is unforgivable."

With that, Professor LaVal left the room.

III.

Detective Talbot reentered, almost colliding with the exiting Professor Ravi LaVal. DJ walked over to Hoa Phan and her sister Thien. Talbot sat down at the head of the table, rubbing his face.

"I'm going to describe a sequence of events," said DJ.

Thien Phan interrupted. "Haven't you done enough? You have ruined my sister's reputation."

"Let's get it over with," said Hoa Phan, wearily placing a hand on her sister's arm. "I don't want to hide this anymore. I'm exhausted and I want it all out in the open."

DJ looked at Hoa Phan's face. Today, no makeup could hide her distress or pain. He refused to feel responsible. He might be salt in an open wound, but the wound was created by willing participants.

"On Thursday afternoon," said DJ, "Will Bloom picked up your dry cleaning from Lau 'N Dry and realized he was holding another man's suit. Not just any man's suit, a specific brand, tailored, and slim cut. He'd seen it before, many times, on President Bill Reese. As you said, Mr. Bloom suffered from sexual addiction. He couldn't be faithful, but he was also emotionally fragile. He fell apart when he suspected the woman he loved had been with someone else. Someone he knew, someone younger, more powerful, someone he was jealous of."

Hoa Phan looked spent. Whatever tears she had shed were over. "What happened with President Reese was a mistake, on both our parts. It only happened once, months before Will and I got together," she said. "I won't go into details, but Bill Reese ended up in my apartment, there was red wine, it spilled all over his suit. He had his gym clothes with him and wore them home. Neither of us wanted to deal with what happened between us, so we agreed to move on, act like it never happened. The suit hung hidden in the back of my closet for months, an awful reminder of that night. I finally decided to get the damn thing out of my apartment, clean it, give it away. Get on with my life. I was ready to move on with everything. I suspected Will was unfaithful to me when I was away. I heard Trish gossiping, always within my earshot. I finally told Will that he would have to commit to me or we were through. That he had to get help with his addiction."

"When did this conversation occur?"

"Last week, before I left for Phoenix. We were supposed to discuss it when I returned from the conference. I still can't believe that he found that receipt.

I place my personal receipts under the desk pad in my office. That he would find it and pick up my dry cleaning was completely out of character."

DJ paced around the table. "He must have found the receipt that Thursday morning when he was in your office. He had an appointment at the Glendale Humane Society and wrote down the details on the back of it. With Dolly Ruiz's help, he'd arranged to adopt a dog, as a gift to you."

Hoa Phan looked confused. "I can't have a dog at my apartment. It doesn't make sense."

"But he had Evidence locked in the bathroom of his house," said DJ. Hearing her name, the dog looked up; finding nothing of interest, laid her head on her paws and closed her eyes. "I think he was going to ask you to move in with him."

Hoa Phan stared at DJ as the truth dawned on her.

"Oh my God," she said. "That would have been an incredible gesture on Will's part. If he hadn't found that receipt, everything might have turned out different."

DJ studied Hoa and wondered if she believed that. People like Will Bloom never really changed.

"Will was supposed to pick me up at the airport at six fifteen last Thursday night. Instead, he called me on my cell phone." Hoa Phan took a deep breath. "He was furious. He accused me of cheating on him with Bill Reese. I was shocked, didn't know how he found out about Bill. He didn't mention the suit. He was too angry. The things he said . . . he called me a whore and worse. I could tell he'd been drinking. He was out of control, out of his mind."

"And what did you do?"

"I was hurt, then angry. Finally, I was frightened. He said terrible things I can't repeat. Or forget. After he hung up, I knew I could never feel the same way about him. It was as if a curtain opened and revealed the man he really was; full of rage, bitterness, and violence. Maybe it was fueled by alcohol, but it was real and dangerous. I called my sister from my rideshare. I told her that Will and I were through, and I asked if I could stay at her apartment that night."

"You thought he might hurt you?"

"I thought he might show up at my apartment," said Hoa. "Either in a drunken rage or full of remorse. Either way, it would be ugly."

Hoa Phan sat up straight. "You know, I thought I could forgive him for the other women, but it wasn't enough. He couldn't forgive me for something that had nothing to with him. And then, the next morning he was dead."

Her sister, Thien, took Hoa's hand, squeezed it and said, "You have been through enough. Let's go."

The sisters began to gather their things and stood up. "But what I don't understand," said Hoa. "What does all this have to do with Will's murder? Or Trish's death? Who killed him? I don't understand."

"I think his behavior on Thursday triggered a chain of events."

DJ thought Will Bloom's violent and self-pitying rage pushed him into dangerous behavior. He had to dominate, take out his rage on someone. That person decided that Will Bloom must die.

"And what about the dog?" Hoa asked. "Are you going to keep her?"

"Yes," said DJ Arias. "If she'll have me." Evidence looked up, her tail thumped the carpeted floor.

The sisters walked toward the door.

"On Friday," said Hoa, "after I heard about Will's death, I asked my sister to pick up the suit from the dry cleaners. I didn't want anyone to know about Bill Reese. Now everyone knows, or soon will."

"Yes," said Thien Phan. "Thanks to you."

DJ said nothing.

"Thien, I made a stupid mistake," said Hoa. "But it's time for me to move on. I hope you realize, Detective Arias, that Bill Reese is a powerful ally and a terrible enemy."

"I'm not impressed," said DJ, "by 'just call me Bill' Reese."

Thien headed into the lobby, followed by Detective Talbot. Hoa paused before she left the room. "You know, Bill Reese is a very good president." She gave DJ the smile that could break your heart. "He's not a perfect man. But who is?"

DJ had no answer for that question.

CHAPTER 48

Breaker Panel

Talbot waited for DJ in the lobby. They were scheduled to meet the electrician on the first floor of Sliming.

"Dolly Ruiz stopped by, sir," he said. "She wants to see you. I told her you would check in with her after our next appointment. She's working from the student center."

"That's interesting. According to Professor LaVal, Dolly Ruiz knows all the secrets." DJ looked at Talbot's pale face and slumped shoulders. "What's wrong with you, Talbot? You look like someone killed your puppy."

DJ looked down at Evidence. "Sorry, girl, wrong choice of words."

The dog wagged her tail.

DJ Arias felt wired, ready to face the day, as if he'd just finished a good hard workout. Talbot looked like he had watched a soccer match and his team lost. "That was a tough meeting, sir."

"Was it? We're closing in on the murderer, Talbot, I feel it. How was the patrol rotation? Remember, eyes on both Fern Lake and Warren Worthington twenty-four hours a day."

"Yes, sir," said Talbot. "Fern Lake and Daniel just returned to Mendoza's house, with the new patrol. Warren Worthington became upset when Officer Lopez was preparing to leave, made quite a ruckus. She agreed to work a double shift and LT SS just approved it."

"God bless Officer Maria Lopez." DJ wasn't ready to invoke the gods for LT SS yet.

They headed down the circular stairway to meet the electrician.

Officer Rodney Johnson met the two men at the bottom of the stairs.

"I'll walk you gentlemen to the closet that houses the breaker panel. The electrician is already here."

Officer Johnson's eyes were bloodshot, his face ashen.

"I can't believe Trish is gone," he said. "I've known her for years. This has been hard on everyone. Particularly Hedy. She's broken up."

Johnson led them down one long corridor, then turned right at another. This side of the building, opposite Will Bloom's office suite, was utilitarian.

Beige walls, chipped paint on metal doors, the ever-present muddy blue carpet. Behind one set of doors to their left was the persistent hum of a mainframe computer. A reminder that Hesperia College was also a business processing data; student grades, application fees, and donations. High ideals had to be paid for.

"Is Hedy here?" asked DJ, looking around.

"I think she's still with President Reese after that meeting." Officer Johnson's face offered no indication of what he thought of the previous hour's activities. Talbot walked ahead out of listening range to a large closet where two metal doors stood open.

"Hedy and Trish Ballentine were close, right?" said DJ as if he already knew the answer. Yesterday, Hedy didn't appear as devastated about Trish as Johnson suggested.

"Yep," said Officer Johnson. "Hedy, Isabella, and Trish were lifers. Knew each other forever . . . knew where all the bodies were buried."

Rodney Johnson stopped, looking shaken.

"Sorry, I didn't mean that. Two of them gone now. I meant they were close and shared everything. Even the kids. Hedy practically adopted Danny. And Isabella was like a second mom to Delores. Trish wasn't into kids as much. She liked Danny, maybe not so much Delores. Particularly lately, I don't think Trish found working with her easy."

They stopped at the battered beige twelve-foot double doors. "Well, here we are," said Officer Johnson. "This is Lars Ivanho, our staff electrician."

"Hello, Detective," Lars said. Talbot had already introduced himself.

DJ still stared at Officer Johnson. He had a memory from ten years ago. Isabella Mendoza in the courtroom crying over her son. Standing next to her was her best friend, Hedy Scacht, and a sullen preteen girl with strawberry-blonde hair, cornflower blue eyes.

"Can you wait for me, Officer Johnson? I want to follow up on what we were just discussing."

"Sure. I'll be outside."

DJ twisted Evidence's leash in his hand and turned his attention to the now open closet that housed the breaker panel. He felt the pieces of the case clicking into place, secrets coming out of hiding. He tried to focus now on the electrician.

"Well," said Lars. "Here it is in all its glory."

DJ looked up. The interior of the closet was dirty beige, painted once decades ago and left to yellow and chip away in neglect. There was a riot of thin red and white wires, thick blue and gray cords, various long and narrow yellowed plastic panels, and one main steel box, flanked by a black-and-white rectangle of switches. On the floor of the closet sat a giant cube with flashing lights, an out-of-date modem.

"It's not pretty," said Lars. "But it works, most of the time. Just don't plug in an electric heater."

"It looks dangerous," said Talbot. "What's that about a heater?"

"Portable heaters eat up electricity. We tell folks not to use them, but it gets cold in this building. People plug them in and poof. It'll flip one of these breakers and the whole floor loses electricity. It's old patchwork technology. The building was constructed in 1961. Back then, there were half the number of offices. As the college grew, floors were subdivided into more offices and they kept adding more wires, more circuit breakers."

"Is this a fire hazard?" asked Talbot.

"Well, I can't say," said Lars. "But to fix it—we'd have to rewire the whole building, replace the breaker panel, all these wires and panels. At that point we may just want to tear it all down and start over."

"Do you think," DJ asked, "that someone could have turned off the electricity in this building by manipulating this breaker panel."

"Well, the closet is locked. Obviously, we don't want everyone having access to it. Now that would be a hazard."

"But if someone had the key," DJ asked, "could they turn off the electricity in this building? Would it be difficult?"

"Well, no. If the closet was unlocked, someone could turn off the electricity pretty easily. It wouldn't be hard if you knew what to do. Just flip the right switch and everything shuts down."

"Would there be an alarm? Would Facilities or Campus Safety be alerted?"

"No, it's old technology, it's autonomous. Someone would have to report it."

"Okay," said DJ. "Which switch?"

"This one," said Lars, pointing to a large gray switch with a red handle at the top of the largest panel. "There's other wires and subpanels, but this one here's the main one. Just like the switch on the electrical panel at your house."

"So it would be easy," said Talbot.

"Yes," said Lars, "but the closet is kept locked."

"And who has the keys?" asked DJ.

"I do," said Lars. "As of now, I'm the only staff electrician. Josef retired in August. Another key is kept in Facilities. But only Jerome Blight has access to that one; he has override keys to buildings that need to be signed out, but master utility keys are in a safe in his office. We like to keep anything related to the campus grid secure. That includes master keys to electrical panels, the underground tunnels, the Chiller—all those are highly restricted."

"I heard about the tunnels when I was here before," said DJ. "They're blocked off, right? No access?"

"Well, there are points of access for Facilities. We have plumbing lines, distribution pumps, and pipes for the Chiller. The tunnels are hidden behind steel doors and securely locked. There's an access point in Sliming, by the elevator on this floor. Years ago, students used to get inside the tunnels, roam underground, have a bit of mischief. We shut that down about fifteen years ago."

"What is a Chiller?" asked Talbot.

"It's the cooling system for campus. It's a large gray building between Campus Safety and Robinson Hall. Water runs through pipes into the Chiller, the water is cooled and sent back out through another set of underground pipes to buildings around campus."

"Okay," said DJ. "Back to the blackout on the night of the murder. So no one but Jerome Blight or you have access to this closet."

"Yes, that's right," said Lars. "Unless someone got the key out of Jerome's safe, but his security is tight."

"And what about Campus Safety?" asked DJ.

"No," said Lars. "They don't have utility keys."

"Okay," said DJ.

"Except for Hedy Scacht, of course. She has master keys for everything."

"What?" asked DJ.

"Well, the head of Campus Safety is responsible if anyone tries to access the campus power grid or get into the tunnels. So, like Jerome, she has keys to everything critical. But Hedy runs a tight ship. She keeps the keys with her at all times."

DJ thought of the large ring of keys she carried with her that first day in the lobby and every day since.

"Hey, Talbot," said DJ. "Why don't you finish up here. I'm going to talk to Officer Johnson outside."

"Sure, boss," said Talbot. "Don't forget Dolly Ruiz wants to see you." He was staring at the riot of red, white, and blue wires with a mixture of dismay and worry. "It looks mighty dangerous."

"It sure does," DJ said as he headed outside to talk to Officer Rodney Johnson.

CHAPTER 49

Delores

Officer Rodney Johnson stood outside the lawn adjacent to Sliming's first-floor exit. DJ freed Evidence from the leash to do her business. He walked over to Johnson, who offered him a cigarette. DJ shook his head.

"I know I shouldn't smoke on campus," Johnson said, "but the kids are gone and I feel like things are spiraling out of control. Two murders. We can't take a hit like this."

"Listen, Johnson," said DJ. "Go back to what you were saying about Hedy, Trish, and Danny's mom."

"Isabella Mendoza," said Johnson. "Yep, Hedy swore to watch over Danny after Isabella was diagnosed with breast cancer. I think the prison sentence did her in. Ummm, no offense, Detective."

"None taken," said DJ. Evidence had returned to his side; he bent down and clipped on her leash. "Tell me, who is Delores?"

"Well, we keep it on the down-low here, it's a big old secret. But you being the police and all, I guess it's okay to say. You know, faculty see Hedy as *the man*, I mean the police, and they don't like the police, no offense."

"Yeah, none taken," DJ said. The Professor LaVals of the world hated the police. But if they were in danger, they would dial nine-one-one and demand to be rescued.

"Delores is Hedy's daughter," said Johnson.

DJ was confused, silently filing through his memory.

"Wait," he said. "I remember when I was here before, Hedy had a kid with her. Wasn't her name Lee or something?"

"That was ten or eleven years ago," said Johnson. "They called her Dee, she goes by Dolly now. Dolly Ruiz. Ruiz, that's her father's last name, I guess. I don't ask. Kids grow up, you know. Choose their own names, their own life."

"Why didn't Hedy tell me Dolly was her daughter?" asked DJ.

"Like I said, it's on the down-down-low. Faculty are on a rant about nepotism here. When President Reese got hired, they got wind his wife was on the payroll and the shit hit the fan. Of course, the trustees negotiated the wife's salary, but didn't tell faculty. Anyway, it was ugly. Now Danny Mendoza, that was different. The head of faculty, Professor LaVal, encouraged President Reese to hire Danny. That was taking care of family. Isabella Mendoza was beloved and dying of cancer. Anyway, people here thought Danny was railroaded. I mean . . ."

"I know," said DJ, "no offense."

"Well, he was the cook's child, a poor Mexican kid, I mean Latino, or whatever they say nowadays. Anyway, people here were pissed that his white frat brothers got off scot-free. No offense . . . well, I was pissed too. That boy took the rap for a bunch of spoiled brats who poured alcohol down his throat. There were protests from the students and faculty. President Jordan White was pushed out; he called it retirement."

"I didn't know that," said DJ.

"After an interim leader," continued Johnson, "President Reese was hired. After the hoo-haw about the president's wife on payroll, it seemed wiser to keep Delores under wraps. The president likes Hedy, she's tough, has his back. And I'm sure it looks good for him to have a woman in the chief security position."

"And looks count for everything with Reese," said DJ.

Johnson shrugged. "I gotta say, Reese has balls, he wasn't going to let the faculty push him around. The man takes care of his own, you gotta say that for him. And Hedy was beside herself with worry. Delores had come back, started to get into trouble."

"Came back from where?"

"Hedy sent Delores to boarding school in Ojai for middle and high school."

"The Thatcher School? That must have been expensive."

"Sure," said Johnson. "But there's scholarships, and Hedy has connections. Besides, nothing was too good for Delores. I don't know that she was a great student. Went to community college, but really kind of drifted after high school. Hung out with the wrong crowd, bad choices and stuff. Anyway, Hedy got her a clerk job in Facilities, the same building as Campus Safety, to keep an eye on her."

"No shit," said DJ, now wishing that he had taken Officer Johnson up on that cigarette, but not wanting to interrupt him.

"It's the ugliest place at Hesperia, no windows, hidden away under the tennis courts. She was now Dolly Ruiz, with a different first and last name. Younger faculty didn't know who she was. And the old-timers, who knew Delores when she was a little girl, kept quiet. They believe in protecting their own. And Hedy has power."

The fiefdom again, hidden players and all their entanglements.

"How did Dolly Ruiz get from Facilities to working in Development with Will Bloom?"

"Well, I put that into the *no good deed goes unpunished category*. Delores, I mean Dolly, got tired of being tucked away in the dungeon, so to speak, and under her mother's thumb. When the president hired a rainmaker, lord knows the college needed money, Will Bloom arrived on campus with a big expense account and approval to hire whoever he wanted. Trish Ballentine was assigned as his executive assistant by the president, she knew how the college ran. Dolly applied for a transfer and Bloom hired her as an office clerk. She moved up quickly, to coordinator, manager, assistant director. Turns out Dolly was whip-smart in office politics; ambitious and hardworking to boot. That didn't sit well with Trish, watching a young girl get promoted from clerk to a management position above her. And Dolly, she hero-worshipped Will Bloom. I wouldn't say that to Hedy, of course."

"Is that why Hedy hated Will Bloom?"

Officer Johnson stopped his loquacious rendering of the past. He cleared his throat and swallowed hard. "Don't know," he said.

"I think you do, Officer Johnson," said DJ. "I'm not asking because I enjoy gossip. This is important. Two people are dead, and I need to know the lay of the land. The real story, not the fairy tale I've been fed by everyone else." DJ could see Officer Johnson's internal struggle as the man dropped his spent cigarette on the ground, stood up straight, cracked his shoulders, his neck, and came to a decision.

"All I know," said Johnson, "is that Hedy was furious that President Reese hired Will Bloom. She said she'd worked with him before. At Claremont—no, Chapman, that's right, it was Chapman. Hedy said her piece, but Reese wanted Bloom. He was aware of the rumors about the man, but he brought in big money wherever he worked. Reese told Hedy that everyone deserved a second chance. Hedy avoided Bloom and vice versa. Then the final insult was when Delores, I mean Dolly, transferred out of Facilities and into Will Bloom's office. She did it all right and proper. Human Resources said there was nothing Hedy could do about it."

"Listen," said DJ. "I need to speak to Hedy right now. You need to reach her ASAP."

Officer Johnson continued grinding the cigarette butt into the grass until it was indistinguishable from dirt.

"Yes, sir," he said. "I've been calling her every ten minutes when you were with Lars. She's not answering. Maybe she's still with the president."

"Try again," said DJ. "Now."

Officer Johnson hit speed dial and then the speaker. The phone rang until the message clicked on. The voice mail was full.

"Please call the president's office," said DJ. "See if she's still there."

Johnson dialed a number, listened and shook his head. "No one's answering."

"Please, keep trying. Call me the minute you find her." DJ handed him his card with his cell phone number.

Officer Johnson's fingers twitched, as if they were mourning the loss of the cigarette. "Yes, sir."

DJ went inside and found Talbot at the electrical closet with Lars. "Excuse us!" DJ pulled the younger detective away, down the hall.

"Please check again on the patrols. Make sure that they have eyes on Fern Lake and Warren Worthington."

"All right," said Talbot. "I checked in with them before we came downstairs."

DJ stared hard at Talbot.

"I'll check on them again, right now."

"And no one in or out. No one checking on the witnesses but you and me. And that includes Hesperia Campus Safety." Already on the phone, Talbot registered surprise, nodded yes. DJ handed Evidence's leash to Talbot. "I'm going to talk to Dolly Ruiz."

DJ quickly crossed campus to the Anderson Student Center housed beneath the cafeteria. He saw a series of offices with glass doors occupied by people he didn't recognize, other denizens of Hesperia College. Dolly was visible in the last office. DJ knocked and the young woman shoved something into a purse that sat on the floor.

"Come in," said Dolly. "Oh, finally. I'd about given up on you." Her face held a mixture of impatience and restrained excitement.

"I came as soon as I could," said DJ. "I need to ask you about your mother."

"My mother? Oh, you finally figured that out," said Dolly. "Brilliant detective work."

DJ entered the small office and closed the door. He was angry at the girl, her mother, and even more furious with himself. He sat opposite Delores "Dolly" Ruiz. The fair skin, blue eyes the color of a Mediterranean sea, the sharp tongue. She was Hedy's daughter, all right, without the heavy makeup, pantsuits, and height.

"Where is your mother?"

"I don't know," said Dolly. "She seems to be missing in action. But that's not why I asked to meet with you."

"Well, that's why I'm here," said DJ.

"Of course, it's always about her. But I think you'll change your mind, Detective," said Dolly, reaching down to her purse and retrieving an interoffice envelope. She pulled out an item and handed it to DJ Arias. It was the small blue notebook.

"I need you to carefully set that down on the desk." DJ took out plastic gloves and an evidence bag.

"Geez," said Dolly. "It's not a bomb. It's just Trish's stupid notebook."

"Where did you find this?"

"It was sitting in our temporary mail cubby."

"Here in this building?"

"No, I set up temp mail slots on Friday; in Sliming, on the third floor. I mean we can't access our offices and we need to get our mail. People send us checks and credit card numbers for donations. They need to get processed."

"Okay," said DJ, "and the notebook?"

"I came in early this morning to meet with Serena before the meeting. I hadn't checked the afternoon mail on Friday, after the police and everything. So, before the meeting, I checked the cubbies and I saw the notebook."

"In this envelope? In your slot?"

"No, just the notebook. It was in Trish's cubby. Isn't that weird? She must have left it here on Friday and someone put it in her mail slot."

DJ thought back to Bill Ballentine's interview at the station. He had said, "She was outside reading through the notebook on the balcony." No, Trish Ballentine had the notebook on Saturday in her condo. The only person who could have brought it to campus was the murderer.

"Where were you on Saturday night? From 9:00 p.m. to midnight?"

"What? I went out for a drink with a friend. I was upset."

"Your friend has a name?"

"Oh, for God's sake, you think I killed Trish Ballentine? Stole her notebook?"

"The friend's name?"

"It was my ex-boyfriend, Jesse. Jesse Luna. Okay. I met him at around nine thirty at Colombo's. We ended up at his apartment. All night. Hedy would be furious. She doesn't like him. She doesn't like anybody I associate with."

"Well, your list of associates is shrinking. Where are these cubbies located?" DJ asked.

Dolly looked sullen, and DJ saw the same adolescent girl who accompanied Hedy to the courtroom all those years ago. How could he have missed that?

"On an empty desk by the third-floor conference room."

"So anyone could have walked by and seen the mail slots? Could have left this notebook in Trish's cubby?"

"I guess so," said Dolly. "Anyone who had business on the third floor."

DJ thought about yesterday afternoon, Professor LaVal and Hedy Scacht rushing to the third floor for a meeting with President Reese.

He placed the notebook into the evidence bag and sealed it. "Why didn't you give this to me before the all-staff? Why did you wait?"

Dolly's face reddened. "I didn't think, I didn't know if it was important."

"You wanted to read it," said DJ. "Did you?"

"Yes," said Dolly. "Trish was always writing in that damn notebook, pasting in things. I wanted to know what she wrote about. You need to read the last entry. I think it explains everything, who had a motive to kill Will Bloom."

"Really, and who is that?"

Dolly leaned forward, her blue eyes glistening, and lowered her voice to a confidential whisper. "It was Serena Rigby."

"And why would Ms. Rigby have a motive?'

"Serena slept with Will. I can't believe it; it was a terrible lapse of judgment on his part. But according to Trish's notebook, it happened last week when Hoa was out of town! Ugh." Dolly trembled with exaggerated disgust.

DJ didn't look surprised, much to Dolly's chagrin.

"Don't you see," said Dolly, "Will must have realized his mistake. And Serena was probably all over him, wanting things, making demands. And then this morning at the meeting, when we learned about Hoa Phan and President Reese, I pieced it all together. Thursday afternoon when he found the suit, Will figured out that Hoa had slept with President Reese. That afternoon, he was like a different person, a wounded animal. You see? He must have gone to Serena for . . . for comfort, and something went terribly wrong! I bet he realized he still loved Hoa and tried to get away from Serena and she killed him in a jealous rage."

DJ stood up. "Come on," he said. "We'll talk while we walk."

"Where are we going?" Dolly asked. "To arrest Serena?" She couldn't keep the excitement from her voice.

"You're going to show me these cubbies. And I need to ask you about your mother."

"My mother? Really? I hand you the murderer and you want to talk about Mother?" DJ walked fast; Dolly had trouble keeping up.

"Do you remember Chapman College?" DJ asked.

"Barely. I was born when Hedy worked there. We came to Hesperia when I was four, I think. By the way, I call her Hedy because no one is supposed to know I'm her daughter."

"Yeah, I got that."

"Yeah, finally." Dolly rolled her eyes and couldn't suppress a giggle. "At least you found the dog."

DJ didn't like Dolly Ruiz. She was like a buoy on the water, bouncing along with no anchor, no sense of depth. Sarcastic, snitching on her colleagues, judgmental of others; Will Bloom's Girl Friday.

"And what about your father?"

Dolly slowed down. The subject seemed to penetrate her tin-plated armor.

"I never met him," said Dolly. "Apparently he was some dude Hedy was sleeping with. He was gone before I was born. Returned to his country of origin, Colombia or some such place. He never bothered to contact me."

"And that's all you know about him?"

"Yep," said Dolly. "That's it. It's been just me and Hedy for twenty-two years. And believe me, I don't blame dear old dad for skipping town, or the country. Hedy is no picnic."

"Seems like she's done a lot for you," said DJ.

"So she tells me, all the time." They were at the third-floor entrance of Sliming.

"All right," said DJ, "show me where you found the notebook."

As they entered the building, DJ texted Talbot to meet them by the third-floor conference room, and asked him to find Reese's assistant, Larissa Wren, to determine if Hedy Scacht was still with the president.

The mail cubby was a portable three-by-four-foot particleboard box with fifteen slots. It sat on an unoccupied U-shaped desk, to the right of the third-floor conference room. One had to walk around the return portion of the desk to reach the mail storage unit, but it was in plain sight. Dolly had used a labeler to designate the various people in the Development office. Will Bloom's name was first, followed by Trish Ballentine, Serena Rigby, Hoa Phan, and Dolly Ruiz. The other slots were inhabited by back-office workers and others relegated to the other side of the building. Will Bloom's cubby was full of correspondence.

"Who sorts the mail into these slots?" DJ asked.

"Trish does, I mean, she did," said Dolly. "Larissa arranged for the receptionist up here to sort the mail until we move back into our offices."

Talbot arrived from the elevator with Evidence in tow. "Hi," he said to Dolly with a shy smile.

"Hello, Detective." Dolly batted her eyelids. DJ watched as the younger man blushed.

After Talbot recovered from the charms of Miss Ruiz, he looked to DJ, addressing his earlier inquiry. "She left an hour ago."

DJ nodded. "Miss Dolly Ruiz has made a discovery." DJ pulled the clear evidence bag from his pocket and showed the blue notebook to Talbot.

"Wait, where was this?" Talbot asked.

"I found it in Trish's mail cubby," said Dolly triumphantly.

"But that's impossible . . ." DJ caught the younger man's eyes, shook his head, warned him to keep quiet. "Oh, I see."

"What's your mother's address?" DJ asked Dolly.

"You are obsessed with my mother," said Dolly. "She lives on Precipice Road, right off campus. Third house on the left, you can't miss it, it's painted pistachio green, like one of her pantsuits."

Talbot looked confused.

"Excuse us, Miss Ruiz," said DJ as he pulled Bobby Talbot into the third-floor entrance, away from Dolly and the receptionist.

"I don't understand," said Talbot. "Who is Dolly's mother?"

DJ quickly filled him in on the conversation with Officer Rodney Johnson, Dolly's discovery of the notebook, her story about Serena Rigby, and where the notebook was found.

"Ask Browning and Butter to question the receptionist and Larissa Wren. Find out if they saw the notebook yesterday or this morning."

"But it's impossible," said Talbot. "Mr. Ballentine said Trish had the notebook on Saturday. And if Dolly is Hedy Scacht's daughter, what does that mean exactly?"

"It means everybody has been hiding the truth, or lying, as we call it. It means the murderer returned the notebook after Trish's death."

"Goddamn," said Talbot. "This place is a puzzle."

DJ looked at his swearing Buddhist partner. He was right, it was a jigsaw puzzle with sharp edges.

"Our witnesses are safe?" DJ asked.

"Yep," said Talbot, "I checked in on my way upstairs."

DJ handed Talbot the notebook, secured in the evidence bag. "Check out the last entries before you lock it up. I'm heading to Hedy Scacht's house since she's missing in action." DJ picked up Evidence in his arms.

"You know who the murderer is?" Talbot asked.

"I'm 99.9 percent sure," said DJ, "that it's not Serena Rigby."

CHAPTER 50

Strange Angels

On Monday morning, Warren Worthington looked downstairs into his living room. The curtains were open. Sunlight bounced off polished wood tables, the empty soda bottles were gone, the pain pills tucked away. His home smelled like peppermint and lemon and appeared to sparkle with good cheer.

Officer Maria Lopez sat in his mother's chair watching his parents' old television. Warren had managed to keep her here for another day, in the same way he had exited the Saints of the Messiah church—by using his voice, just like the therapist had taught him. Officer Lopez jumped up at commercials, tidied another corner of the living room or ducked into the kitchen, opening and straightening cupboards. He was happy, living the life he had read about in his comic books.

Warren took a shower and dug out a clean T-shirt and pair of sweatpants from a drawer. It took him a long time to dress, but he could still manage it alone. He wasn't a doodlebug yet.

He heard the crackle of the radio downstairs. "Hey, Ricardo," said Officer Lopez. "Would you be a good partner and get me a *grande café* with cream and sugar and a couple of breakfast sandwiches?"

"No can do, Maria," said Officer Hermosillo. "I can't leave you."

"Well, Rico," said Maria Lopez, "unless you do as I request, I'm ending this partnership. I never want to see you again unless you get me a *grande café* with cream and sugar. It's morning, late morning at that, and I need it. Make that two *cafés*."

No answer.

"There's no caffeine in this house, only soda pop and something called Sanka from the last century. I'll buy yours. We have twelve more hours to go and I'm about to nod off."

Maria heard Hermosillo sigh, she was wearing him down. And she knew he also needed the coffee.

"Look, Rico, there's a Char Burger drive-through two minutes away, right down the street on York. Please, I'm begging you. Two *grande cafés* for me, and two for you. And get us breakfast burgers, and one for Mr. Worthington too. It will take you ten minutes tops."

More silence, then the crackle of the radio clicking on and off. "Please, *mi amigo.*"

"Ten-four," said Officer Hermosillo. "But if the bogeyman comes while I'm gone, it's your head."

"Whachya talking about, Rico. I ain't afraid of no ghosts."

"All right, lock up everything. I'll be back in ten."

"Locked and loaded my friend," Officer Maria Lopez flexed her muscles, did a little victory dance.

Warren, watching from the top of the stairs, was thrilled by this conversation and the impending breakfast sandwich. Warren managed his slide down the stairway, butt on one handrail, his good leg and hand braking his descent.

"Hey, Mr. Worthington," said Maria Lopez, "don't break a leg. Not on my watch. I'm here to protect you."

Warren smiled, a big lopsided toothy grin, as he landed perfectly intact on the first floor. He knew protecting people was futile, but he humored her.

After the accident, his mother claimed a guardian angel had protected him. When the surgeries and therapy ended, his heavenly guardian, weary at his lack of progress, must have flown off to a more promising ward.

That's when Warren become his own angel. The first time it happened, he was asleep. The long scars on his back burned and itched that night, the wings sprouted along the raised wounds on his back, then, as he pulled himself up, they unfurled, feathers and quills in a majestic spread. Like a dream, he was aloft, no stumbling about, no leaning on a cane. He flew. At first hitting his head, bumping into walls, soaring to the vaulted roof above the living room, scraping against the plaster.

"Okay, Mr. Worthington," said Officer Lopez, "you got your wish! It's official. Me and my partner are here for the next twelve hours."

"Thhhaaank hyou," he said. This morning, the two long scars on his back twinged with expectation. He held back the unfurling of his wings; it was a secret he kept to himself.

"No need to thank me. Now you sit down, okay? Okay! I have a surprise for you. Breakfast is coming, sir. What do you think of that? You are too thin, my friend. A strong wind could blow you away! Yep. A breakfast sandwich, and it's going to be delicious."

She managed to high-five Warren's right hand. Warren guffawed happily, his inner wings twitching with good cheer.

That first night, as he flew around the house, he found a rat in the kitchen, caught in Pa's mousetrap. The hammer bolt had slammed down just above its tail, right at the rectum. It squirmed in agony. Warren hovered above it, loosened the hammer's grip, freed the creature, who stopped and stared at Warren. He knew rats didn't talk, but still he heard, "Thank you, friend. One day I'll pay you back."

The next morning, Pa was furious.

"Damn rat must have chewed off its own tail."

"Language, Henry!" Ma had said.

This morning, Warren nodded at Officer Lopez and sat down in his favorite chair, imagining how delicious breakfast would taste.

"You're looking good, Mr. Worthington. Now, I've tidied up around here. I like to keep busy. You've got plenty of food in the fridge and pantry. But a word to the wise, for your future visitors. You need coffee. Some caffeine, Mr. Worthington. Okay? Okay! Now, I've thrown out anything that's expired."

Officer Lopez continued her monologue as she moved into the kitchen. The pitter-patter of her voice soothed him. Warren wasn't worried about visitors. No one came to *the haunted hole* and stayed after Mrs. Mendoza passed away, except for Officer Lopez, who was a perfect successor to Mrs. Mendoza and even answered her own questions.

Warren had carried down a DC comic book, *The Sword of Azrael*, not one of his favorites, but he had unearthed it last night when he had talked to the sad detective. He leafed through its pages as he listened to Officer Lopez. There was a knock on his front door. It was a quick rat-tat-tat-tat. Warren started to rise to answer it.

Officer Lopez came running out of the kitchen. "No, no. I got it," she said, holding a dish towel. "It's the surprise!"

Warren stayed put and looked down at the comic book. The figure of Azrael, a tall, square-shouldered, hooded figure, stared back at him from the page.

"Rico?" Office Lopez said. "That you?"

"Ten-four," a deep muffled voice answered.

Warren heard the locks click open. Then a crash as the door slammed hard against the wall. He struggled to turn toward the front entrance.

Officer Maria Lopez was a heap on the floor. And in the doorway, backlit by the sunlight of a glorious morning, was a tall, hulking figure: the silhouette of Azrael, the assassin, the angel of death.

The monster.

CHAPTER 51

Precipice Drive

Danny stood outside. He had pulled on a pair of dirty work pants and old T-shirt. Because of the murders, he was off work during the fall break from Hesperia. Watering the azaleas and other flowers, he checked out his own yard. One of the officers from the police unit waved at him, then yawned. A different set of LAPD partners had rotated in after the all-staff meeting.

Fern was inside the house talking to her father on the phone. She hadn't contacted him about Thursday night or her involvement in the case. It had only been reported in the *Los Angeles Times* this morning. Somehow, by a miracle of luck and probably by the manipulations of President Reese, the Friday discovery of Will Bloom's death at Hesperia had slipped through the weekend news cycle of professional football, a mass shooting in El Paso, Texas, and another national political scandal.

Deep in his high school football season, Fern's father, Coach Lake, had missed the president's late Friday afternoon email about early dismissal. Since the news had started to slip out in the media this morning, Fern's father had been calling and texting her nonstop.

"I don't want to tell him about my professor," said Fern.

"You don't have to," Danny said. "But you need to talk to him and tell him what happened to you in the olive grove."

"He'll want to drive out here and take me home."

"Well, you're over twenty-one. If you want to stay here, he can't make you leave. I don't think the police will let you go anyway."

Danny watched the water quench the dusty flowerbeds. The bubble that Fern and Danny had lived in for the past few days was about to burst, the real world would come rushing in. It was as inevitable as the ache in his chest.

Ten years of loneliness had heightened and accelerated his emotions into a compressed few days. Because of the murders, Fern and Danny had tumbled through a fast-forward relationship; meeting each other, facing secrets and mistakes, reconciliations, bared emotions, amazing sex, and mutual feelings that were developing into friendship and something deeper. He cared for and about this woman. And now Danny, an ex-convict, might have to meet her father. He didn't want to think about that right now.

He took the clippers to the hedge bordering his yard, looked down his block to the corner and across the street to Mr. Worthington's house. Danny felt fingers of unease creep up his spine. It was strange, the black-and-white police car was gone. The rear of a white Cadillac Escalade, brake lights flashing stood in front of the house facing the wrong direction. He dropped the clippers and ran into the street.

The SUV, tires peeling against the asphalt, tore away. Danny recognized that white Escalade with the winking panther logo, knew it was Hesperia Campus Safety. Worse, he knew the driver.

The two cops in the police car facing the opposite way looked up, and in their rearview mirror, saw Danny standing in the street. He turned and ran to them, frantically waving his arms.

The shard in the pocket of the dirty work pants he had thrown on to do yard work seemed to come alive, like a penknife stabbing his thigh.

Talbot took the blue notebook down to the Wick conference room. It was an oblong steno pad with a metal coil on top; the front cover was blue, the back cover thick cardboard. With gloved hands, he opened it, carefully flipping through the pages, briefly reading what caught his eye, until he reached the later entries. There were a few taped in copies of old receipts, but mostly written text.

Trish's handwriting was ornate, lots of curlicues, each "i" dotted with an open circle.

Talbot felt he was reading the diary of a teenager instead of tales from a dead woman.

If the handwriting was sweet, the content was not. There were lists of women, Shirley Jones, Bettina Lorek, Mindy Duran, more names Talbot didn't know, and one he did, Ravi LaVal. Trish had noted times of day they entered Will Bloom's office and when they exited, or didn't. If the women stayed past 5:00 p.m., the hour Trish left for home, she wrote COB (Close of Business). There were three- and four-hour lunches listed by woman, hour and date, the state of dress or undress on return. Phone messages were next, the name of the woman, dates with tally marks following it, presumably the number of times they called, as one might keep score in a cribbage match.

There was a whole subheading on Hoa Phan, copies of hotel and restaurant receipts with sloppy handwritten messages, one presumably in Bloom's handwriting that said *Will loves Hoa* with a crudely drawn heart and arrow. Will Bloom must have turned in the original receipts for recompense, either not caring or not worried that anyone would take notice or care. Bloom really did believe he was untouchable.

In the last few months of his life, when he was presumably in a relationship with Hoa Phan, there were notably fewer women listed, but he hadn't stopped. As if Will Bloom had to keep up his job as a womanizer even if his heart wasn't in it.

The last entry was narrative, short sentences and timestamps on Serena Rigby. So here was the source of the woman's scarlet blush. October fifteenth, the final week of Bloom's life. *Monday–WB in and out of SR's office. SR flushed and bothered coming out of WB's office. Tuesday–WB entering SR's office at 4:00 p.m.* The magic hour of five o'clock must have arrived, *SR and WB still locked in Rigby's office past COB. Voices heard within* was the last entry of that day. Talbot had a vision of Trish, ear to door, holding her steno pad and pen ready to take notes.

There was a final entry, *Wednesday–SR came in late this morning resembling a fat orange tabby, sated from drinking too much cream.*

A dramatic flourish, thought Talbot.

WB avoided SR. SR standing outside WB's office, ready to . . . the next page was blank, the writing cut off in midstream. Talbot searched for the rest of the sentence, the remainder of the sad short romance of WB and SR. The rest of the pages were untouched, no more entries.

Talbot closed the notebook, then, with gloved hands, held it by its covers, letting the pages dangle free. Then he did the opposite, held only the pages, gave it a shake, letting the covers fall free. There was something tangled in the metal coil between two pages. A minute shred of paper, caught between the written and empty sheets, as if a page or pages had been torn off, leaving behind a sliver of evidence. Someone had edited the story of Will Bloom's final days. The murderer didn't want the last entries to be read.

Talbot's cell phone buzzed.

DJ stood at the house on Precipice Drive, three doors down from the corner, on the left, painted pistachio green. There were piles of leaves scattered across the lawn. Evidence sniffed at several packages addressed to Ms. Hedy Scacht sitting on the small front porch, stepped over and pushed aside.

DJ rang the doorbell, then knocked loudly. No one answered. He tried the door; it was locked. He and Evidence moved around the house and peered through the front window. It was not the pristine home he expected of Hedy Scacht. There was a jacket draped across a sofa. Muddy tennis shoes sitting on the floor, dirt tracked on a beige carpet.

He and Evidence walked to the side of the house. He pushed into the thick shrubbery below a window and peered in. A messy dining room table was visible; a dish with a half-eaten croissant, a coffee cup stained with bright pink lipstick. Pushed into the center of the table, a half-empty glass of amber liquid that looked like whiskey sat next to an overflowing ashtray, as if the occupant had taken up chain-smoking. Next to the ashtray stood a bottle of red nail polish.

DJ had an image of Hedy this morning and her short scarlet nails. That was wrong, wasn't it? When he first saw Hedy on Friday, and in his memories of her form ten years ago, she had incredibly long tapered nails; he had wondered how she could do her job and maintain them. But on Friday, one of her nails was missing; the chink in her armor, he had thought.

The women DJ now dated had long painted nails. He wasn't a fan. They called them something—acrylics? That's right. They fussed over their talons. If there was a chip or a nick, they cried out as if wounded. DJ thought it was ridiculous.

Sure enough, on the table, next to a bowl of liquid, the discarded acrylic fingernails, looking like claws, were lined up. DJ counted them. There were nine; they were metallic silver, pulled off and discarded like the afterthought of a torturer.

The phone call came in from Talbot. The patrol at Danny Mendoza's house had reported in; there was an emergency with the other patrol. Something went down on the street in front of Mr. Worthington's house.

"Goddamn it," DJ said as he and Evidence jumped into his car. The last sentence Talbot said reverberated through his brain.

"The front door was open. Officer Lopez was down and no one can find Warren Worthington."

CHAPTER 52

Missing

DJ was at Warren Worthington's house in eight minutes. There were flashing lights from three patrol cars and an ambulance. Several neighbors were held back by a police officer. Inside, Officer Maria Lopez sat on the couch, pressing a cold compress to her head. Several LAPD officers and a medic stood around her. DJ put Evidence down on the floor.

Bobby Talbot waved him over to where he stood by Lopez.

"What happened?" DJ asked.

"Sir?" asked Officer Lopez. She looked confused as to her surroundings and who exactly DJ was. "Somebody was at the door."

"We found her," said a young police officer. "She was face down at the threshold, unconscious. Looks like she took a hit on the head."

Lopez's partner, Officer Ricardo Hermosillo, stood in the corner of the living room looking guilty. Three sloshed coffee cups and cold breakfast burgers sat discarded on a table.

"Officer Hermosillo went for coffee and food," said Talbot.

DJ stared him down and the young officer recoiled.

"I was only gone for nine minutes, maybe ten," said Hermosillo.

"Long enough," said DJ. He looked at Talbot. "Warren Worthington?"

"He's missing," said Talbot. "We have patrols searching the neighborhood and campus."

"No, no," said Officer Lopez, holding the compress to her left cheek and eye. "It's my fault. I needed coffee. I remember now. I heard a knock on the door. I thought it was Rico, bringing the coffee and food. I called out to him, someone answered ten-four, so I unlocked the deadbolts and then wham. Poor Mr. Worthington, it's my fault!"

"Indeed," said DJ. Talbot felt the contained rage emanating from Arias. Somehow, it was worse than the humiliation he had doled out a few days earlier.

"Tell me," DJ said to Officer Maria Lopez. "Did you at least see who did this to you? Can you identify them?"

"No," said Lopez. "It happened so fast, by the time I got to the third dead bolt and started to open the door, the perp slammed it into my face, cold-cocked me. I don't remember anything after that until the other patrol came in and revived me."

"So no ID," said DJ, "from anyone." His voice was intense. He had everyone's attention as the room grew quiet.

"Actually," said Talbot, "we do have something. Please, come with me." Talbot led the way into the kitchen. Before he followed, DJ stared into each face of the room's occupants, telegraphing his disgust.

The kitchen caught DJ off guard. With new light bulbs and a good scrubbing, it was now bright yellow. He looked around at the immaculate sink, tidy shelves, and clean floor.

"What happened in here?" he asked.

"Officer Lopez happened," said Talbot. He stood next to a small kitchen table and several chairs that had miraculously arisen from the previous clutter. In one of them sat Danny Mendoza. He looked miserable.

"He's the witness?" DJ asked Talbot. The younger detective nodded. "Who was it?" asked DJ. "Did you see who took Warren Worthington?"

Danny sat slumped in the chair. He didn't respond.

"Daniel, you are going to have to answer Detective Arias's questions," said Talbot.

Danny shook his head as if waking from a nightmare.

"What? I didn't see a person, just the car. I was doing work in my front yard. I looked down the street toward Mr. Worthington's house. I noticed the patrol car was gone. I saw the red lights of an SUV. It was Hesperia Campus Safety."

"Did you see the driver?" DJ asked.

"No, I ran into the street. I started jogging toward the truck, but it peeled off and drove away. I went to the patrol car at my house, told them what I saw."

"Wait, why didn't they see what was happening?"

"They were facing in the opposite direction. Away from Mr. Worthington's house. The SUV was already gone."

"Goddamn it," said DJ.

"The officers told me to stay put, made a U-turn, and sped to Warren's house."

"That's when they found Officer Lopez down," said Talbot, "and Mr. Worthington was missing."

"So you didn't see the perp either. We have no identification."

Talbot looked at Danny. "Tell Detective Arias," he prompted.

"I know the SUV. It's a white Cadillac Escalade. It was recovered by the police last year, reconditioned and given to Hesperia College to be used for Campus Safety. It has the Hesperia logo, the panther's face, on the back door."

"Okay," said DJ. "And who drives that car?" He already knew but needed to hear it from a witness.

"Only one person drives the Escalade."

"And that person is?"

"Look, she's not my mother, and she has issues with her own kid, but she's been in my corner through thick and thin. I can't imagine what came over her."

"The name, Danny!"

"Hedy. Hedy Scacht. Only Hedy drives the Escalade. She peeled down the street and sped away. I think she was heading toward campus."

"The murderer has been under our noses this whole time," said DJ. "She's cleaning up witnesses."

"I can't believe it," said Danny. "Why would she hurt Trish or Mr. Worthington?"

"Interesting you didn't mention Will Bloom," DJ said. "Why? Any other secrets you're hiding? You knew all along that Dolly Ruiz was Hedy's daughter."

"It wasn't my secret to tell. I've known Dolly since she was a kid. Our mothers were best friends."

"But you never told us about Dolly, did you, Danny?"

"Why would I?" Danny asked. "I'm not your snitch. Besides, I was worried about myself. You were trying to railroad me back to prison."

DJ took a step toward Danny. "Well, it's not too late."

Danny stood up, ready to defend himself.

"Goddamn it, calm down, both of you," said Talbot.

"Well, the Buddhist swears again," said DJ. The exhausted Talbot shook his head as if DJ were a pitiful old bull that had wandered into the kitchen and broken all the china.

"Can we focus on what's important right now?" said Talbot. "Finding Mr. Worthington."

"Before it's too late," said DJ, feeling chastened. "Wait, is Fern Lake safe?"

"Yes, we have an officer sitting with her inside the house. With specific instructions not to leave her alone."

"And make sure they don't answer the door," said DJ.

"Yes, they know. Now," said Talbot to Danny, "you thought the SUV was headed to campus. Can you think of where Hedy Scacht would go? Where would she hide? Mr. Worthington is vulnerable. We need to find him ASAP."

Danny sat back down at the table, his head in his hands.

"Hedy knows the campus better than anyone. There are a hundred places to hide: outbuildings, tunnels. With the students gone, there are ten residence halls with empty lounges, basements, parking garages. Hedy has keys to everything."

"All right," said DJ, getting himself under control. "Let's set up a command center in the conference room, call up Campus Safety and as many officers as Northeast can spare and search every inch of Hesperia."

"What about me?" Danny asked. "Do you want me to help search?"

Talbot and DJ exchanged looks, Talbot's concerned, DJ's unreadable.

"No," said DJ. "We'll have Campus Safety and the LAPD. I want you to sit tight with Fern Lake. In case your benefactor decides to come back looking for her."

Danny looked relieved. He wanted to be alone with Ferencia Lake, before her father and the world came rushing in. He couldn't fathom hunting down Hedy, a woman his mother had trusted in life and after her death to watch over him.

DJ left the house, slid into his Toyota Highlander with Evidence riding shotgun. He felt sick. He couldn't lose another witness, his only witness.

He conjured up the image of Warren Worthington. Something about the man had gotten to him. The intelligent eyes staring out from the destroyed body, seeing the world through his comic books. Managing to live alone in that crumbling house, walking through the neighborhood at night. Warren had kept going, collecting Christmas ornaments and shit in that old roller bag.

Warren Worthington was a survivor. DJ hoped against hope that he could survive Hedy Scacht.

CHAPTER 53

Passage

Sky, clouds, the tops of trees. Everything was speeding by.

Was Warren flying? Something was wrapped around his face, under his nose. It smelled sickly sweet. The dark came again.

He was bumped awake. He looked up and out the window; white buildings, red roofs. Then trees and branches scratched at the window.

Warren was on his back. He lay on the floor of an SUV, between the back and front seats, a rope coiled loosely around his body and legs. He bounced up and down. The center hump of the carpeted floor hit his spine, the raised scars burned, his wings curtailed, unable to unfurl. His arms were pinned beneath him, his legs useless. The worst had happened. He was a doodlebug. Unable to grab something, anything to pull himself up.

Someone was talking.

"He saw me. Goddamn it. You know I didn't want to do it. I had no choice. You heard her, she laughed. At me! And now I need to do this. This last thing and then it's done. No one needs to know. But someone knows. Your son. He saw me. He knows, he knows, he knows, he knows."

Warren didn't care what the voice was saying. Not really. He watched the world outside fly by the window. It was kind of beautiful, like a movie. Then everything stopped. He heard the screech of brakes. His body slammed hard against the bottom of the back seat. The SUV reversed course, then came to a halt. His body jerked again. Everything was dark.

He heard breathing, heavy breathing, as if the monster had run several miles. Because it was the monster, it had easily overpowered him. He remembered that now. The monster had invaded his home, hurt Officer Lopez, then came for him.

And now the voice started screaming.

CHAPTER 54

Search Party

By 3:00 p.m., the LAPD and Campus Safety had secured the perimeter of campus and were organized into two search units. Browning and Butter led the police team; Talbot, with Luke Benson, headed up Campus Safety. From the Wick Conference Room, DJ directed their efforts, manned communications, and indicated cleared locations by drawing an X on a large campus map Facilities had provided. They had first cleared Hedy's house. It was empty.

The police unit searched the northern boundary of campus, beginning with Malo Hill, the soccer and baseball fields, and their adjacent outbuildings. Campus Safety began on the eastern side of lower campus, closest to Danny and Warren's neighborhood. This area included a science building, the alumni house, and the softball and football fields.

At 4:35 p.m., Campus Safety found the abandoned white Cadillac Escalade in an old garage behind the Athletic Facilities. Before AstroTurf was installed, mowing and aeration equipment for the football field had been stored inside. The garage had stood empty for years, overgrown trees and shrubs obscured the access road behind the stadium with its thin asphalt tributary to Facilities. After a quick inventory, one golf cart was reported missing from the Facilities parking lot.

With the 3:00 p.m. early dismissal, Hesperia was now a ghost town haunted by LAPD and Campus Safety officers on foot and in cars crisscrossing campus. No one had sighted Hedy, Warren, or the golf cart.

The search was now focused on concentric circles, outward from the area where the golf cart had been housed. One team searched the music buildings and olive grove. The other took on the Facility and Campus Safety offices, a bunker-like building beneath the tennis courts. Windowless and connected by long hallways, it was a maze of small boxlike spaces. It took thirty-five minutes and a unit of five officers to clear it.

By then, dusk had fallen. The adjacent athletic facilities with locker and weight rooms, offices, and outbuildings were another tangle of spaces that needed to be searched. As if by magic, the campus lit up, all the exterior lights turned on by Jerome Blight, the Facilities director.

The officers had reconvened on the football field, ready to head to Sliming for a meal, flashlights, and jackets. Officer Kathy Browning looked through a chain-link fence at the old service road with the abandoned garage and area of overgrown shrubbery that bordered the street. Barely visible in the descending gloom sat a squat, dusty shack, its windows papered over with aluminum foil.

"What is that?" Browning asked Luke Benson, who stood close by. "I don't see any exterior lights."

"The rat lab," said Benson. "It's off the main electrical grid. No one wants to search that. Besides, we don't have the key, not even Hedy. That's the psychology department's bailiwick."

Kathy Browning stared at Luke. "Someone needs to check it out," she said. "Once we get the flashlights."

"I'll flip you for that one," said Luke Benson.

"I sincerely hope you lose," said Kathy Browning.

The rest of campus would need to be searched tonight.

At 6:30 p.m., Talbot, Officers Browning and Butter, and Luke Benson were gathering the searchers inside the Wick Conference Room. DJ stood outside Sliming with Evidence, watching them trudge in. They looked tired and defeated.

It was a cold night, a scent of rain in the air. DJ thought he heard far-off thunder above the San Gabriel Mountains, but maybe it was dread pounding in his ears. The president's office had approved voluntary overtime for the cafeteria workers so they could make sandwiches and provide hot coffee for the troops. With the lights activated, Hesperia glowed in the dark like a starship in space.

As the searchers ate dinner, Talbot came outside with two coffees and handed one to DJ.

"We've got an officer with Dolly Ruiz," said Talbot. "She's secured in the third-floor conference room. Dolly is phoning Hedy every fifteen minutes or so. No answer, and her mailbox is full."

DJ looked up to the third floor of Sliming, the cockpit of this glowing campus spaceship.

"And Worthington?" DJ asked. "He doesn't have a cell phone?"

"He has one of those RAZ phones, for people with disabilities. It's sitting in his house on a table by the door."

"Yeah, I figured as much," said DJ, watching the building lights flicker like candles across campus.

The elevator doors opened, and President Bill Reese strode into the lobby, his gimlet eyes, beneath the gleaming head of hair, taking in the activity of the conference room. He had ditched the Brooks Brothers suit for a tight blue windbreaker and black jeans.

He saw the two detectives through the glass walls and stepped outside. Reese addressed himself to Detective Bobby Talbot.

"I came down for an update on the search. I find it impossible to believe that Hedy Scacht has anything to do with any of this."

"I'm sure it's difficult to hear, sir," said Talbot, "but it's our working assumption."

"But why? Why would she do something like this?" Reese asked. "I trusted her completely."

"She hated Will Bloom," said DJ. "Hedy told me that he was a notorious womanizer. She'd worked with him before."

"People may disapprove of others, but they don't go around murdering them," Reese said coldly, still not addressing DJ.

"Some do," said DJ.

Reese's penetrating blue eyes slid over to DJ. "And therefore, we have men like you," said Reese as though he addressed a peasant who cleaned up sewer waste.

"You hired a sexual predator," DJ said, "because you wanted the money he could raise. Your director of Campus Safety, a very powerful and seasoned woman, warned you about Will Bloom. She told you he was bad news, but you ignored her. Men like me have to clean up after men like you."

"I've said it before, but consider it a promise. When this is over, my mission will be to make sure that you never work another murder case in your life. You'll be cleaning toilets at your precinct house."

DJ shook his head at President Reese.

"You're not thinking clearly. You placed your complete trust in Hedy Scacht. You made her the law at Hesperia. She has the key to every door on campus and the safety of all your students, faculty, and staff in her hands. She has murdered two employees on your watch. And God help us, she doesn't murder a private citizen, a disabled man who has no defenses."

President Reese opened his mouth to say something but couldn't find the words to counter DJ Arias.

"I don't think your old friend, the chief of police," said DJ, "will be taking your suggestions, or even your phone calls, for that matter, once this story hits the media."

President Reese had gone white, with fury or dawning comprehension—it was difficult to tell.

Talbot was too exhausted to stop DJ, and part of him agreed with his partner. Will Bloom had been a narcissist, a predator, a destroyer. After reading Trish Ballentine's notebook, Talbot had felt a worm turn in his gut; all the women Will Bloom dallied with, then discarded, leaving behind a trail of broken relationships. Everyone knew it. President Reese had to know, but they all ignored it, made excuses because Bloom brought in money. It was easier and to their advantage to look the other way.

DJ's cell phone buzzed. It was Campus Safety Officer Rodney Johnson. "Detective Arias," said Johnson, "I got a message. From Hedy. I'm one minute away from Sliming. You need to hear it."

"All right," said DJ. "I'm standing outside."

DJ looked at Talbot. "Hedy sent a message to Rodney Johnson. He's on his way."

A few minutes later Officer Johnson walked up to the three men.

"Let's move inside the lobby," said Talbot. "It's freezing out here."

Under the interior lights, it appeared Rodney Johnson had aged five years in the past few hours. His face was ashen, his eyes bloodshot. He held out his phone and put it on speaker.

"She didn't call, just sent the message." He hit play.

"ROMEO/JULIET, it's HOTEL/SIERRA. By now, you've probably heard some things about me, about what I've done. You know what I always say, *You can apologize or you can fix it.* I did what I had to do. I explained myself to the one person I owed an answer. I sent her a letter. It's up to her to judge me. Anyway, please give this message to Dr. Doom."

Rodney paused the message and looked up at DJ.

"That's you," he said.

"Yeah, I know," said DJ, "no offense."

Rodney clicked on the speaker again.

"I'll be waiting for Arias in the Chiller. Tell him he has to come alone with no weapons. If he does that, I'll think about turning myself in. If he comes with anyone else, I'm armed, and I'll do damage. He's already seen what I'm capable of, so tell him not to fuck with me."

There was a pause. "ROMEO, one more thing. I know the news about Delores, I mean Dolly, is out there. Don't blame yourself or Danny. You're not snitches, or rats. I couldn't hide anymore. Believe me, you can't keep things inside forever. Goodbye, ROMEO. HOTEL/SIERRA, over and out."

"Okay, that's it." Officer Rodney Johnson sniffled. "I got the keys from Jerome Blight. To the Chiller."

"Wait," said Talbot. "Remind me again, what's the Chiller?"

"It's the utility building," said Johnson, "tucked into the hillside below Robinson Hall. It takes in heat, converts it, and sends cold water through underground pipes all across campus. Regulates the temperature, keeps everything cool."

"It's dark inside and cavernous," said President Reese, "even during the day. It houses huge pipes and pumping stations. There's a hundred places to hide in there."

DJ glanced at Reese. With the phone message, he had quickly slipped from disbelief that Hedy was their suspect to giving intel on the building she was holed up in.

"All right," DJ said to Talbot and Johnson. "Let's get moving. Johnson, think about the best way for me to get inside the Chiller. Talbot, let's discuss how to proceed with the troops. We need to arm everyone with the flashlights, keep a group focused on finding Warren Worthington. Hedy didn't mention him in that message. We have to hope that he's still alive, out there somewhere."

The three other men, Talbot, Johnson, and Reese, met his eyes. Their faces were grim. When one of their own, a person who swore to keep people safe, went bad, there weren't enough flashlights to chase away the dark.

CHAPTER 55

Sacrament

Hedy stared at her phone, then threw it high up toward the branches. It arced over the chain-link fence and disappeared into scrub and a bog of leaves.

She wouldn't be traced, wouldn't need it again.

Slipping out of her hiding place behind the shed, she stayed low, close to the perimeter fence, and crossed the road. She unlocked the door and entered into darkness and the hum of water.

Like a baptism. You end up where you began, she thought.

Parts of herself had fallen away: the phone, her elegant long fingernails, her friend Isabella Mendoza, her daughter.

Hedy felt no kindness from her daughter. She knew there was the sinew of connection, commonality of blood.

Well, kindness was hard, and didn't she know it. Hard as a diamond, just as rare.

Hedy had felt no kindness toward her own parents. Her father used to drink. He was a bad man when he drank, almost lost his family. Her mother, Delores, always apologized for him.

When Hedy was four and her brother seven, he sobered up. Her mother said they had to put the past behind them, not think about the bad things. Those memories were locked away, in a vault, inside her chest. Her mother's finger circled her own chest, tapped her heart with a closed fist. "Locked, no key."

But now, in the hum of the Chiller, Hedy remembered the angels' singing. She remembered everything; the bitter bright of the winter day, the crisp air, the motor's whine as gears shifted, the lavender scent of Mother's Jean Nate perfume.

Hedy was almost four, sitting in the back seat of their old VW van. She heard the angels, a sustained heavenly chorus. It made her smile. They sang to her at odd times. That day they were glorious and loud. She wondered why no one else heard the chime of their voices.

"Do you hear them, Mama?"

Her mother didn't answer. Father was driving, drunk again. The old VW van screeched around the corner like a tin can skidding on ice.

"Mama, Mama, do you hear them?" she asked again. "The angels are singing to me, Mama!"

Her mother sat very still.

"Mama?" Hedy whined and kicked at the back of her mother's seat. Mama stared straight ahead.

The slap from her father was backhanded and hard. It rattled Hedy's teeth. A welt from his school ring rippled across the apple of her cheek. Hedy's father used to pitch for his high school baseball team. Power with a deadly aim.

Hedy was stunned, she heard crying. It was her mother, knowing she would be next. Her brother sat beside Hedy, eyes closed, a dark bloom on the crotch of his pants. Father's right arm swung wildly toward her mother, his left hand pulled at the steering wheel, sending the van into a jagged turn. The old metal tin can skittered across the center line, hit a patch of loose shoulder dirt, tilted sideways, then rolled over and over again.

Time tumbled, slowed down. Hedy and her brother's arms, hands, and tops of their heads banged against the roof, the sides, the floor of the van. Their bodies, Hedy on top of her brother, finally piled against the sliding door. The angels sang even louder, a crescendo of voices that drowned out her mother's screams, her father's curses, her brother's silence. The turn signal stuttered, clicked, then died. Hedy heard the far-off sirens coming closer. Inside, the van was quiet. The angels stopped singing. She never heard them again.

That was the bad thing they never talked about. Her father almost lost his family. It was a secret, locked away.

Father stopped drinking; he took up chain-smoking and attended meetings every night, then every other night. Each time he looked at Hedy, his haunted eyes searched her face, then darted away. He was looking for the scar his ring had made. But it wasn't visible. The scar was inside.

And when another bad thing happened, years later, when she was older, Hedy said nothing. No one would have believed her anyway, not twenty-two years ago, a woman accusing a man everyone loved. There were no sexual assault advocates, no hotlines. She had no women friends to hold her hand or wipe her tears.

Besides, all her life Hedy had been expecting the next wound. When it came, she put it away inside, where it scabbed over and curdled into silence.

The hum of water, the turbines churning brought her back into the present. A baptism. No, the time had come for confession. Not to a priest or a haunted weakling like her father. She wanted an equal, someone who locked up people who did bad things. Someone fearless. DJ Arias would hear her confession and then Hedy would decide what to do next.

The years of her life had passed so quickly. Some days were astonishing, some beautiful. When her daughter was born, Hedy had counted five fingers on each hand, stared into the eyes of a baby who saw the world for the first time.

There were also terrible times; the rape, hurt, shame. These she locked away into the vault, where silence burgeoned, black dust covering every surface.

She had learned that worse than anger and pain were their absence; the numb, the void, the null. Walking through life as a sleepwalker. But under the scabbed-over wounds, Hedy's scars seethed sharp and bright.

And when the rage surfaced, erupted, lifted its ruthless head, fury reigned. Hedy had roared. The bloodletting; the smell of copper, strangled cries, ripping flesh. She had done what she had to do.

Now she was spent. The little girl with the welt on her soul stood alone and silent.

No kindness offered. No angel sang.

She circled her chest, her fist pounded her heart.

With a gun in her pocket, she waited.

CHAPTER 56

Chiller

DJ Arias walked across the deserted campus, down an exterior stairway to a road that overlooked the football field and tennis courts.

He had entrusted Talbot to keep Evidence safe.

"If anything happens to me, contact Dr. Lillian Sing. She's my vet, and my ex-wife." Lillian may have written off DJ, but she'd never turn away an orphaned dog.

The night was cold, crystal clear. The biting air slipped between DJ's clothes and skin, penetrated his bones. On his right stood Robinson Hall, the largest auditorium on campus. Exterior lamps illuminated the neoclassical entrance and its four columns.

Further down, level with the road on the opposite side, DJ saw the flat roof of a building tucked into the hillside below. It was the Chiller.

The roof was fenced with an access gate. It was open. Just for him. He stepped onto its smooth concrete surface; two robot-shaped vents spewed out hot air, and gray buzzing boxes stood sentry at each corner of the building. He walked over to a walled ledge and looked out.

Suspended above the empty football field and tennis courts, floodlights burned bright like stars fallen to earth. Looking down, DJ figured the height of the building was three stories above the road below.

He had discussed the two points of entry with Officer Johnson. The bottom entrance would place him in the belly of the beast, exposed with no place to hide, the red exit light above the door heralding his arrival. The access point from the roof would place him inside an alcove where his eyes could adjust to the dark. He would need to descend a long steel stairway into the bowels of the building. Both ways made him vulnerable if Hedy wanted to shoot, but this route would give him time to assess the situation.

He didn't need the keys that Officer Johnson provided. The roof entrance was cracked open. Just for him. One way or the other, the case was coming to a close.

DJ's gun was tucked into the back of his waistband, his down jacket covering its bulk. Walking through the door of the Chiller, he paused in the alcove and waited for his pupils to adjust to the dark interior.

"Hedy," he called out. "It's DJ Arias. I got your message. I'm here, alone, like you asked."

He walked to the top of the stairway, paused, took a breath, then slowly began to descend. Emergency lights glowed from the bottom floor, muted by purple glass encased in steel grids. Hedy's override key had cut off any bright lights.

Massive white pipes ran the length of the immaculate interior. Signage was placed on the piping and walls. Green arrows pointed west. Blue arrows ran perpendicular. Red arrows pointed east.

DJ heard the pervasive hum of the Chiller's pumps, water pouring in, churning turbines stripping away heat; frigid water spewing out through underground tunnels to cool buildings and residence halls. He was inside a massive organ, the heart of campus.

It was a good place to hide.

"Stop right there," Hedy said. "Arms up where I can see them."

With the unfamiliar acoustics and the turbines' hum, he wasn't sure where her voice originated. DJ stopped at the bottom step, lifted his hands.

"Hedy," he said. "Let's talk. We can find a way to bring this to a peaceful end."

"It's too late for that."

"Where's Warren Worthington, Hedy? If he's alive, that will count in your favor."

"Always such a sweet talker," she said, ignoring his interest in Mr. Worthington. "The two other deaths swept under the rug, huh?"

"I imagine Will Bloom was self-defense. Right?"

A humorless cackle emanated from the shadows behind him; he turned toward the unsettling sound. "Yeah, self-defense, twenty-two years too late."

DJ needed to keep her talking. "I don't know what that means, tell me."

"You're forgetting Trish Ballentine," she said, again ignoring his attempt to lead the conversation. "But you aren't really forgetting Trish, are you?" There was a pause. "I won't."

DJ turned left; arms raised.

Her voice ricocheted like a basketball bouncing across a warped wood floor.

"Trish Ballentine was a busybody, right?" DJ said. "Couldn't mind her own business."

"A busybody," said Hedy. "Angry she had to work for Will Bloom, pissed at Dolly being promoted above her." Then in a deadly accurate Southern accent, *"Fortune has passed me by,"* Hedy said, mocking Trish Ballentine. "She made me fight her for that damn notebook."

"Hedy," DJ said, walking a few steps away from the stairway. "Come out. Let's talk."

"But it wasn't just the notebook. Trish was such a bitch. She said, *Like mother, like daughter.* Then she laughed. At me."

DJ heard the agitation in the woman's voice. She was defending her actions, even now.

"Hedy, let's get you out of here. Up to the roof. Let's get some air."

"Do you understand? That stupid cow laughed. At what happened to me. Everything repeating, repeating, repeating itself."

"Hedy," he said. "Let's go somewhere quiet where we can talk."

"How is Delores?" Hedy asked. "I hate that name Dolly. What a fucking ridiculous name. Is she okay?"

"Dolly, Delores, is safe. She's worried about you."

"Is she? I don't think she'll ever forgive me. And I did it all for her."

"Give her time."

DJ couldn't think of anything more encouraging to say about Dolly, Delores Ruiz. "Besides, you have a lot to live for. Delores isn't everything."

There was a long pause.

"She is to me," said Hedy.

DJ turned that over in his mind. Deserved or not, Dolly Ruiz was the object and downfall of Hedy's life.

Hedy walked into a spot of bruised light. She held a gun.

"You don't know what it's like to love someone more than yourself. Worry about them day and night. Would die to protect them."

DJ slowly turned, hands up, and faced her.

"Well then, you have a reason to end this. Peacefully. Your daughter needs you."

"I tried to tell her about Will Bloom. What he was, the monster inside. But all she saw was the shiny bright exterior; the cocktails, the witty banter, the 'fun.' How could I say such terrible things about Will. Poor Will."

"She's young." DJ didn't say "and spoiled." Not a spoiled brat. No, Dolly Delores Ruiz was damaged, something inside of her missing.

"I couldn't tell her," Hedy said, "the truth."

DJ still didn't know what pushed Hedy Scacht over the edge. He inched forward. Hedy kept the gun pointed at him, but she seemed to be looking through him, into a past that wasn't pretty.

"Hedy, what happened to you? All those years ago?"

"What happened?" she asked. "I met Will Bloom at Chapman College. And I died."

One shaft of dim light fell on Hedy Scacht's face. "Inside."

Her eyes had the cold silver sheen he'd seen at the meeting, a sea turned to ice. DJ shivered. There was something inhuman about those eyes. He wondered if they were the last thing Will Bloom and Trish Ballentine saw before their death. If they would be the last thing he saw.

"But then my daughter was born. She was a miracle. Everything changed. I became a different person. I kept it all together like a machine. Click, click, click." Hedy nodded the barrel of the gun from DJ's heart to his head. She chuckled.

The sound and action unsettled DJ.

"You knew Will Bloom at Chapman?" he asked.

"Just an acquaintance."

"What happened?"

"He got into trouble. I found out later that he was sleeping with a student. Only none of us knew that then. It was kept confidential. The trouble men get into is always confidential, isn't it?"

"I'm afraid it often is," said DJ.

"A group of us had met for cocktails. And Will Bloom joined us. I only saw that shiny bright exterior. He was charming, gracious, polite. He said he was being run out of Chapman, unfairly. I felt sorry for him."

"And what happened?"

Hedy spoke in a monotone voice, seemingly disinterested in the goings-on she described. "He walked me home and I offered him a nightcap. He was a vampire waiting at the threshold and I invited him inside. I didn't see what he was until it was too late. He must have been drinking all day. The anger, the rage, the need to destroy was burning inside of him, just under the skin. I can still feel that monster on top of me, inside of me. Holding me down, grunting like a pig. Even now, with a sword through his heart, he's still holding me down."

DJ didn't know what to say.

"Hedy. I'm sorry." And he was. That men committed such terrible deeds was why DJ became a cop.

"Two years ago," Hedy continued, "Will Bloom arrived at Hesperia and acted like we were just old acquaintances. He'd wiped away his memory of what he did to me all those years ago. I was just another fuck in the scorched earth of Will Bloom's indiscretions."

DJ stayed quiet. Hedy wasn't looking into the past anymore, she was re-living it.

"And then my daughter. She runs right into the arms of that monster."

"Did you tell Dolly? What he did to you?"

"I never told anyone," said Hedy. "Except Isabella Mendoza. She said I should tell Dolly, but how could I? I'd told my daughter a fairy tale about her father, and she would know it was all a lie, an unforgivable lie. It was too late."

DJ was missing something, some part of Hedy's story eluded him.

"A fairy tale?"

"I'd made up a story. About a man who had to leave the country—his visa expired, he had family issues in Colombia, and was never heard from again."

"You mean Dolly's father," said DJ. "The man named Ruiz. He wasn't real?"

"Oh, there was a man with that name, and he did have to return to Colom-bia, but he wasn't her father."

"He wasn't," repeated DJ, "her father."

"And when Isabella died, my secret was safe. And I knew what I had to do. Before it was too late."

"Your secret?" Something was forming at the back of DJ's mind, dark, sick, and loathsome.

"But it was already too late. I saw them, Thursday afternoon. I was in Dol-ly's office waiting for her. You can see right into Will Bloom's window through the courtyard when the drapes are open."

"What did you see?"

Her voice faltered. "He grabbed Dolly, pulled her to him, and then he kissed her," said Hedy. "And that was it. All the pieces fell into place. And I knew what I had to do."

DJ said nothing, waited for her to continue.

"I'd run into him earlier, in the hallway. He was already three sheets to the wind. I told him I was stopping by after work. I needed to talk to him. You know what Bloom said to me? 'Coming back for more?'" She emitted a mirth-less laugh. "And I said, 'Yes, I've been thinking about it for years.' And it was true. I had been thinking about what I would do to him if I had the chance."

"And what did you do?" DJ asked.

"It was easy. I threw the switch, shut down the lights, made sure every-one else was out of Sliming. I entered the courtyard through the other door.

When he left to go to the bathroom, I took down that ridiculous sword and waited outside. He was wasted, trying to get himself ready for a repeat conquest, one more fuck. His back was facing me, he was trying to get it up. It was pathetic. All the pain that man caused, and all the pain he was going to cause hung between his legs, and he couldn't get it up. It was really a mercy killing. He was a destroyer of women. So I ended it. For him, for me. For Delores."

DJ saw it all as she described it. If he wasn't a cop he might see the poetic justice in the act. But he was a cop, and he had a job to do.

"I understand why you did it, Hedy," said DJ. "You wanted to save your daughter from Will Bloom, from what he did to you."

Hedy snapped out of her reverie and returned to the present. She bent her head to one side as if studying a new specimen of insect: Phylum Arthropoda Arias. "You still don't understand, do you?"

"I do," he said. But he stared at Hedy's silver eyes, everything human leached away. "I mean, I think so." DJ didn't want to examine the hideous thought that had formed in his mind.

Hedy shook her head. "Men are thick as a cord of wood," she said.

DJ didn't respond since the gun Hedy held was still trained on his heart.

"Trish knew or guessed. She had written things in that notebook about Dolly and Will Bloom, how close they were, how 'kindred.' And about me. I'd been trying to see Bloom for days, to reason with him. He was going to promote Dolly again and then he would own her. Trish recorded my phone calls, my attempts to see him in her stupid blue notebook. I couldn't have that. I couldn't be connected to Bloom before he died. Even worse, she figured it out. That night, fighting over the notebook, she said, *history repeating itself.*"

"History repeating," said DJ to himself. Those words again.

"And then in that goddamn hick accent she said, 'Oh my God, this time he'd be sleeping with his own daughter!'"

There it was. DJ could think of nothing to say.

"Then she laughed," said Hedy. "At me."

DJ felt sick to his stomach. The insatiable Will Bloom devouring female after female, until he finally consumed his own flesh and blood.

And Trish Ballentine, keeping score of Bloom's victims in her notebook, her morbid excitement at his death. Trish laughed; proud she had figured out a puzzle. Ignorant that she was putting a stake through the heart of the woman she laughed at. DJ inched toward Hedy, one hand outstretched.

"Don't come any closer," she warned.

DJ stopped and lowered his arm.

"Hedy, I'm sorry. For everything that happened to you."

"You think I'll get a pass for killing an incestuous bastard and that piece of Southern taffy?"

"I think people will understand," said DJ. "I do."

"No one will understand. No one must ever know."

"And your daughter?"

"I sent her a version of the truth with the ugliest parts missing."

Missing, that word again associated with Delores "Dolly" Ruiz. Something had been missing inside of her for years. And when Dolly found the missing piece of the puzzle, she was like a moth to the light.

"You need to put the gun down and come with me."

"You need to turn around and go back up those stairs. I'll be right behind you."

DJ was 99 percent sure that Hedy wouldn't shoot him in the back. But he was betting on a woman who had lost everything. To a monster. It had taken twenty-two years for the past to catch up to Will Bloom. And when it did, Hedy had become the monster.

"Hedy, where is Warren Worthington?" DJ asked as he slowly walked up the metal stairway. "Is he okay?"

"Have you met Worthington?" Hedy asked. "He didn't start out okay."

"Is he alive?" DJ asked.

"You know, he thinks he has wings? He thinks he's a fucking angel."

"Where is he, Hedy?" They were at the exterior door.

"Outside, now!" she barked.

DJ was worried. If everything was going the way Talbot and DJ had planned, the roof and the road along Robinson Hall would be empty. If no one had screwed up or panicked. DJ stepped out onto the Chiller's roof and tried not to sigh in relief. No one was in sight. Hedy followed behind him out the door.

"Turn around." She aimed the gun at DJ's chest. Outside, in the ambient light he could see it was a Glock 23 she held in her right hand with its short blood-red fingernails. He should have known that first day, with that lone fingernail torn off the nail bed, that something was wrong with her. Christ, the woman never had a hair out of place since he had met her ten years ago.

Hedy wasn't looking into the ugly past anymore, she was fully in the present, assessing her situation and him. It occurred to DJ that he was the only one alive who knew her secret. He couldn't twitch without her responding; he certainly couldn't pull his gun.

"Don't think about it," she said as if reading his mind. "I'll do it."

"Do what?" he asked. "Shoot me?"

"That's the idea," she said.

"Hedy, where's Warren Worthington? I can't believe you would hurt him."

"He can identify me. I escaped Sliming through the tunnel, then exited by the olive grove. If it wasn't for that half-wit and the stupid girl, I would have gotten away. And the murder of Will Bloom would have been an unsolved mystery."

"Worthington is an innocent."

"He's a witness," said Hedy. "Not an innocent or an angel." She eked out a sad smile and said, "More like a stool pigeon."

DJ had to make his move. Hedy was facing him and Robinson Hall, but behind her, DJ could detect the faint reflection of red and blue lights from the street three stories below the Chiller. They should have cut the lights, but there's always someone wanting to show off.

"You know what they say about pigeons, right?" Hedy asked.

DJ answered without thinking, "Rats with wings." Something ticked in DJ's brain. Hedy cocked the gun, and DJ jumped forward.

He tried to wrestle the weapon away from her. The gun went off, grazing the bone of his arm. It felt like a thousand wasp stings. He fell back, wrenched by pain. She took control of the gun, stuck the barrel against the soft hollow beneath her chin.

"Hedy," he said. "Don't."

The world-weary smile reappeared for a second. "Don't worry about Worthington," Hedy said. "He flew away."

She pulled the trigger. The back part of her head blew into the air, a miniature firework display of brain splatter and blood.

DJ ran to her. He knelt down and tried to stanch the bleeding around her head. Police were rushing in.

He held up his good hand.

"I'm okay," he said. "Hedy Scacht is down."

DJ looked down at her and whispered, "Your secret is safe with me."

Her eyes, open, pale and facing the sky, were cold and distant as the stars.

CHAPTER 57

Wings

Warren Worthington didn't fly away.

Officer Rodney Johnson had puzzled over Hedy's voice mail, particularly the last part addressed to ROMEO. He decided it was a coded message.

Convincing Talbot to accompany him, Johnson carried giant bolt cutters across the football field, through the rusted gate, and onto the thin trail between overgrown shrubs and trees. Talbot carried a powerful LED flashlight as they arrived at the dirty beige building with peeling paint and aluminum foil covered windows. It was the last place on earth he wanted to enter.

Unlike the rest of campus, this building was dark, and it hummed.

"It's on its own grid," said Johnson, "and hooked up to several backup generators."

"Why does it have its own electrical and generators?" Talbot asked.

"Rats are a nightmare, but worse than live rats are rooms full of dead ones."

Talbot felt queasy. He tried to practice his breathing, calm his nerves. These last four days had taken their toll. There were two murder victims, and their prime suspect had just shot his partner and then killed herself. A witness was missing. Now he was being led into a shack full of vermin, the Rat Lab.

"Wasn't Officer Benson going to do this search?"

"Yeah, well, he lost the bet to your Officer Browning. He was going to leave it till the very end. But I have a hunch."

"A hunch. That's great." Talbot held the light and his breath as Officer Johnson checked the door. There was a large broken padlock hanging from a latch. It had been smashed and pulled open, perhaps with a tire iron. The lock's shackle had been repositioned; whether to impede the rats' escape or something else, they were about to find out.

Johnson opened the door; a faint scent of ammonia tickled their nostrils.

"Shine the light here," Johnson said. There were several light switches, and Johnson hit them all. The small room lit up, along with the whir of a machine.

Talbot thought he heard movement behind one or more doors in a hallway to his right. It appeared they had time-traveled back to a nineteen-eighties sci-fi movie. Old cassette players, wires, and empty Big Gulp cups littered the floor. An ancient Dell computer buzzed and clicked, lights blinking, on a makeshift table.

"I hear something moving in one of those rooms," said Talbot.

"Um-hmm," said Johnson. "Lots of things moving."

Talbot involuntarily shuddered while Johnson led him to the first door in the dingy hallway. There was a constant scratching sound, something clawing to get out. Johnson opened the door, turned on the lights, and the ammonia stung their nostrils.

There were dozens of rats in stacked cages, mamas surrounded by blind flesh-colored pups. Older babies swarmed at their mothers' nippled bellies, vampire feet grasping and pink rat tails curling in satisfaction. Talbot felt an imaginary trail of sharp claws skitter along his spine. He felt sick.

Warren Worthington was not here.

Thank God, thought Talbot. They moved to the next room and opened the door.

There was slightly less of an ammonia stink, and here each rat had their own cage. Some of these cages were labeled "DRUG."

"They experiment on them with sugar and caffeine," said Officer Johnson.

Talbot burped up an aftertaste of the sweetened coffee he drank in lieu of eating dinner. Maybe it was time to switch to herbal tea.

Again, no Warren Worthington.

Finally, they stood before the last room at the end of the hall. Talbot didn't hear anything behind this door.

"This last room is a testing lab."

Johnson unlocked it and turned on the light.

On the floor among makeshift mazes and scattered LEGOs lay Warren Worthington, with one leg splayed and the other bent awkwardly backward. The white-blonde eyelashes fluttered; his pale blue eyes opened. He was alive.

Warren cradled something in his good hand.

With effort, Worthington pulled himself up into a semi-sitting position. He opened his cupped hand and stroked at something with his claw-like fingers.

A rat's startled black eyes stared at the two men standing at the door and squeaked.

Warren Worthington squinted at Rodney Johnson and Bobby Talbot. He rocked his torso back and forth with a smile that could have lit up the room without the fluorescents.

"Uhh foun meh!" he said, as if they were playing a particular thorny game of hide and seek.

Worthington whispered to the rat who had nestled more snugly into Warren's chest.

"Ith's okeh," he said.

The rat was missing its tail.

"Ith okeh," Warren repeated. "Monstheh gonne."

Talbot looked to Johnson.

"Can he keep that?" Talbot asked.

"Fine by me," Johnson said. "This college could do with one less rat."

EPILOGUE

CHAPTER 58

The Unforgiven

Hedy Scacht—actually, the remains of Hedda Gertrude Scacht—ensconced in a handsome wood and brass casket, was being lowered into her final resting place during a graveside service at Forest Lawn. It was a quickly arranged ceremony. DJ, with his injured left arm in a sling, stood behind a gathering of mourners. It was a good crowd for a murderer.

Jerome Blight stood next to the Campus Safety officers in attendance, seven tall men and one woman, dressed in dark blue uniforms, their faces grim. Rodney Johnson, a.k.a ROMEO/JULIET, wept, tears running down his face.

Hoa Phan, who had resigned from Hesperia, stood with her sister, Thien, on one side and Dolly Ruiz on the other. DJ was surprised that Hoa decided to attend, but perhaps witnessing the burial made sense. Funerals provided finality and Will Bloom was being buried on the East Coast in a family plot. Hoa's lovely face was crumpled and tearstained. She reminded DJ of a flower succumbing to overwhelming elements, rain, wind, love, regret.

Dolly Ruiz, eyes closed and swaying in her own mysterious rhythm, held Hoa's other hand. DJ didn't know what version of truth was in the letter her mother wrote or if Dolly had read it.

For his part, DJ kept his promise. After Hedy's suicide, he had told Dolly Ruiz that an incident with Will Bloom at Chapman had deeply scarred her mother. He couldn't go into details, but it involved a student. Dolly had said nothing, circled her chest with her finger, then fist to heart, she had closed her eyes. DJ wondered if Dolly Ruiz was more aware of Will Bloom's character than he had first believed.

Today, Dolly appeared to be weathering her personal storm. A few tears raked her cheeks. More likely, the hurricane hadn't made land. From DJ's experience, the tumult would be great, the damages deep and damning. He would not be a witness to it, and for that, he was grateful.

Professor Ravi LaVal had moved to Dolly's other side and held her left hand. The four women stood intertwined and impenetrable, like a chain-link fence around Hedy's grave, guarding one of their own. Hedy, in her own way, had tried to protect them from Will Bloom. The denizens of the castle closing rank.

An older man stood separate and behind the women. He had introduced himself to various mourners as Hedy's older brother. Dolly and her uncle acknowledged each other, but barely spoke.

Serena Rigby stood alone, fidgeting with her ill-fitting black jacket. She surveyed the crowd with her persistent glum expression, no doubt looking to see if President Bill Reese would attend. He was a no-show.

Danny Mendoza and Fern Lake stood nearest the casket. Hedy Scacht had been his mother's best friend, and Danny stood up for her like the son she never had. Danny's arm wound around Fern Lake's waist, and in his other hand he held a white rose. *White for sympathy*, thought DJ.

At the end of the preacher's remarks, Danny walked to the grave, where Hedy's casket was already interred. He dropped the flower and something small that caught a flash of sunlight. DJ thought it might be a piece of jewelry from his mother, Isabella Mendoza.

Danny said a few words. "Hedy, you were my mother's best friend, my protector and advocate. You were loved and respected by many of us here." Danny looked up and caught Dolly's eye. She nodded. "And you were loved by my mother," Danny continued as he choked up. "And by me."

Fern Lake reached out, touched Danny's back and they fell into an embrace. *Still in love*, thought DJ. *Still fucking*. A melancholy came over DJ, who stood alone and perhaps always would.

From where he stood, DJ could see the roof of his own house nestled in the neighborhood below the green lawn and headstones. Hedy Scacht's burial site was two football fields away from DJ's home. It was a good thing that his Grandma had taught him to honor the dead, some of them might be in attendance.

He thought of Trish Ballentine, who couldn't stop herself from mocking the horror in another woman's life. And the spirit of Daniel's mother, Isabella Mendoza, felt tangible, a shadow flitting through the trees.

At every intersection of death, religion, and ceremony, DJ searched for his dead cousin Frankie. It was just like his cousin to never show.

Something moved at the edge of DJ's vision. Then he felt the nuzzle of a wet nose against his pant leg. He looked down to see Evidence pawing at his calf. He reached down with his good arm to pick her up, rubbed his face against hers, and felt her tongue lick his cheek.

DJ looked behind him to see if Lillian had dropped off his dog. He had planned to pick up Evidence from her home after the funeral. But she was nowhere in sight.

Rolf, the veterinarian's assistant, stood by the road, leaning against a compact sports car. He was out of his scrubs and wore a blazer over a gray T-shirt and black jeans; he waved. Rolf looked handsome, buff, and older. DJ wondered if he was more than an assistant to his ex-wife.

Lillian wasn't his anymore. DJ knew that. He forced himself to mouth the words, "thank you" to the younger man. He kept the *fuck you if you mess with Lillian* to himself.

Turning away, he looked again at the small gathering of mourners. Hedy Scacht had taken two lives. Her acts were unforgivable. Still, the unforgiven had to be buried.

DJ pressed Evidence gently to his chest. She gave a murmuring sound of contentment.

"You don't know what it's like to love someone more than yourself," Hedy had said.

But now, maybe he did.

CHAPTER 59

Danny

DJ had one last task after the funeral; to meet his partner, Bobby Talbot, at Hesperia College. Bobby was wrapping up final paperwork, closing their command center, and returning the Wick Conference Room back to its denizens, to the pursuit of excellence and superior beings.

After he left Forest Lawn, DJ drove through Char #8 for a hamburger and fries. He sat in the parking lot and shared his meal with Evidence.

On his way to Hesperia, DJ passed the exact spot where Warren Worthington had been kidnapped and glanced at *the haunted hole*. He stopped the car.

Danny Mendoza stood watering the lawn of Warren Worthington's house, now resplendent with green sod and geranium flowers at its border. There was a makeshift ramp that skimmed the stairs onto the porch.

DJ and Evidence hopped out of the car, walked up to the yard, and stared at the house that now gleamed in the afternoon sunlight. The shutters had been straightened and affixed to the walls. The overgrown bougainvillea had been cut back; other ragged shrubs pulled out. There was a scent of lumber and fertilizer in the air.

"Wow," said DJ. "This place looks great."

"It's amazing what a good power wash, a hammer and nails, and yard work can accomplish," Danny said. He had changed into casual clothes.

DJ was impressed. Evidence peed on the lawn.

"So, where's the girl?" DJ asked, looking around.

"Ferencia Lake went home to spend some time with her dad."

"You met the father. How did that go?"

"Better than expected," said Danny. "But then, I don't expect much."

"Me neither," said DJ. "Has Fern met Warren Worthington?"

Danny shook his head. "Just briefly. It's not easy for her, after everything that happened."

DJ looked at Danny.

"I talked to Professor LaVal at the gravesite. She said Fern Lake is a very good student. Has a bright future, maybe in academia."

"She's a finalist for a Fulbright," said Danny. "Professor LaVal's helping her prepare for interviews. I think she'll get it. Then Fern will spend next year in London."

"And what will you do?" asked DJ.

"I'll be here," said Danny. "If she comes back, I'll be here."

"Don't hold your breath."

Danny turned and looked at the older man. He almost said, "I held my breath for ten long years. Maybe for years before that."

Instead, Danny turned off the hose.

"I got my AA in prison, and I've always wanted to finish my degree. I'm applying to Cal Poly Pomona for landscape architecture. I worked out a schedule with Hesperia. Maybe one day I'll start my own business."

DJ had a vision of Danny in his mother's old beater minivan, fighting the traffic on the San Bernardino freeway. Cal Poly, a state school, sprawled across a scrubby Pomona hillside, an old estate with Arabian horses turned into a middle-class learning mecca for the masses. And every afternoon Daniel would continue to toil in Hesperia College's pristine soil.

"Cal Poly, huh?" said DJ. "That's a haul."

"It's not bad. Heading against traffic."

DJ looked at the younger man. He was about to give Daniel his world-weary advice on love, work, and the cultural chasms of education that people like DJ and Danny faced. They had to fight for everything they got, then clean up the messes in the vaulted world of people like President Bill Reese, Professor Ravi LaVal, and now his precious Fern Lake.

Evidence nudged his shin. DJ looked down into her Yoda-like face.

Who was DJ Arias to murder hope? Somewhere deep in the dustbin of his heart, he still felt a spark of it. DJ kept quiet.

"Besides," said Danny, "I'll have plenty to keep me busy. I have a new responsibility."

A medical van pulled up and its doors opened. Danny walked up to the van and watched Warren Worthington descend on its lift. Danny took over the wheelchair and rolled him up the walkway toward the house.

"Warren was at the doctor."

"How are you doing, Warren?" DJ asked.

"Okeh," he said. "Legths hurth. Back betther, wingths gohnne."

DJ thought about the comic book, *The Avenging Angel*, and Hedy's comment that Warren believed he could fly.

"Let's get you walking first," Danny said, "then you can think about the other things."

Warren Worthington eked out a groan and frown that DJ guessed was his version of a polite "you don't know what the fuck you're talking about." He held something in the curled fingers of his damaged hand.

"What's that?" DJ asked.

"Warren has a pet," Danny said. "He calls him Angel."

DJ looked down into the black eyes and twitching nose of a gray and white rat. It was missing its tail.

"Anghel," Warren repeated.

"A rat named Angel," said DJ. That made sense to him. "Well, Warren," he said, squeezing his shoulder, "I hope your leg heals up fast."

To Danny, he offered his uninjured hand. Danny took it and they shook.

"Good luck," DJ said with a crooked smile. "I'll see you around."

He and Evidence walked toward his car and got in.

"I certainly hope not," Danny said to himself as DJ's old black SUV disappeared down the street.

Danny thought about the long silver acrylic nail he had shoved into his pocket the morning he saw Will Bloom's dead body.

Danny did it without thinking. Did some part of him know? A series of split-second thoughts flashed through his mind that morning; *dead man, murdered man, something glittery on the carpet, acrylic nail, pick it up, hide it*. It wasn't just any man. It was Will Bloom, the man who had raped Hedy Scacht, the man who was Dolly Ruiz's father.

In the sacred quiet of Isabella Mendoza's hospice, her last days on earth, she had told Danny her secrets, and one of Hedy's too. The terrible secret that made sense of Hedy and Dolly's relationship, the bleakness that had sunk into Hedy's eyes, the weight on her shoulders these past few years. Danny didn't know Will Bloom; he did not mourn him. He grieved for Hedy Scacht, her life and death, the violence that had propelled her toward darkness and revenge.

Did Danny know that Hedy had murdered Will Bloom? He had asked himself that a hundred times since Hedy's death. No, he had never imagined that. He still couldn't understand how or why Hedy had killed Trish Ballentine. Did Trish know her secret? Some questions had no answers.

The acrylic nail had stayed in the pocket of his work pants. A sharp penetrating shard of evidence, almost forgotten until the day he saw Hedy kidnap Warren in her SUV.

Danny had dropped the long silver nail into Hedy's grave along with the white rose. Her secrets were buried with her. And one of Danny's too.

"T-t-ired," said Warren.

"All right, bud, let's get you inside," said Danny as he positioned the wheelchair toward the house.

Danny had never seen himself as a caretaker, but that is what he was. Tending the roses that bloomed white and scarlet across Hesperia's campus, pulling weeds that invaded flowerbeds, seeding lawns, clipping errant branches. Making sure that Ferencia Lake finished out her senior year and participated in the interviews to become a Fulbright scholar. He would watch over Dolly Ruiz as her mother, Hedy, had protected him.

And now he would take care of Warren; take over where his mother left off, bring him casseroles and cookies. Check on his health and well-being. He'd already brought in someone to clean the place. It's what his mother had expected of him. It was what he expected of himself.

And one day, who knows, perhaps he would see Warren Worthington fly. He was the avenging angel after all, the hero who had saved Fern Lake.

And Fern Lake had saved Danny.

Worthington smiled at Danny. "Tthhannk you."

He smiled back. Danny Mendoza. Hollow no more.

Danny pushed him up the makeshift wooden ramp and into the house, no longer *the haunted hole*, but Warren's home.

Biographical Note

DC Frost is a second-generation Angelino. For almost twenty years, she has worked at a small private liberal arts college in the heart of Los Angeles. Denise loves and respects Southern California, a melting pot of class and culture that is often misrepresented and misunderstood in popular fiction and media. DC lives in Eagle Rock, California, with her husband, who is an NPR journalist and reporter, and three rescue dogs. DC and her husband have an adult son, a filmmaker, who resides in Los Angeles.